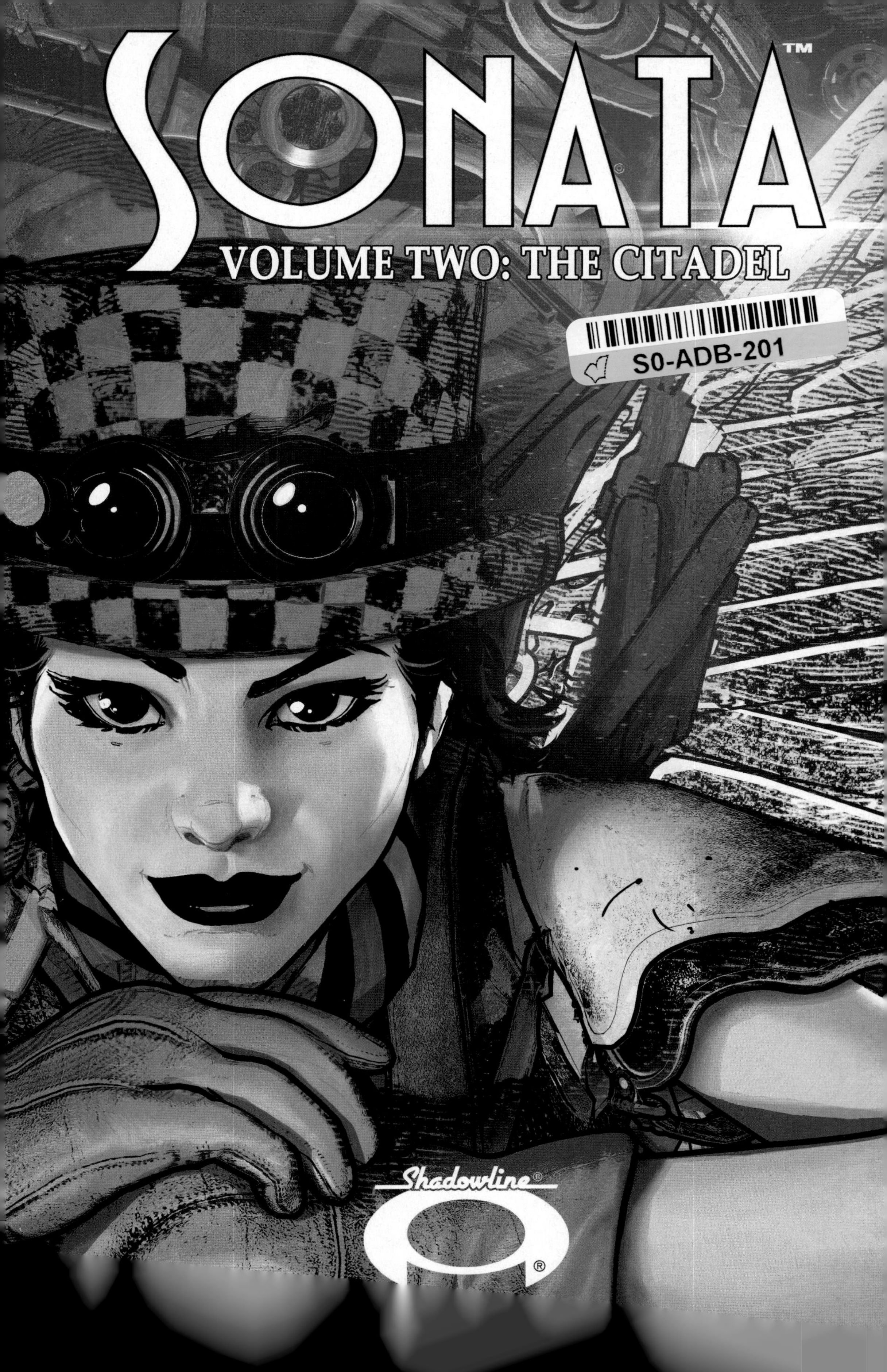
SONATA™
VOLUME TWO: THE CITADEL
Shadowline®

First printing: September 2020   ISBN: 978-1-5343-1617-1

SONATA, VOL. 2: THE CITADEL. Published by Image Comics, Inc. Office of publication: 2701 NW Vaughn St., Suite 780, Portland, OR 97210. Copyright © 2020 ANOMALY PRODUCTIONS, INC. All rights reserved. Contains material originally published in single magazine form as SONATA #7-12. "Sonata," its logos, and the likenesses of all characters herein are trademarks of Anomaly Productions, Inc., unless otherwise noted. "Image" and the Image Comics logos are registered trademarks of Image Comics, Inc. Shadowline® and its logos are registered trademarks of Jim Valentino. No part of this publication may be reproduced or transmitted, in any form or by any means (except for short excerpts for journalistic or review purposes), without the express written permission of Brian Haberlin, or Image Comics, Inc. All names, characters, events, and locales in this publication are entirely fictional. Any resemblance to actual persons (living or dead), events, or places, without satirical intent, is coincidental. Printed in the USA. International Rights/Foreign Licensing: Christine Meyer at christine@gfloystudio.com.

image COMICS PRESENTS

SONATA™

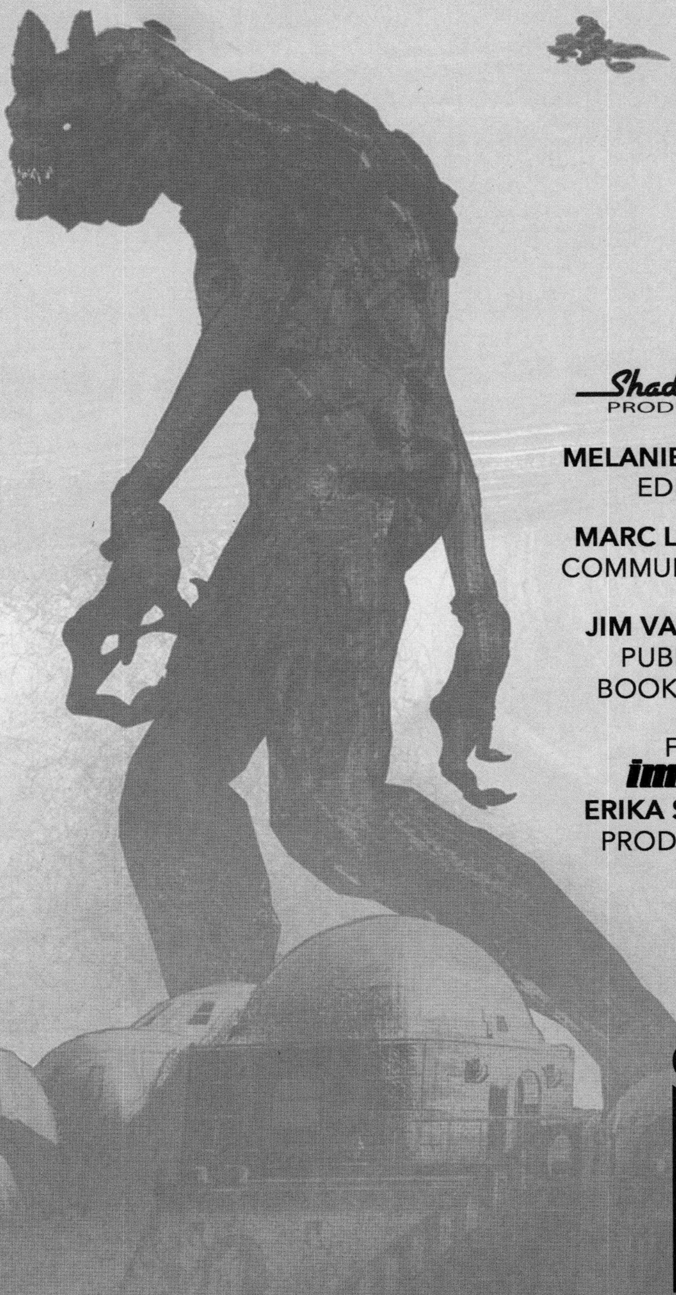

FOR
ANOMALY PRODUCTIONS

STORY
DAVID HINE &
BRIAN HABERLIN

ART
BRIAN HABERLIN

COLORS
GEIRROD VAN DYKE

COVERS
BRIAN HABERLIN &
GEIRROD VAN DYKE
JAY ANACLETO

LETTERS
FRANCIS TAKENAGA

PRODUCTION
HANNAH WALL
DIANA SANSON
CHRISTIAN PRECIADO

A
Shadowline®
PRODUCTION

MELANIE HACKETT
EDITOR

MARC LOMBARDI
COMMUNICATIONS

JIM VALENTINO
PUBLISHER
BOOK DESIGN

FOR
image®
ERIKA SCHNATZ
PRODUCTION

IMAGE COMICS, INC.
Robert Kirkman—Chief Operating Officer
Erik Larsen—Chief Financial Officer
Todd McFarlane—President
Marc Silvestri—Chief Executive Officer
Jim Valentino—Vice President
Eric Stephenson—Publisher/Chief Creative Officer
Jeff Boison—Director of Sales & Publishing Planning
Jeff Stang—Director of Direct Market Sales
Kat Salazar—Director of PR & Marketing
Drew Gill—Cover Editor
Heather Doornink—Production Director
Nicole Lapalme—Controller
IMAGECOMICS.COM

Unpublished art for SONATA TV pitch

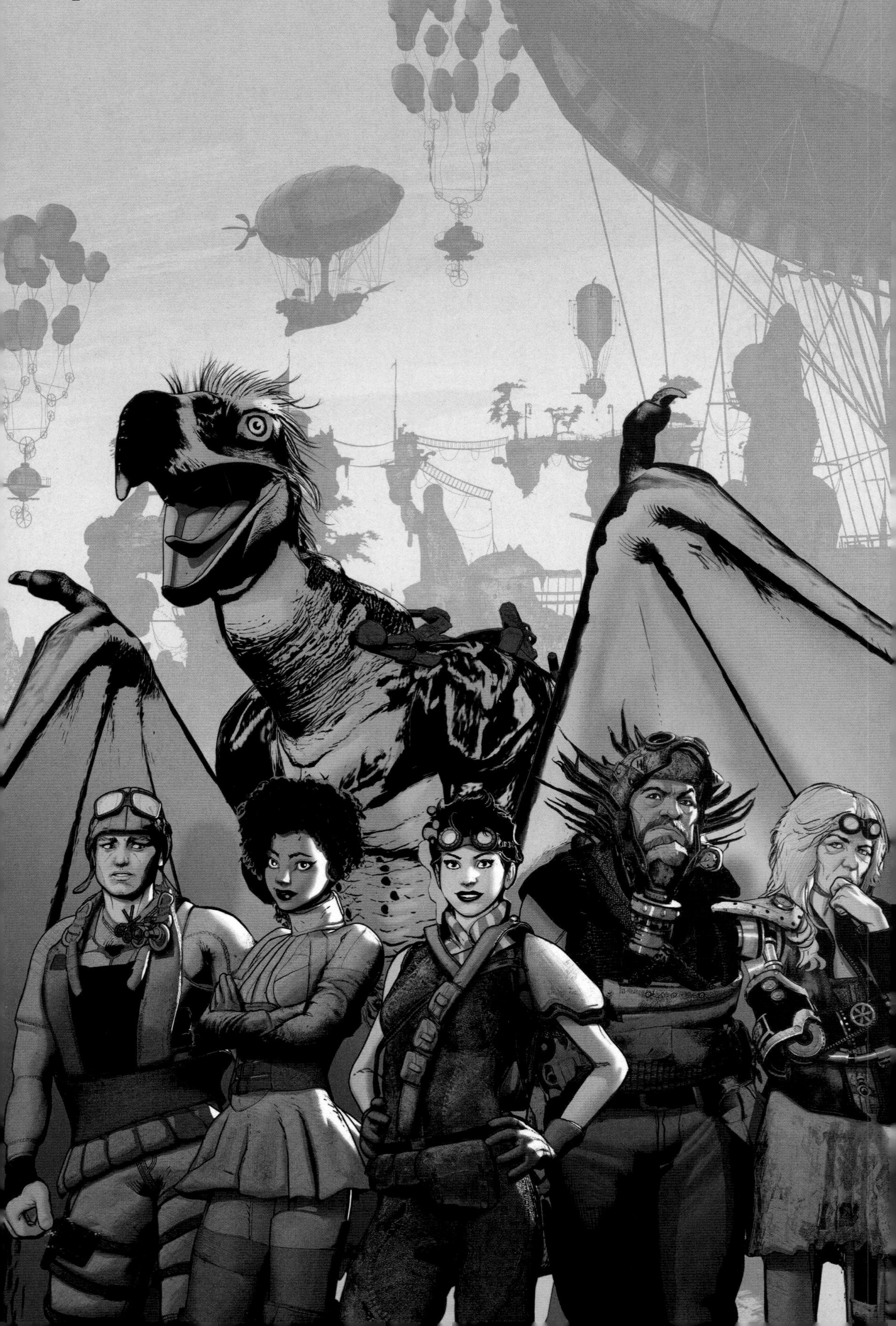

Issue #7 Cover A

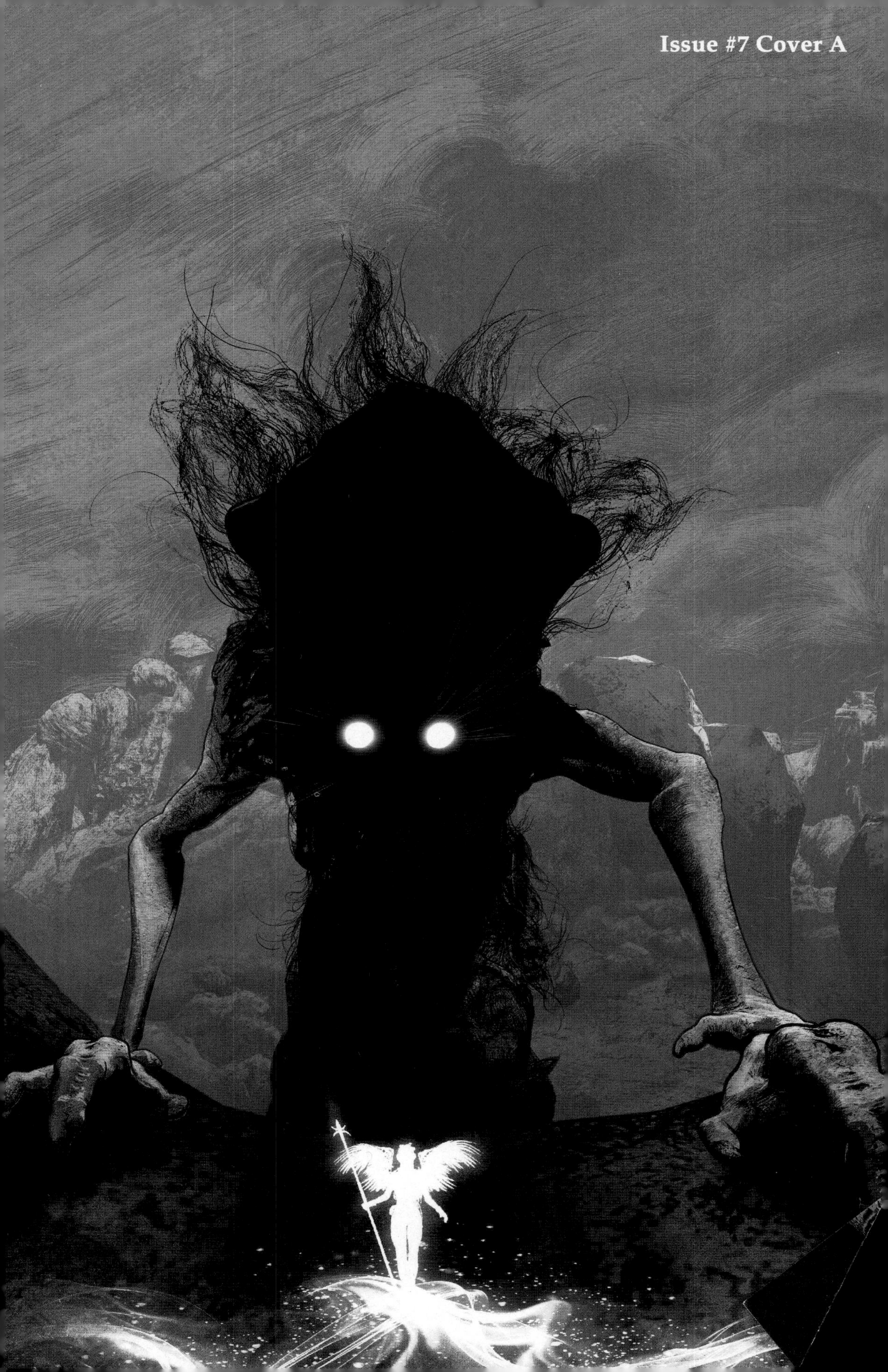

Issue #7 Cover B

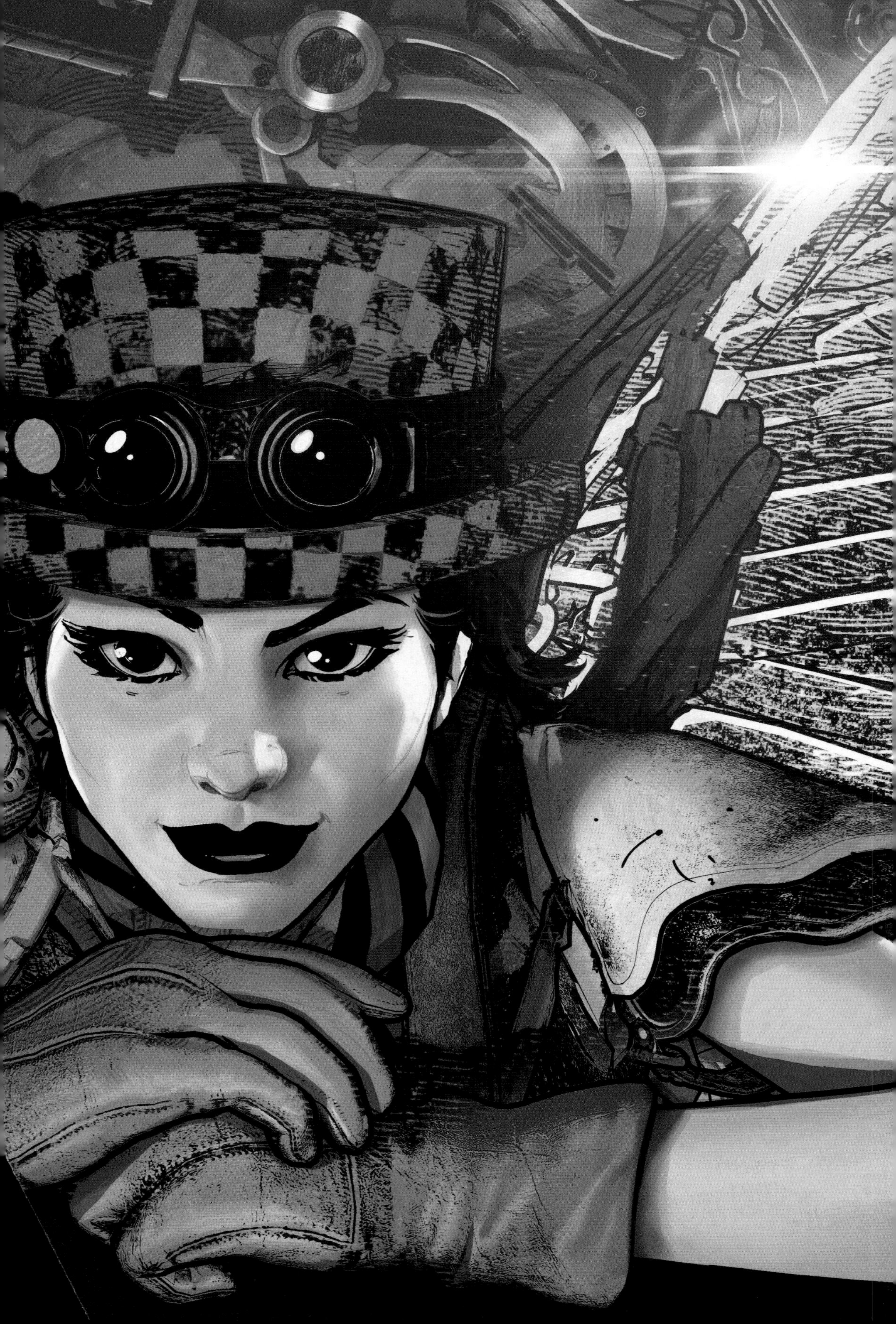

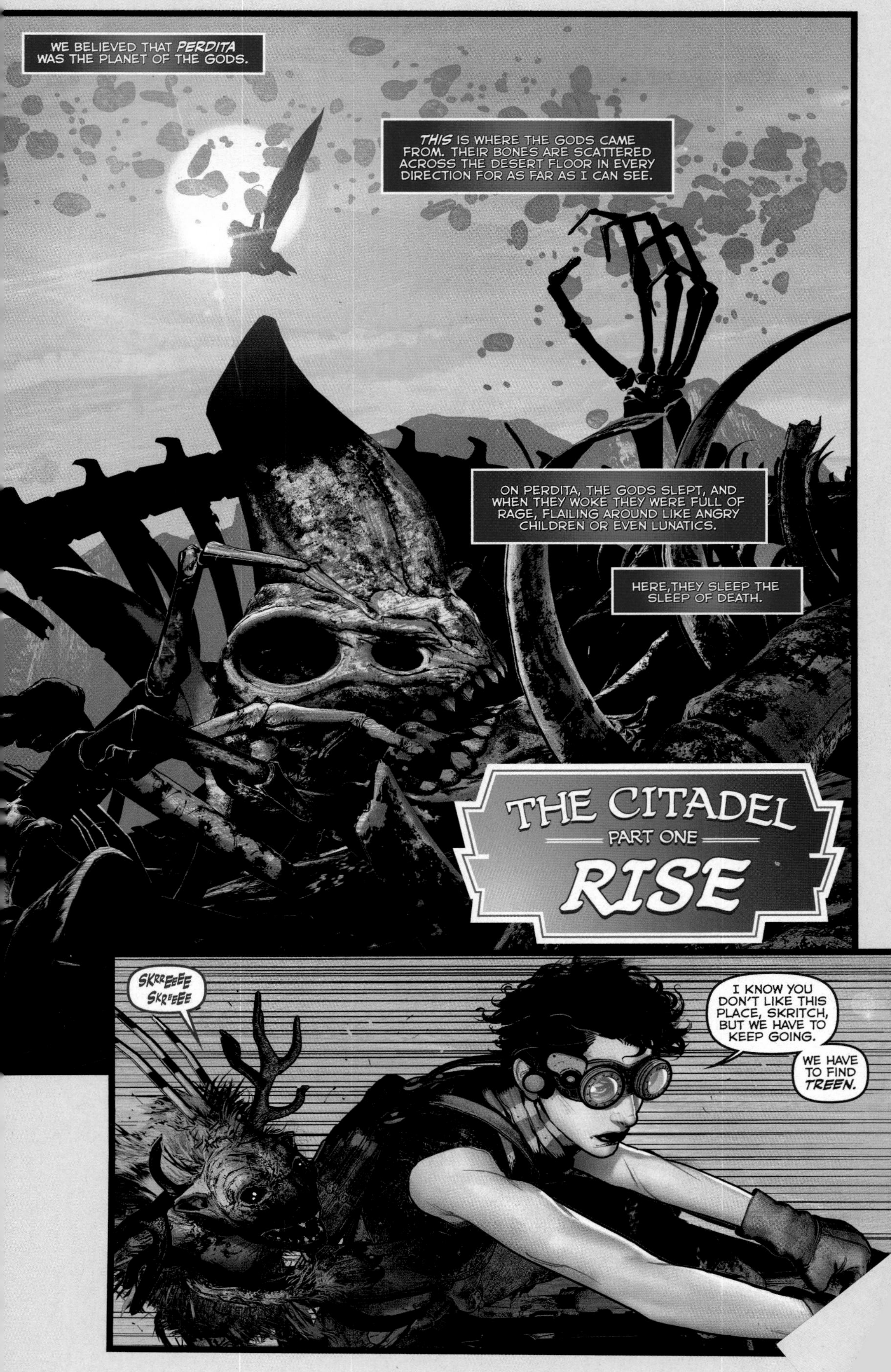
WE BELIEVED THAT PERDITA WAS THE PLANET OF THE GODS.
THIS IS WHERE THE GODS CAME FROM. THEIR BONES ARE SCATTERED ACROSS THE DESERT FLOOR IN EVERY DIRECTION FOR AS FAR AS I CAN SEE.
ON PERDITA, THE GODS SLEPT, AND WHEN THEY WOKE THEY WERE FULL OF RAGE, FLAILING AROUND LIKE ANGRY CHILDREN OR EVEN LUNATICS.
HERE, THEY SLEEP THE SLEEP OF DEATH.
THE CITADEL
PART ONE
RISE
SKRREEEE SKREEEE
I KNOW YOU DON'T LIKE THIS PLACE, SKRITCH, BUT WE HAVE TO KEEP GOING.
WE HAVE TO FIND TREEN.

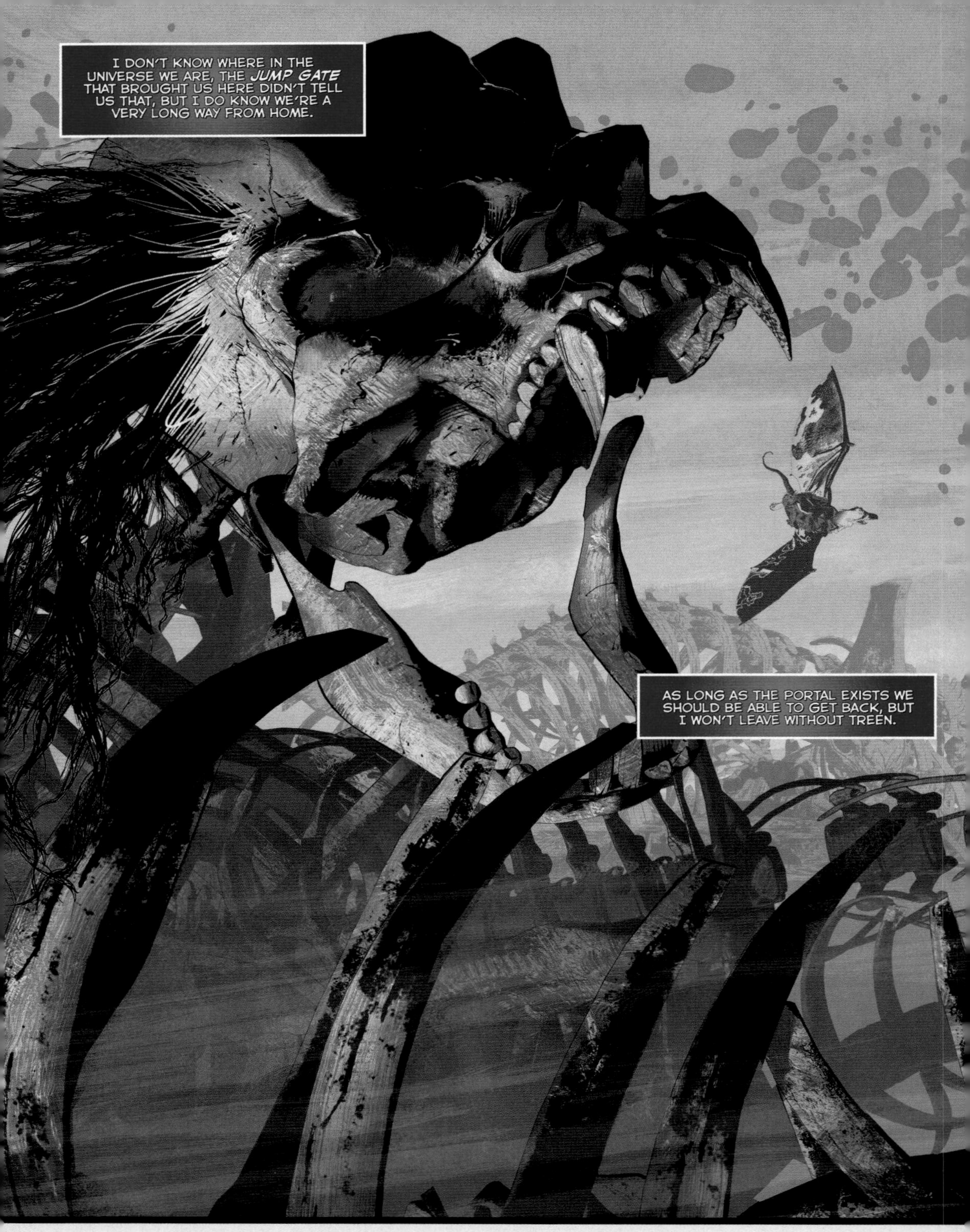
I DON'T KNOW WHERE IN THE UNIVERSE WE ARE, THE *JUMP GATE* THAT BROUGHT US HERE DIDN'T TELL US THAT, BUT I DO KNOW WE'RE A VERY LONG WAY FROM HOME.
AS LONG AS THE PORTAL EXISTS WE SHOULD BE ABLE TO GET BACK, BUT I WON'T LEAVE WITHOUT TREEN.

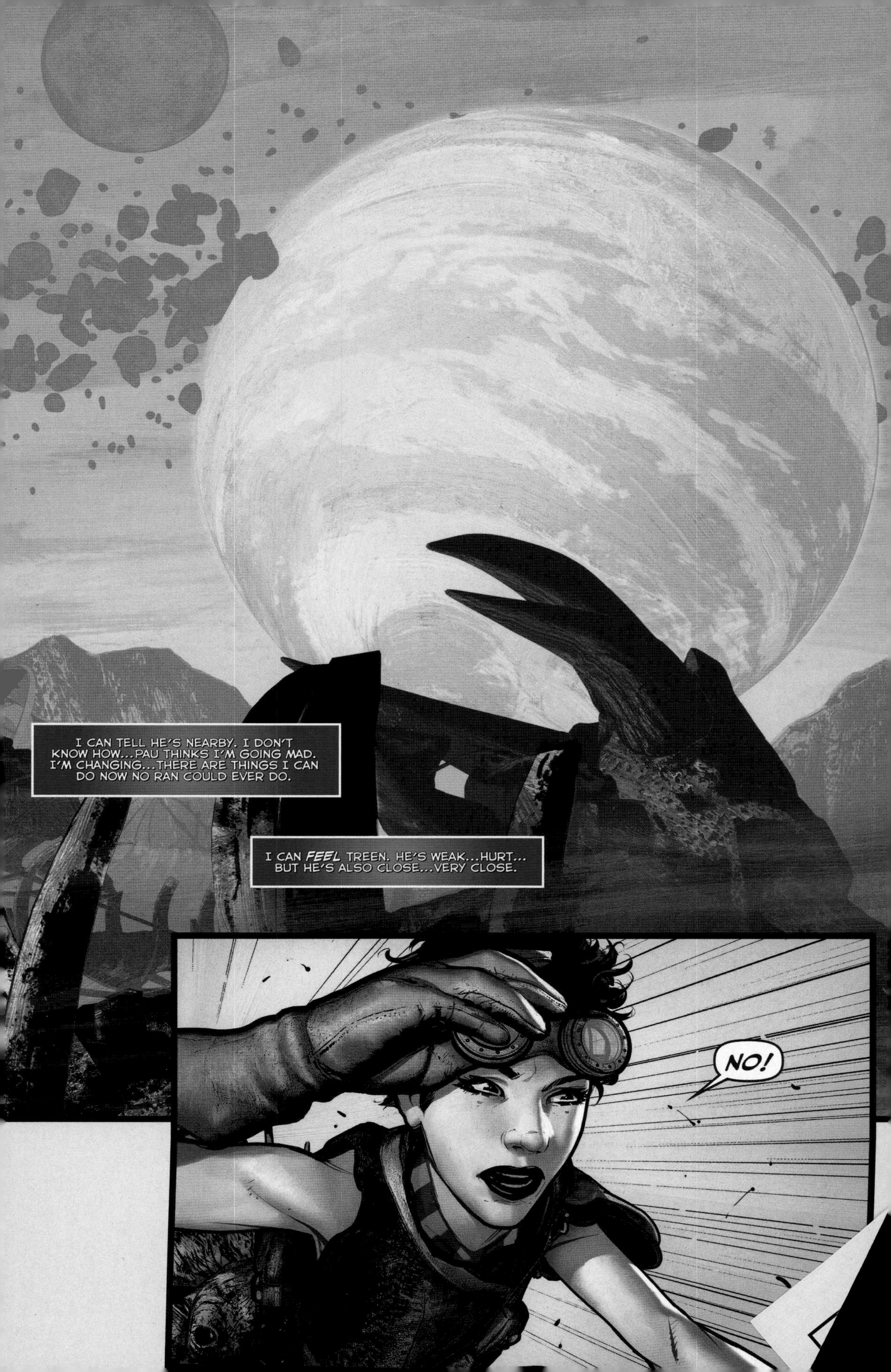

I CAN TELL HE'S NEARBY. I DON'T KNOW HOW...PAU THINKS I'M GOING MAD. I'M CHANGING...THERE ARE THINGS I CAN DO NOW NO RAN COULD EVER DO.
I CAN *FEEL* TREEN. HE'S WEAK...HURT... BUT HE'S ALSO CLOSE...VERY CLOSE.
NO!

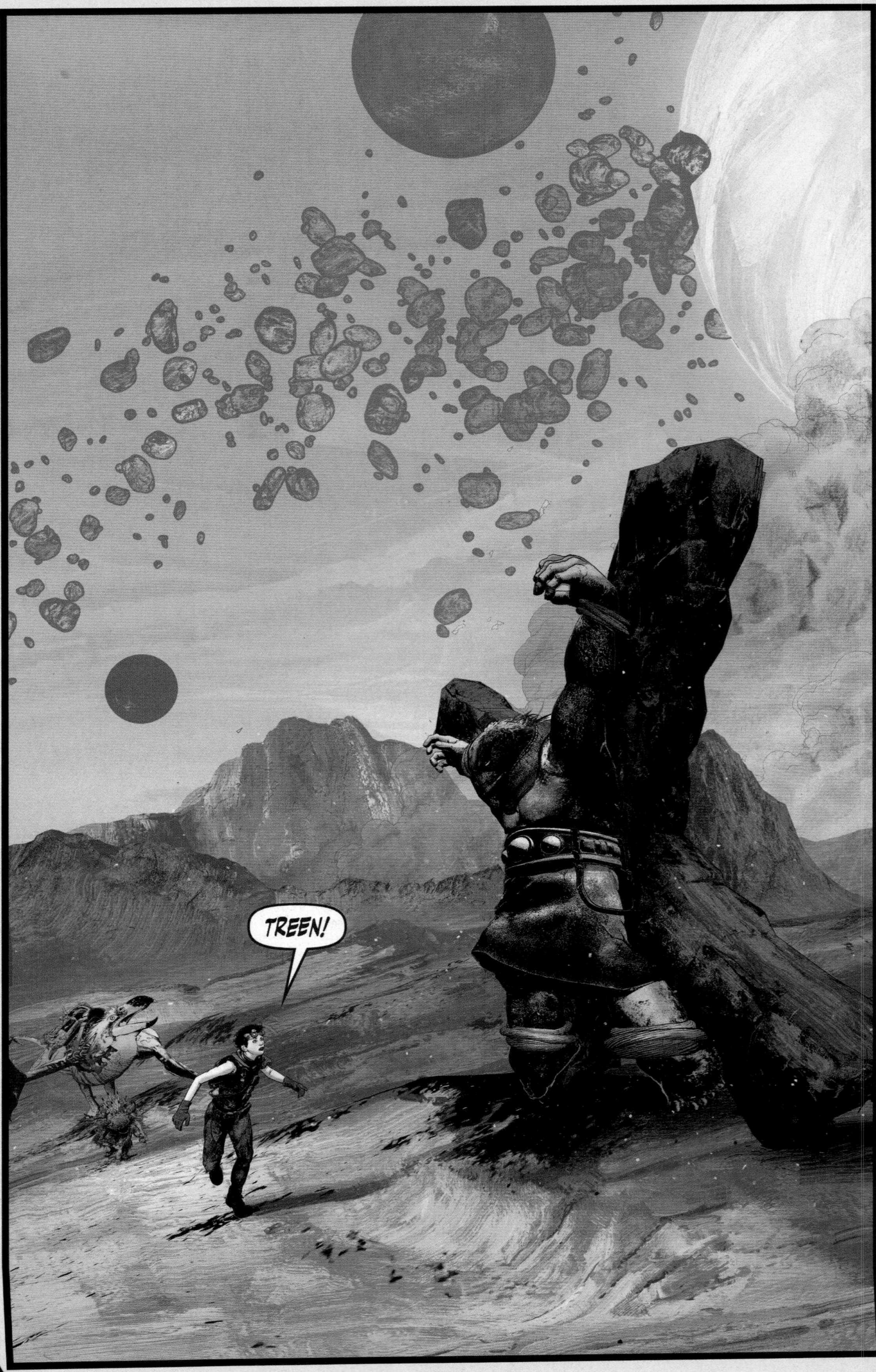
TREEN!

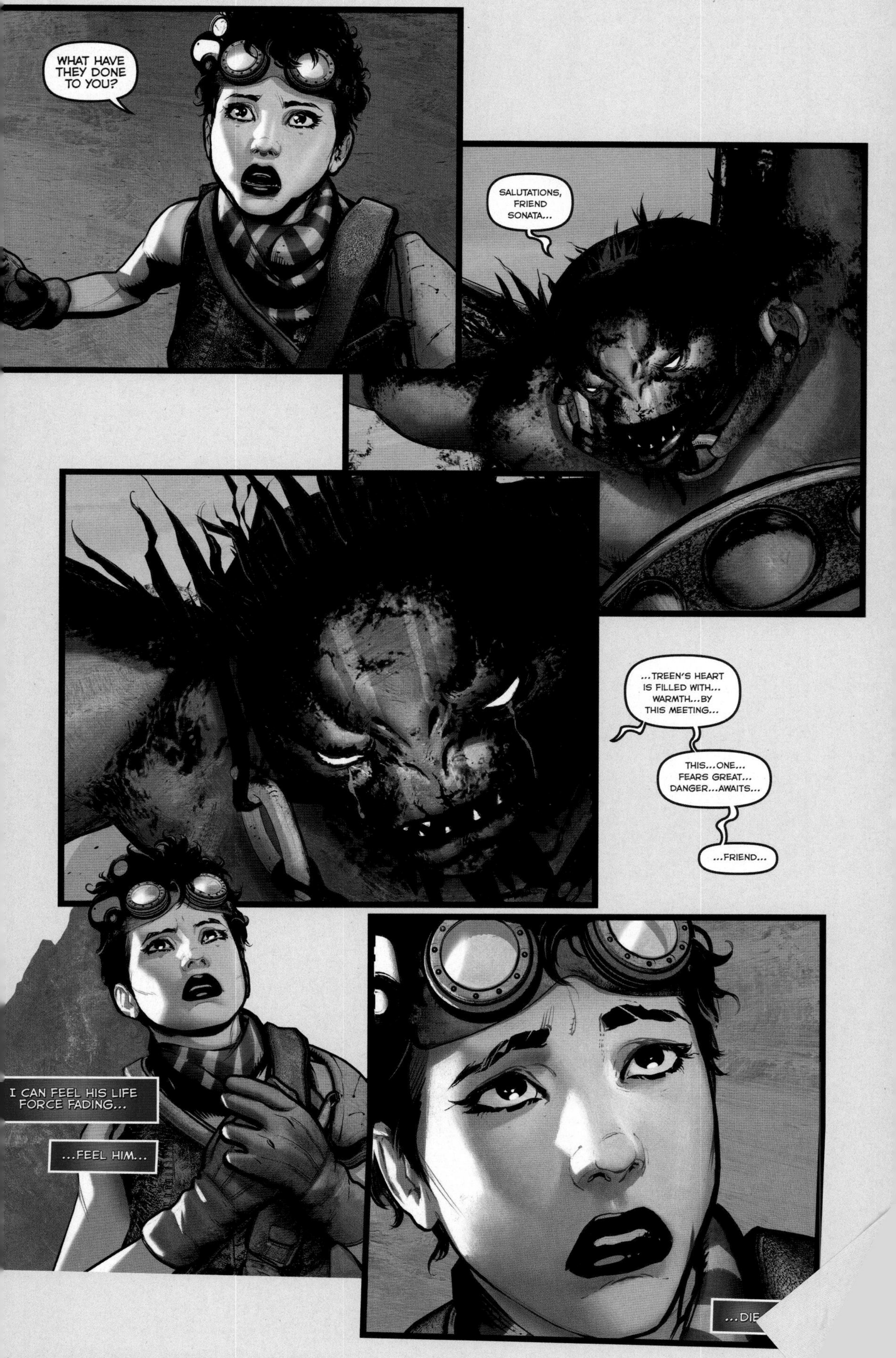
WHAT HAVE THEY DONE TO YOU?
SALUTATIONS, FRIEND SONATA...
...TREEN'S HEART IS FILLED WITH... WARMTH...BY THIS MEETING...
THIS...ONE... FEARS GREAT... DANGER...AWAITS...
...FRIEND...
I CAN FEEL HIS LIFE FORCE FADING...
...FEEL HIM...
...DIE

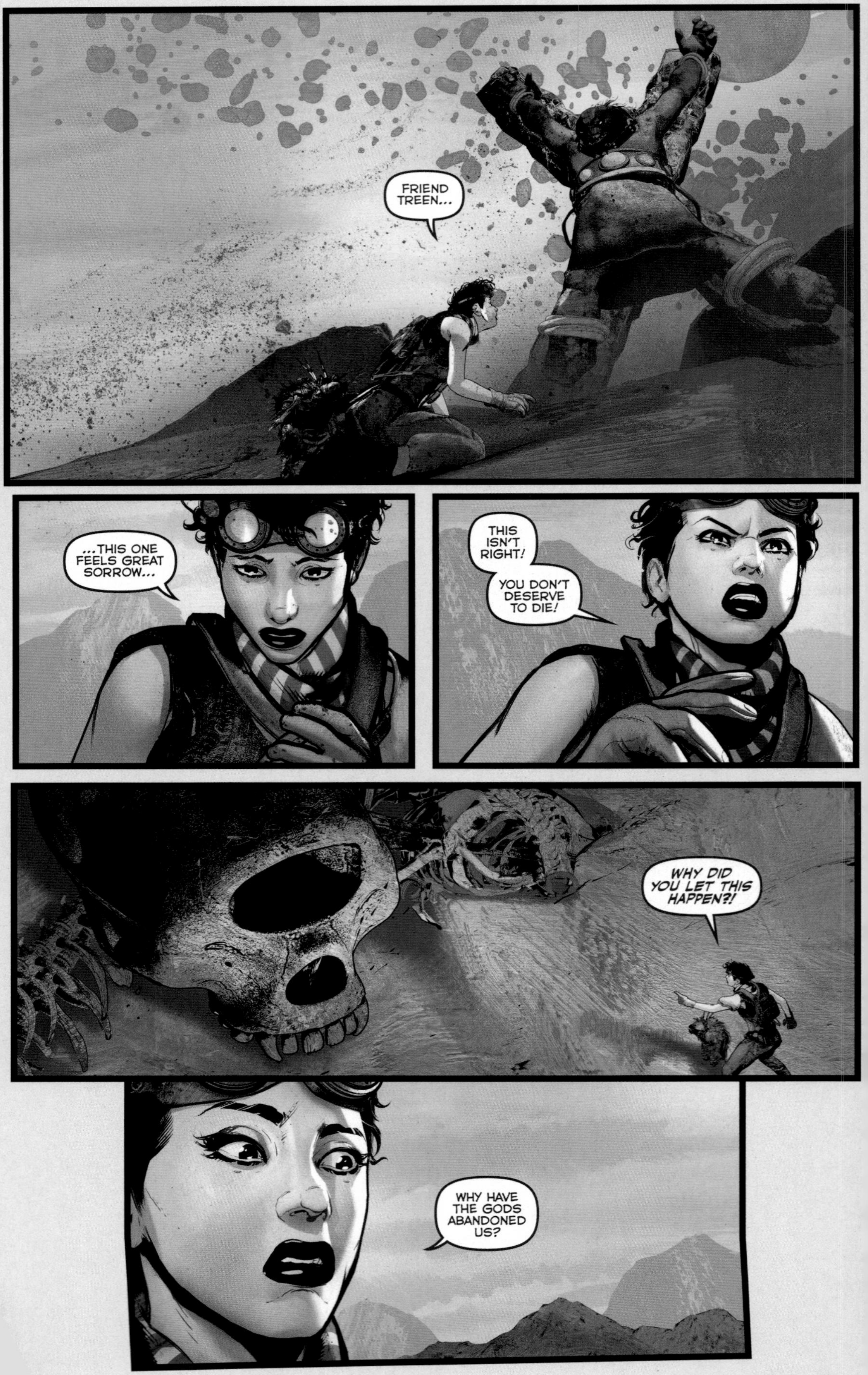
FRIEND TREEN...
...THIS ONE FEELS GREAT SORROW...
THIS ISN'T RIGHT!
YOU DON'T DESERVE TO DIE!
WHY DID YOU LET THIS HAPPEN?!
WHY HAVE THE GODS ABANDONED US?

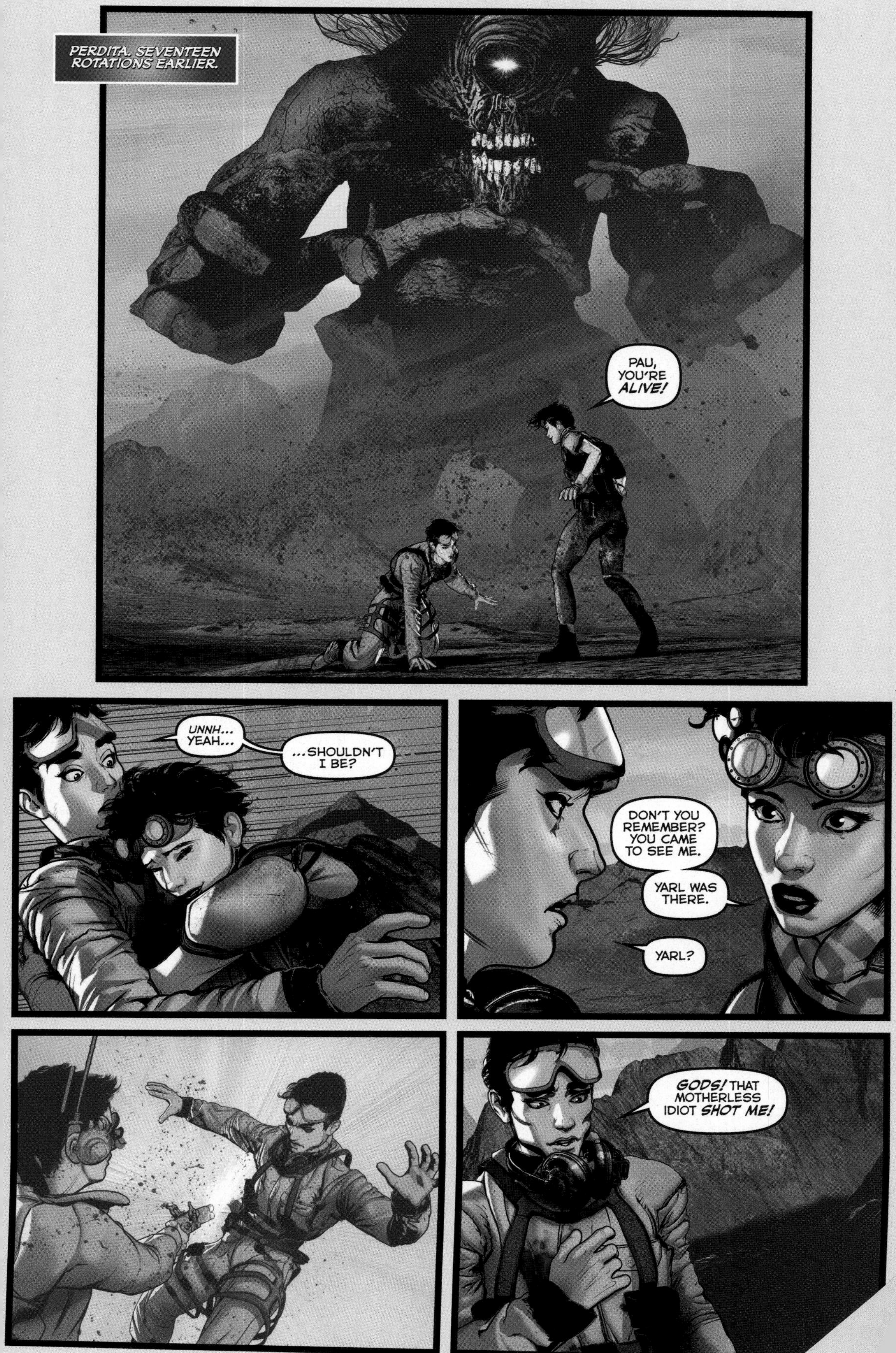
PERDITA. SEVENTEEN ROTATIONS EARLIER.
PAU, YOU'RE *ALIVE!*
UNNH... YEAH...
...SHOULDN'T I BE?
DON'T YOU REMEMBER? YOU CAME TO SEE ME.
YARL WAS THERE.
YARL?
GODS! THAT MOTHERLESS IDIOT *SHOT ME!*

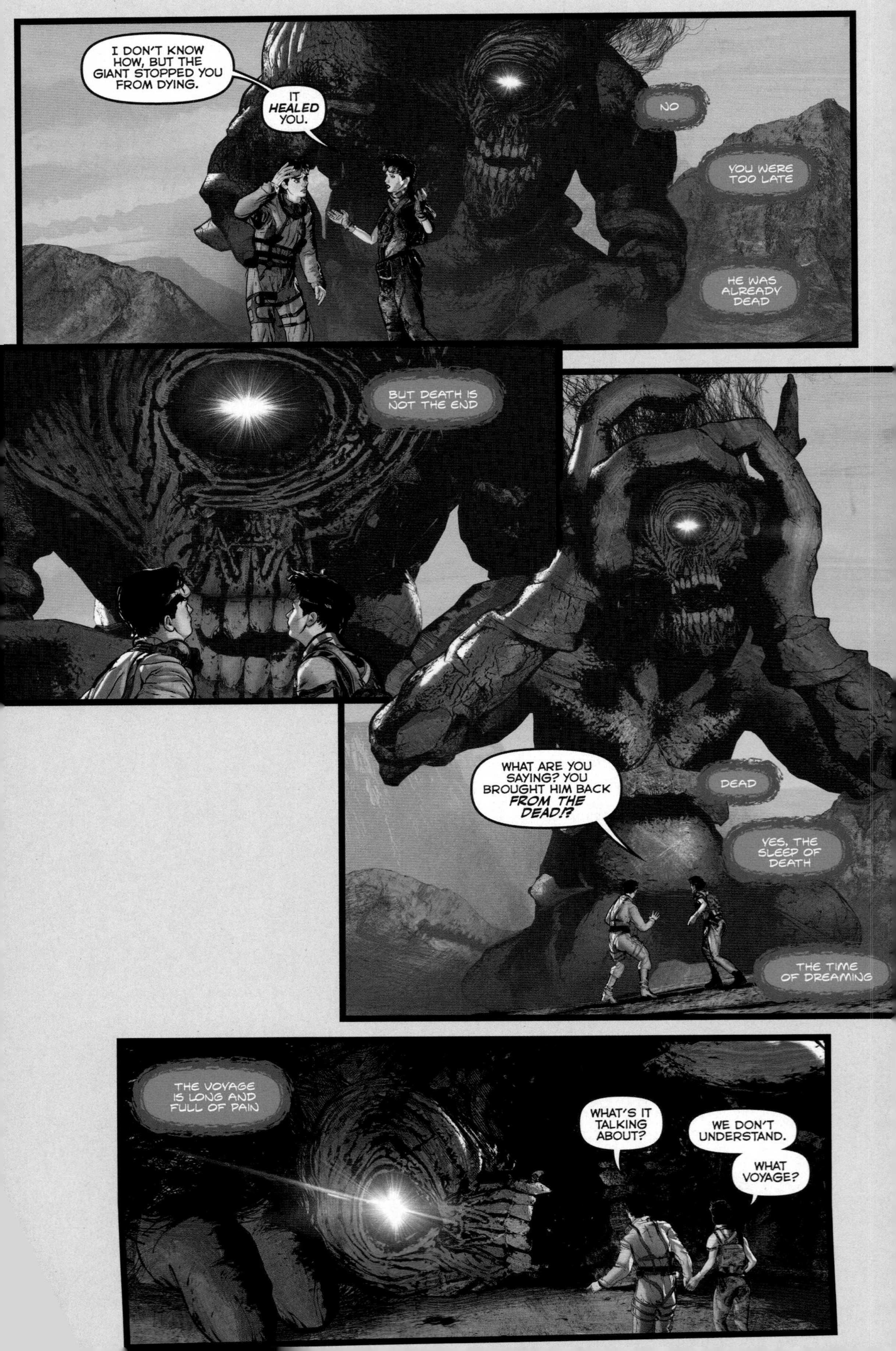
I DON'T KNOW HOW, BUT THE GIANT STOPPED YOU FROM DYING.
IT *HEALED* YOU.
NO
YOU WERE TOO LATE
HE WAS ALREADY DEAD
BUT DEATH IS NOT THE END
WHAT ARE YOU SAYING? YOU BROUGHT HIM BACK *FROM THE DEAD!?*
DEAD
YES, THE SLEEP OF DEATH
THE TIME OF DREAMING
THE VOYAGE IS LONG AND FULL OF PAIN
WHAT'S IT TALKING ABOUT?
WE DON'T UNDERSTAND.
WHAT VOYAGE?

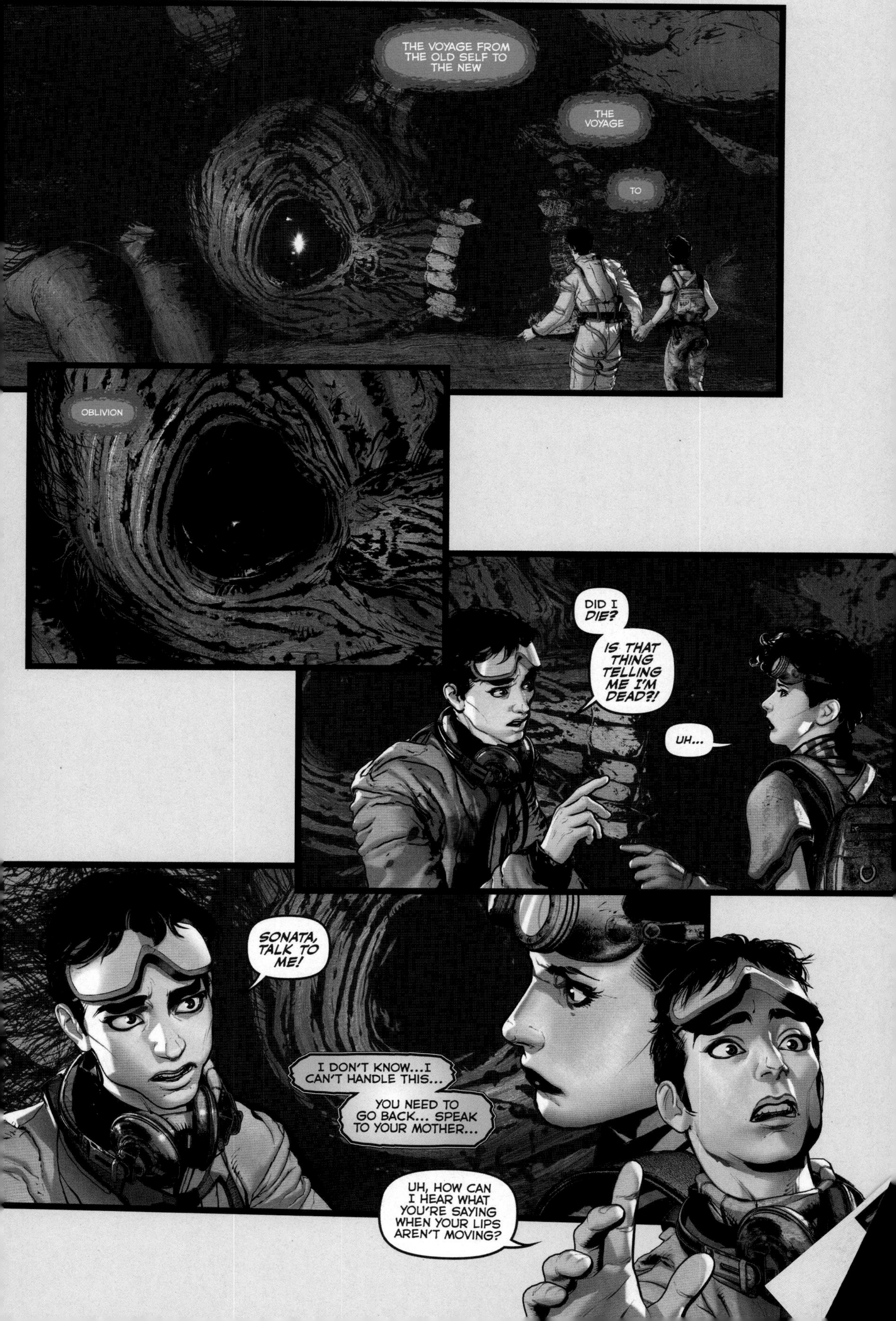
THE VOYAGE FROM THE OLD SELF TO THE NEW
THE VOYAGE
TO
OBLIVION
DID I DIE?
IS THAT THING TELLING ME I'M DEAD?!
UH...
SONATA, TALK TO ME!
I DON'T KNOW...I CAN'T HANDLE THIS...
YOU NEED TO GO BACK... SPEAK TO YOUR MOTHER...
UH, HOW CAN I HEAR WHAT YOU'RE SAYING WHEN YOUR LIPS AREN'T MOVING?

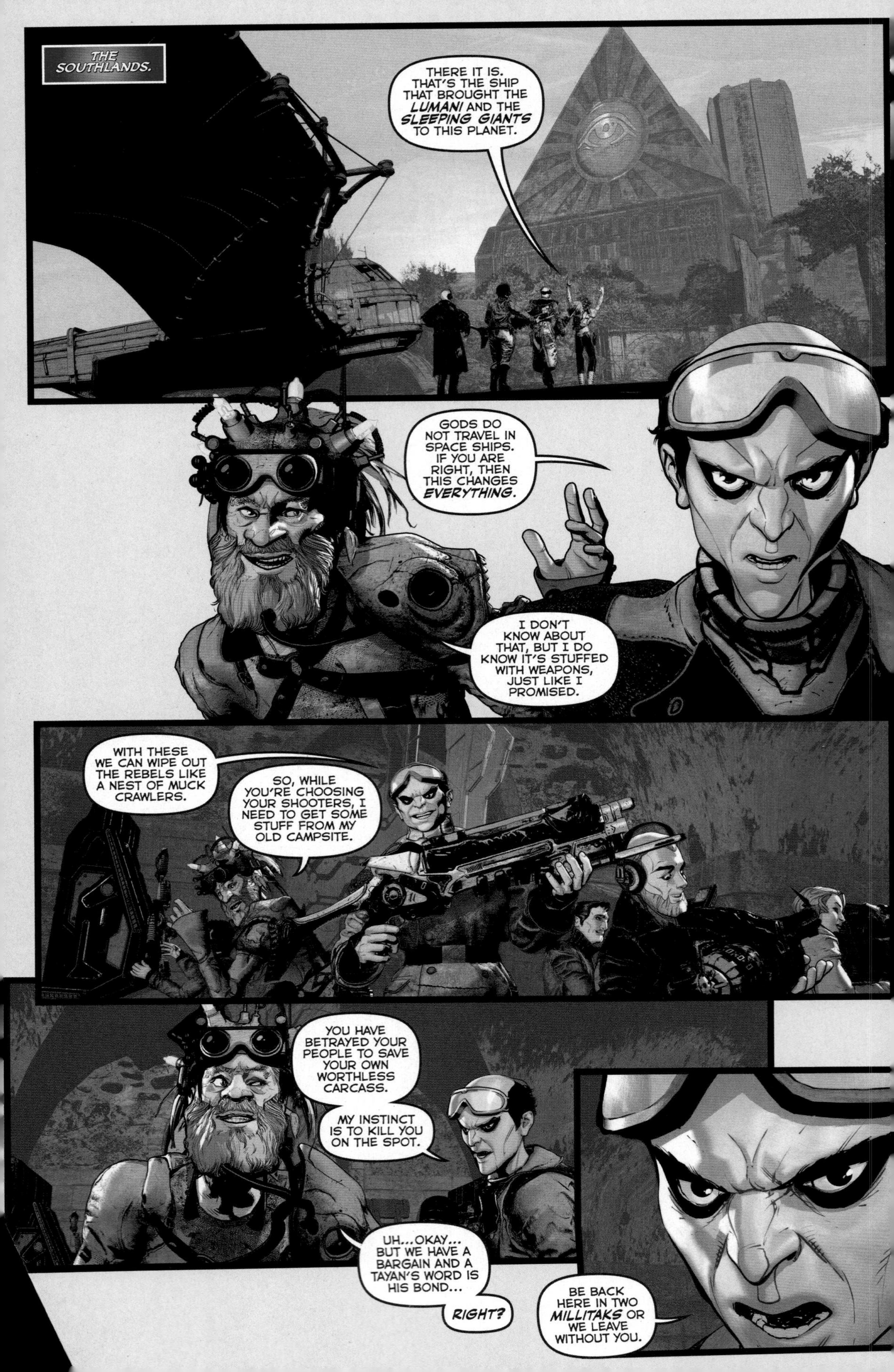
THE SOUTHLANDS.
THERE IT IS. THAT'S THE SHIP THAT BROUGHT THE LUMANI AND THE SLEEPING GIANTS TO THIS PLANET.
GODS DO NOT TRAVEL IN SPACE SHIPS. IF YOU ARE RIGHT, THEN THIS CHANGES EVERYTHING.
I DON'T KNOW ABOUT THAT, BUT I DO KNOW IT'S STUFFED WITH WEAPONS, JUST LIKE I PROMISED.
WITH THESE WE CAN WIPE OUT THE REBELS LIKE A NEST OF MUCK CRAWLERS.
SO, WHILE YOU'RE CHOOSING YOUR SHOOTERS, I NEED TO GET SOME STUFF FROM MY OLD CAMPSITE.
YOU HAVE BETRAYED YOUR PEOPLE TO SAVE YOUR OWN WORTHLESS CARCASS.
MY INSTINCT IS TO KILL YOU ON THE SPOT.
UH...OKAY... BUT WE HAVE A BARGAIN AND A TAYAN'S WORD IS HIS BOND...
RIGHT?
BE BACK HERE IN TWO MILLITAKS OR WE LEAVE WITHOUT YOU.

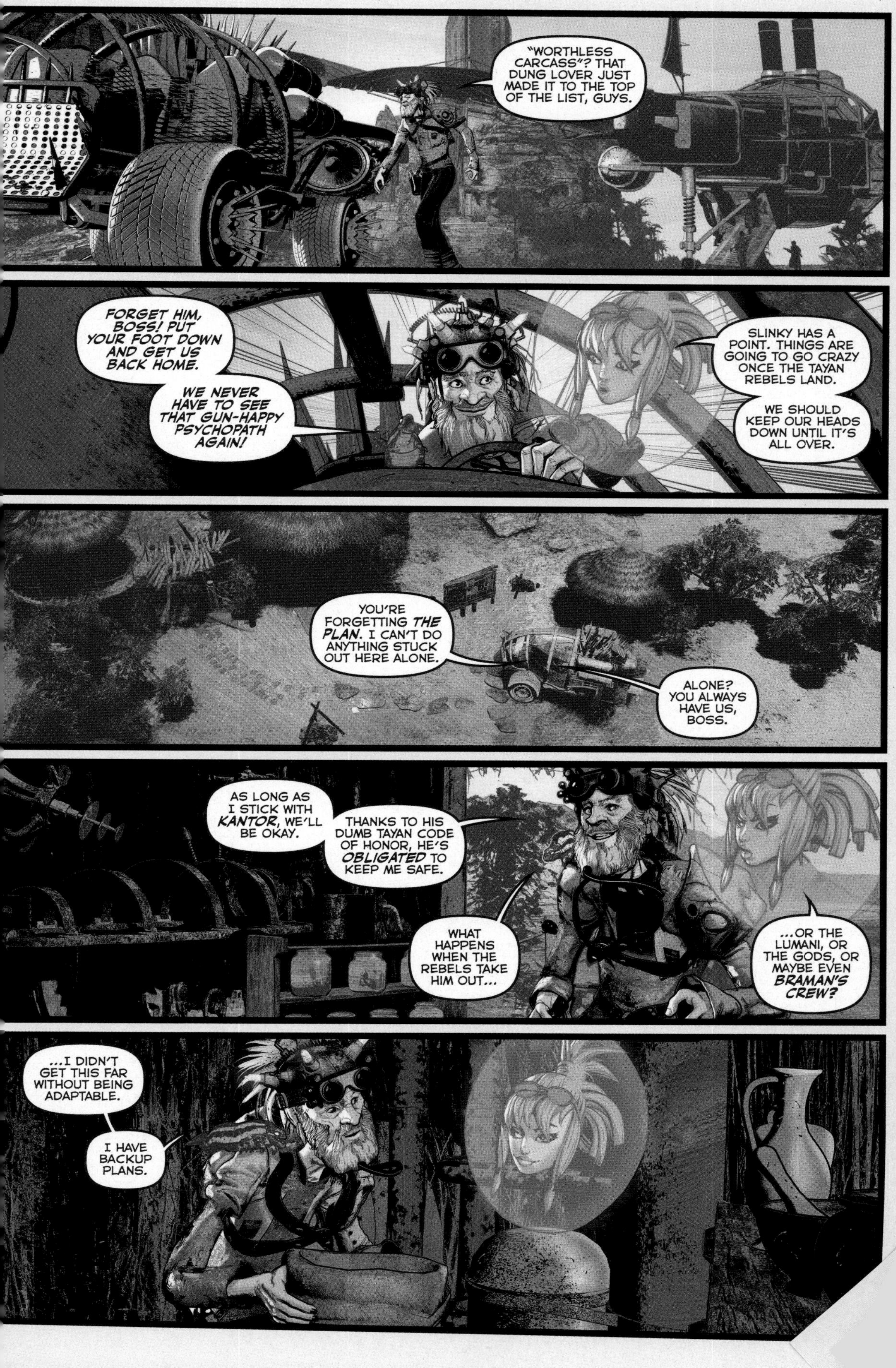
"WORTHLESS CARCASS"? THAT DUNG LOVER JUST MADE IT TO THE TOP OF THE LIST, GUYS.
FORGET HIM, BOSS! PUT YOUR FOOT DOWN AND GET US BACK HOME.
WE NEVER HAVE TO SEE THAT GUN-HAPPY PSYCHOPATH AGAIN!
SLINKY HAS A POINT. THINGS ARE GOING TO GO CRAZY ONCE THE TAYAN REBELS LAND.
WE SHOULD KEEP OUR HEADS DOWN UNTIL IT'S ALL OVER.
YOU'RE FORGETTING THE PLAN. I CAN'T DO ANYTHING STUCK OUT HERE ALONE.
ALONE? YOU ALWAYS HAVE US, BOSS.
AS LONG AS I STICK WITH KANTOR, WE'LL BE OKAY.
THANKS TO HIS DUMB TAYAN CODE OF HONOR, HE'S OBLIGATED TO KEEP ME SAFE.
WHAT HAPPENS WHEN THE REBELS TAKE HIM OUT...
...OR THE LUMANI, OR THE GODS, OR MAYBE EVEN BRAMAN'S CREW?
...I DIDN'T GET THIS FAR WITHOUT BEING ADAPTABLE.
I HAVE BACKUP PLANS.

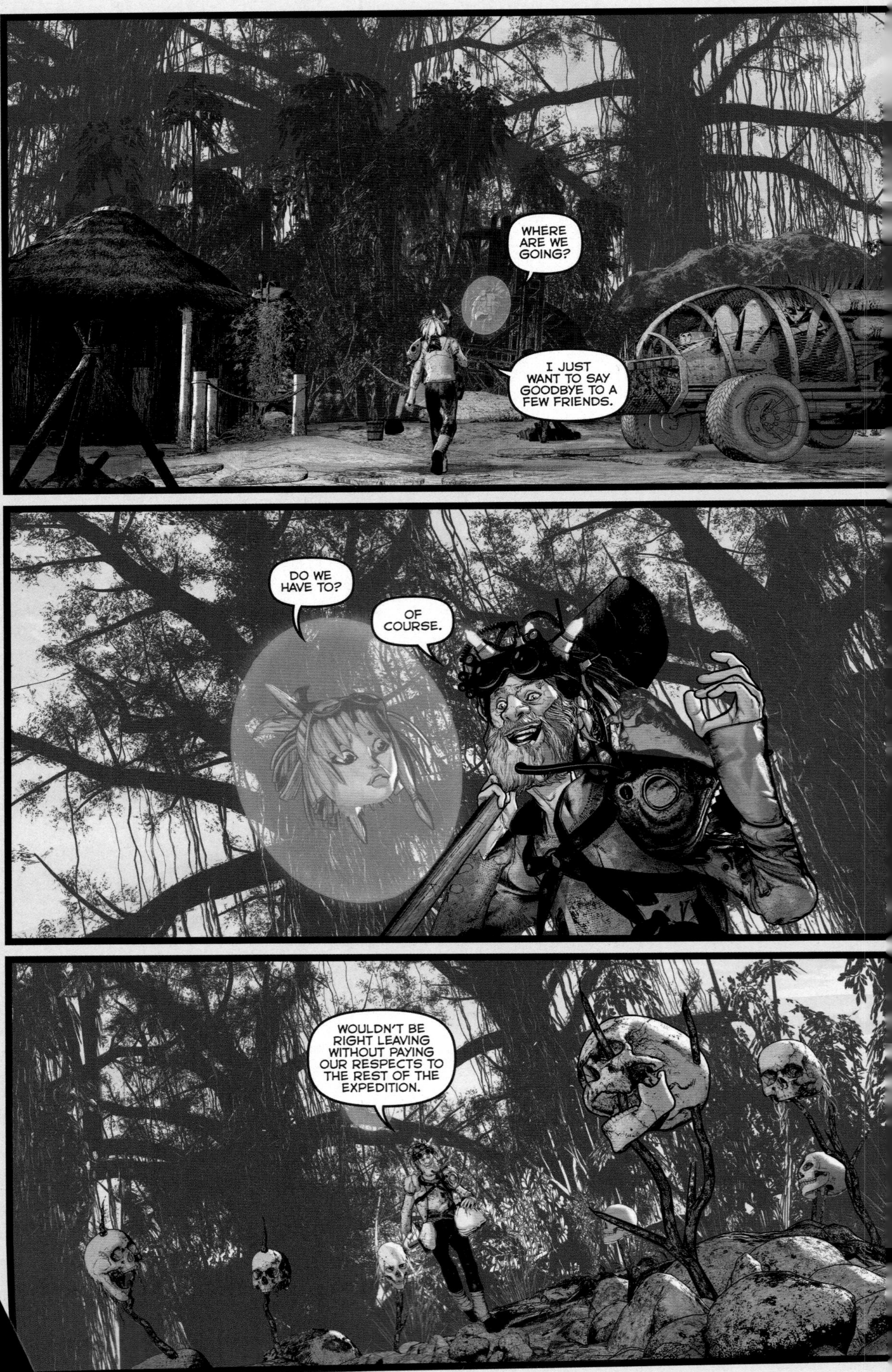
WHERE ARE WE GOING?
I JUST WANT TO SAY GOODBYE TO A FEW FRIENDS.
DO WE HAVE TO?
OF COURSE.
WOULDN'T BE RIGHT LEAVING WITHOUT PAYING OUR RESPECTS TO THE REST OF THE EXPEDITION.

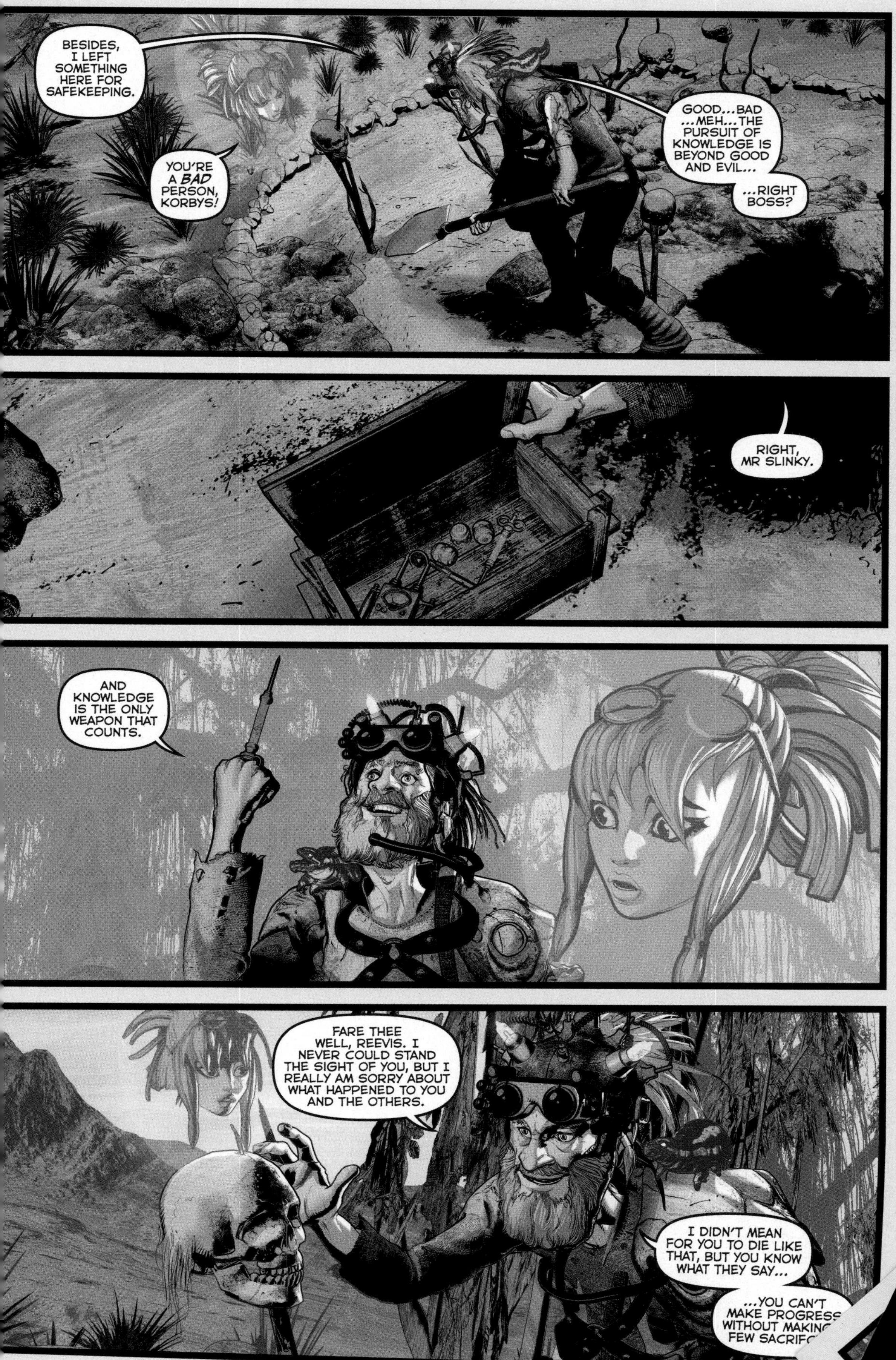
BESIDES, I LEFT SOMETHING HERE FOR SAFEKEEPING.
YOU'RE A *BAD* PERSON, KORBYS!
GOOD...BAD ...MEH...THE PURSUIT OF KNOWLEDGE IS BEYOND GOOD AND EVIL...
...RIGHT BOSS?
RIGHT, MR SLINKY.
AND KNOWLEDGE IS THE ONLY WEAPON THAT COUNTS.
FARE THEE WELL, REEVIS. I NEVER COULD STAND THE SIGHT OF YOU, BUT I REALLY AM SORRY ABOUT WHAT HAPPENED TO YOU AND THE OTHERS.
I DIDN'T MEAN FOR YOU TO DIE LIKE THAT, BUT YOU KNOW WHAT THEY SAY...
...YOU CAN'T MAKE PROGRESS WITHOUT MAKING FEW SACRIF

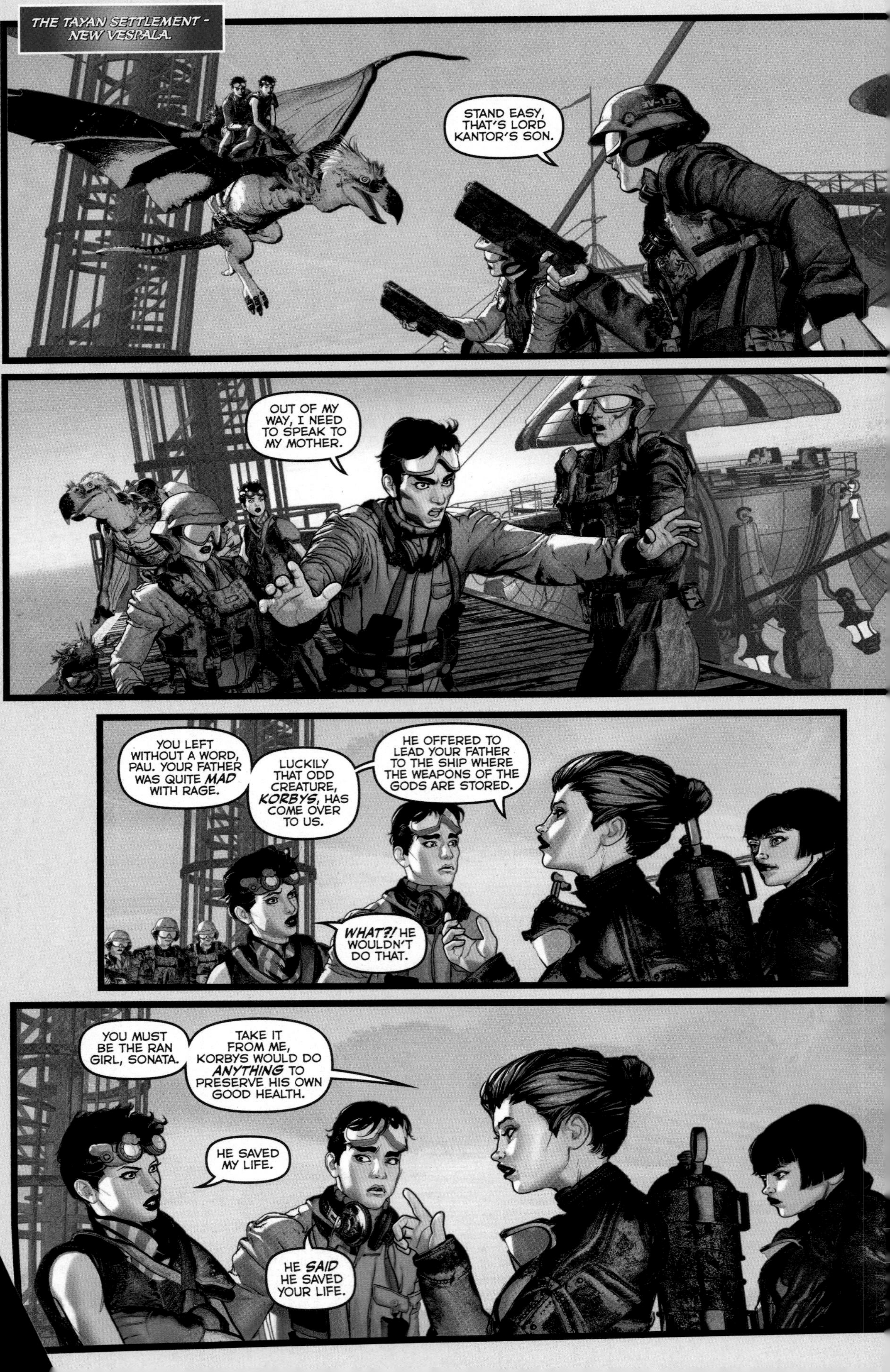
THE TAYAN SETTLEMENT - NEW VESPALA.
STAND EASY, THAT'S LORD KANTOR'S SON.
OUT OF MY WAY, I NEED TO SPEAK TO MY MOTHER.
YOU LEFT WITHOUT A WORD, PAU. YOUR FATHER WAS QUITE MAD WITH RAGE.
LUCKILY THAT ODD CREATURE, KORBYS, HAS COME OVER TO US.
HE OFFERED TO LEAD YOUR FATHER TO THE SHIP WHERE THE WEAPONS OF THE GODS ARE STORED.
WHAT?! HE WOULDN'T DO THAT.
YOU MUST BE THE RAN GIRL, SONATA.
TAKE IT FROM ME, KORBYS WOULD DO ANYTHING TO PRESERVE HIS OWN GOOD HEALTH.
HE SAVED MY LIFE.
HE SAID HE SAVED YOUR LIFE.

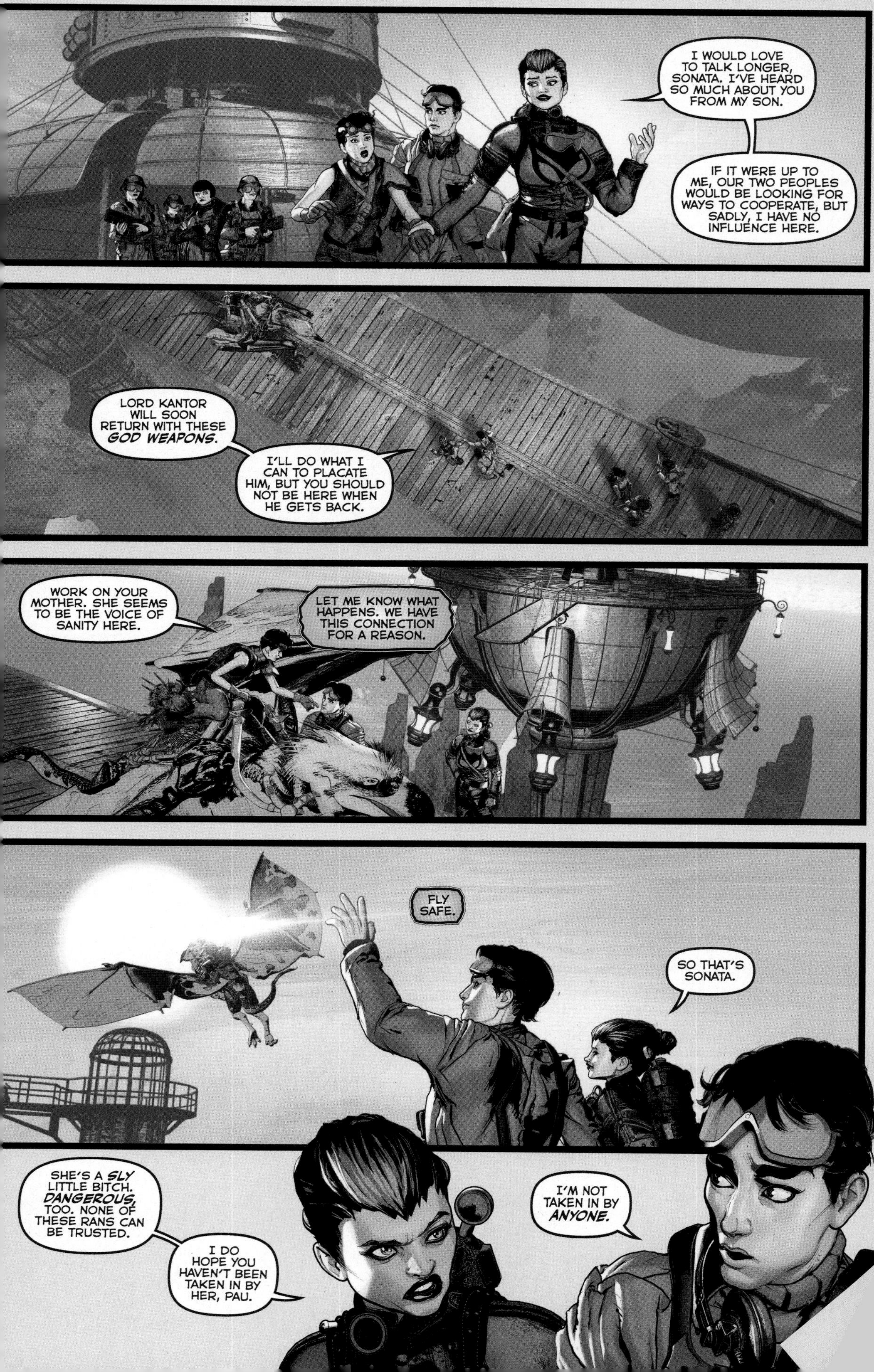
I WOULD LOVE TO TALK LONGER, SONATA. I'VE HEARD SO MUCH ABOUT YOU FROM MY SON.
IF IT WERE UP TO ME, OUR TWO PEOPLES WOULD BE LOOKING FOR WAYS TO COOPERATE, BUT SADLY, I HAVE NO INFLUENCE HERE.
LORD KANTOR WILL SOON RETURN WITH THESE *GOD WEAPONS*.
I'LL DO WHAT I CAN TO PLACATE HIM, BUT YOU SHOULD NOT BE HERE WHEN HE GETS BACK.
WORK ON YOUR MOTHER. SHE SEEMS TO BE THE VOICE OF SANITY HERE.
LET ME KNOW WHAT HAPPENS. WE HAVE THIS CONNECTION FOR A REASON.
FLY SAFE.
SO THAT'S SONATA.
SHE'S A ***SLY*** LITTLE BITCH. ***DANGEROUS,*** TOO. NONE OF THESE RANS CAN BE TRUSTED.
I DO HOPE YOU HAVEN'T BEEN TAKEN IN BY HER, PAU.
I'M NOT TAKEN IN BY *ANYONE*.

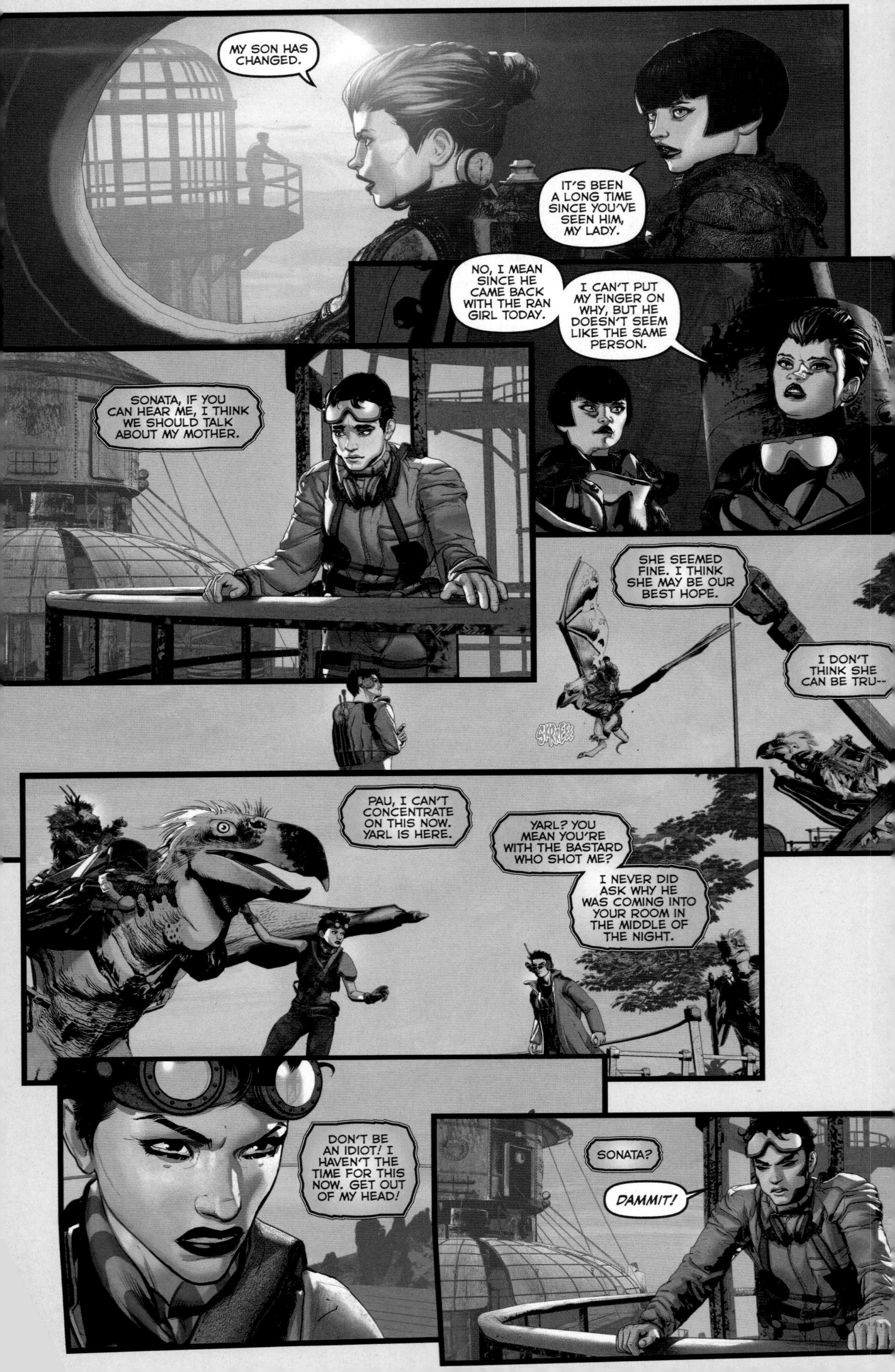
MY SON HAS CHANGED.
IT'S BEEN A LONG TIME SINCE YOU'VE SEEN HIM, MY LADY.
NO, I MEAN SINCE HE CAME BACK WITH THE RAN GIRL TODAY.
I CAN'T PUT MY FINGER ON WHY, BUT HE DOESN'T SEEM LIKE THE SAME PERSON.
SONATA, IF YOU CAN HEAR ME, I THINK WE SHOULD TALK ABOUT MY MOTHER.
SHE SEEMED FINE. I THINK SHE MAY BE OUR BEST HOPE.
I DON'T THINK SHE CAN BE TRU--
SKREEE
PAU, I CAN'T CONCENTRATE ON THIS NOW. YARL IS HERE.
YARL? YOU MEAN YOU'RE WITH THE BASTARD WHO SHOT ME?
I NEVER DID ASK WHY HE WAS COMING INTO YOUR ROOM IN THE MIDDLE OF THE NIGHT.
DON'T BE AN IDIOT! I HAVEN'T THE TIME FOR THIS NOW. GET OUT OF MY HEAD!
SONATA?
DAMMIT!

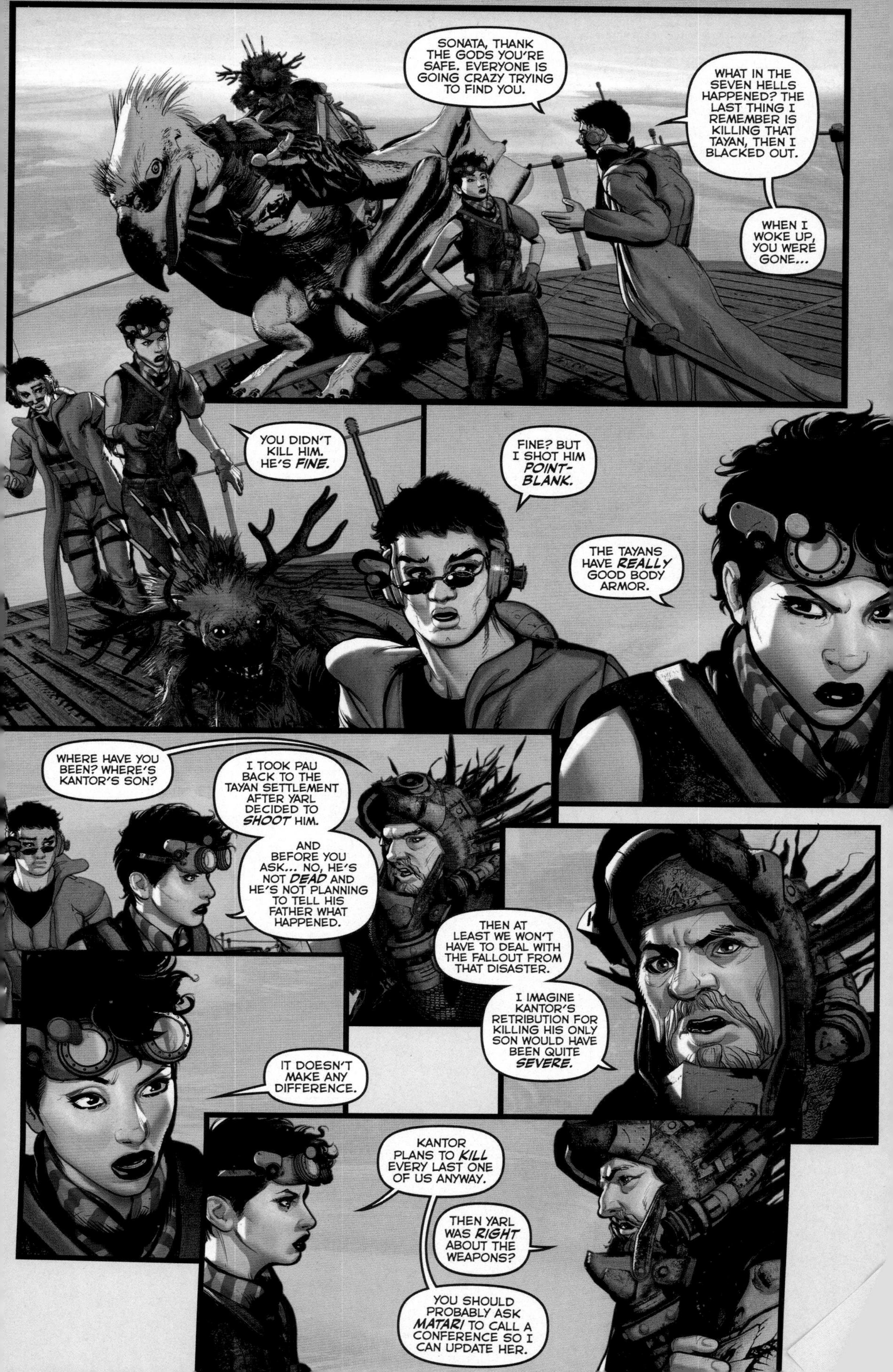
SONATA, THANK THE GODS YOU'RE SAFE. EVERYONE IS GOING CRAZY TRYING TO FIND YOU.
WHAT IN THE SEVEN HELLS HAPPENED? THE LAST THING I REMEMBER IS KILLING THAT TAYAN, THEN I BLACKED OUT.
WHEN I WOKE UP, YOU WERE GONE...
YOU DIDN'T KILL HIM. HE'S FINE.
FINE? BUT I SHOT HIM POINT-BLANK.
THE TAYANS HAVE REALLY GOOD BODY ARMOR.
WHERE HAVE YOU BEEN? WHERE'S KANTOR'S SON?
I TOOK PAU BACK TO THE TAYAN SETTLEMENT AFTER YARL DECIDED TO SHOOT HIM.
AND BEFORE YOU ASK... NO, HE'S NOT DEAD AND HE'S NOT PLANNING TO TELL HIS FATHER WHAT HAPPENED.
THEN AT LEAST WE WON'T HAVE TO DEAL WITH THE FALLOUT FROM THAT DISASTER.
I IMAGINE KANTOR'S RETRIBUTION FOR KILLING HIS ONLY SON WOULD HAVE BEEN QUITE SEVERE.
IT DOESN'T MAKE ANY DIFFERENCE.
KANTOR PLANS TO KILL EVERY LAST ONE OF US ANYWAY.
THEN YARL WAS RIGHT ABOUT THE WEAPONS?
YOU SHOULD PROBABLY ASK MATARI TO CALL A CONFERENCE SO I CAN UPDATE HER.

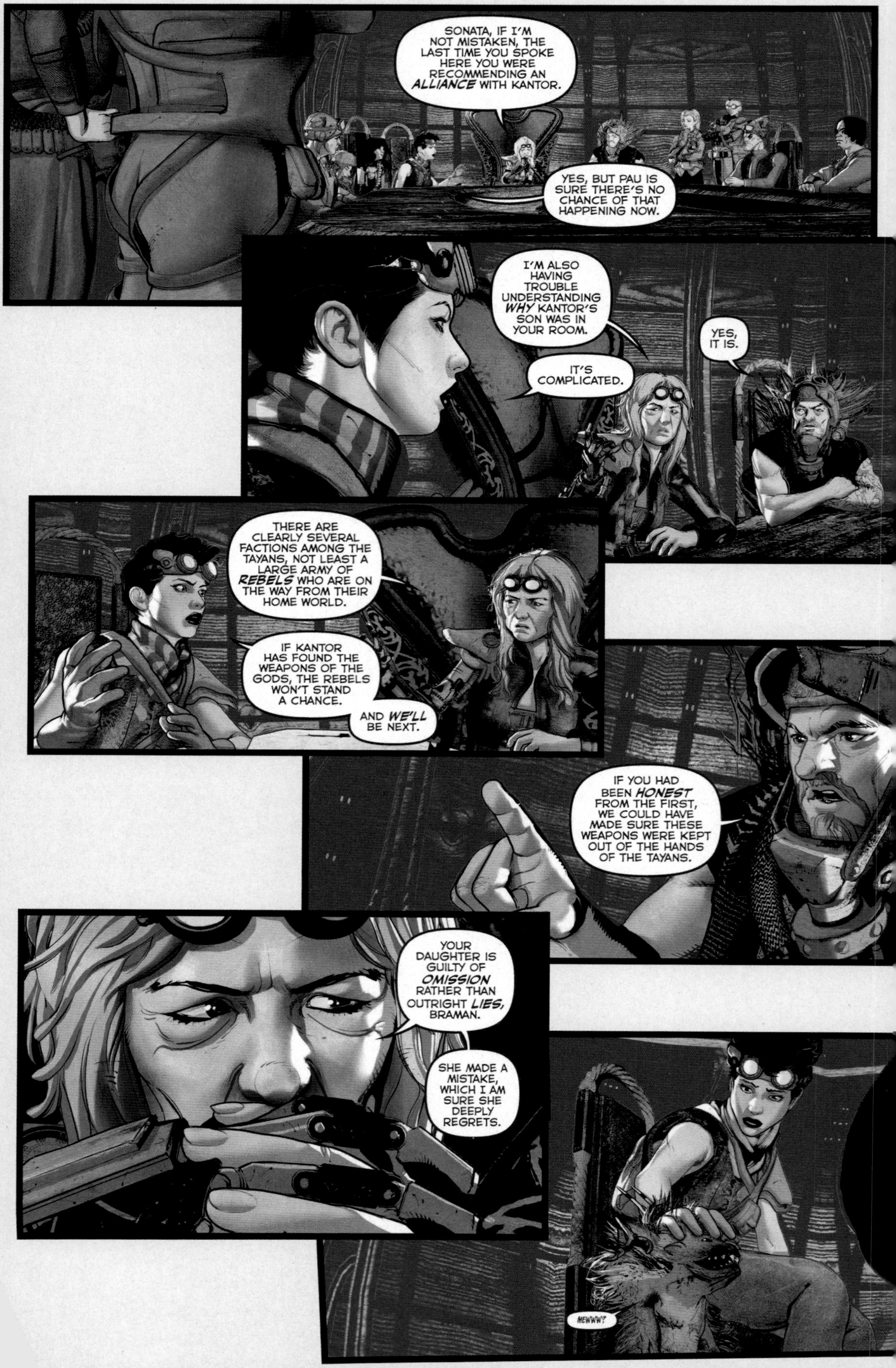
SONATA, IF I'M NOT MISTAKEN, THE LAST TIME YOU SPOKE HERE YOU WERE RECOMMENDING AN *ALLIANCE* WITH KANTOR.
YES, BUT PAU IS SURE THERE'S NO CHANCE OF THAT HAPPENING NOW.
I'M ALSO HAVING TROUBLE UNDERSTANDING *WHY* KANTOR'S SON WAS IN YOUR ROOM.
IT'S COMPLICATED.
YES, IT IS.
THERE ARE CLEARLY SEVERAL FACTIONS AMONG THE TAYANS, NOT LEAST A LARGE ARMY OF *REBELS* WHO ARE ON THE WAY FROM THEIR HOME WORLD.
IF KANTOR HAS FOUND THE WEAPONS OF THE GODS, THE REBELS WON'T STAND A CHANCE.
AND *WE'LL* BE NEXT.
IF YOU HAD BEEN *HONEST* FROM THE FIRST, WE COULD HAVE MADE SURE THESE WEAPONS WERE KEPT OUT OF THE HANDS OF THE TAYANS.
YOUR DAUGHTER IS GUILTY OF *OMISSION* RATHER THAN OUTRIGHT *LIES,* BRAMAN.
SHE MADE A MISTAKE, WHICH I AM SURE SHE DEEPLY REGRETS.
MEWWW?

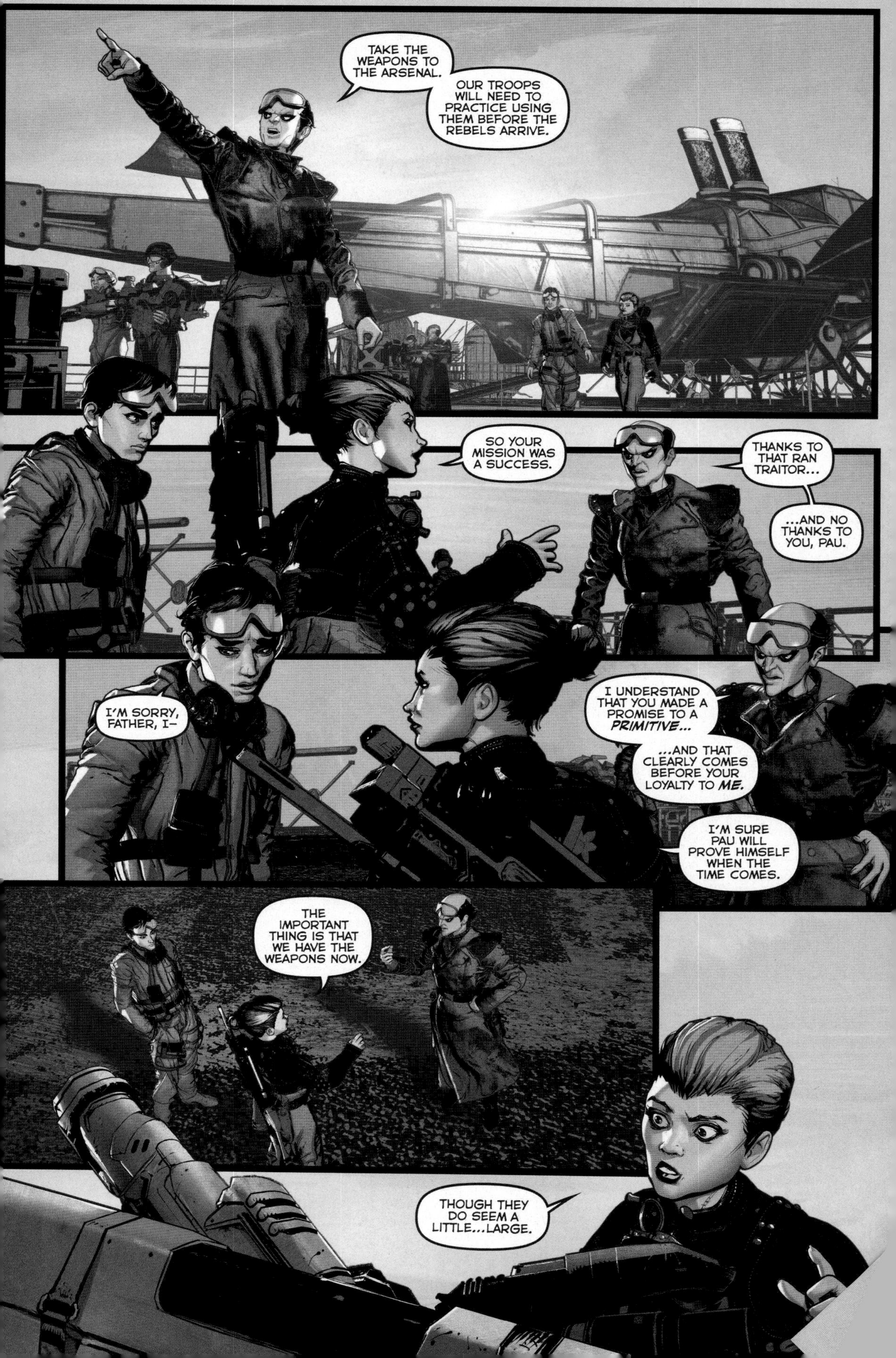
TAKE THE WEAPONS TO THE ARSENAL.
OUR TROOPS WILL NEED TO PRACTICE USING THEM BEFORE THE REBELS ARRIVE.
SO YOUR MISSION WAS A SUCCESS.
THANKS TO THAT RAN TRAITOR...
...AND NO THANKS TO YOU, PAU.
I'M SORRY, FATHER, I-
I UNDERSTAND THAT YOU MADE A PROMISE TO A *PRIMITIVE*...
...AND THAT CLEARLY COMES BEFORE YOUR LOYALTY TO *ME.*
I'M SURE PAU WILL PROVE HIMSELF WHEN THE TIME COMES.
THE IMPORTANT THING IS THAT WE HAVE THE WEAPONS NOW.
THOUGH THEY DO SEEM A LITTLE...LARGE.

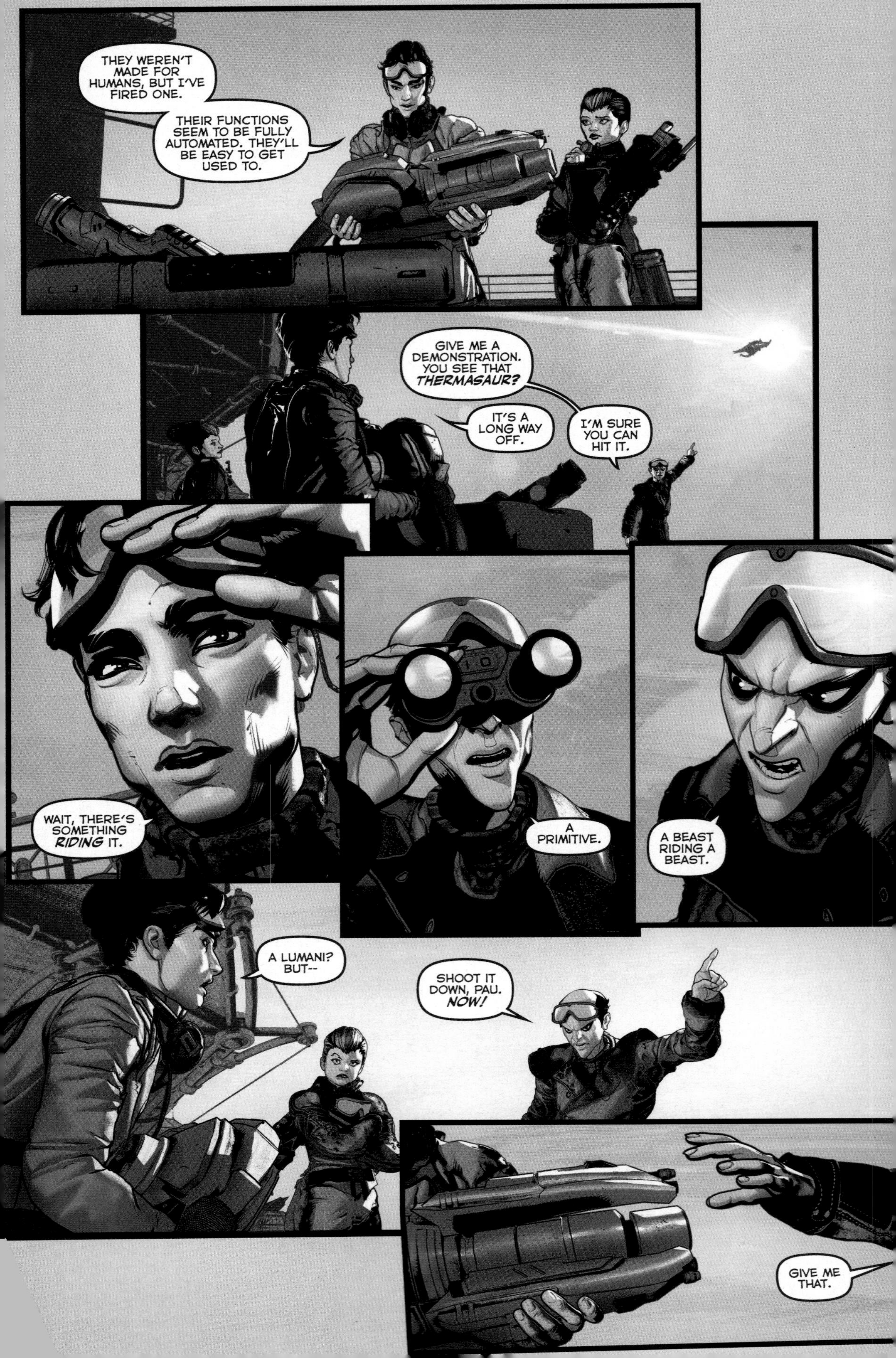
THEY WEREN'T MADE FOR HUMANS, BUT I'VE FIRED ONE.
THEIR FUNCTIONS SEEM TO BE FULLY AUTOMATED. THEY'LL BE EASY TO GET USED TO.
GIVE ME A DEMONSTRATION. YOU SEE THAT *THERMASAUR?*
IT'S A LONG WAY OFF.
I'M SURE YOU CAN HIT IT.
WAIT, THERE'S SOMETHING *RIDING* IT.
A PRIMITIVE.
A BEAST RIDING A BEAST.
A LUMANI? BUT--
SHOOT IT DOWN, PAU. *NOW!*
GIVE ME THAT.

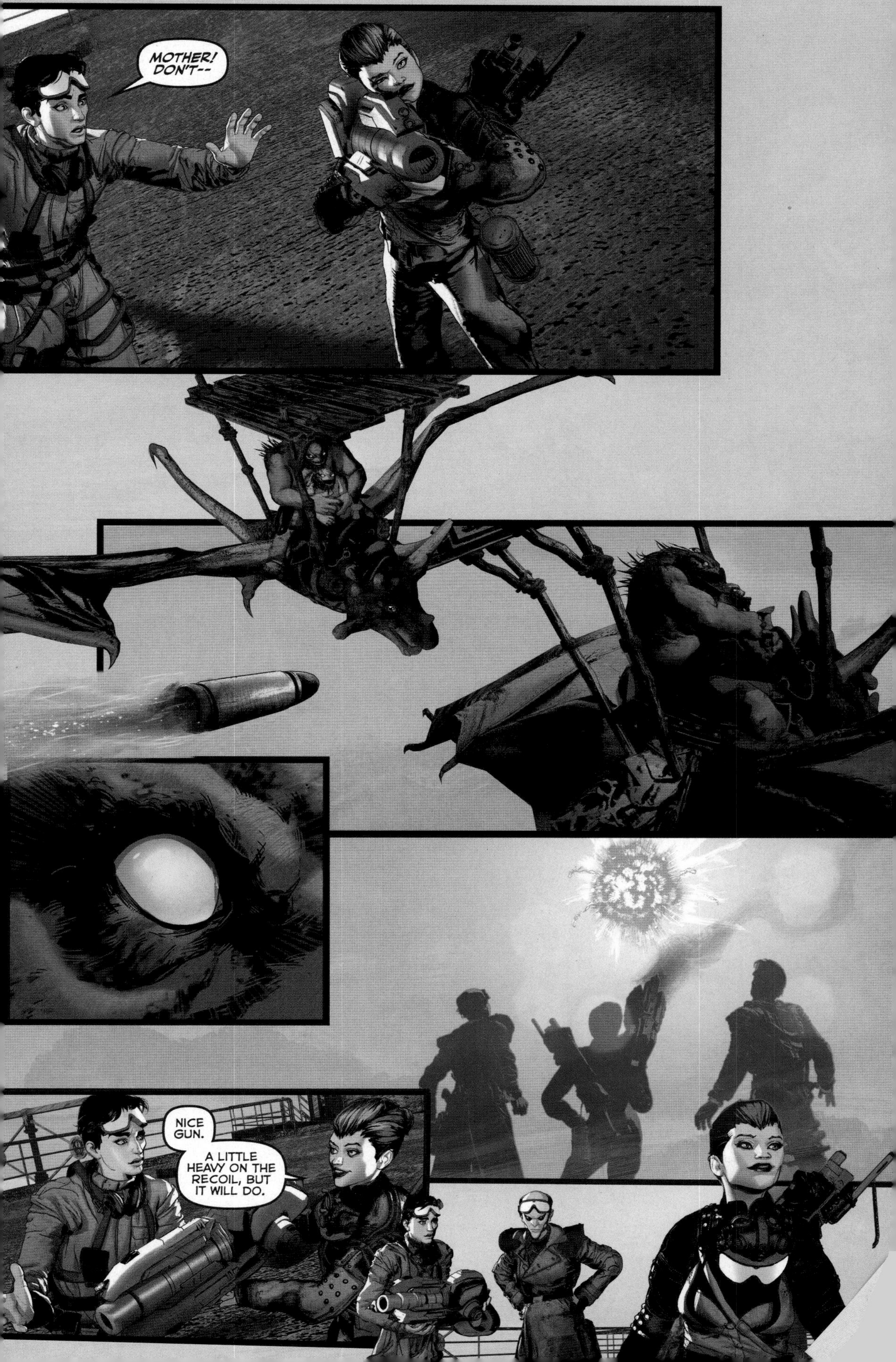
MOTHER! DON'T--
NICE GUN.
A LITTLE HEAVY ON THE RECOIL, BUT IT WILL DO.

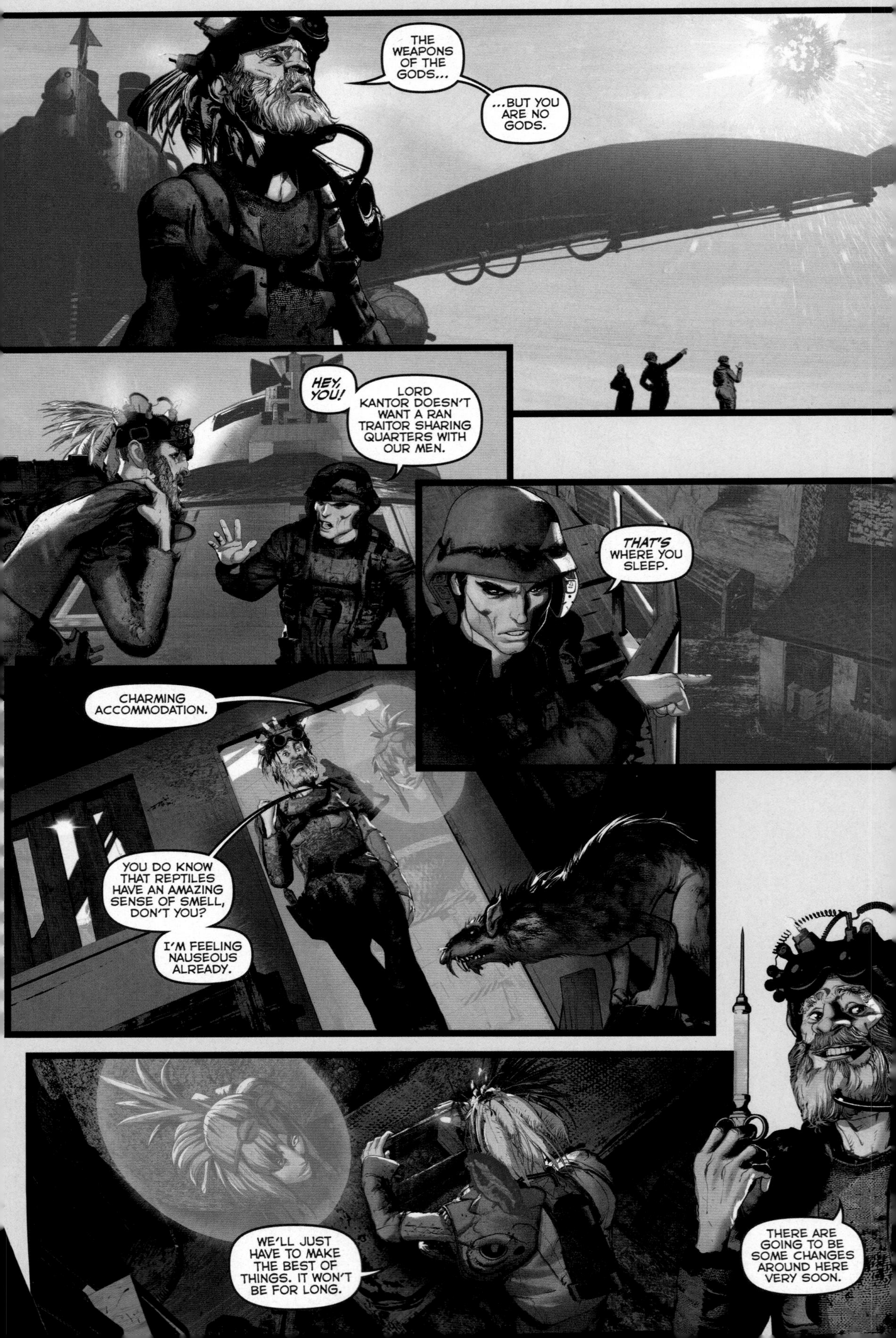

THE WEAPONS OF THE GODS...
...BUT YOU ARE NO GODS.
HEY, YOU!
LORD KANTOR DOESN'T WANT A RAN TRAITOR SHARING QUARTERS WITH OUR MEN.
THAT'S WHERE YOU SLEEP.
CHARMING ACCOMMODATION.
YOU DO KNOW THAT REPTILES HAVE AN AMAZING SENSE OF SMELL, DON'T YOU?
I'M FEELING NAUSEOUS ALREADY.
WE'LL JUST HAVE TO MAKE THE BEST OF THINGS. IT WON'T BE FOR LONG.
THERE ARE GOING TO BE SOME CHANGES AROUND HERE VERY SOON.

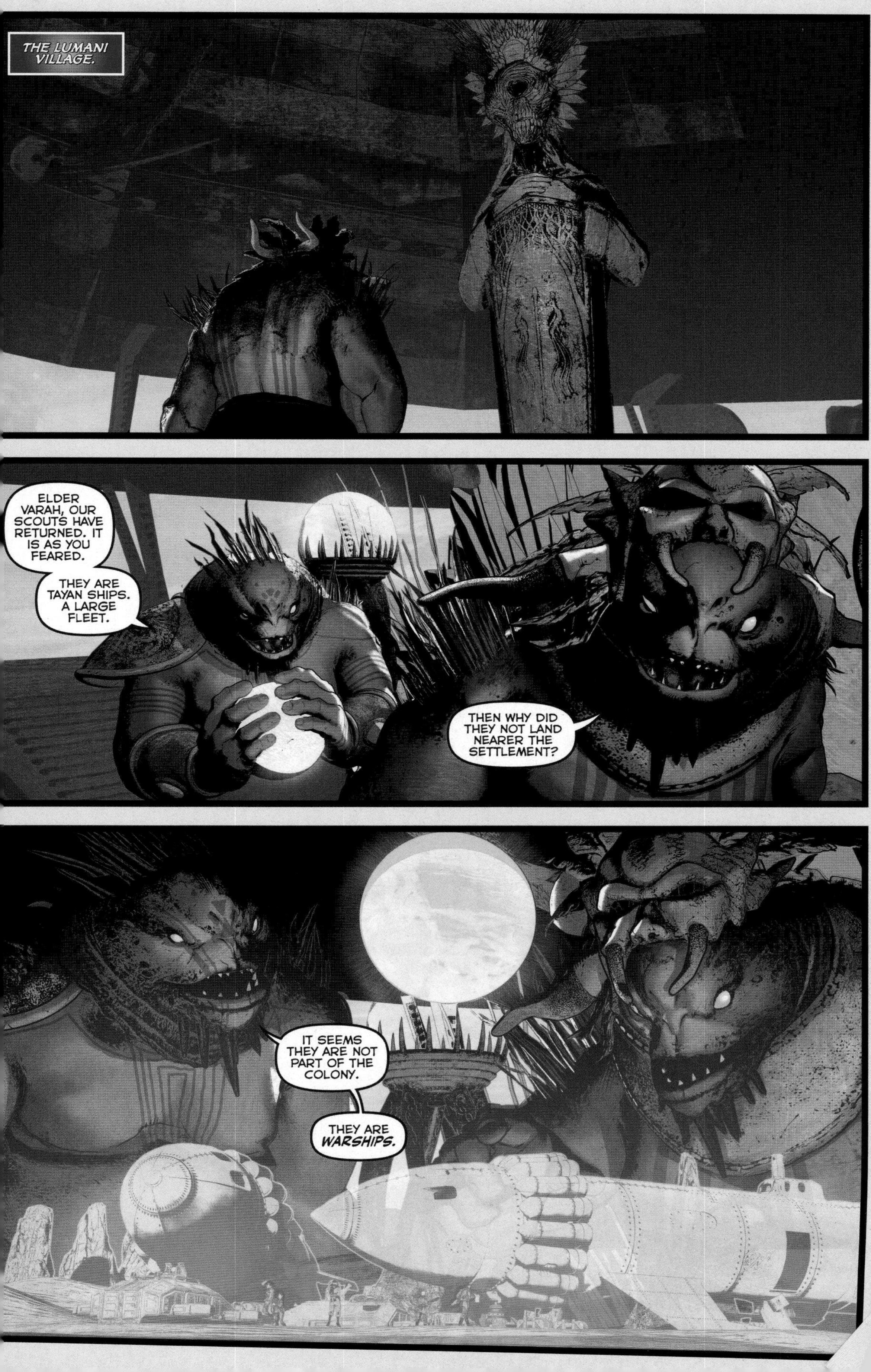
THE LUMANI VILLAGE.
ELDER VARAH, OUR SCOUTS HAVE RETURNED. IT IS AS YOU FEARED.
THEY ARE TAYAN SHIPS. A LARGE FLEET.
THEN WHY DID THEY NOT LAND NEARER THE SETTLEMENT?
IT SEEMS THEY ARE NOT PART OF THE COLONY.
THEY ARE *WARSHIPS.*

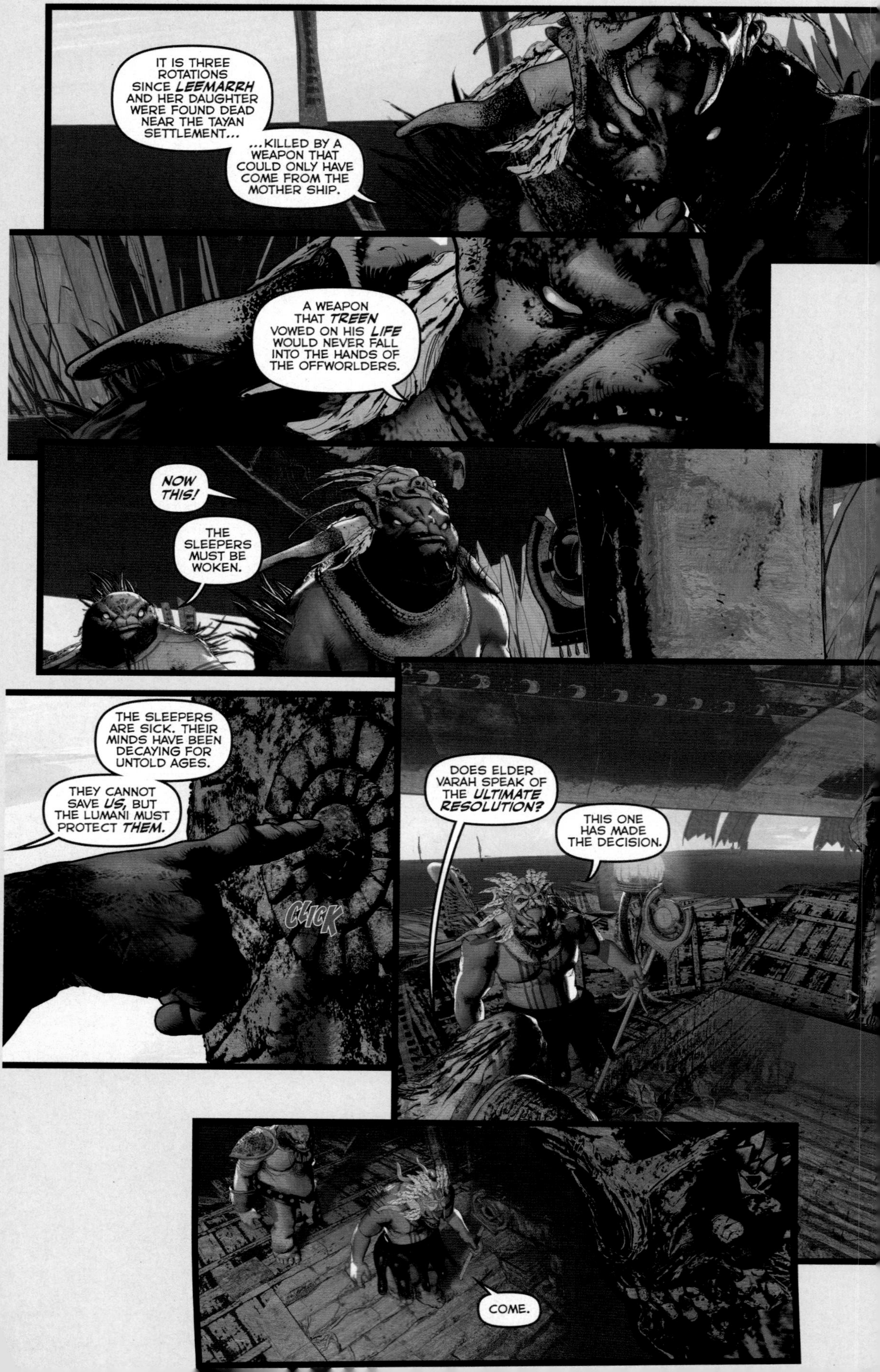
IT IS THREE ROTATIONS SINCE LEEMARRH AND HER DAUGHTER WERE FOUND DEAD NEAR THE TAYAN SETTLEMENT...
...KILLED BY A WEAPON THAT COULD ONLY HAVE COME FROM THE MOTHER SHIP.
A WEAPON THAT TREEN VOWED ON HIS LIFE WOULD NEVER FALL INTO THE HANDS OF THE OFFWORLDERS.
NOW THIS!
THE SLEEPERS MUST BE WOKEN.
THE SLEEPERS ARE SICK. THEIR MINDS HAVE BEEN DECAYING FOR UNTOLD AGES.
THEY CANNOT SAVE US, BUT THE LUMANI MUST PROTECT THEM.
CLICK
DOES ELDER VARAH SPEAK OF THE ULTIMATE RESOLUTION?
THIS ONE HAS MADE THE DECISION.
COME.

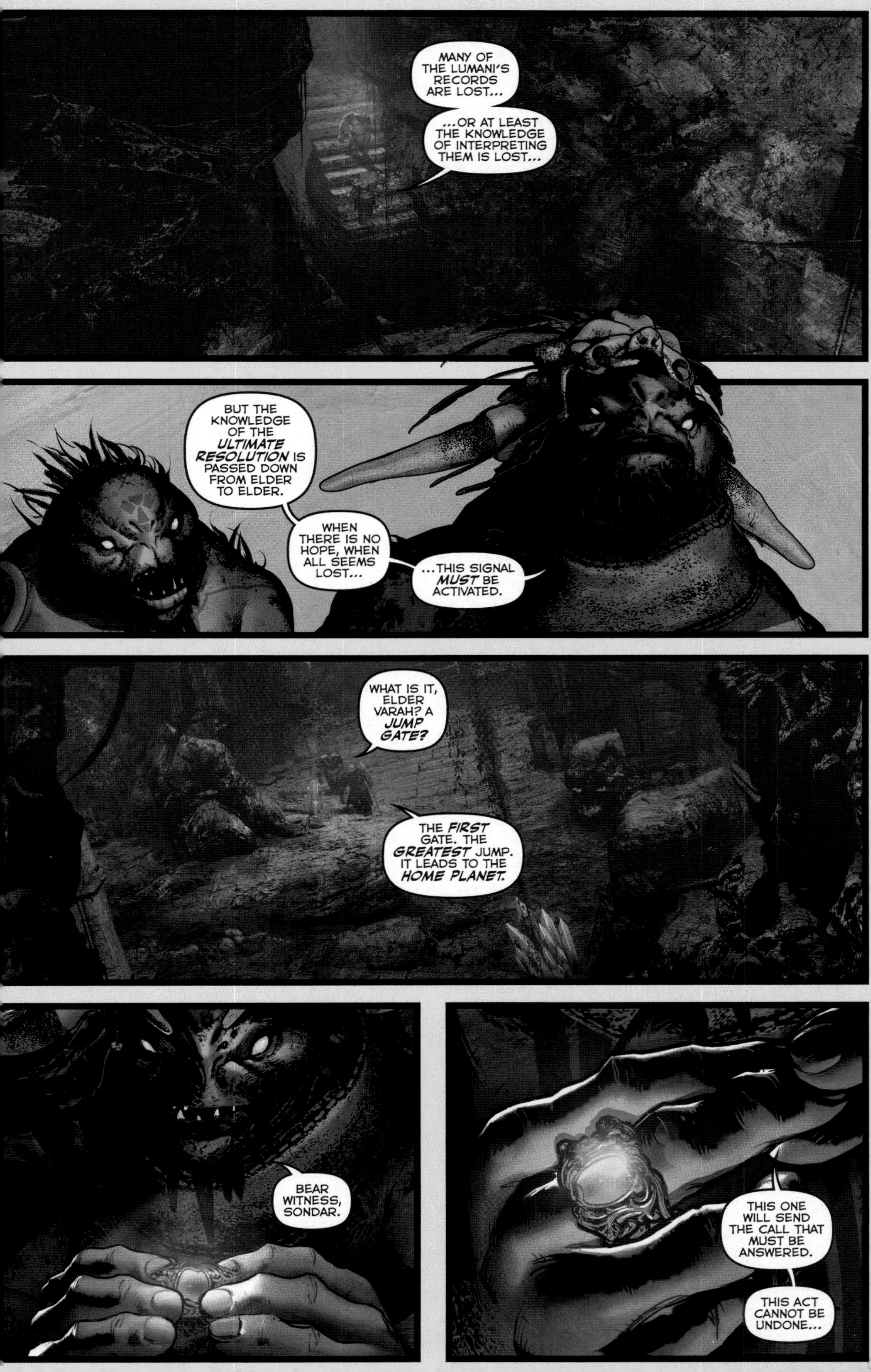
MANY OF THE LUMANI'S RECORDS ARE LOST...
...OR AT LEAST THE KNOWLEDGE OF INTERPRETING THEM IS LOST...
BUT THE KNOWLEDGE OF THE *ULTIMATE RESOLUTION* IS PASSED DOWN FROM ELDER TO ELDER.
WHEN THERE IS NO HOPE, WHEN ALL SEEMS LOST...
...THIS SIGNAL *MUST* BE ACTIVATED.
WHAT IS IT, ELDER VARAH? A *JUMP GATE?*
THE *FIRST* GATE. THE *GREATEST* JUMP. IT LEADS TO THE *HOME PLANET.*
BEAR WITNESS, SONDAR.
THIS ONE WILL SEND THE CALL THAT MUST BE ANSWERED.
THIS ACT CANNOT BE UNDONE...

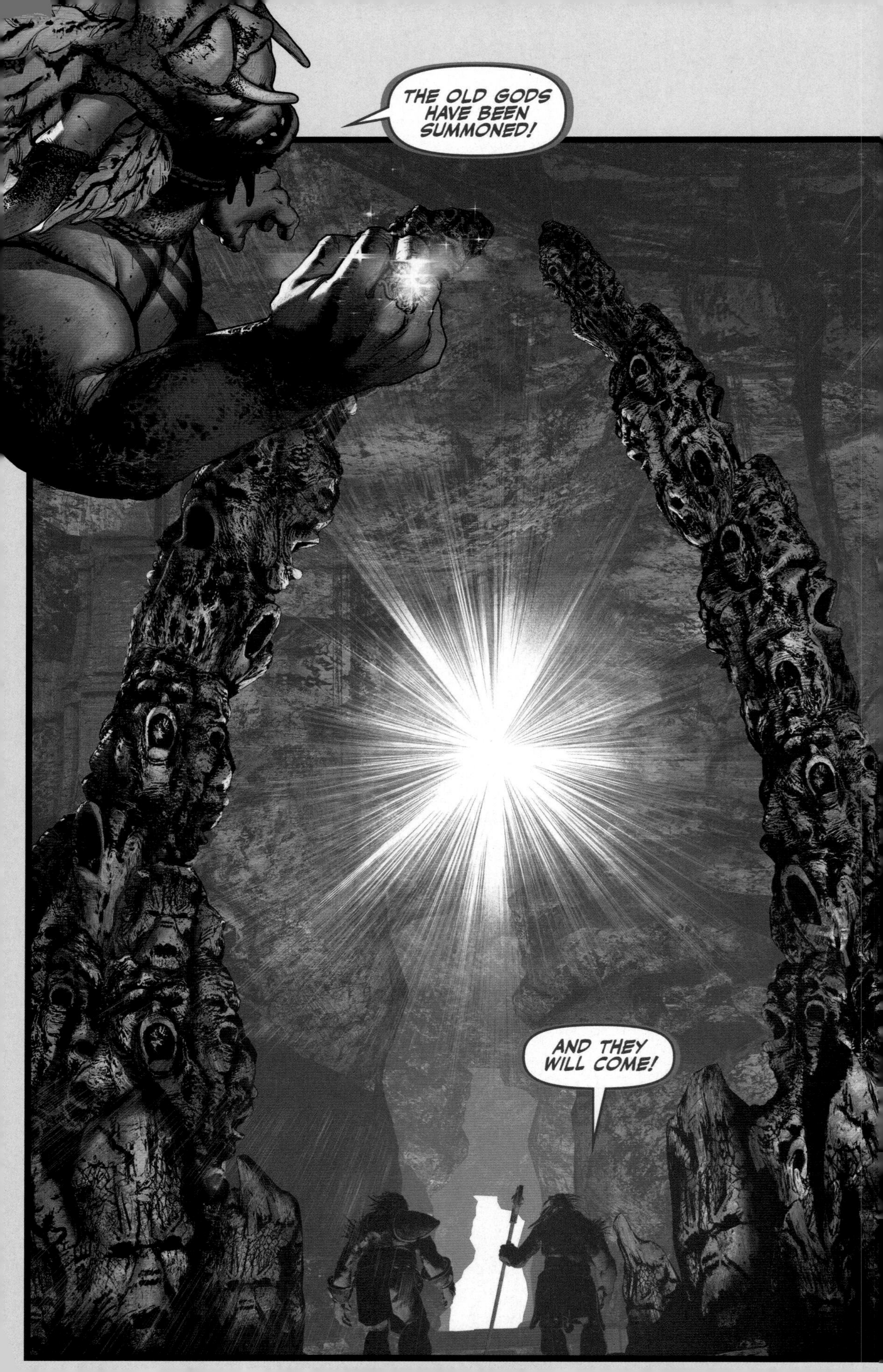
THE OLD GODS HAVE BEEN SUMMONED!
AND THEY WILL COME!

Issue #8 Cover A

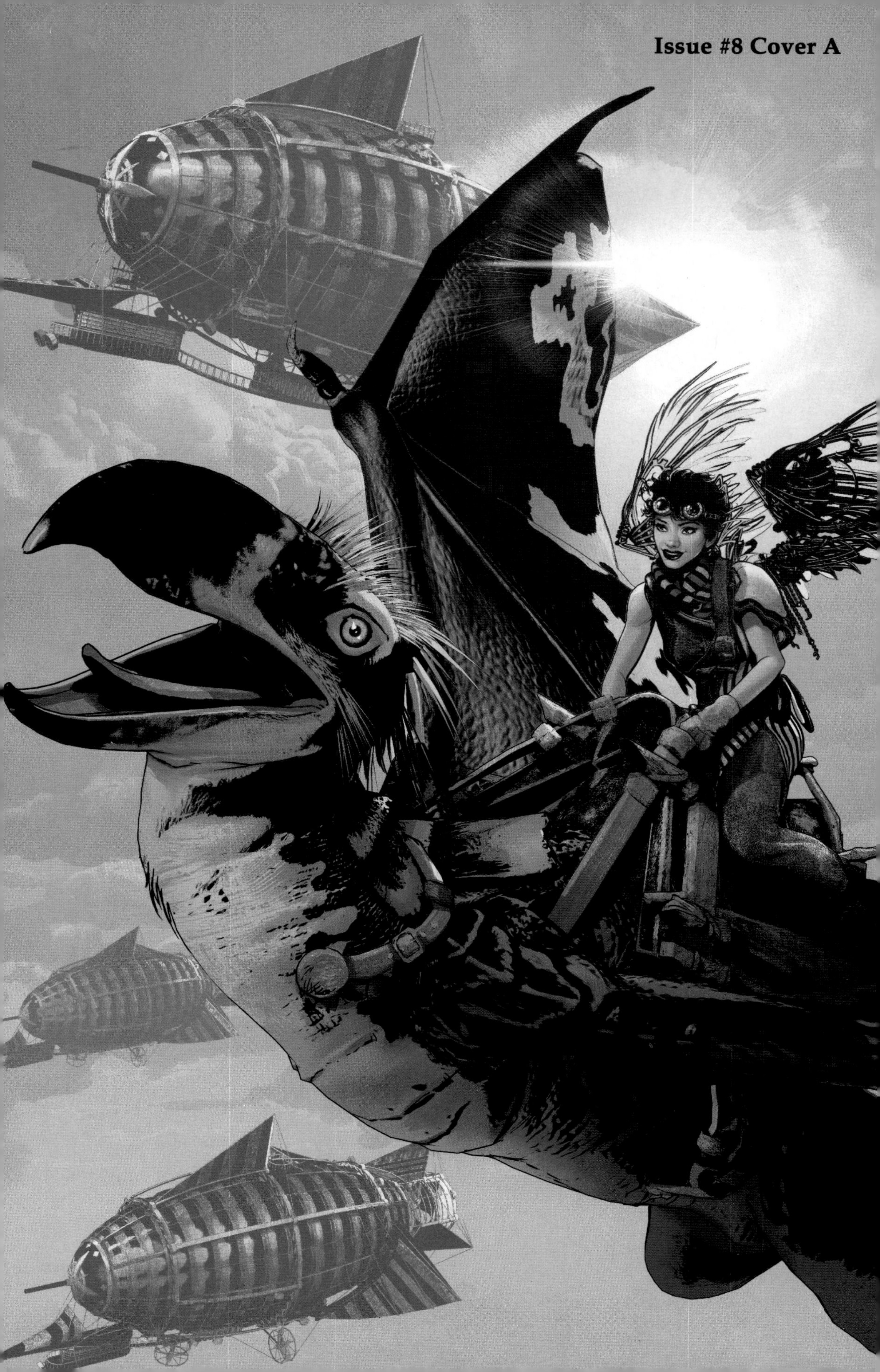

Issue #8 Cover B

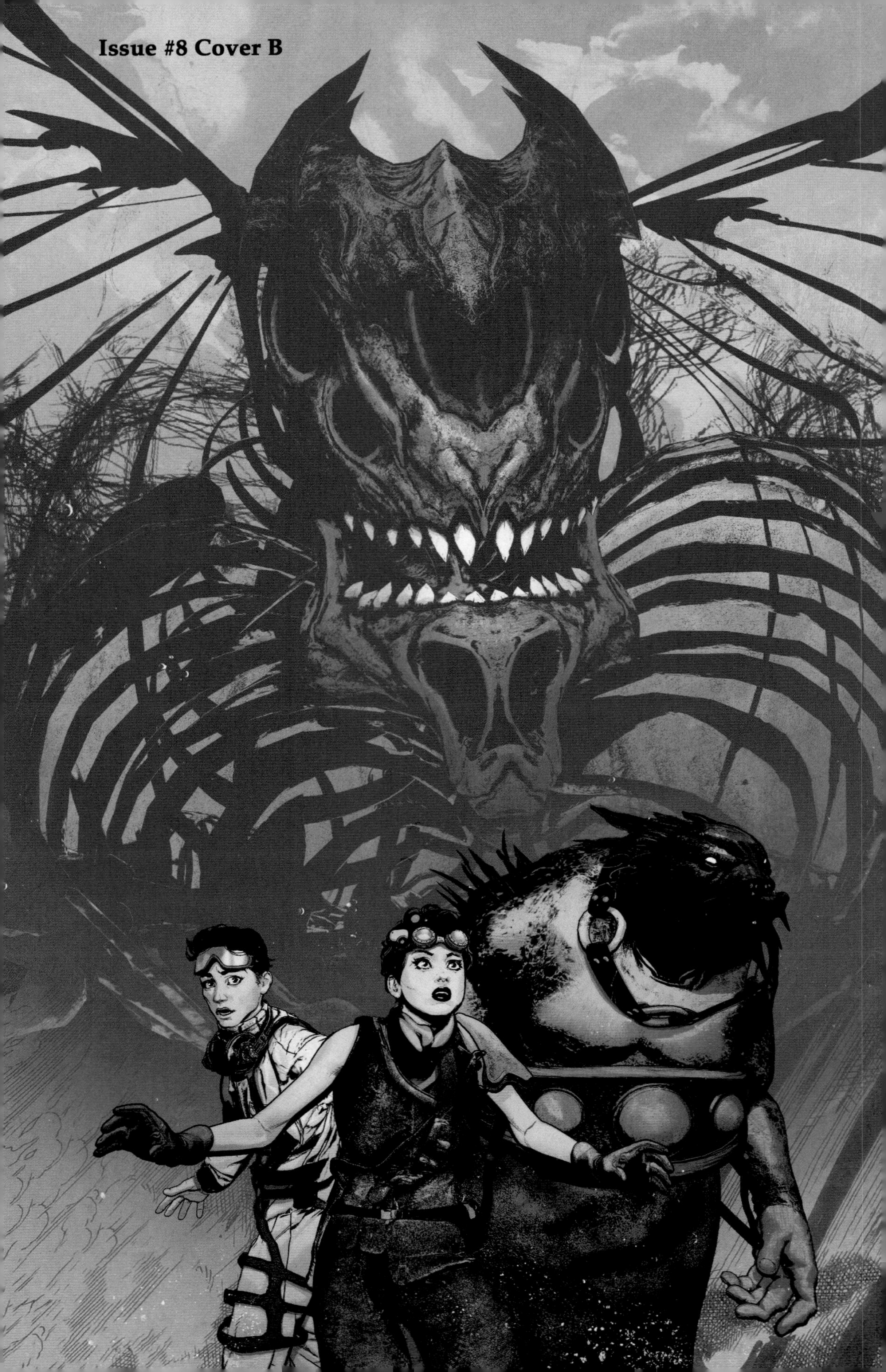

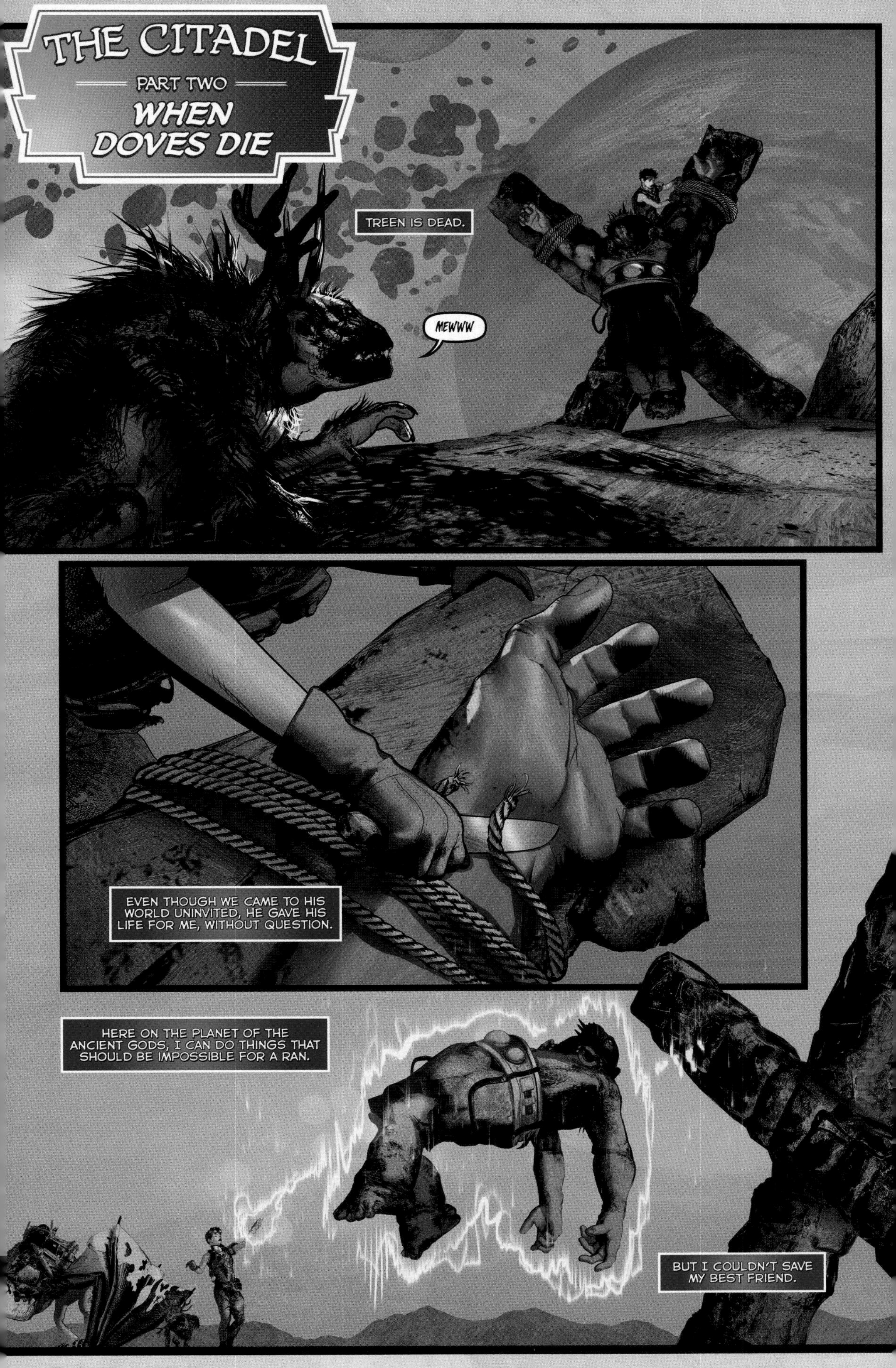
THE CITADEL
PART TWO
WHEN DOVES DIE
TREEN IS DEAD.
MEWWW
EVEN THOUGH WE CAME TO HIS WORLD UNINVITED, HE GAVE HIS LIFE FOR ME, WITHOUT QUESTION.
HERE ON THE PLANET OF THE ANCIENT GODS, I CAN DO THINGS THAT SHOULD BE IMPOSSIBLE FOR A RAN.
BUT I COULDN'T SAVE MY BEST FRIEND.

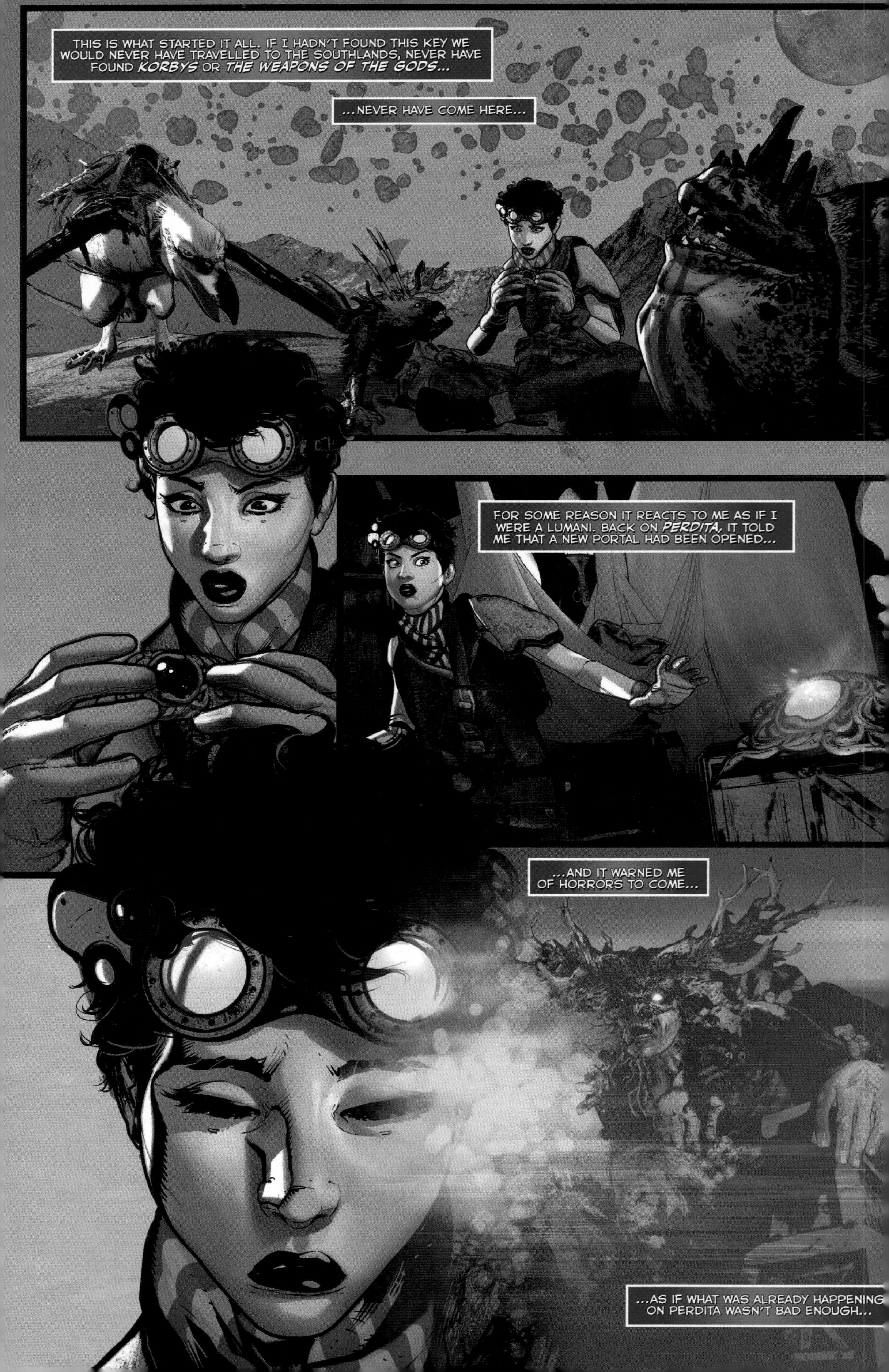
THIS IS WHAT STARTED IT ALL. IF I HADN'T FOUND THIS KEY WE WOULD NEVER HAVE TRAVELLED TO THE SOUTHLANDS, NEVER HAVE FOUND KORBYS OR THE WEAPONS OF THE GODS...
...NEVER HAVE COME HERE...
FOR SOME REASON IT REACTS TO ME AS IF I WERE A LUMANI. BACK ON PERDITA, IT TOLD ME THAT A NEW PORTAL HAD BEEN OPENED...
...AND IT WARNED ME OF HORRORS TO COME...
...AS IF WHAT WAS ALREADY HAPPENING ON PERDITA WASN'T BAD ENOUGH...

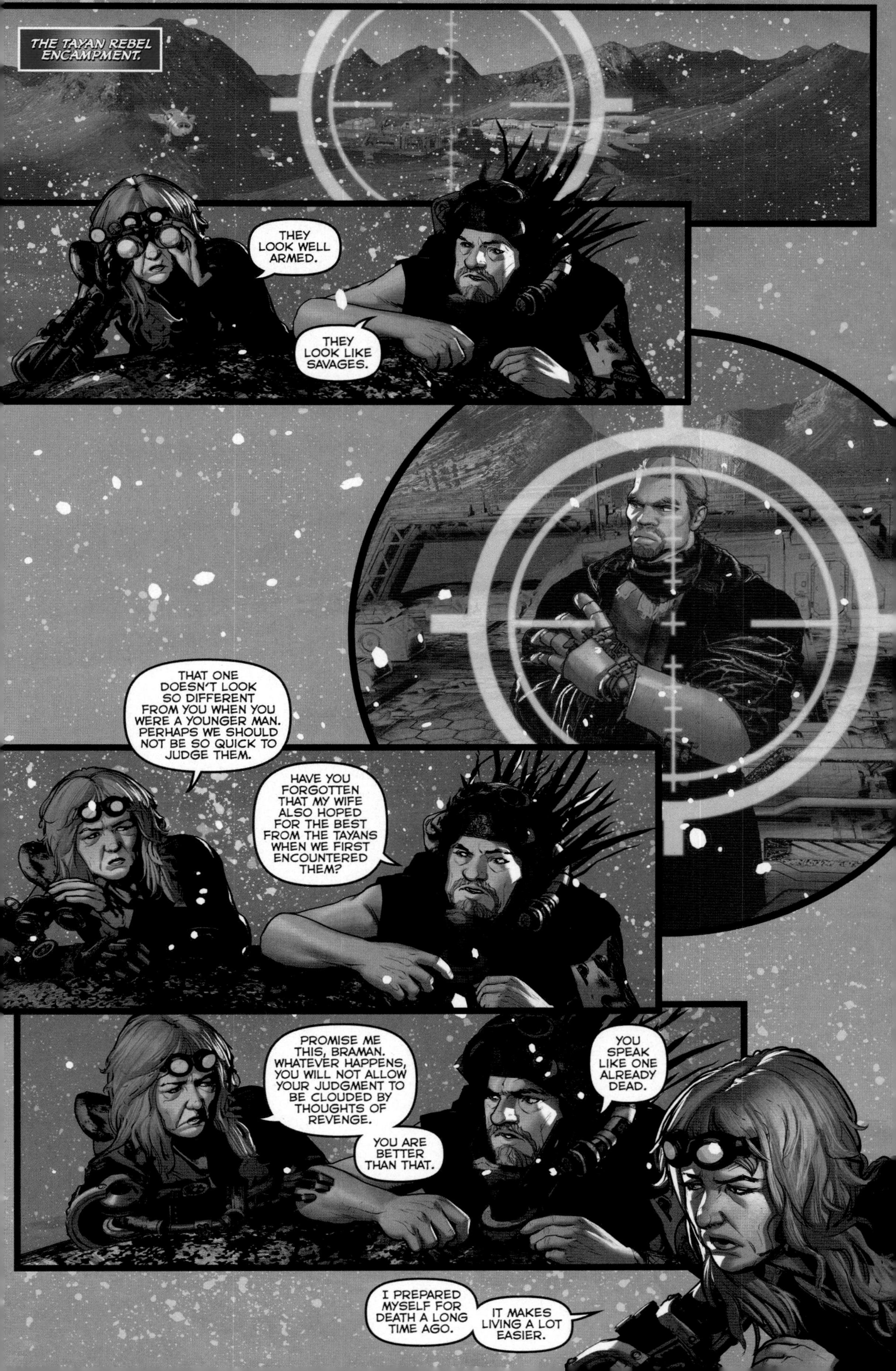
THE TAYAN REBEL ENCAMPMENT.
THEY LOOK WELL ARMED.
THEY LOOK LIKE SAVAGES.
THAT ONE DOESN'T LOOK SO DIFFERENT FROM YOU WHEN YOU WERE A YOUNGER MAN. PERHAPS WE SHOULD NOT BE SO QUICK TO JUDGE THEM.
HAVE YOU FORGOTTEN THAT MY WIFE ALSO HOPED FOR THE BEST FROM THE TAYANS WHEN WE FIRST ENCOUNTERED THEM?
PROMISE ME THIS, BRAMAN. WHATEVER HAPPENS, YOU WILL NOT ALLOW YOUR JUDGMENT TO BE CLOUDED BY THOUGHTS OF REVENGE.
YOU ARE BETTER THAN THAT.
YOU SPEAK LIKE ONE ALREADY DEAD.
I PREPARED MYSELF FOR DEATH A LONG TIME AGO.
IT MAKES LIVING A LOT EASIER.

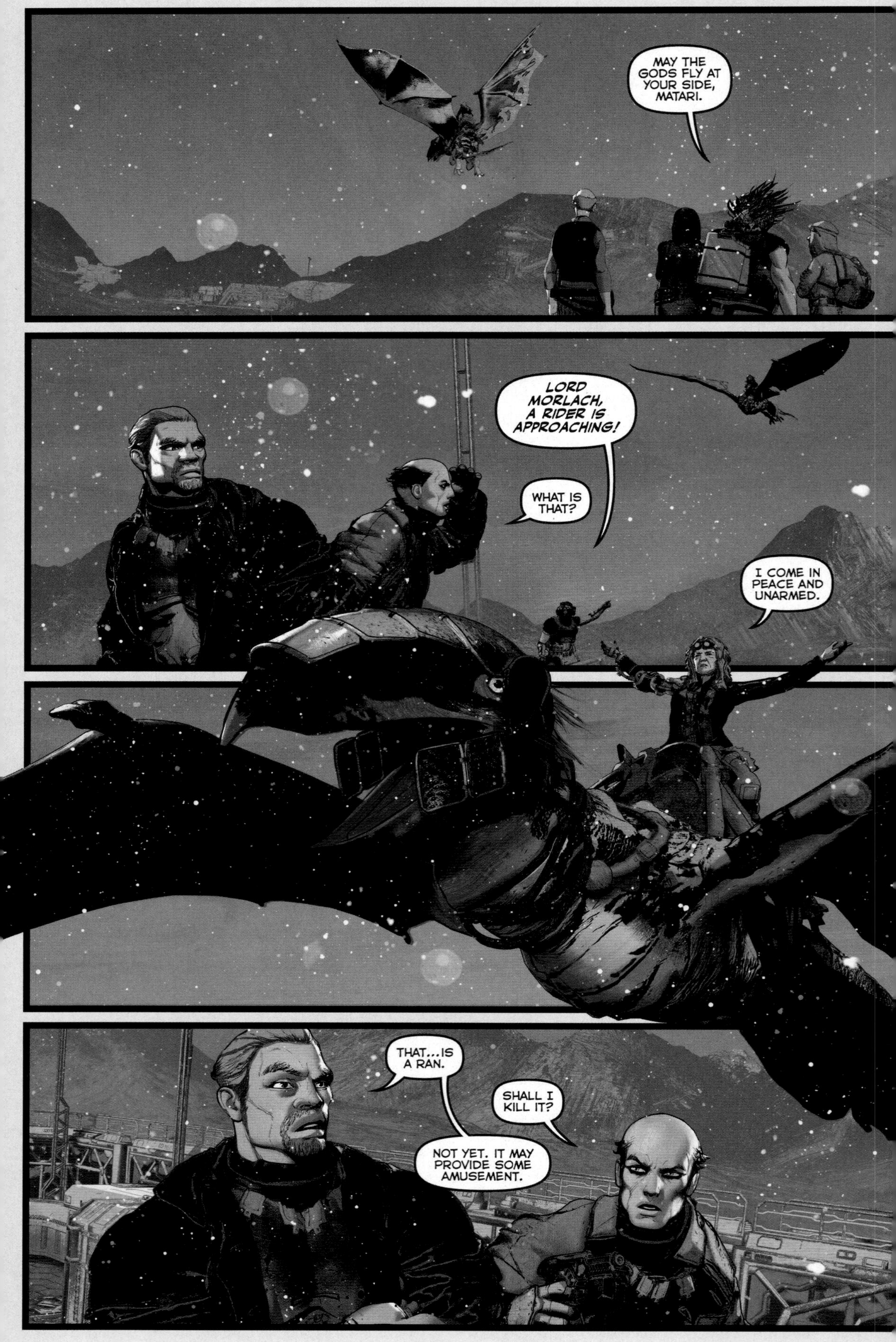
MAY THE GODS FLY AT YOUR SIDE, MATARI.
LORD MORLACH, A RIDER IS APPROACHING!
WHAT IS THAT?
I COME IN PEACE AND UNARMED.
THAT...IS A RAN.
SHALL I KILL IT?
NOT YET. IT MAY PROVIDE SOME AMUSEMENT.

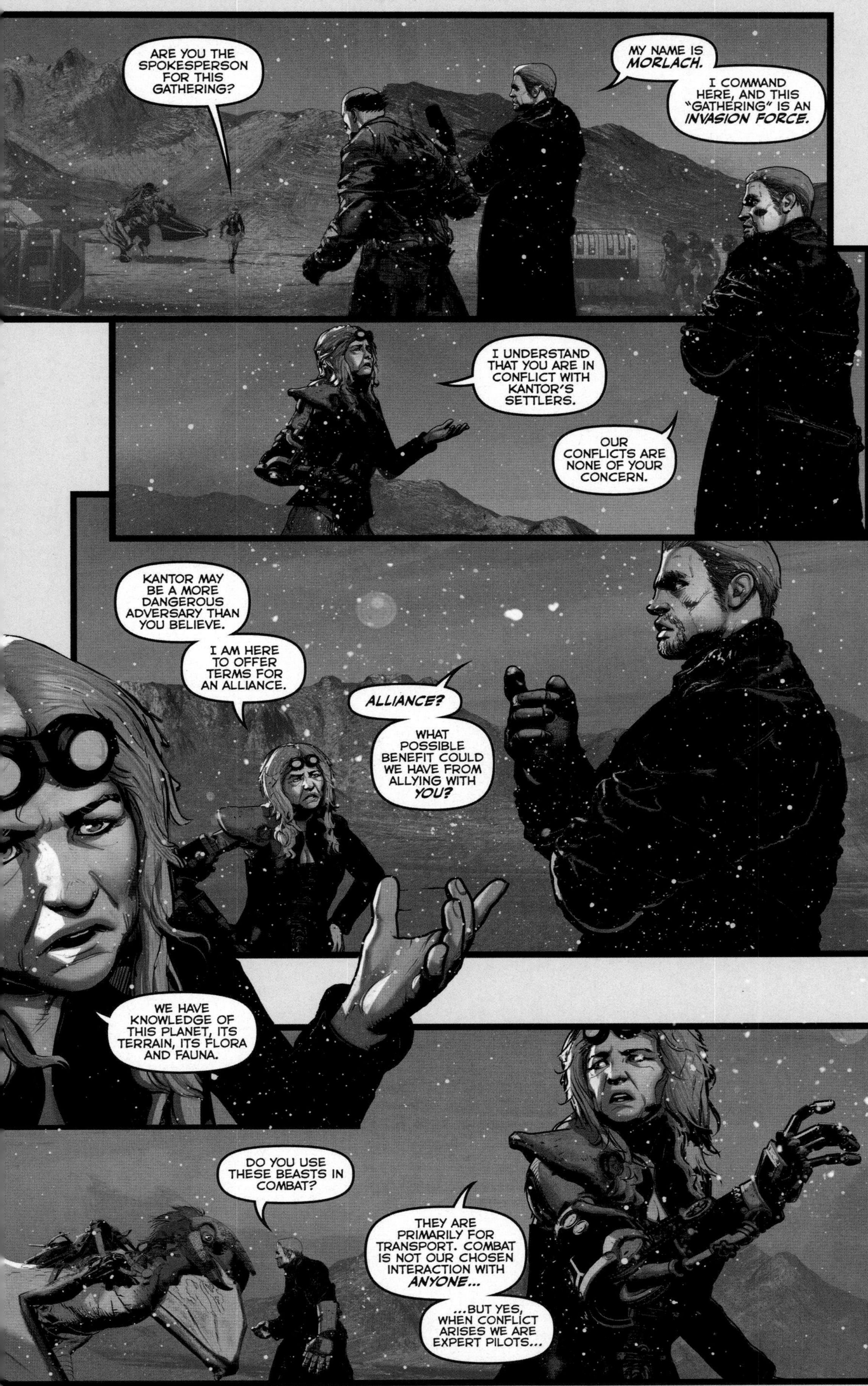
ARE YOU THE SPOKESPERSON FOR THIS GATHERING?
MY NAME IS MORLACH.
I COMMAND HERE, AND THIS "GATHERING" IS AN INVASION FORCE.
I UNDERSTAND THAT YOU ARE IN CONFLICT WITH KANTOR'S SETTLERS.
OUR CONFLICTS ARE NONE OF YOUR CONCERN.
KANTOR MAY BE A MORE DANGEROUS ADVERSARY THAN YOU BELIEVE.
I AM HERE TO OFFER TERMS FOR AN ALLIANCE.
ALLIANCE?
WHAT POSSIBLE BENEFIT COULD WE HAVE FROM ALLYING WITH YOU?
WE HAVE KNOWLEDGE OF THIS PLANET, ITS TERRAIN, ITS FLORA AND FAUNA.
DO YOU USE THESE BEASTS IN COMBAT?
THEY ARE PRIMARILY FOR TRANSPORT. COMBAT IS NOT OUR CHOSEN INTERACTION WITH ANYONE...
...BUT YES, WHEN CONFLICT ARISES WE ARE EXPERT PILOTS...

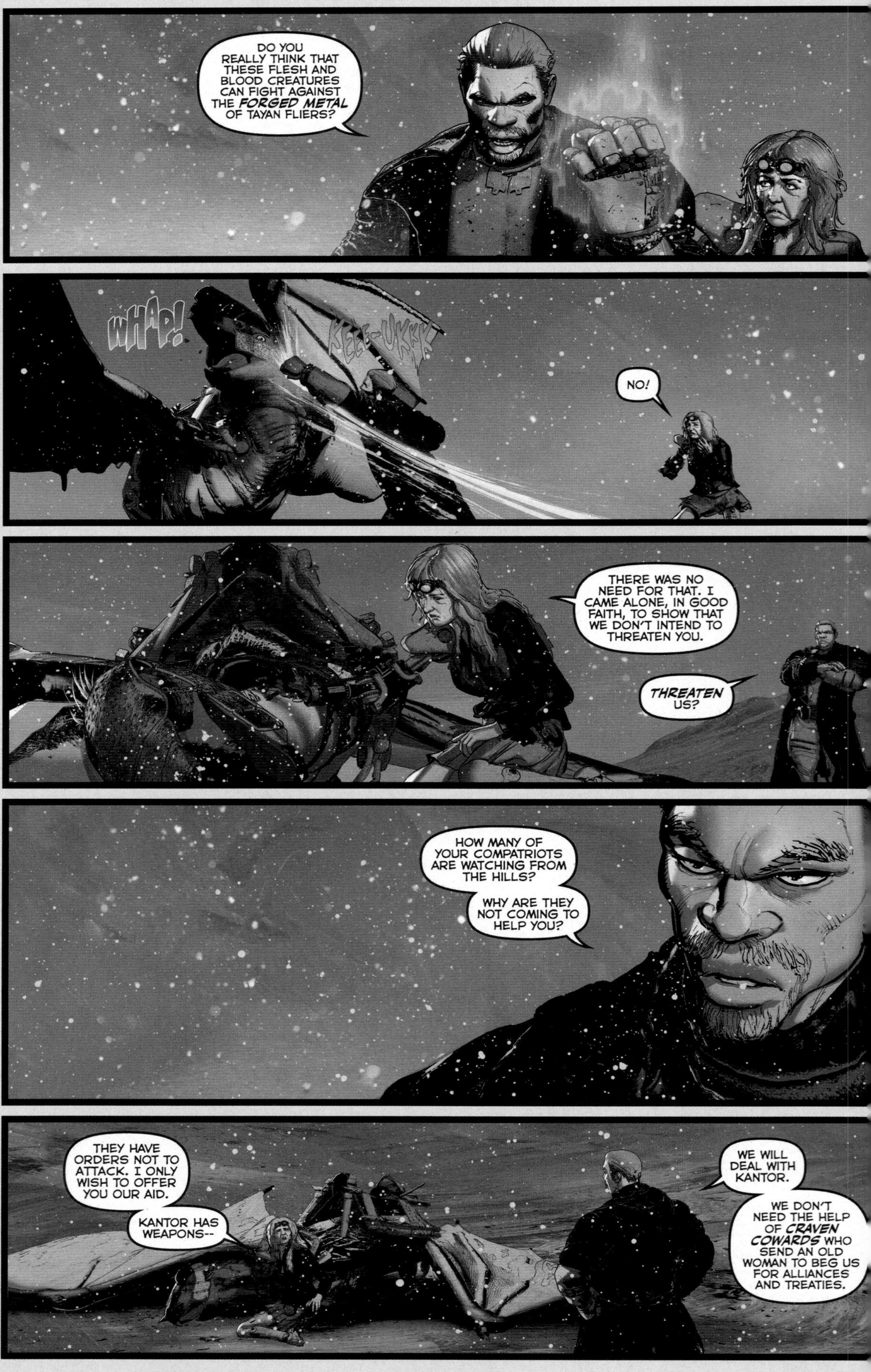
DO YOU REALLY THINK THAT THESE FLESH AND BLOOD CREATURES CAN FIGHT AGAINST THE *FORGED METAL* OF TAYAN FLIERS?
WHAP!
KEEE-UKKK
NO!
THERE WAS NO NEED FOR THAT. I CAME ALONE, IN GOOD FAITH, TO SHOW THAT WE DON'T INTEND TO THREATEN YOU.
THREATEN US?
HOW MANY OF YOUR COMPATRIOTS ARE WATCHING FROM THE HILLS?
WHY ARE THEY NOT COMING TO HELP YOU?
THEY HAVE ORDERS NOT TO ATTACK. I ONLY WISH TO OFFER YOU OUR AID.
KANTOR HAS WEAPONS--
WE WILL DEAL WITH KANTOR.
WE DON'T NEED THE HELP OF *CRAVEN COWARDS* WHO SEND AN OLD WOMAN TO BEG US FOR ALLIANCES AND TREATIES.

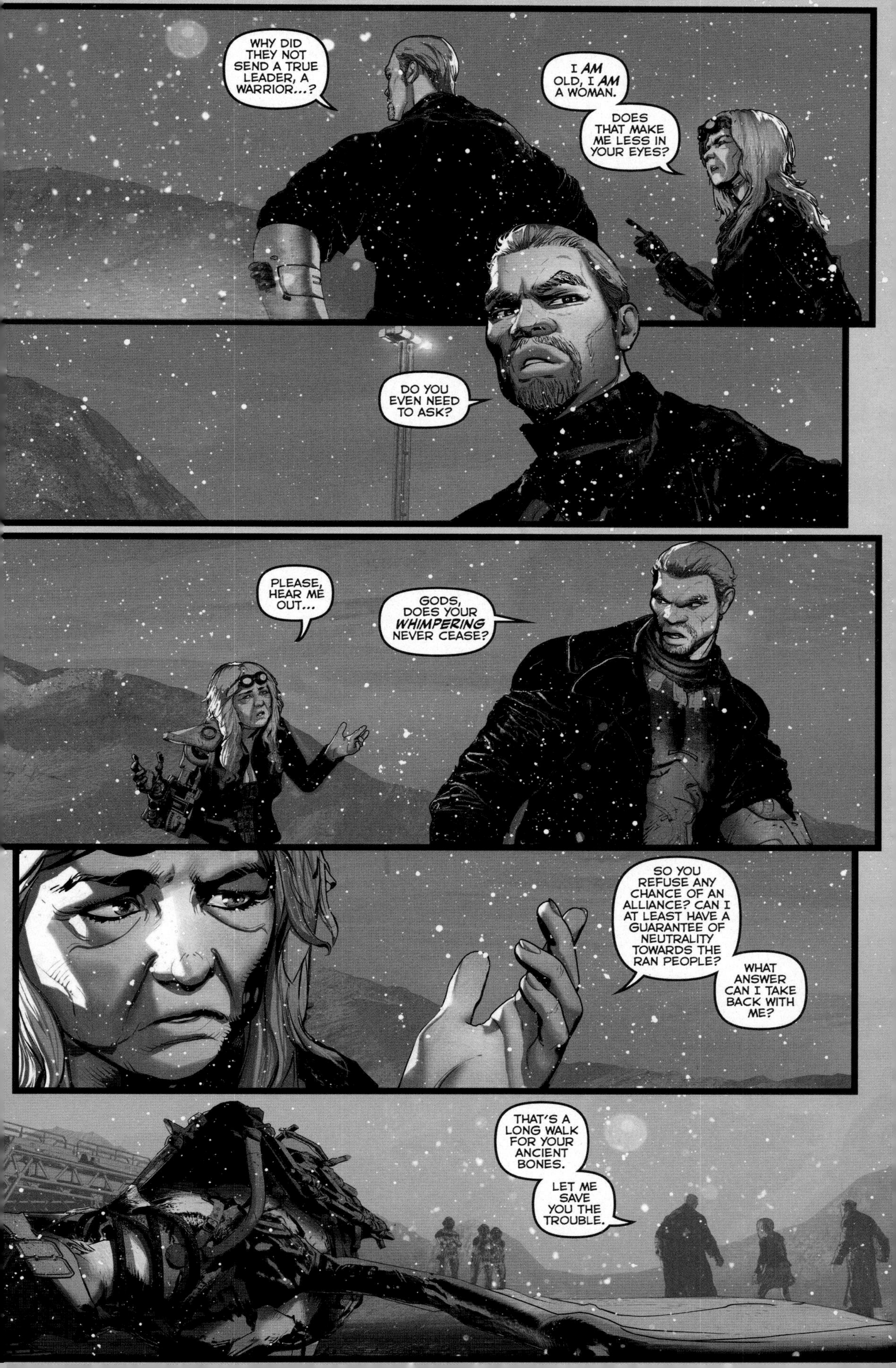
WHY DID THEY NOT SEND A TRUE LEADER, A WARRIOR...?
I AM OLD, I AM A WOMAN.
DOES THAT MAKE ME LESS IN YOUR EYES?
DO YOU EVEN NEED TO ASK?
PLEASE, HEAR ME OUT...
GODS, DOES YOUR WHIMPERING NEVER CEASE?
SO YOU REFUSE ANY CHANCE OF AN ALLIANCE? CAN I AT LEAST HAVE A GUARANTEE OF NEUTRALITY TOWARDS THE RAN PEOPLE?
WHAT ANSWER CAN I TAKE BACK WITH ME?
THAT'S A LONG WALK FOR YOUR ANCIENT BONES.
LET ME SAVE YOU THE TROUBLE.

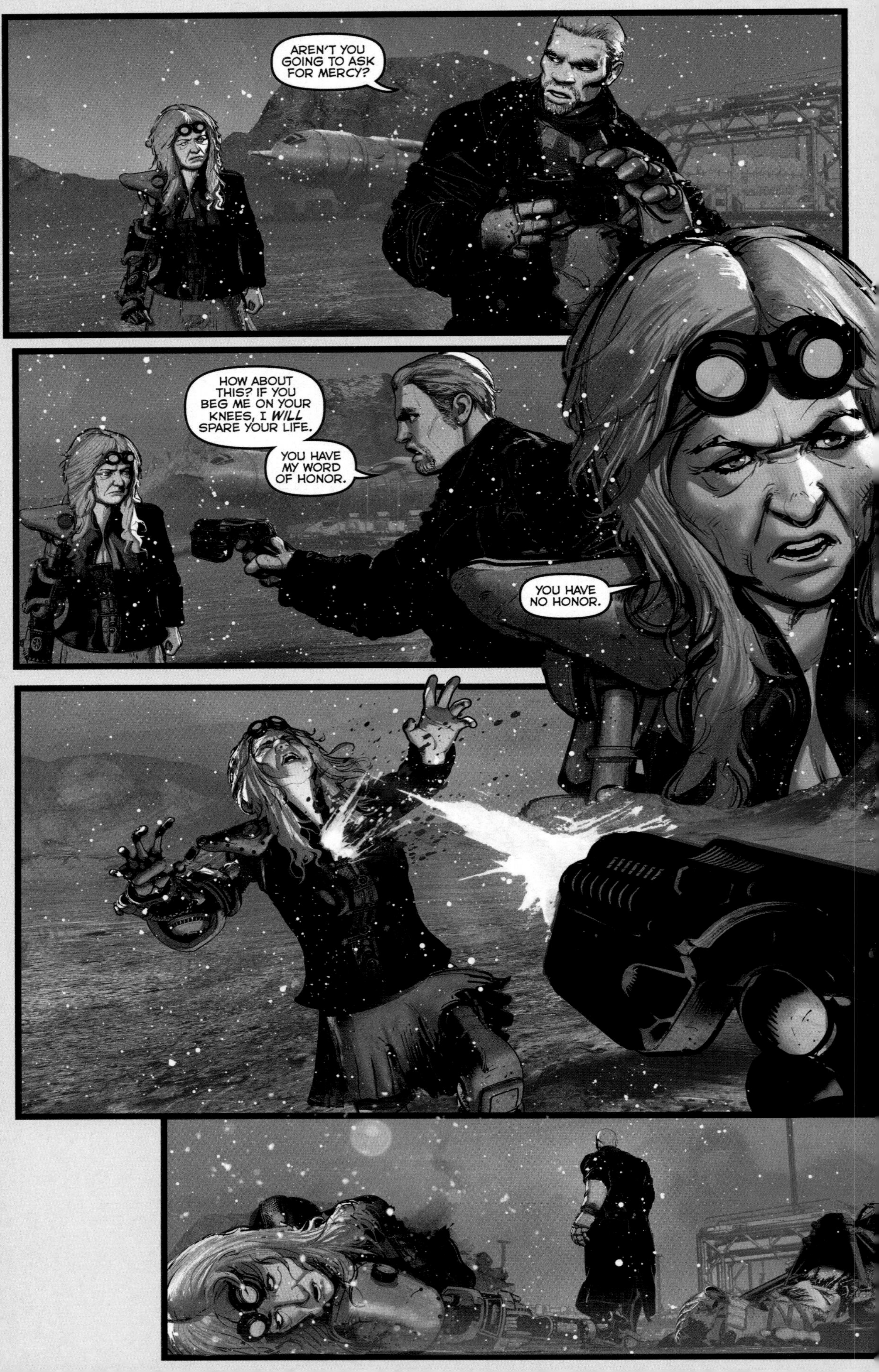
AREN'T YOU GOING TO ASK FOR MERCY?
HOW ABOUT THIS? IF YOU BEG ME ON YOUR KNEES, I *WILL* SPARE YOUR LIFE.
YOU HAVE MY WORD OF HONOR.
YOU HAVE NO HONOR.

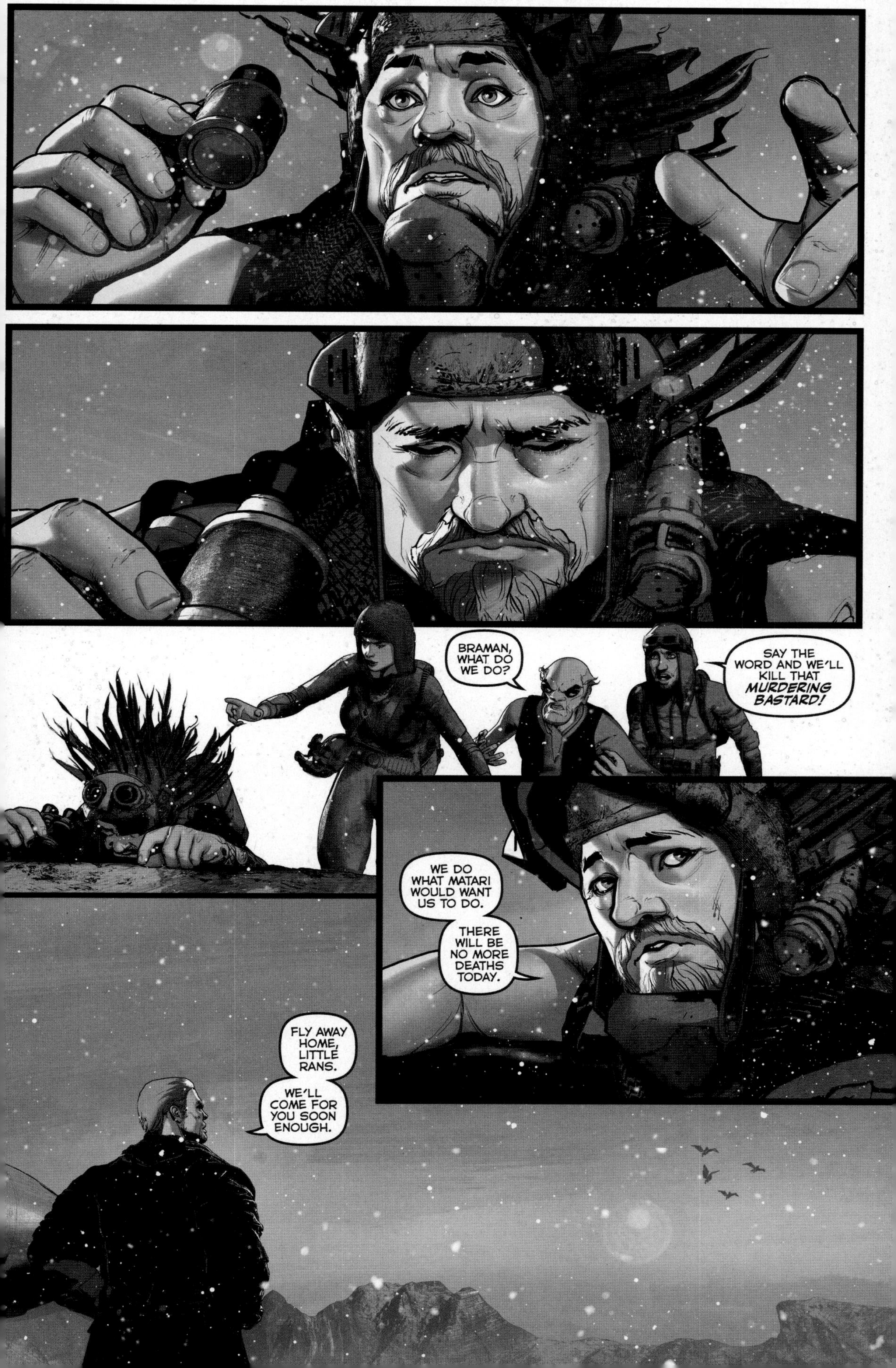
BRAMAN, WHAT DO WE DO?
SAY THE WORD AND WE'LL KILL THAT *MURDERING BASTARD!*
WE DO WHAT MATARI WOULD WANT US TO DO.
THERE WILL BE NO MORE DEATHS TODAY.
FLY AWAY HOME, LITTLE RANS.
WE'LL COME FOR YOU SOON ENOUGH.

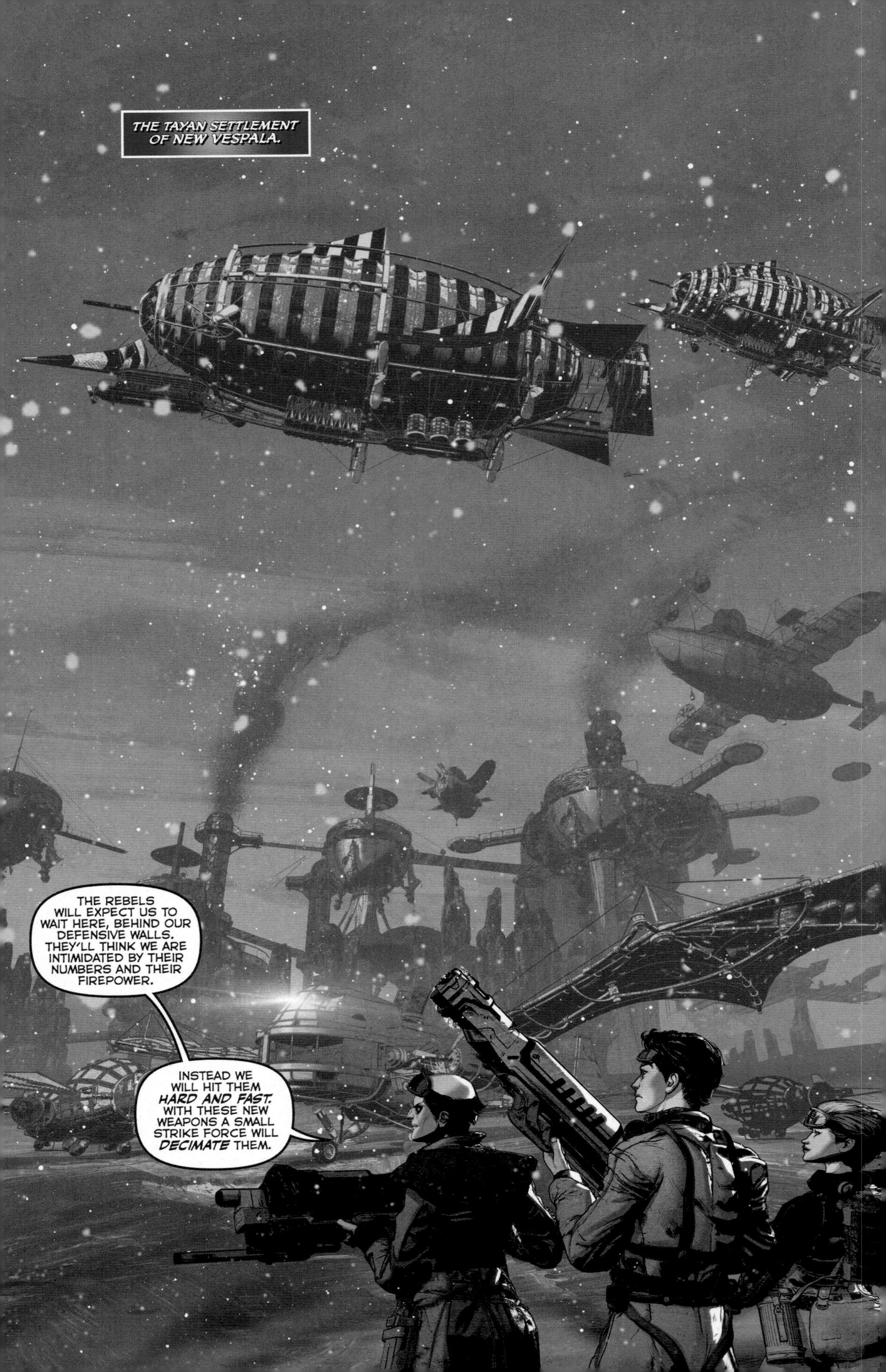
THE TAYAN SETTLEMENT OF NEW VESPALA.
THE REBELS WILL EXPECT US TO WAIT HERE, BEHIND OUR DEFENSIVE WALLS. THEY'LL THINK WE ARE INTIMIDATED BY THEIR NUMBERS AND THEIR FIREPOWER.
INSTEAD WE WILL HIT THEM HARD AND FAST. WITH THESE NEW WEAPONS A SMALL STRIKE FORCE WILL DECIMATE THEM.

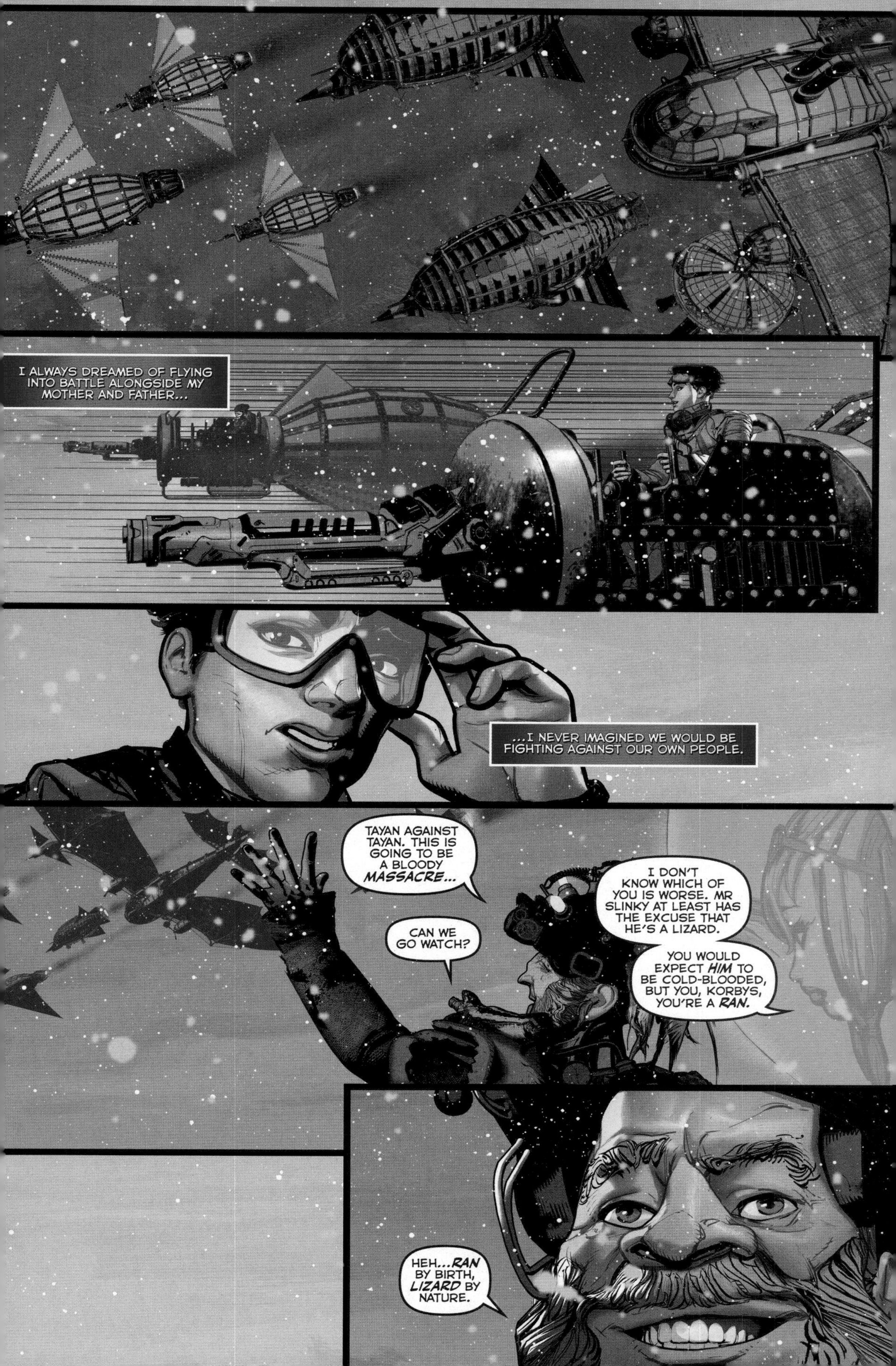
I ALWAYS DREAMED OF FLYING INTO BATTLE ALONGSIDE MY MOTHER AND FATHER...
...I NEVER IMAGINED WE WOULD BE FIGHTING AGAINST OUR OWN PEOPLE.
TAYAN AGAINST TAYAN. THIS IS GOING TO BE A BLOODY *MASSACRE*...
CAN WE GO WATCH?
I DON'T KNOW WHICH OF YOU IS WORSE. MR SLINKY AT LEAST HAS THE EXCUSE THAT HE'S A LIZARD.
YOU WOULD EXPECT *HIM* TO BE COLD-BLOODED, BUT YOU, KORBYS, YOU'RE A *RAN*.
HEH...*RAN* BY BIRTH, *LIZARD* BY NATURE.

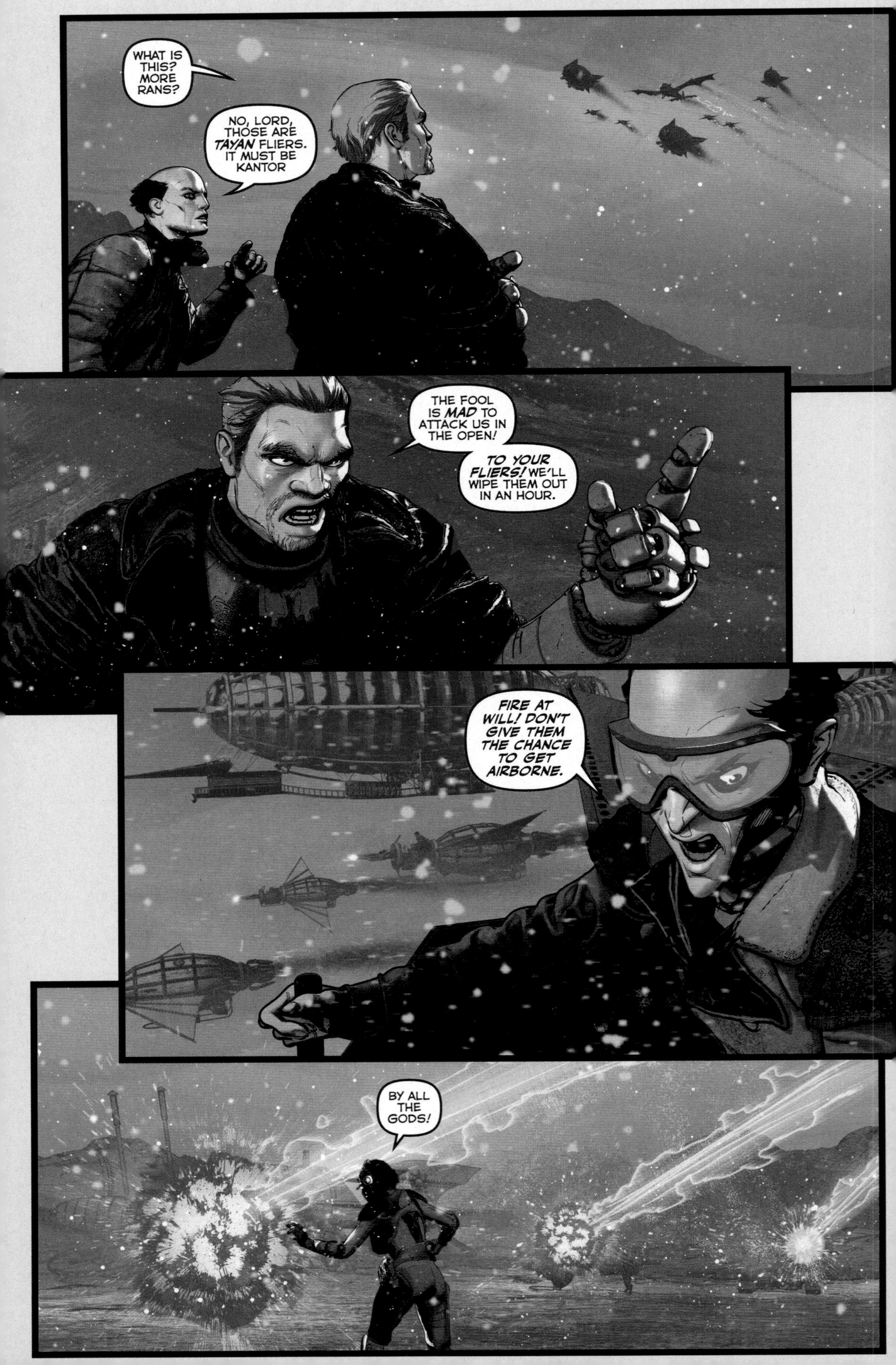
WHAT IS THIS? MORE RANS?
NO, LORD, THOSE ARE *TAYAN* FLIERS. IT MUST BE KANTOR
THE FOOL IS *MAD* TO ATTACK US IN THE OPEN!
TO YOUR FLIERS! WE'LL WIPE THEM OUT IN AN HOUR.
FIRE AT WILL! DON'T GIVE THEM THE CHANCE TO GET AIRBORNE.
BY ALL THE GODS!

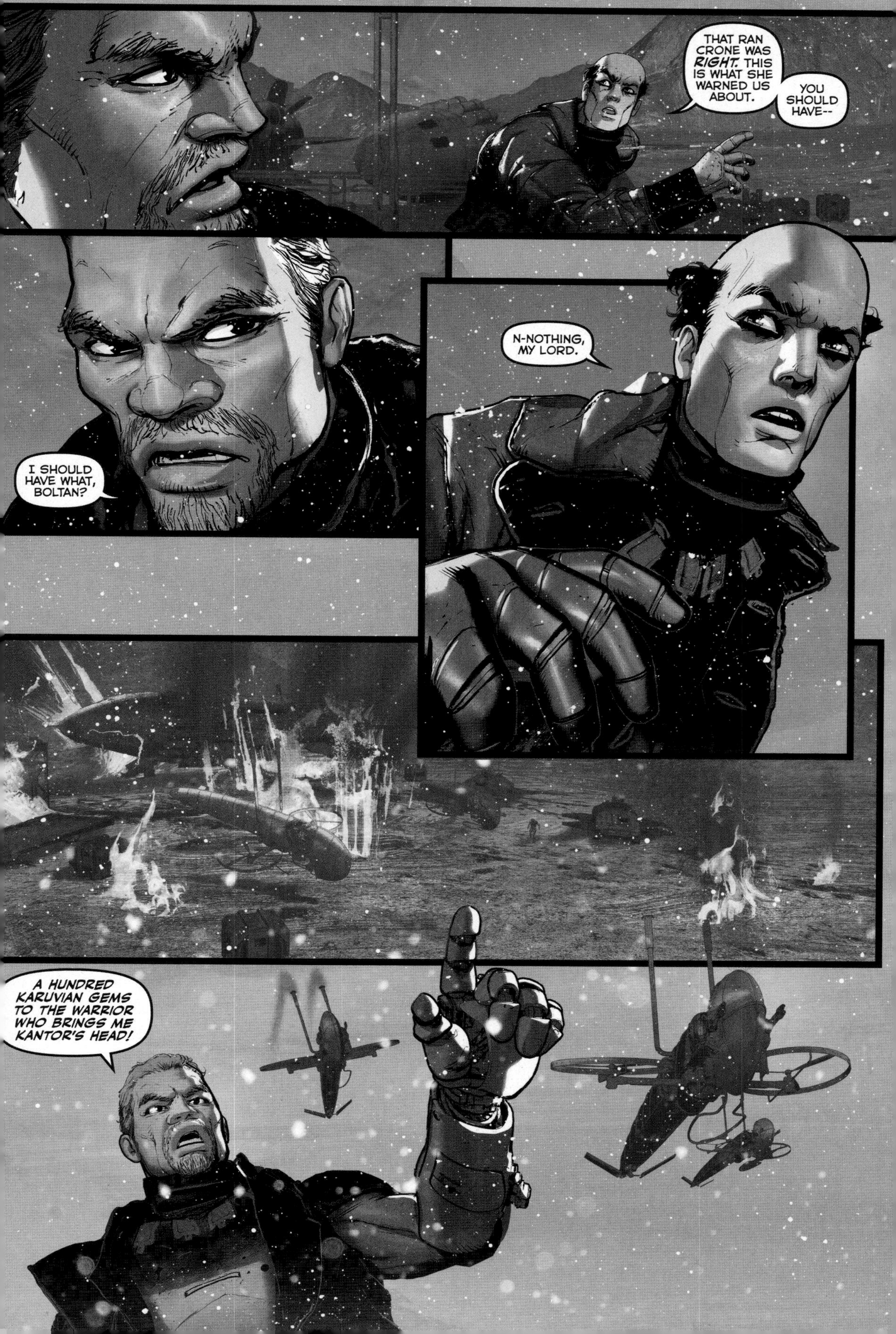
THAT RAN CRONE WAS *RIGHT.* THIS IS WHAT SHE WARNED US ABOUT.
YOU SHOULD HAVE--
I SHOULD HAVE WHAT, BOLTAN?
N-NOTHING, MY LORD.
A HUNDRED KARUVIAN GEMS TO THE WARRIOR WHO BRINGS ME KANTOR'S HEAD!

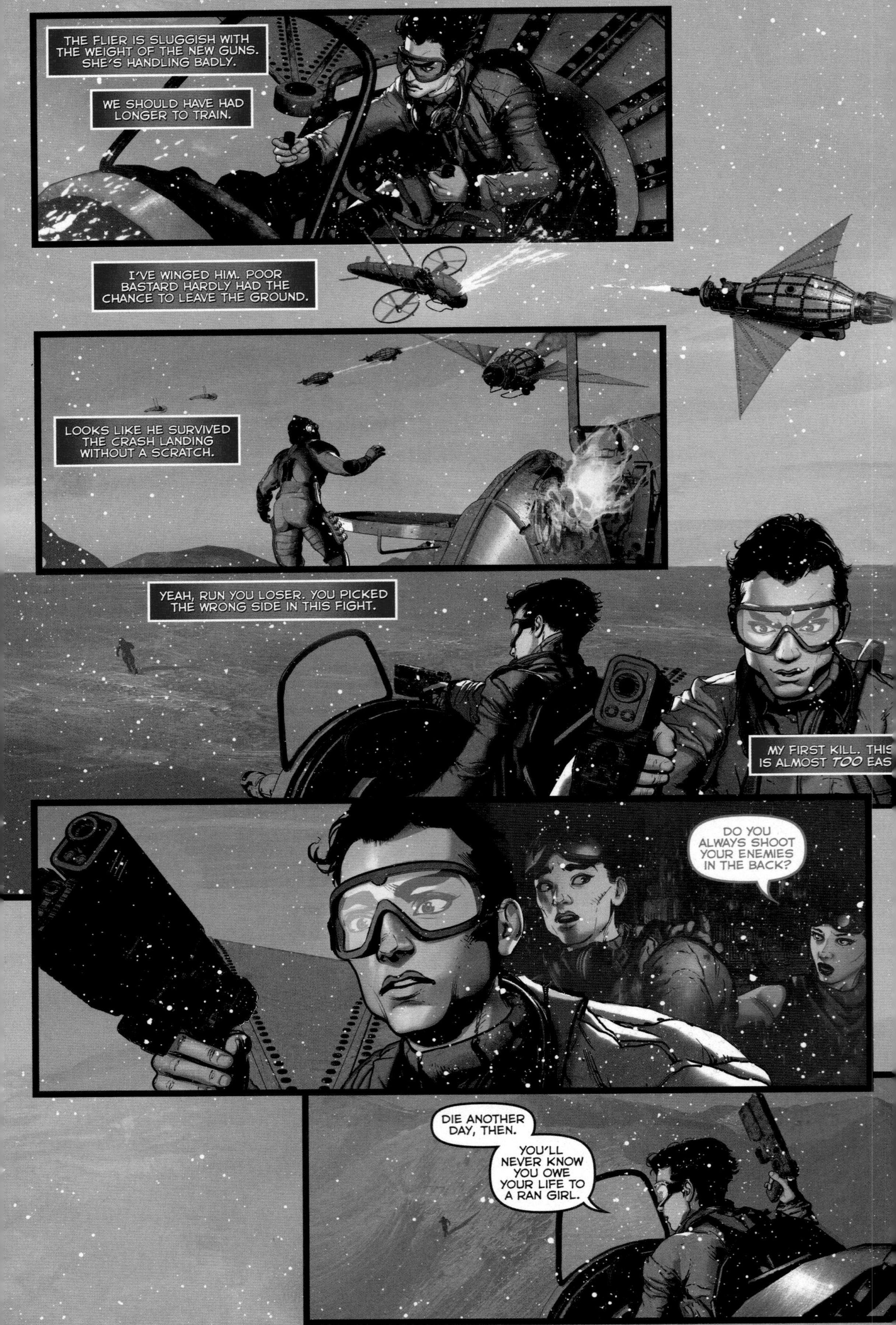
THE FLIER IS SLUGGISH WITH THE WEIGHT OF THE NEW GUNS. SHE'S HANDLING BADLY.
WE SHOULD HAVE HAD LONGER TO TRAIN.
I'VE WINGED HIM. POOR BASTARD HARDLY HAD THE CHANCE TO LEAVE THE GROUND.
LOOKS LIKE HE SURVIVED THE CRASH LANDING WITHOUT A SCRATCH.
YEAH, RUN YOU LOSER. YOU PICKED THE WRONG SIDE IN THIS FIGHT.
MY FIRST KILL. THIS IS ALMOST *TOO* EAS
DO YOU ALWAYS SHOOT YOUR ENEMIES IN THE BACK?
DIE ANOTHER DAY, THEN.
YOU'LL NEVER KNOW YOU OWE YOUR LIFE TO A RAN GIRL.

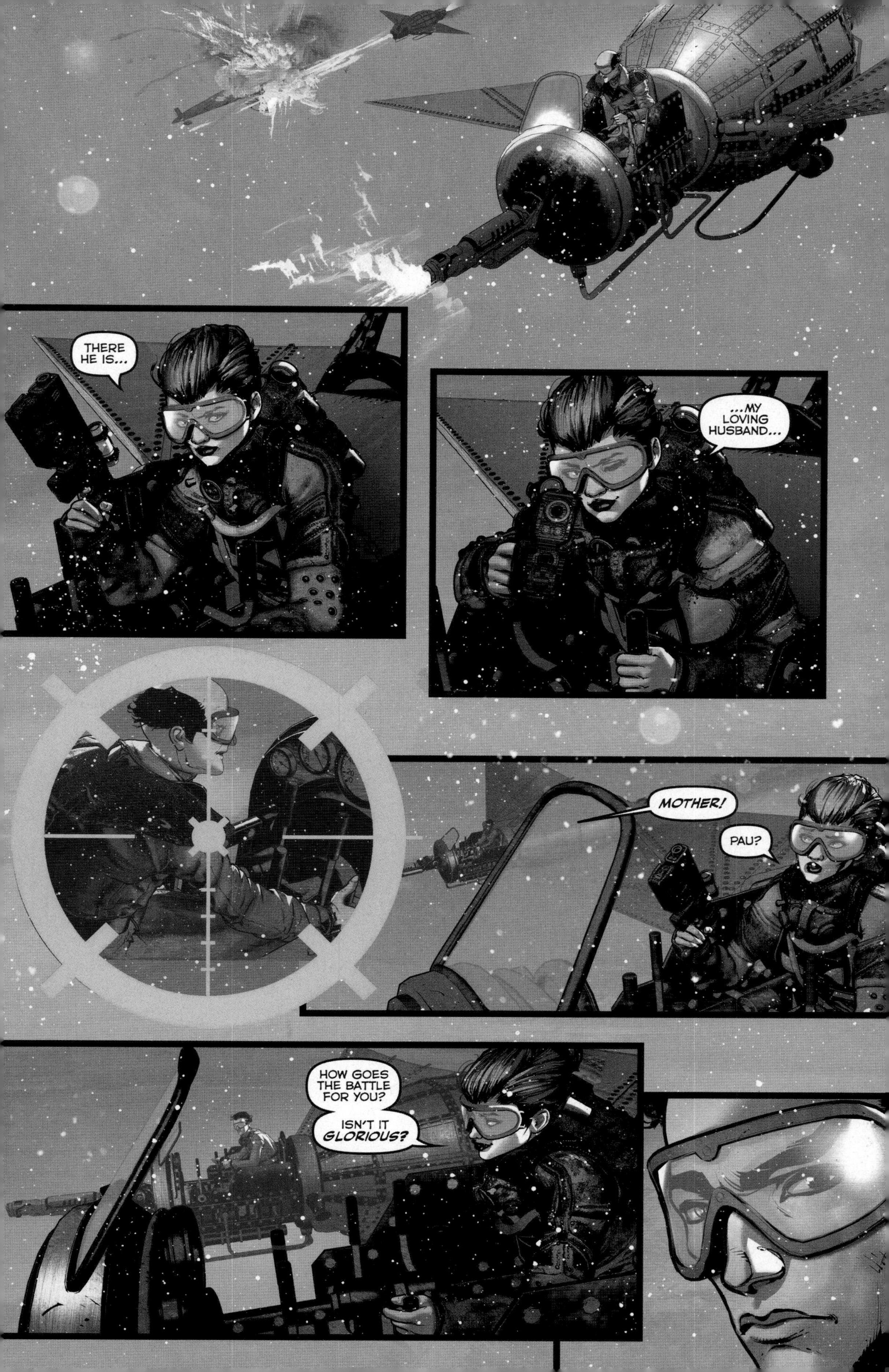
THERE HE IS...
...MY LOVING HUSBAND...
MOTHER!
PAU?
HOW GOES THE BATTLE FOR YOU?
ISN'T IT GLORIOUS?

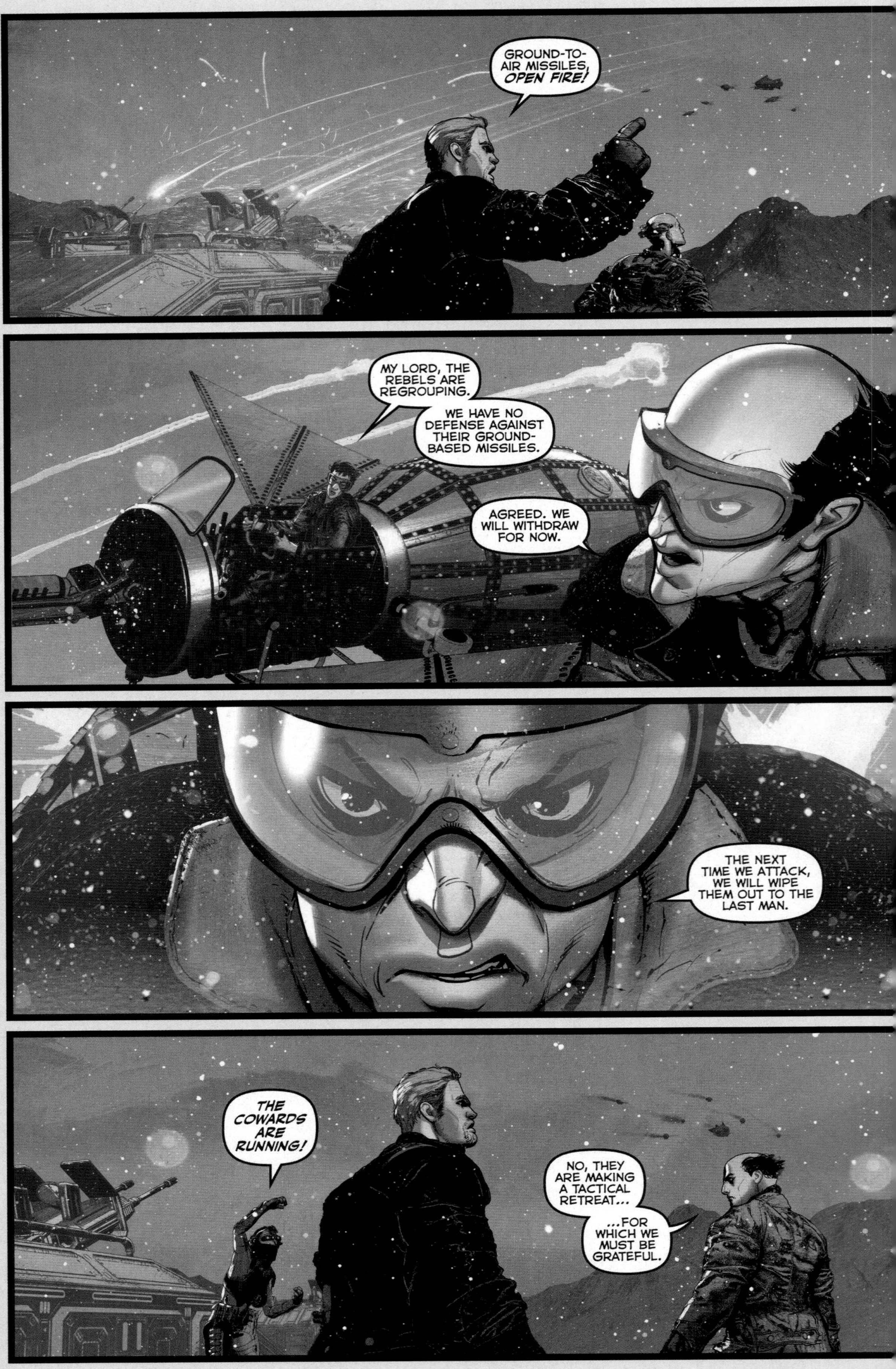
GROUND-TO-AIR MISSILES, OPEN FIRE!
MY LORD, THE REBELS ARE REGROUPING.
WE HAVE NO DEFENSE AGAINST THEIR GROUND-BASED MISSILES.
AGREED. WE WILL WITHDRAW FOR NOW.
THE NEXT TIME WE ATTACK, WE WILL WIPE THEM OUT TO THE LAST MAN.
THE COWARDS ARE RUNNING!
NO, THEY ARE MAKING A TACTICAL RETREAT...
...FOR WHICH WE MUST BE GRATEFUL.

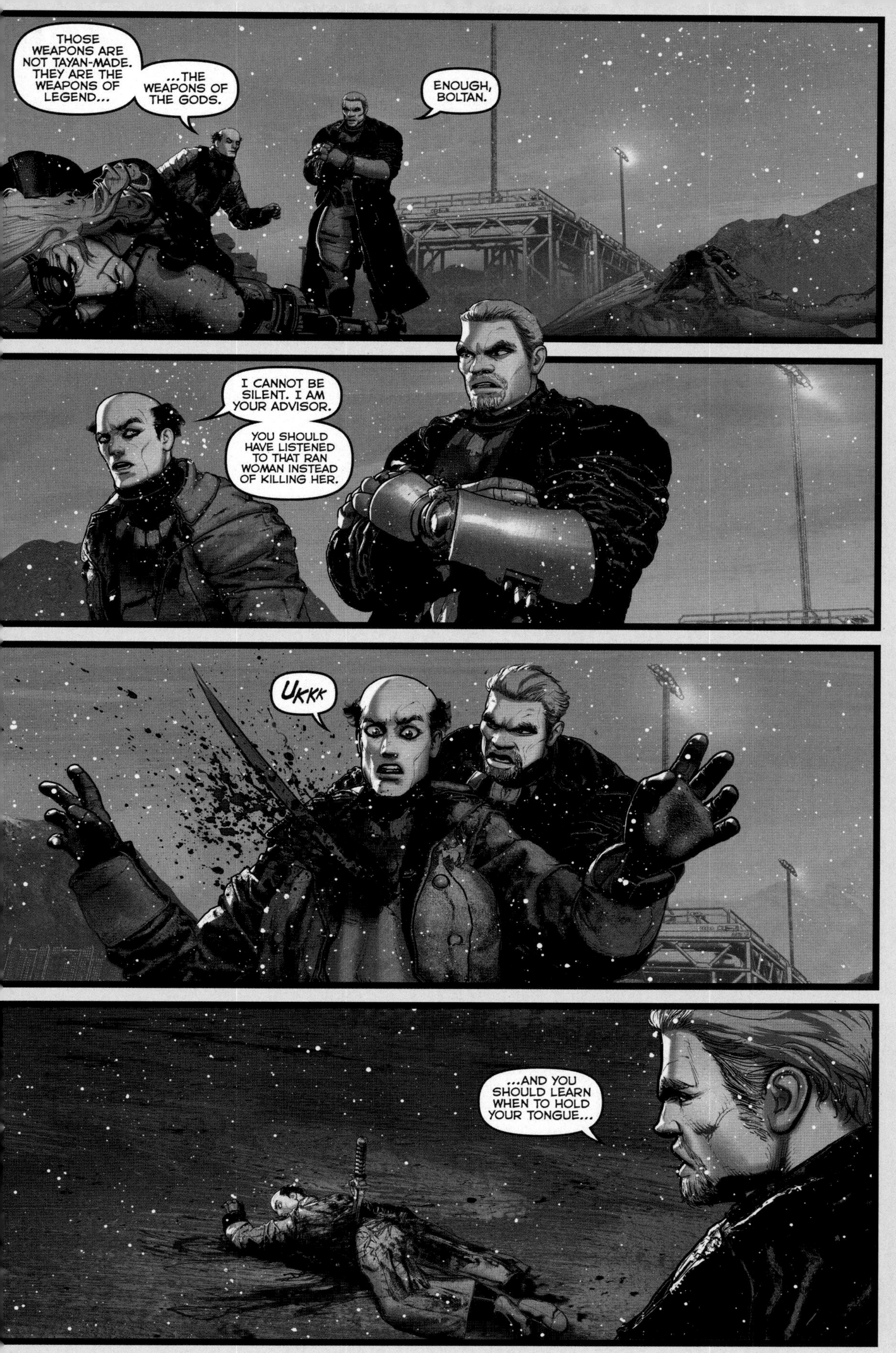
THOSE WEAPONS ARE NOT TAYAN-MADE. THEY ARE THE WEAPONS OF LEGEND...
...THE WEAPONS OF THE GODS.
ENOUGH, BOLTAN.
I CANNOT BE SILENT. I AM YOUR ADVISOR.
YOU SHOULD HAVE LISTENED TO THAT RAN WOMAN INSTEAD OF KILLING HER.
UKKK
...AND YOU SHOULD LEARN WHEN TO HOLD YOUR TONGUE...

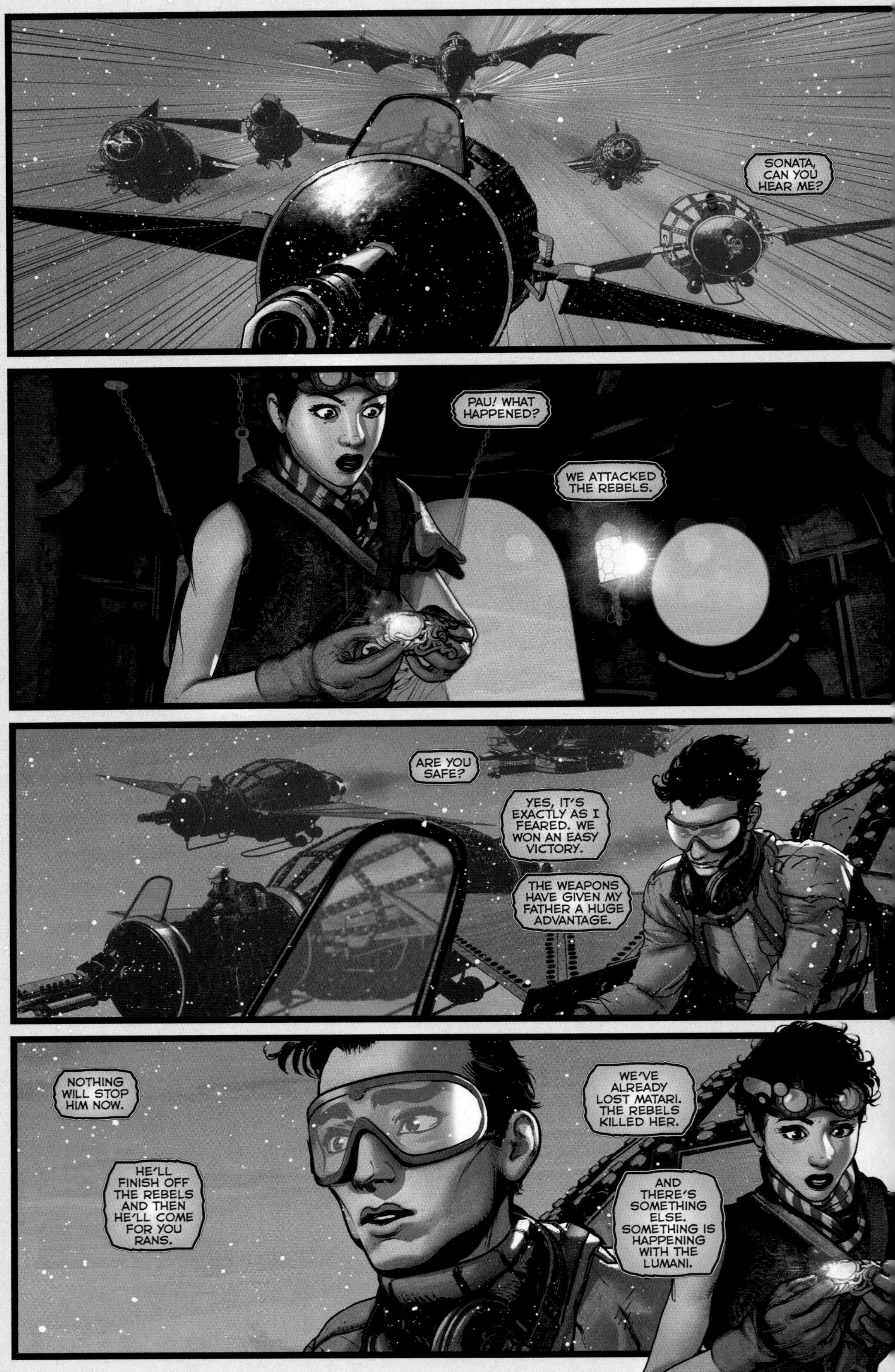
SONATA, CAN YOU HEAR ME?
PAU! WHAT HAPPENED?
WE ATTACKED THE REBELS.
ARE YOU SAFE?
YES, IT'S EXACTLY AS I FEARED. WE WON AN EASY VICTORY.
THE WEAPONS HAVE GIVEN MY FATHER A HUGE ADVANTAGE.
NOTHING WILL STOP HIM NOW.
HE'LL FINISH OFF THE REBELS AND THEN HE'LL COME FOR YOU RANS.
WE'VE ALREADY LOST MATARI. THE REBELS KILLED HER.
AND THERE'S SOMETHING ELSE. SOMETHING IS HAPPENING WITH THE LUMANI.

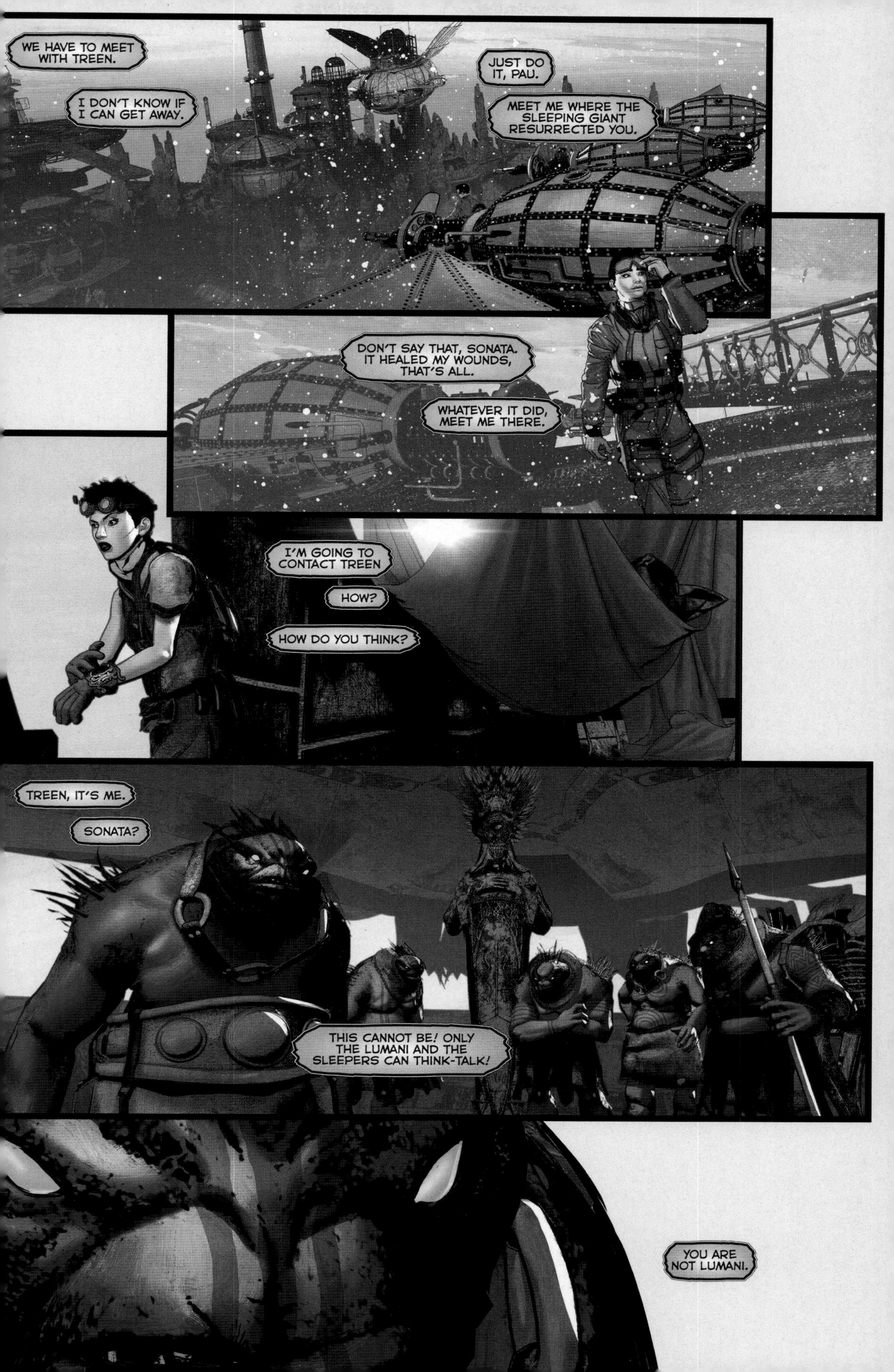
WE HAVE TO MEET WITH TREEN.
I DON'T KNOW IF I CAN GET AWAY.
JUST DO IT, PAU.
MEET ME WHERE THE SLEEPING GIANT RESURRECTED YOU.
DON'T SAY THAT, SONATA. IT HEALED MY WOUNDS, THAT'S ALL.
WHATEVER IT DID, MEET ME THERE.
I'M GOING TO CONTACT TREEN
HOW?
HOW DO YOU THINK?
TREEN, IT'S ME.
SONATA?
THIS CANNOT BE! ONLY THE LUMANI AND THE SLEEPERS CAN THINK-TALK!
YOU ARE NOT LUMANI.

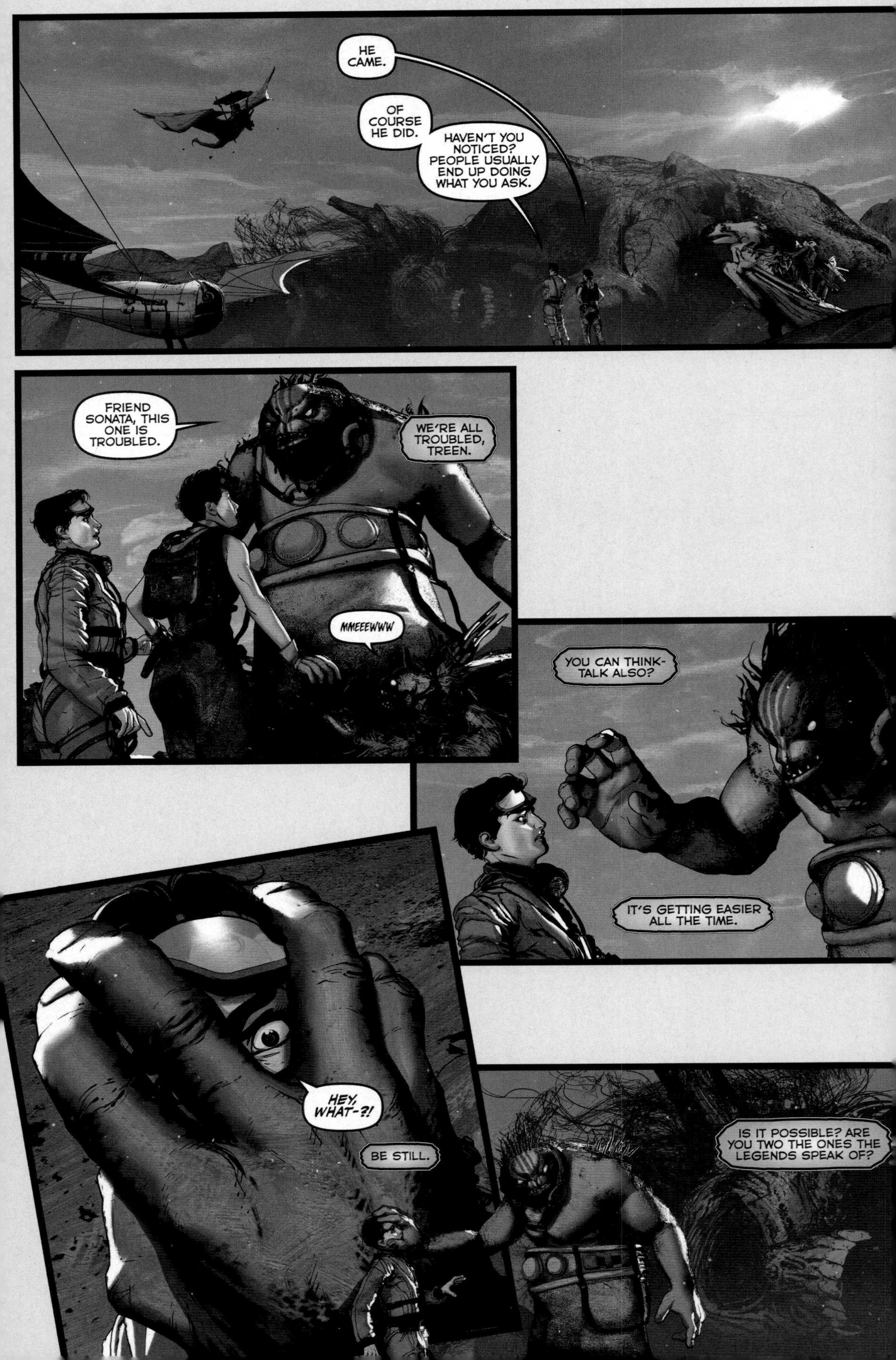
HE CAME.
OF COURSE HE DID.
HAVEN'T YOU NOTICED? PEOPLE USUALLY END UP DOING WHAT YOU ASK.
FRIEND SONATA, THIS ONE IS TROUBLED.
WE'RE ALL TROUBLED, TREEN.
MMEEEWWW
YOU CAN THINK-TALK ALSO?
IT'S GETTING EASIER ALL THE TIME.
HEY, WHAT-?!
BE STILL.
IS IT POSSIBLE? ARE YOU TWO THE ONES THE LEGENDS SPEAK OF?

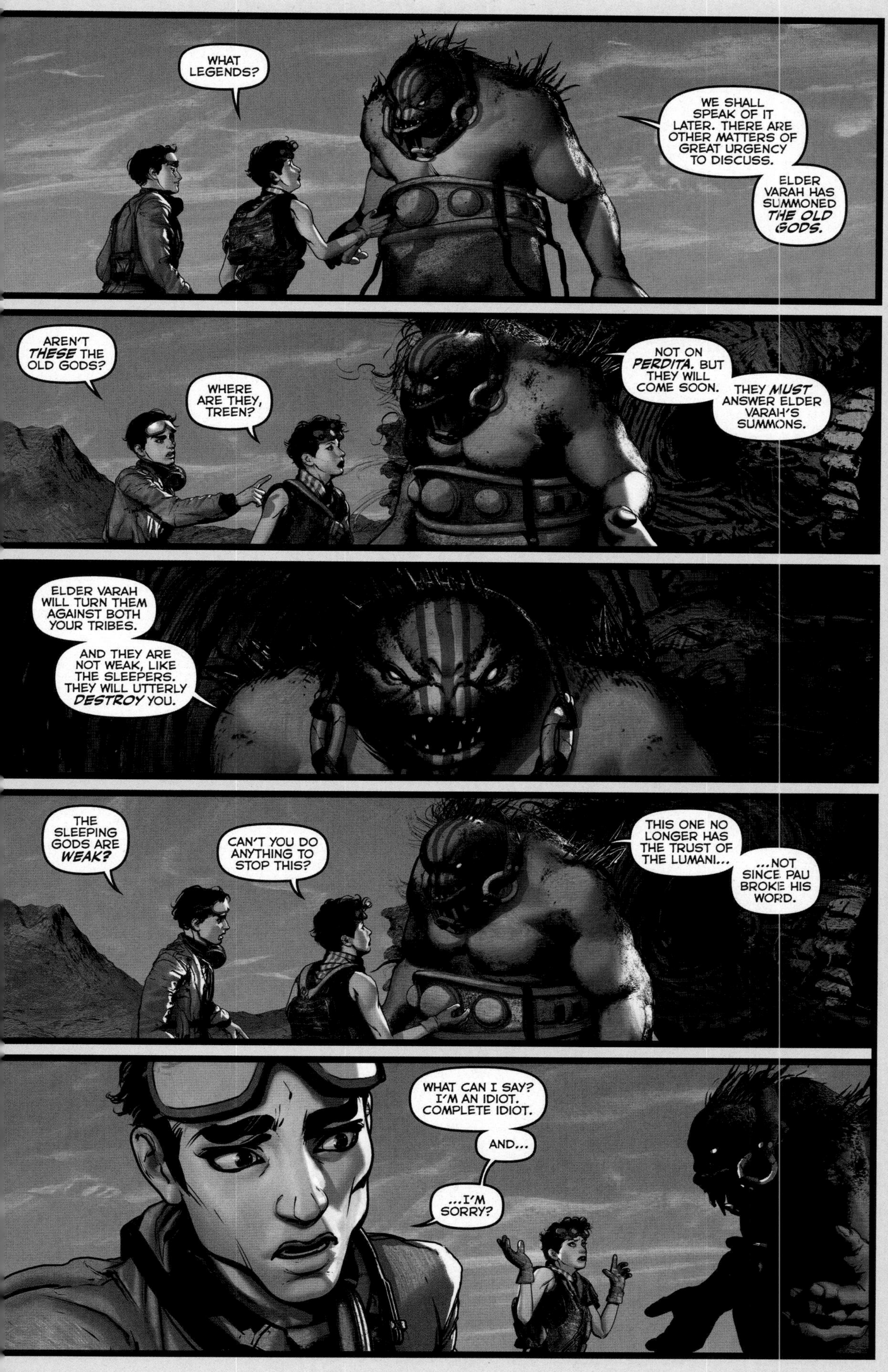
WHAT LEGENDS?
WE SHALL SPEAK OF IT LATER. THERE ARE OTHER MATTERS OF GREAT URGENCY TO DISCUSS.
ELDER VARAH HAS SUMMONED *THE OLD GODS.*
AREN'T *THESE* THE OLD GODS?
WHERE ARE THEY, TREEN?
NOT ON *PERDITA*. BUT THEY WILL COME SOON.
THEY *MUST* ANSWER ELDER VARAH'S SUMMONS.
ELDER VARAH WILL TURN THEM AGAINST BOTH YOUR TRIBES.
AND THEY ARE NOT WEAK, LIKE THE SLEEPERS. THEY WILL UTTERLY *DESTROY* YOU.
THE SLEEPING GODS ARE *WEAK?*
CAN'T YOU DO ANYTHING TO STOP THIS?
THIS ONE NO LONGER HAS THE TRUST OF THE LUMANI...
...NOT SINCE PAU BROKE HIS WORD.
WHAT CAN I SAY? I'M AN IDIOT. COMPLETE IDIOT.
AND...
...I'M SORRY?

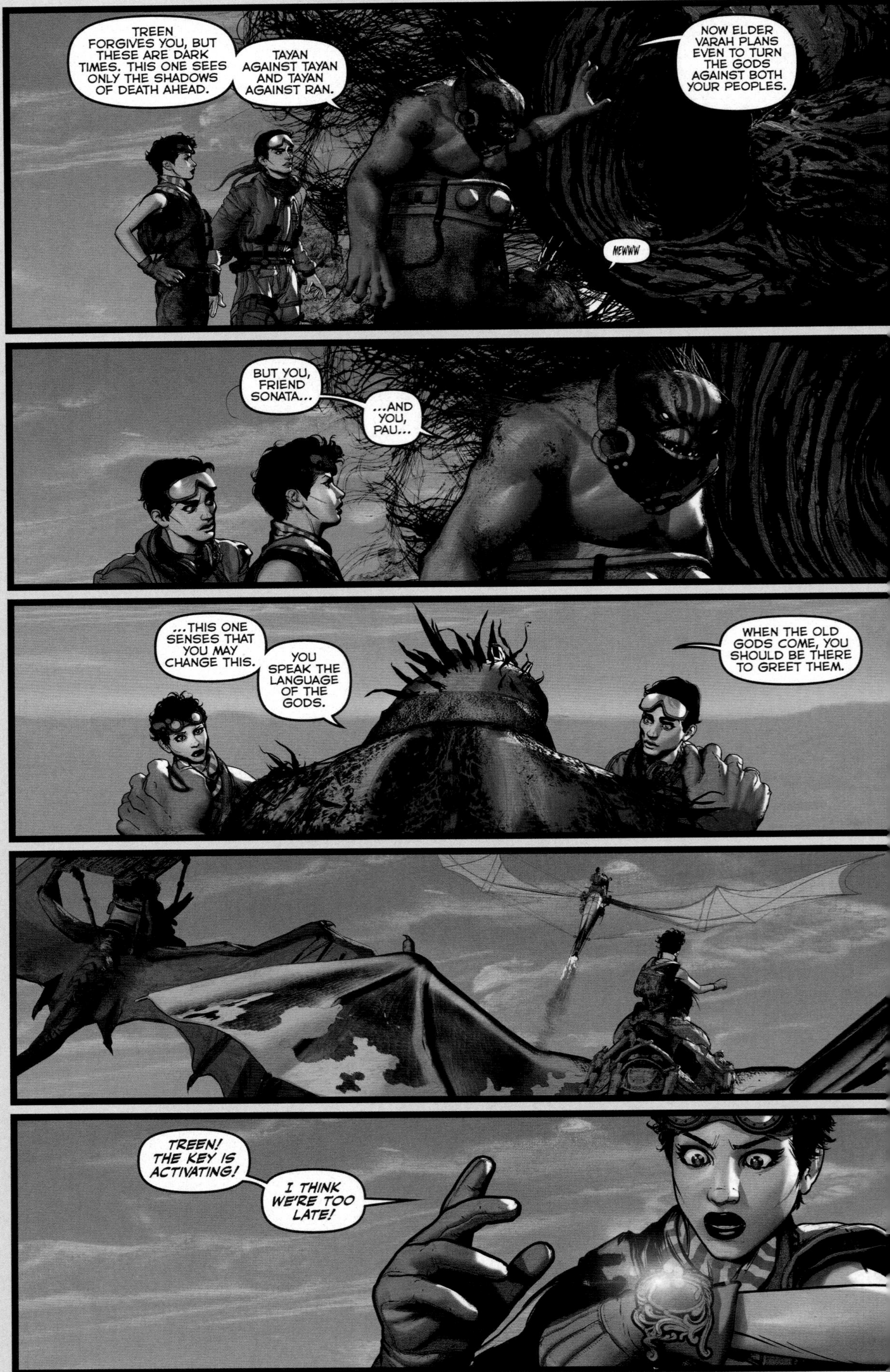
TREEN FORGIVES YOU, BUT THESE ARE DARK TIMES. THIS ONE SEES ONLY THE SHADOWS OF DEATH AHEAD.
TAYAN AGAINST TAYAN AND TAYAN AGAINST RAN.
NOW ELDER VARAH PLANS EVEN TO TURN THE GODS AGAINST BOTH YOUR PEOPLES.
MEWWW
BUT YOU, FRIEND SONATA...
...AND YOU, PAU...
...THIS ONE SENSES THAT YOU MAY CHANGE THIS.
YOU SPEAK THE LANGUAGE OF THE GODS.
WHEN THE OLD GODS COME, YOU SHOULD BE THERE TO GREET THEM.
TREEN! THE KEY IS ACTIVATING!
I THINK WE'RE TOO LATE!

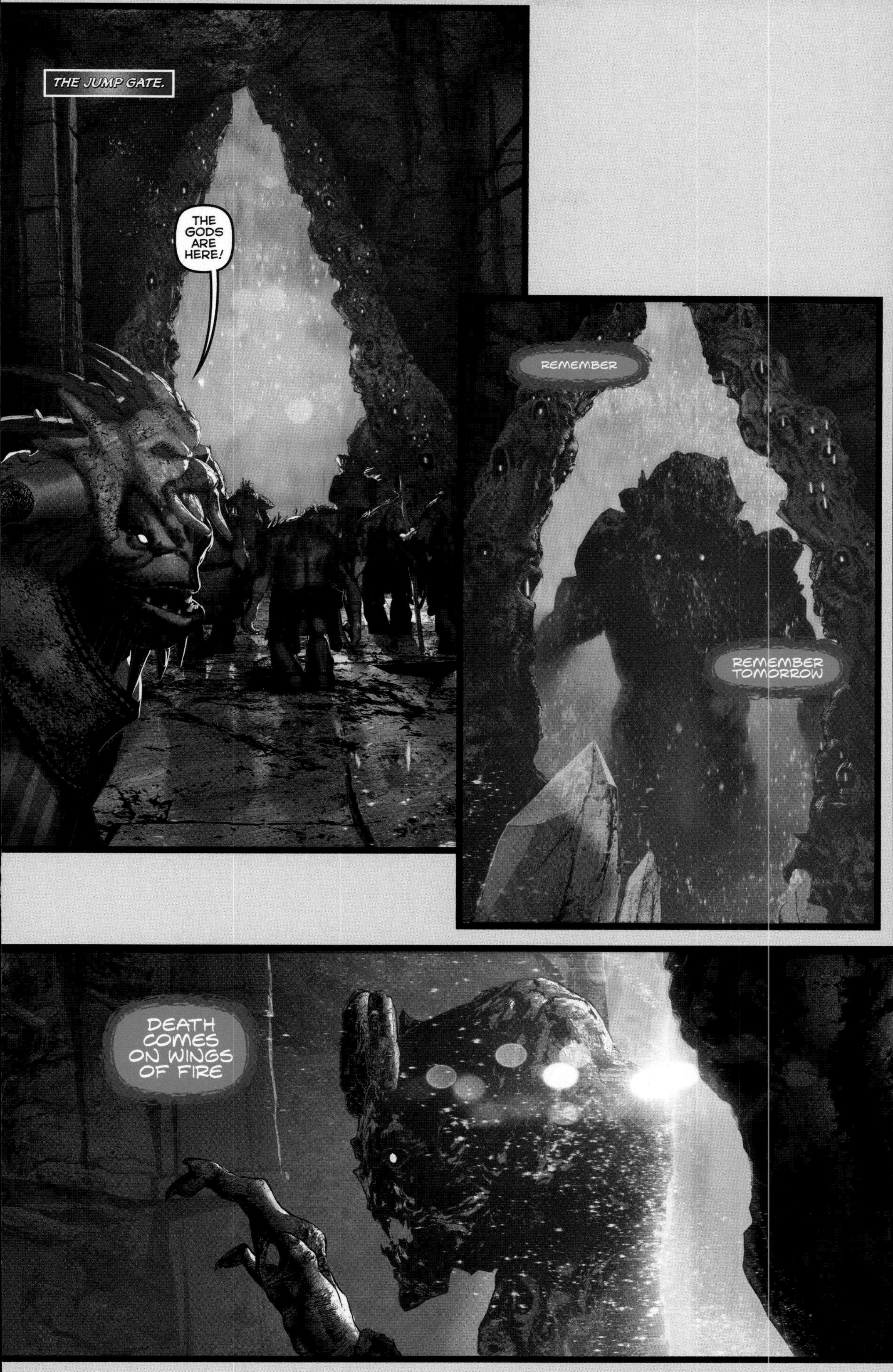
THE JUMP GATE.
THE GODS ARE HERE!
REMEMBER
REMEMBER TOMORROW
DEATH COMES ON WINGS OF FIRE

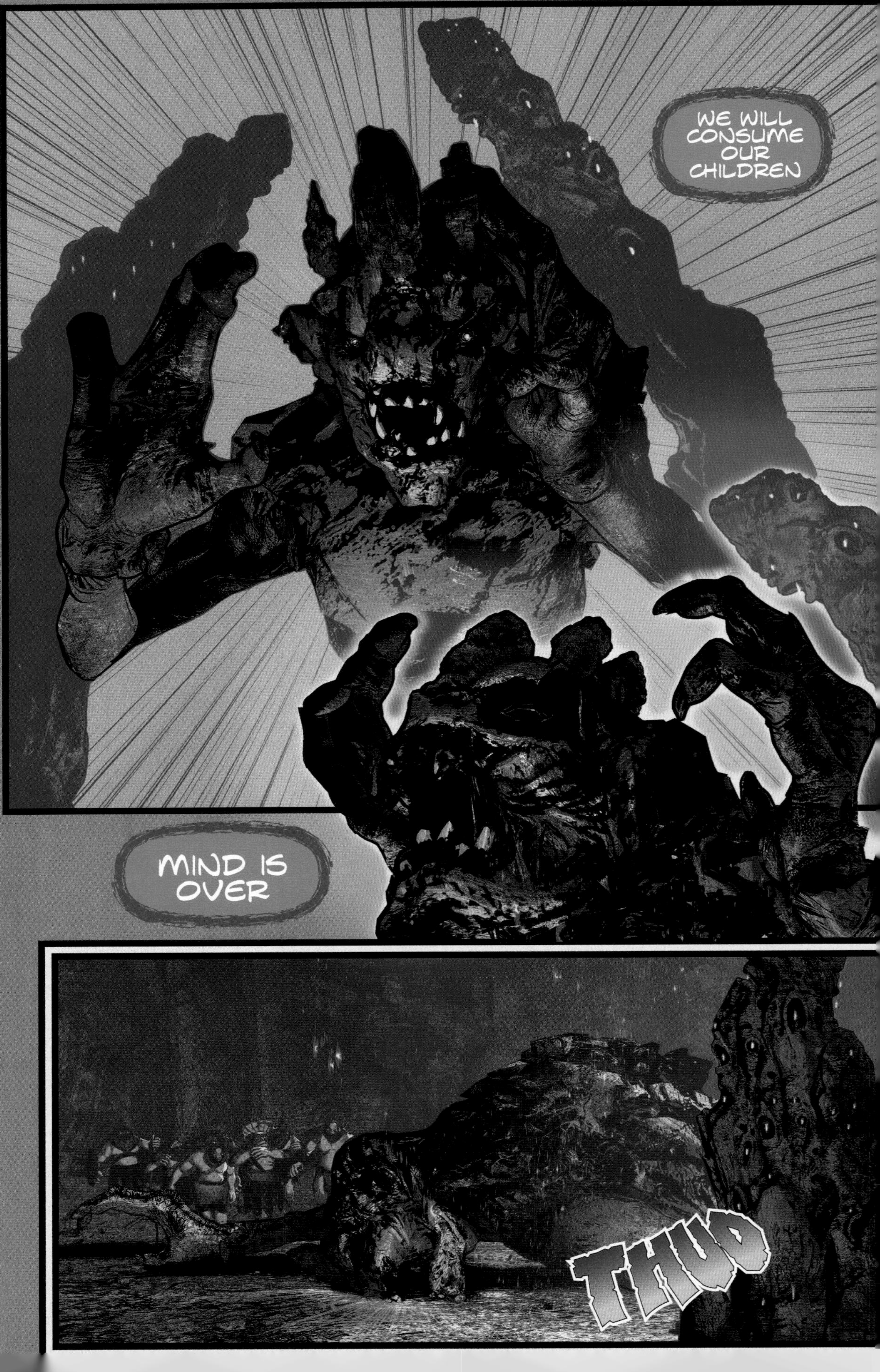
WE WILL CONSUME OUR CHILDREN
MIND IS OVER
THUD

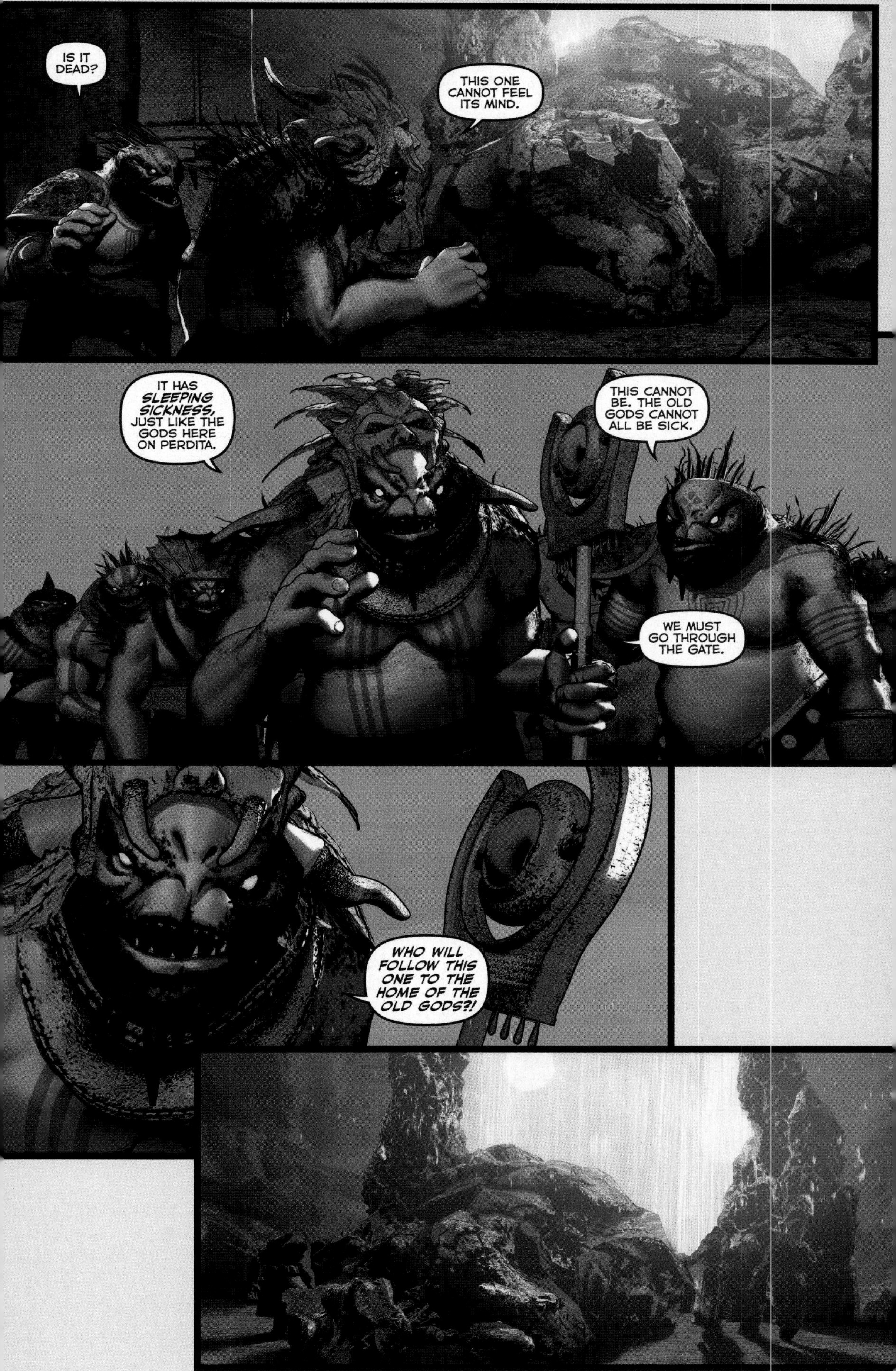
IS IT DEAD?
THIS ONE CANNOT FEEL ITS MIND.
IT HAS *SLEEPING SICKNESS,* JUST LIKE THE GODS HERE ON PERDITA.
THIS CANNOT BE. THE OLD GODS CANNOT ALL BE SICK.
WE MUST GO THROUGH THE GATE.
WHO WILL FOLLOW THIS ONE TO THE HOME OF THE OLD GODS?!

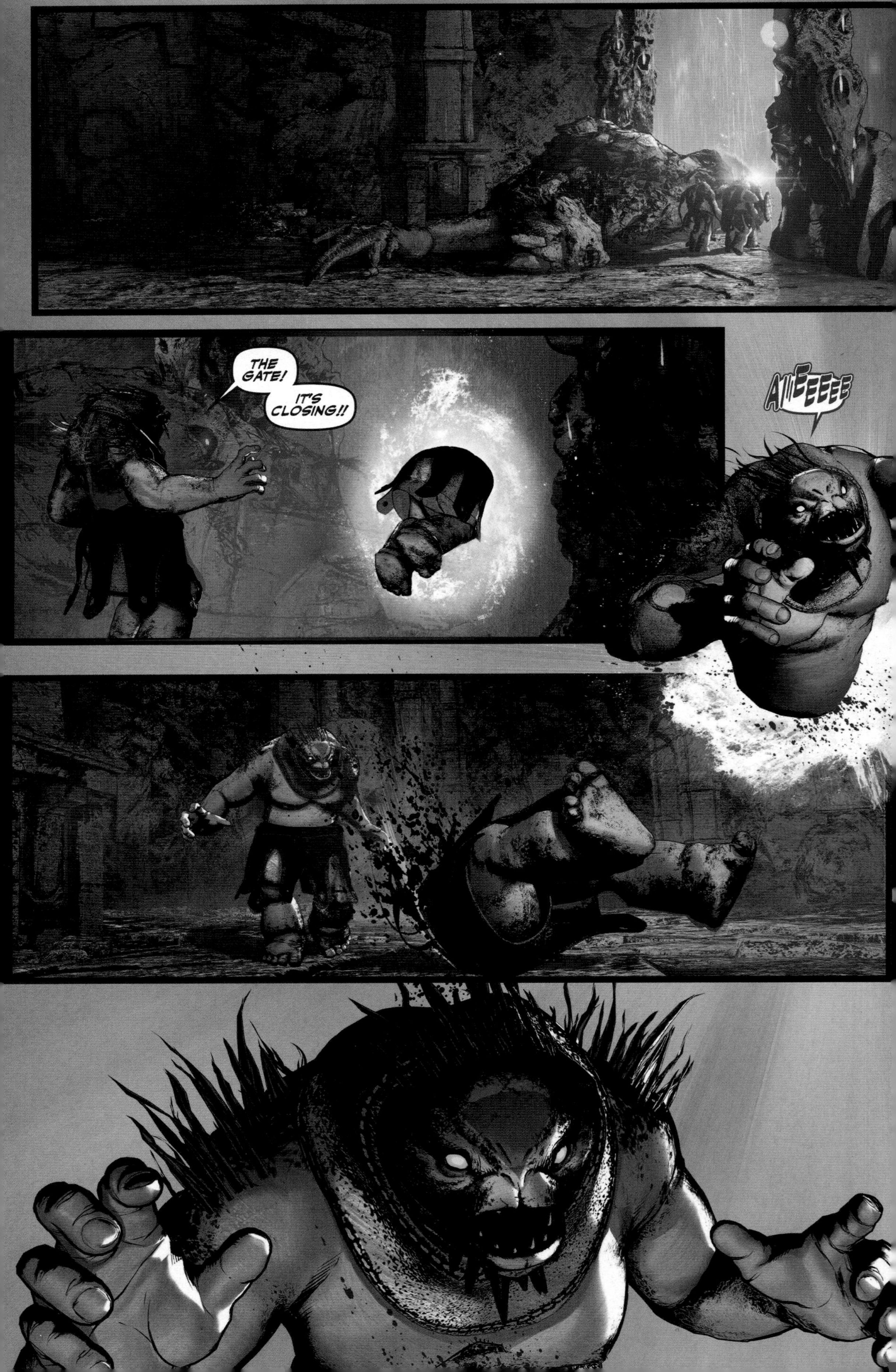
THE GATE!
IT'S CLOSING!!
AIIEEEEE

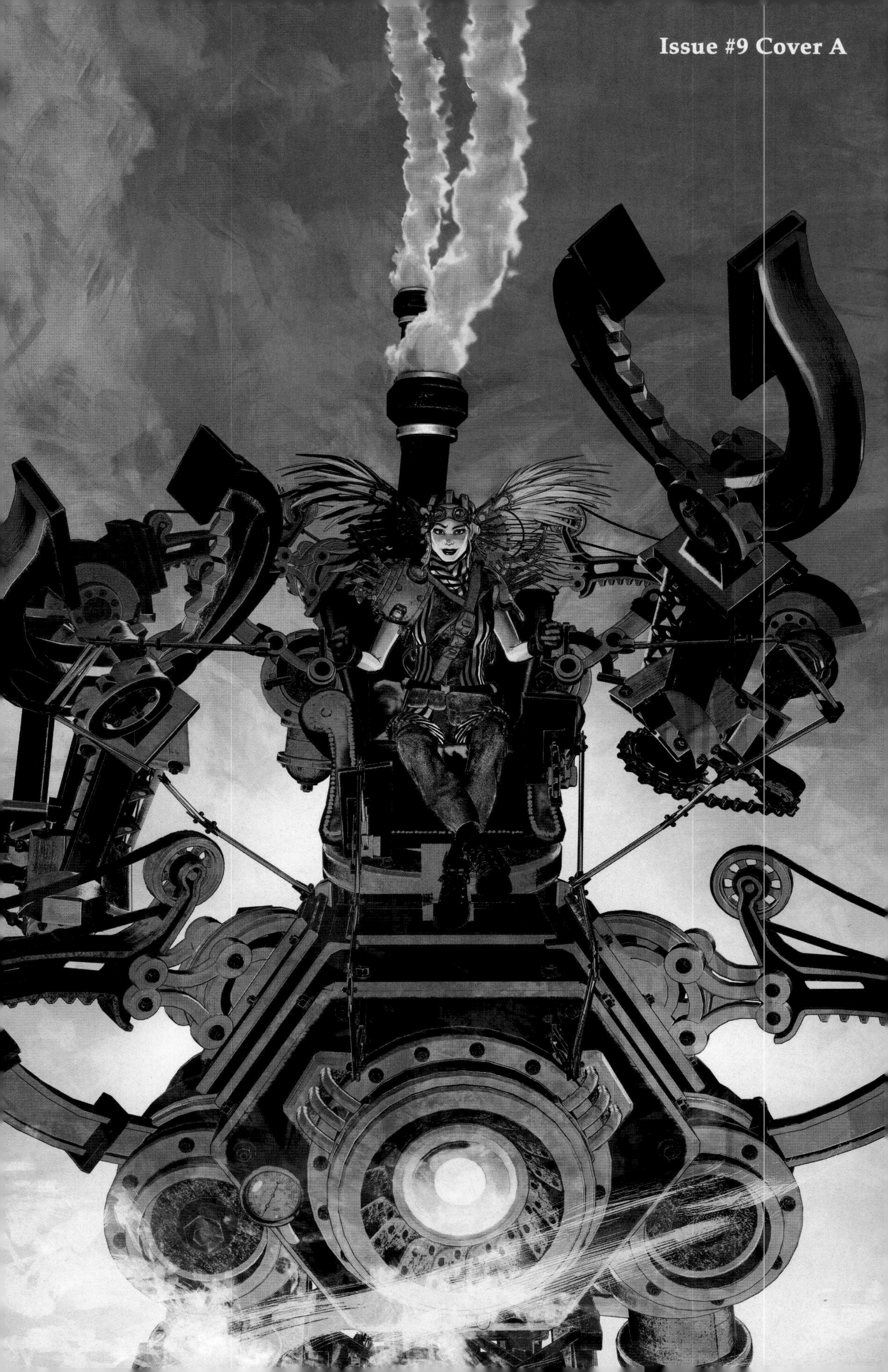

Issue #9 Cover B

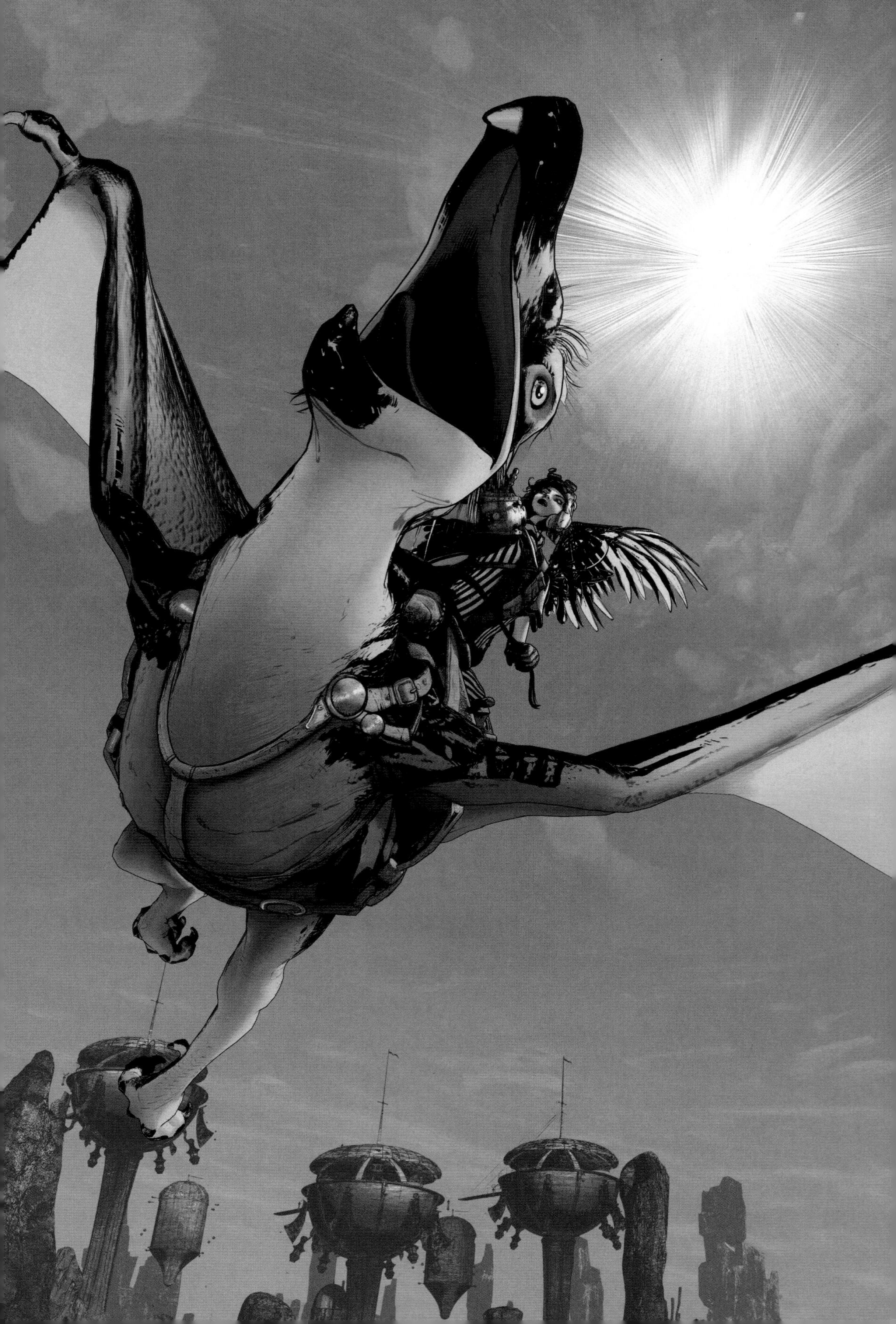

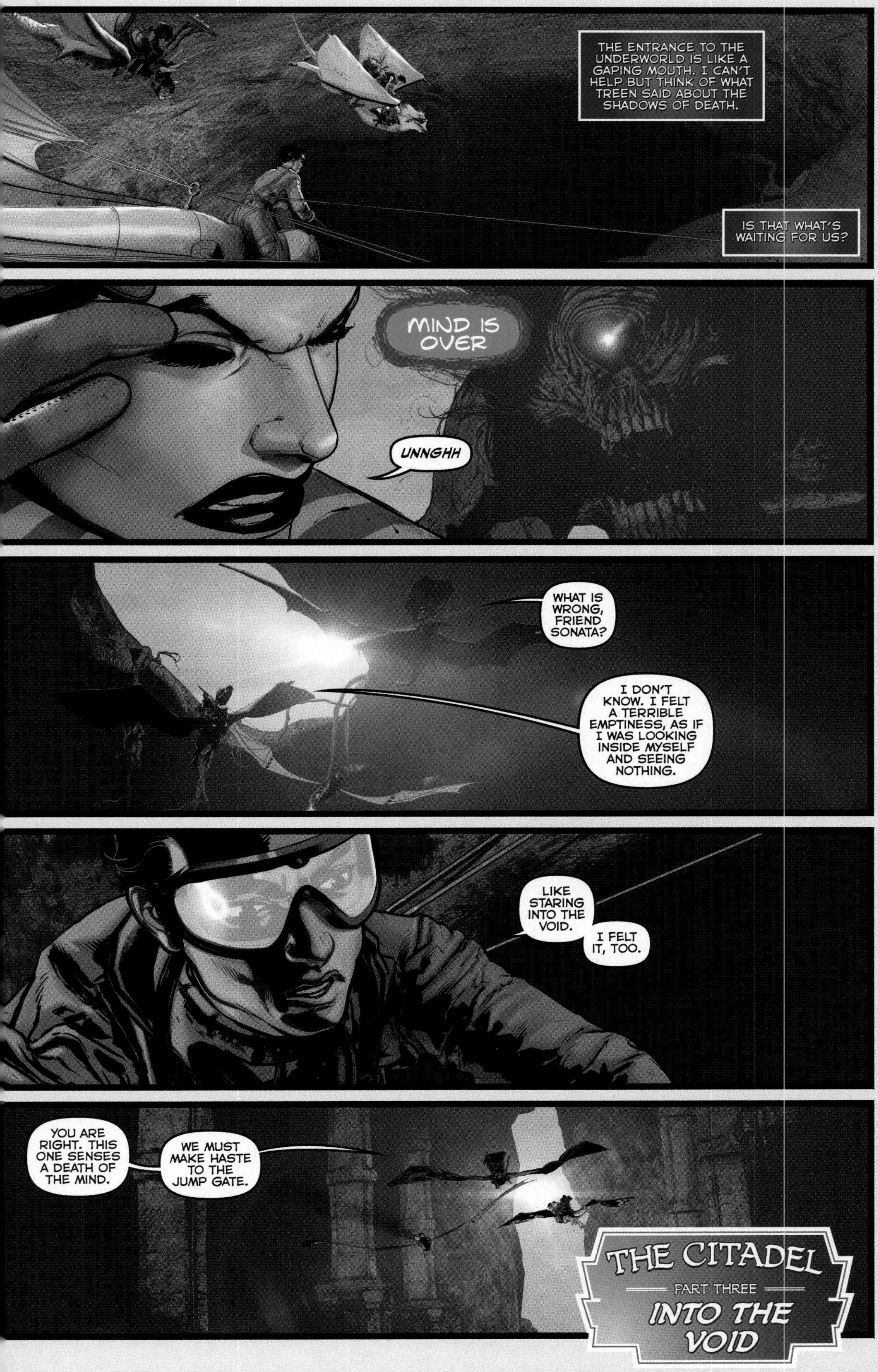

THE ENTRANCE TO THE UNDERWORLD IS LIKE A GAPING MOUTH. I CAN'T HELP BUT THINK OF WHAT TREEN SAID ABOUT THE SHADOWS OF DEATH.
IS THAT WHAT'S WAITING FOR US?
MIND IS OVER
UNNGHH
WHAT IS WRONG, FRIEND SONATA?
I DON'T KNOW. I FELT A TERRIBLE EMPTINESS, AS IF I WAS LOOKING INSIDE MYSELF AND SEEING NOTHING.
LIKE STARING INTO THE VOID.
I FELT IT, TOO.
YOU ARE RIGHT. THIS ONE SENSES A DEATH OF THE MIND.
WE MUST MAKE HASTE TO THE JUMP GATE.
THE CITADEL
PART THREE
INTO THE VOID

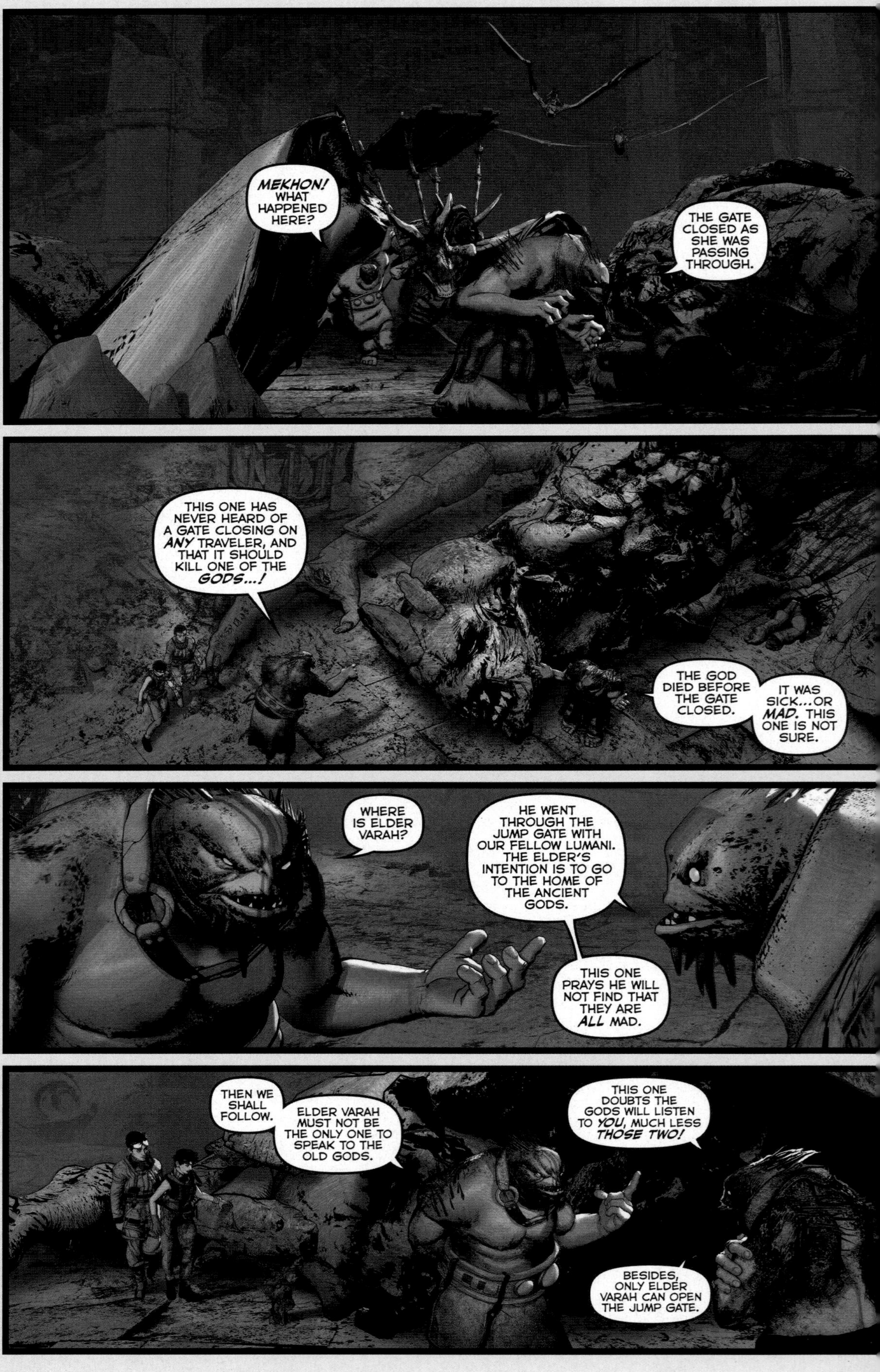
MEKHON! WHAT HAPPENED HERE?
THE GATE CLOSED AS SHE WAS PASSING THROUGH.
THIS ONE HAS NEVER HEARD OF A GATE CLOSING ON ANY TRAVELER, AND THAT IT SHOULD KILL ONE OF THE GODS...!
THE GOD DIED BEFORE THE GATE CLOSED.
IT WAS SICK...OR MAD. THIS ONE IS NOT SURE.
WHERE IS ELDER VARAH?
HE WENT THROUGH THE JUMP GATE WITH OUR FELLOW LUMANI. THE ELDER'S INTENTION IS TO GO TO THE HOME OF THE ANCIENT GODS.
THIS ONE PRAYS HE WILL NOT FIND THAT THEY ARE ALL MAD.
THEN WE SHALL FOLLOW.
ELDER VARAH MUST NOT BE THE ONLY ONE TO SPEAK TO THE OLD GODS.
THIS ONE DOUBTS THE GODS WILL LISTEN TO YOU, MUCH LESS THOSE TWO!
BESIDES, ONLY ELDER VARAH CAN OPEN THE JUMP GATE.

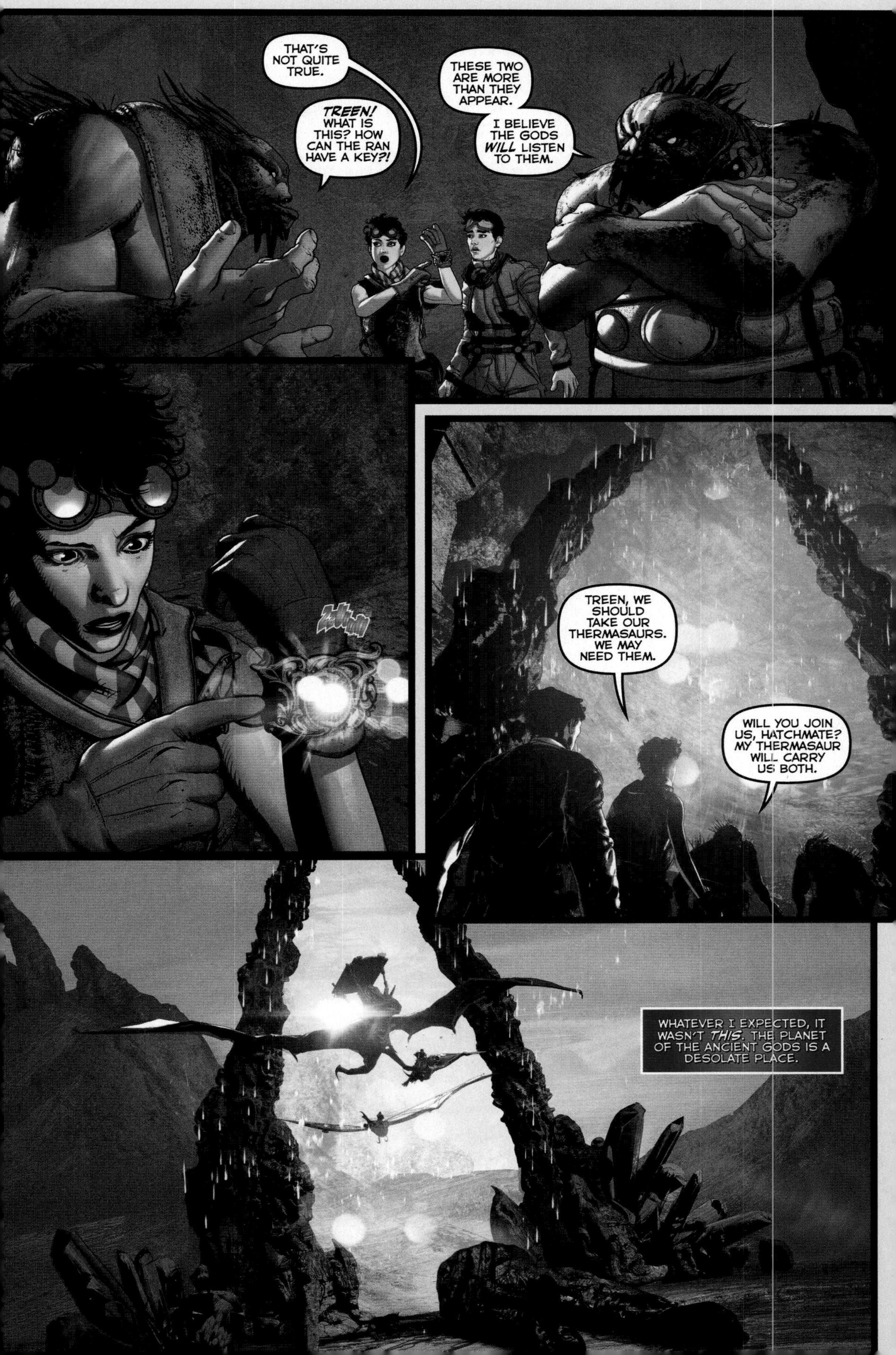
THAT'S NOT QUITE TRUE.
TREEN! WHAT IS THIS? HOW CAN THE RAN HAVE A KEY?!
THESE TWO ARE MORE THAN THEY APPEAR.
I BELIEVE THE GODS WILL LISTEN TO THEM.
TREEN, WE SHOULD TAKE OUR THERMASAURS. WE MAY NEED THEM.
WILL YOU JOIN US, HATCHMATE? MY THERMASAUR WILL CARRY US BOTH.
WHATEVER I EXPECTED, IT WASN'T THIS. THE PLANET OF THE ANCIENT GODS IS A DESOLATE PLACE.

WHAT IS THAT, SOME KIND OF *SCULPTURE?*

NOT A SCULPTURE.

BY ALL THE GODS, THOSE ARE BONES!

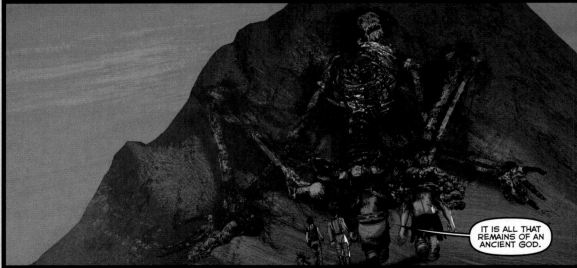

IT IS ALL THAT REMAINS OF AN ANCIENT GOD.

THIS ONE ALWAYS BELIEVED THAT THE GODS ARE IMMORTAL. NOW HERE IS ANOTHER THAT HAS DEPARTED THIS LIFE.

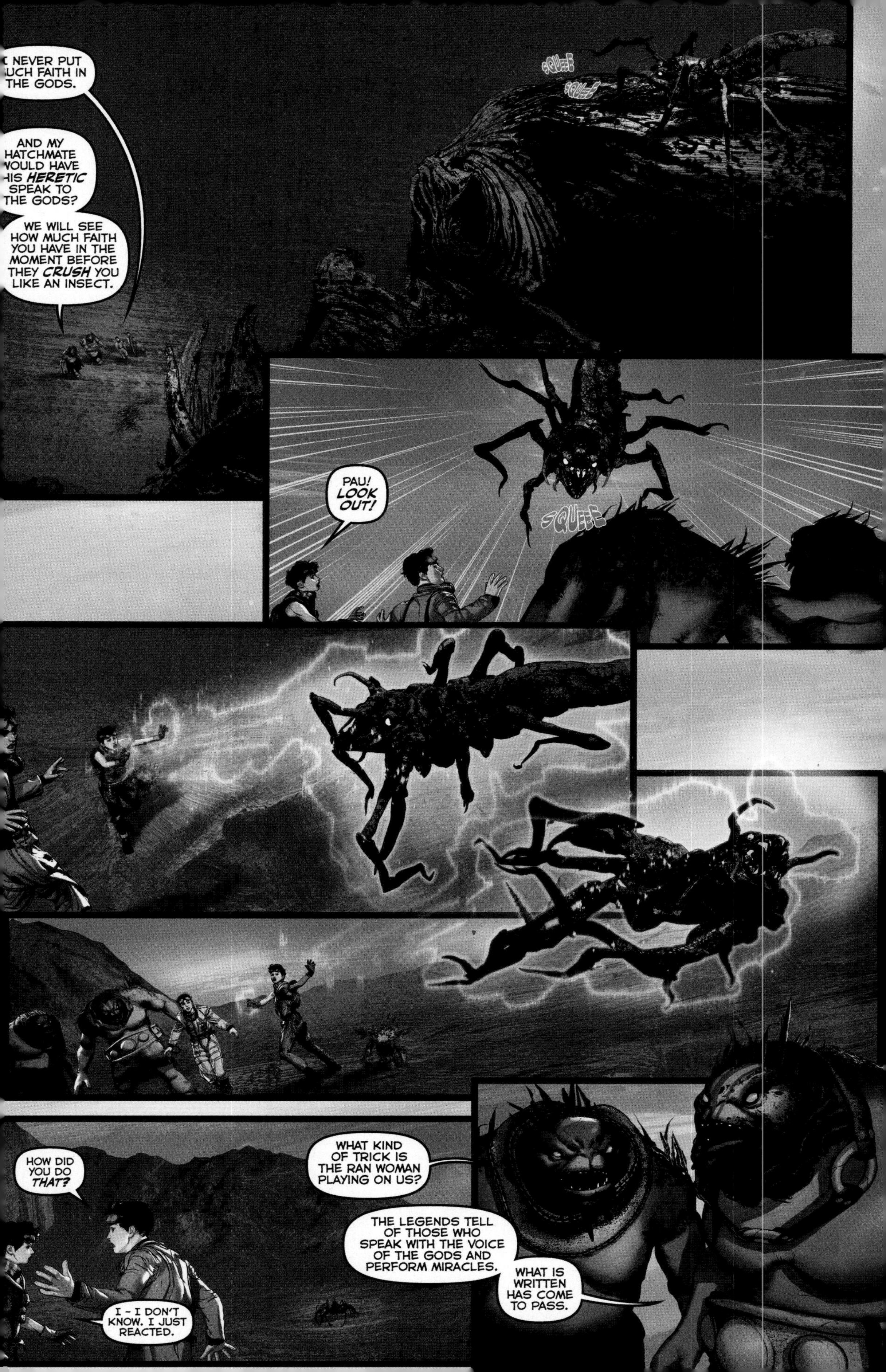

NEVER PUT UCH FAITH IN THE GODS.
AND MY HATCHMATE VOULD HAVE IS *HERETIC* SPEAK TO THE GODS?
WE WILL SEE HOW MUCH FAITH YOU HAVE IN THE MOMENT BEFORE THEY *CRUSH* YOU LIKE AN INSECT.
SQUEE
SQUEE
PAU! *LOOK OUT!*
SQUEEE
HOW DID YOU DO *THAT?*
I - I DON'T KNOW. I JUST REACTED.
WHAT KIND OF TRICK IS THE RAN WOMAN PLAYING ON US?
THE LEGENDS TELL OF THOSE WHO SPEAK WITH THE VOICE OF THE GODS AND PERFORM MIRACLES.
WHAT IS WRITTEN HAS COME TO PASS.

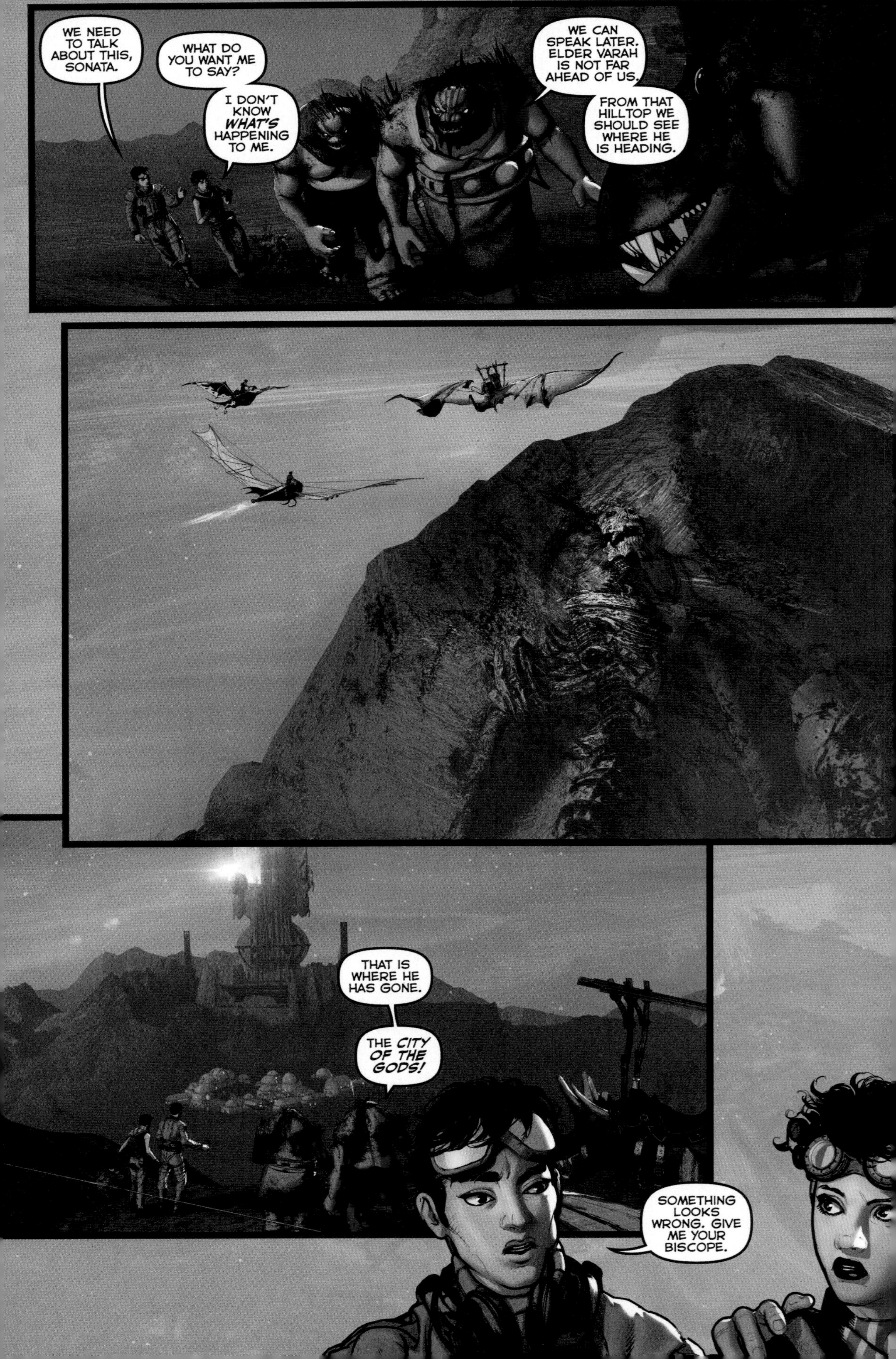
WE NEED TO TALK ABOUT THIS, SONATA.
WHAT DO YOU WANT ME TO SAY?
I DON'T KNOW *WHAT'S* HAPPENING TO ME.
WE CAN SPEAK LATER. ELDER VARAH IS NOT FAR AHEAD OF US.
FROM THAT HILLTOP WE SHOULD SEE WHERE HE IS HEADING.
THAT IS WHERE HE HAS GONE.
THE *CITY OF THE GODS!*
SOMETHING LOOKS WRONG. GIVE ME YOUR BISCOPE.

THERE ARE TWO SEPARATE CITIES.
"THE LARGER BUILDINGS LOOK DESERTED, THERE'S NO SIGN OF LIFE, NO LIGHTS."
"THE SMALLER TOWNSHIP IS LUMANI."
THEY LOOK DIFFERENT. THE BUILDINGS, THE WAY THEY'RE DRESSED.
THEY APPEAR TO BE ALMOST *CIVILIZED*.
"CIVILIZED?" WHAT'S THAT SUPPOSED TO MEAN?

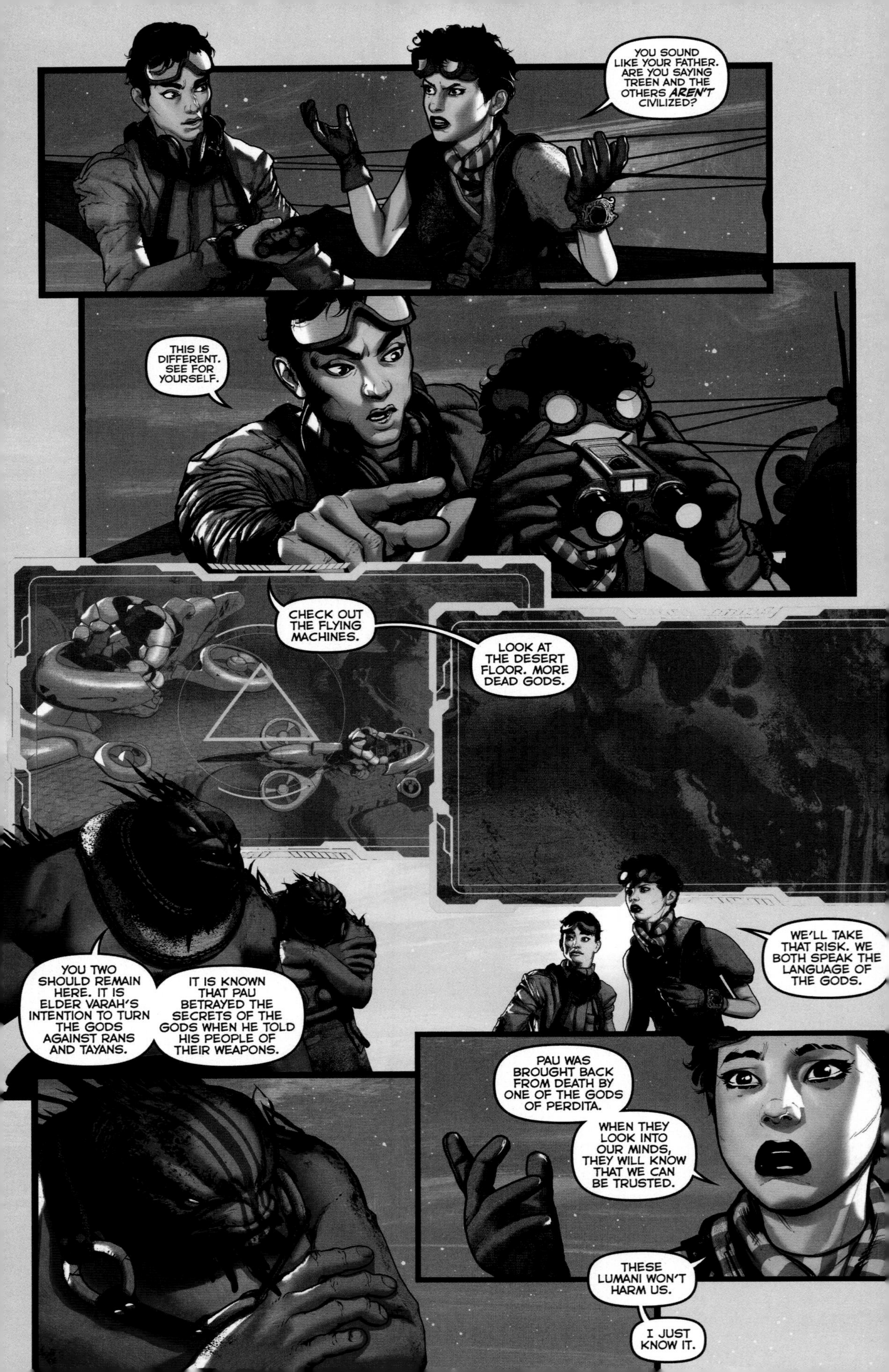
YOU SOUND LIKE YOUR FATHER. ARE YOU SAYING TREEN AND THE OTHERS *AREN'T* CIVILIZED?
THIS IS DIFFERENT. SEE FOR YOURSELF.
CHECK OUT THE FLYING MACHINES.
LOOK AT THE DESERT FLOOR. MORE DEAD GODS.
YOU TWO SHOULD REMAIN HERE. IT IS ELDER VARAH'S INTENTION TO TURN THE GODS AGAINST RANS AND TAYANS.
IT IS KNOWN THAT PAU BETRAYED THE SECRETS OF THE GODS WHEN HE TOLD HIS PEOPLE OF THEIR WEAPONS.
WE'LL TAKE THAT RISK. WE BOTH SPEAK THE LANGUAGE OF THE GODS.
PAU WAS BROUGHT BACK FROM DEATH BY ONE OF THE GODS OF PERDITA.
WHEN THEY LOOK INTO OUR MINDS, THEY WILL KNOW THAT WE CAN BE TRUSTED.
THESE LUMANI WON'T HARM US.
I JUST KNOW IT.

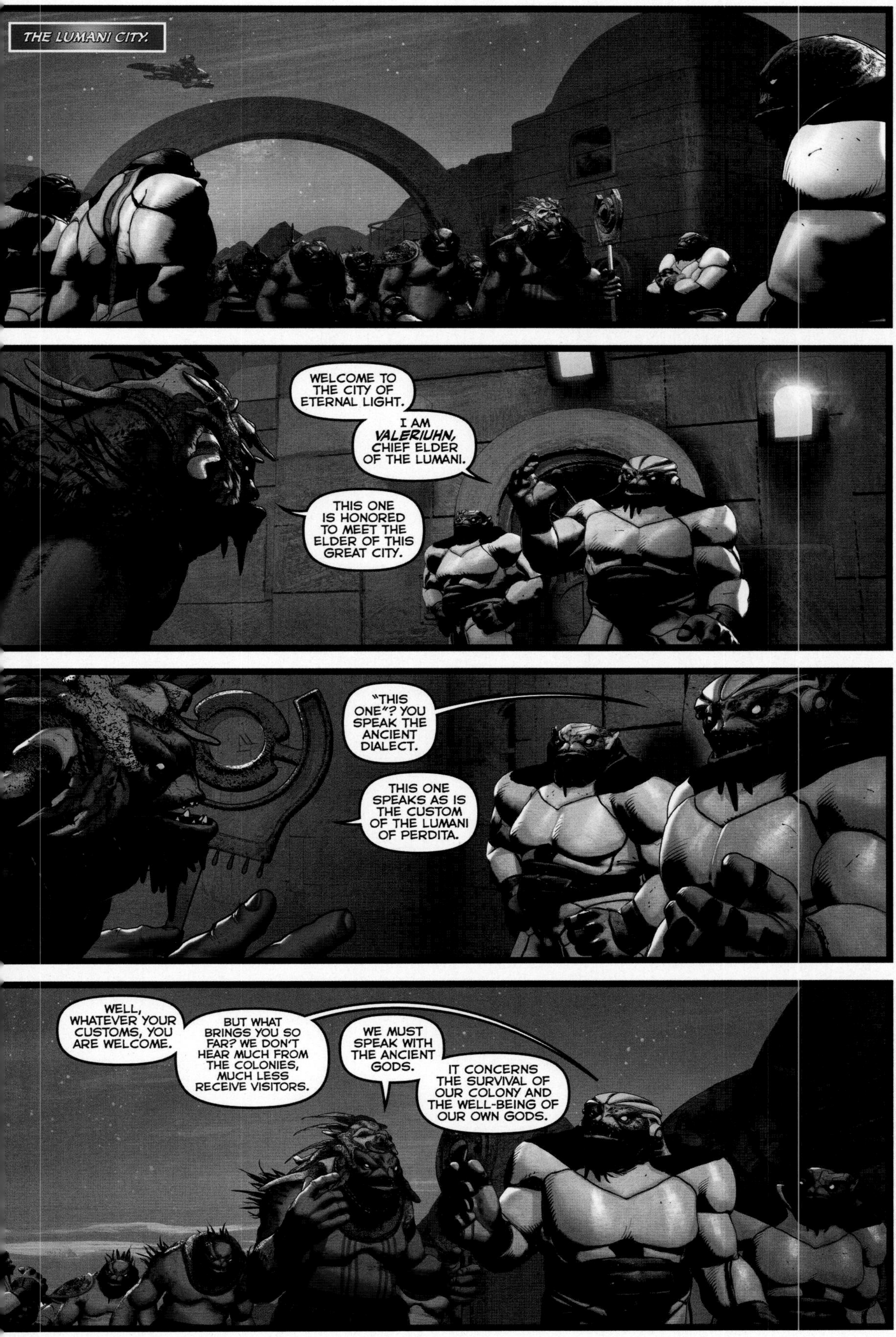
THE LUMANI CITY.
WELCOME TO THE CITY OF ETERNAL LIGHT.
I AM VALERIUHN, CHIEF ELDER OF THE LUMANI.
THIS ONE IS HONORED TO MEET THE ELDER OF THIS GREAT CITY.
"THIS ONE"? YOU SPEAK THE ANCIENT DIALECT.
THIS ONE SPEAKS AS IS THE CUSTOM OF THE LUMANI OF PERDITA.
WELL, WHATEVER YOUR CUSTOMS, YOU ARE WELCOME.
BUT WHAT BRINGS YOU SO FAR? WE DON'T HEAR MUCH FROM THE COLONIES, MUCH LESS RECEIVE VISITORS.
WE MUST SPEAK WITH THE ANCIENT GODS.
IT CONCERNS THE SURVIVAL OF OUR COLONY AND THE WELL-BEING OF OUR OWN GODS.

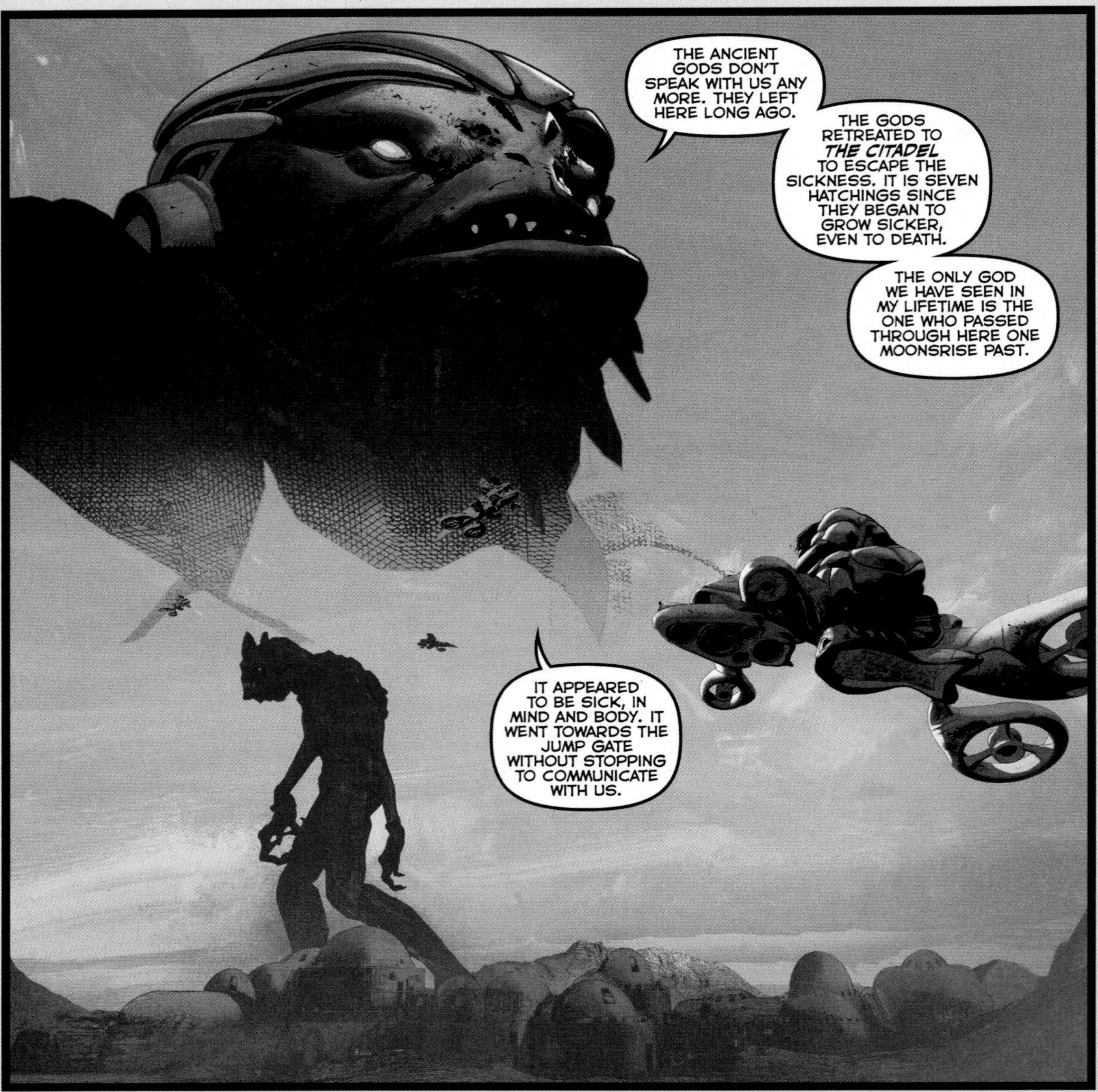
THE ANCIENT GODS DON'T SPEAK WITH US ANY MORE. THEY LEFT HERE LONG AGO.
THE GODS RETREATED TO *THE CITADEL* TO ESCAPE THE SICKNESS. IT IS SEVEN HATCHINGS SINCE THEY BEGAN TO GROW SICKER, EVEN TO DEATH.
THE ONLY GOD WE HAVE SEEN IN MY LIFETIME IS THE ONE WHO PASSED THROUGH HERE ONE MOONSRISE PAST.
IT APPEARED TO BE SICK, IN MIND AND BODY. IT WENT TOWARDS THE JUMP GATE WITHOUT STOPPING TO COMMUNICATE WITH US.

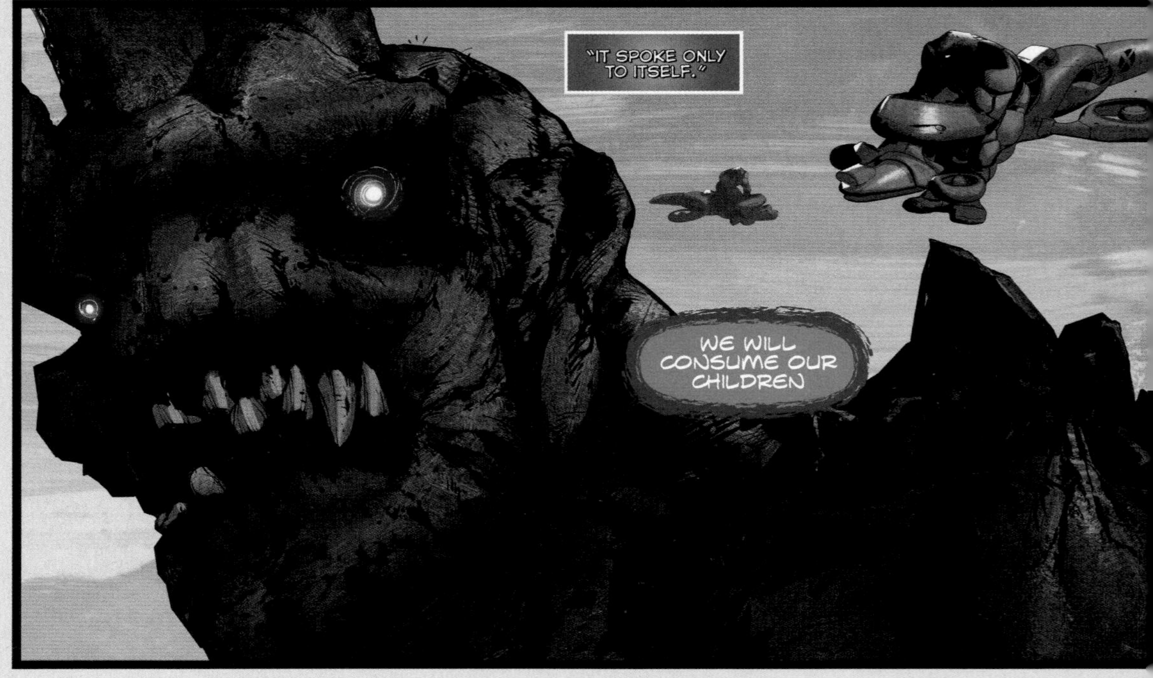
"IT SPOKE ONLY TO ITSELF."
WE WILL CONSUME OUR CHILDREN

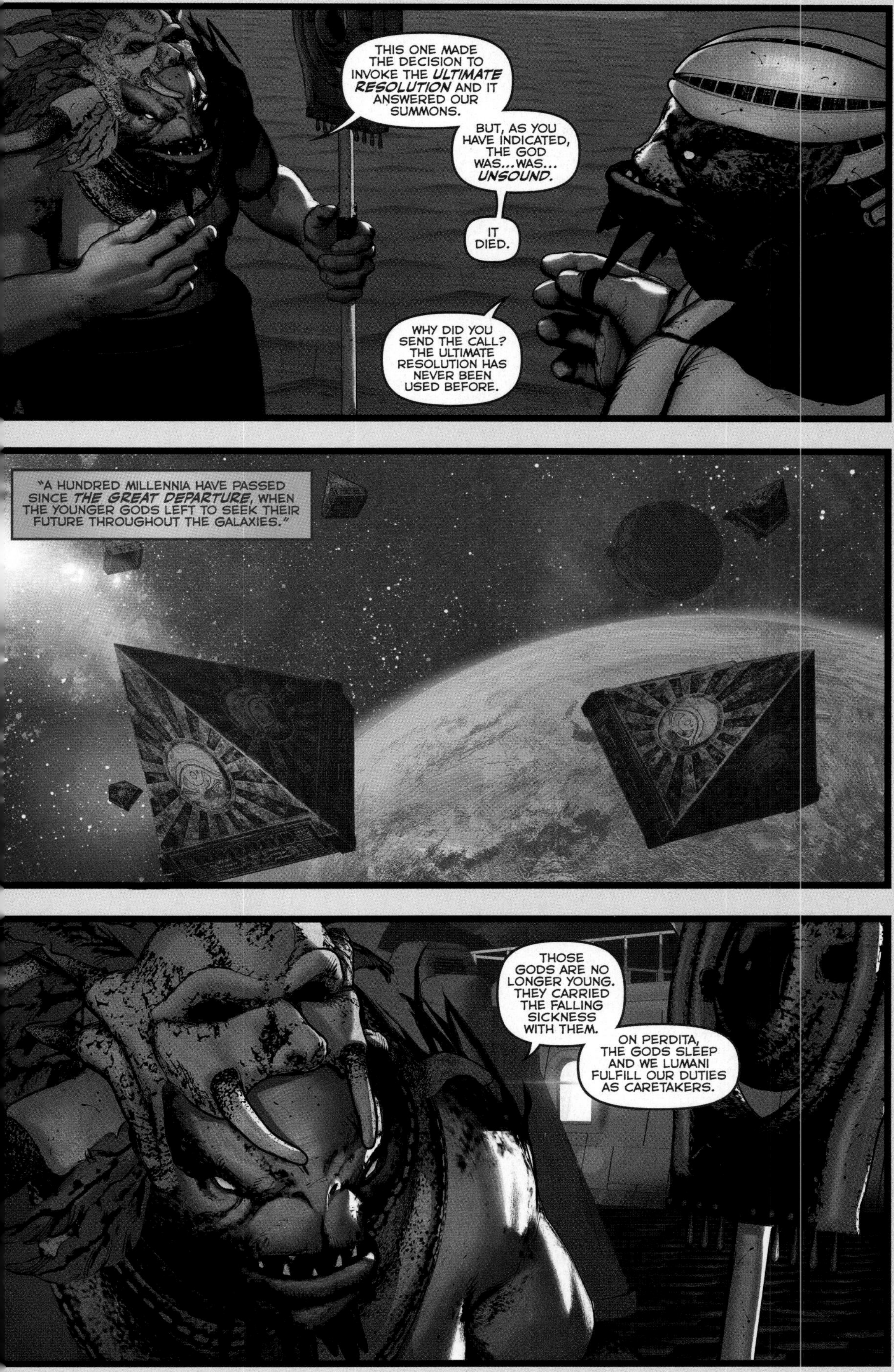
THIS ONE MADE THE DECISION TO INVOKE THE *ULTIMATE RESOLUTION* AND IT ANSWERED OUR SUMMONS.
BUT, AS YOU HAVE INDICATED, THE GOD WAS...WAS... *UNSOUND.*
IT DIED.
WHY DID YOU SEND THE CALL? THE ULTIMATE RESOLUTION HAS NEVER BEEN USED BEFORE.
"A HUNDRED MILLENNIA HAVE PASSED SINCE *THE GREAT DEPARTURE*, WHEN THE YOUNGER GODS LEFT TO SEEK THEIR FUTURE THROUGHOUT THE GALAXIES."
THOSE GODS ARE NO LONGER YOUNG. THEY CARRIED THE FALLING SICKNESS WITH THEM.
ON PERDITA, THE GODS SLEEP AND WE LUMANI FULFILL OUR DUTIES AS CARETAKERS.

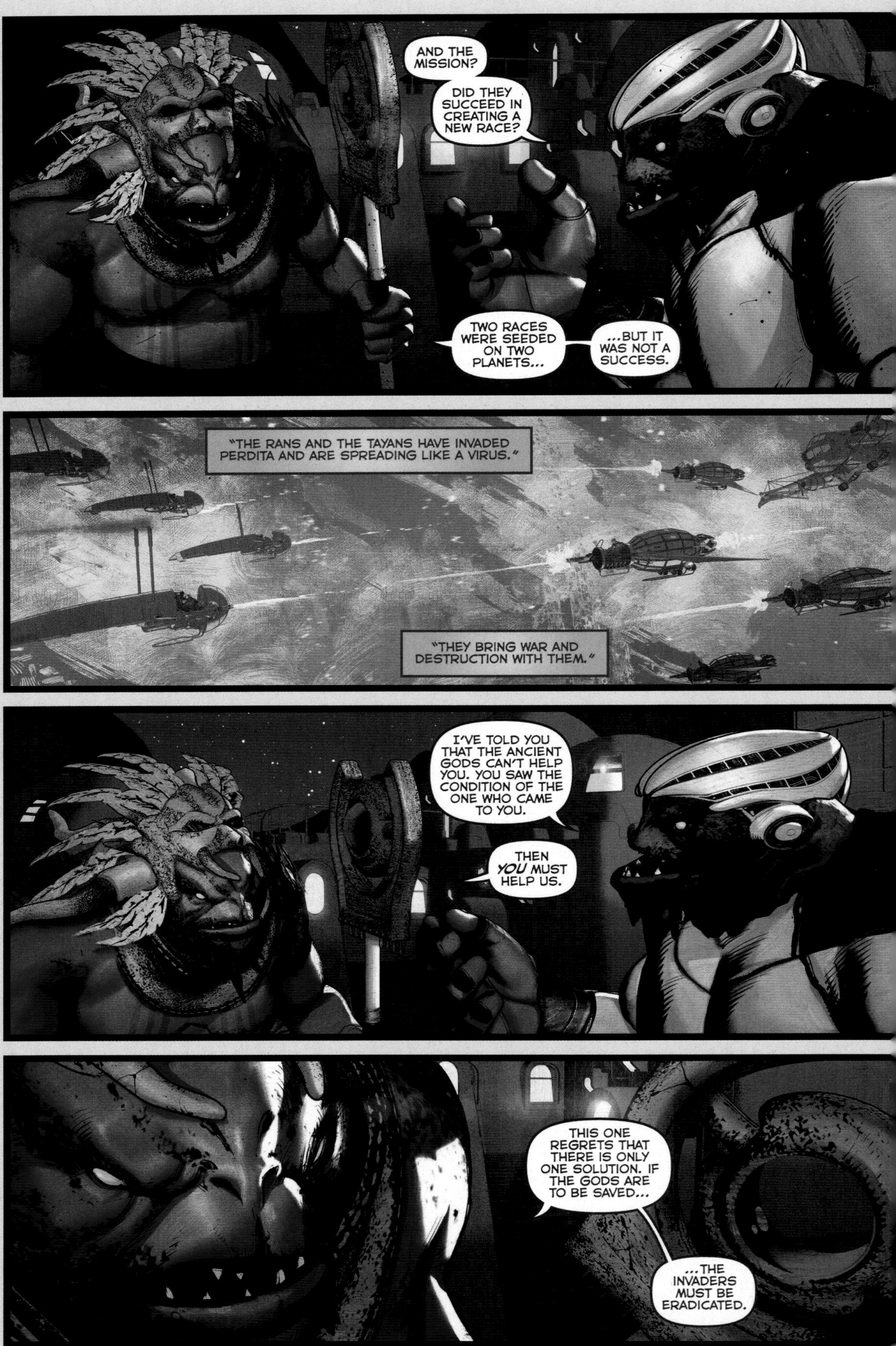
AND THE MISSION?
DID THEY SUCCEED IN CREATING A NEW RACE?
TWO RACES WERE SEEDED ON TWO PLANETS...
...BUT IT WAS NOT A SUCCESS.
"THE RANS AND THE TAYANS HAVE INVADED PERDITA AND ARE SPREADING LIKE A VIRUS."
"THEY BRING WAR AND DESTRUCTION WITH THEM."
I'VE TOLD YOU THAT THE ANCIENT GODS CAN'T HELP YOU. YOU SAW THE CONDITION OF THE ONE WHO CAME TO YOU.
THEN *YOU* MUST HELP US.
THIS ONE REGRETS THAT THERE IS ONLY ONE SOLUTION. IF THE GODS ARE TO BE SAVED...
...THE INVADERS MUST BE ERADICATED.

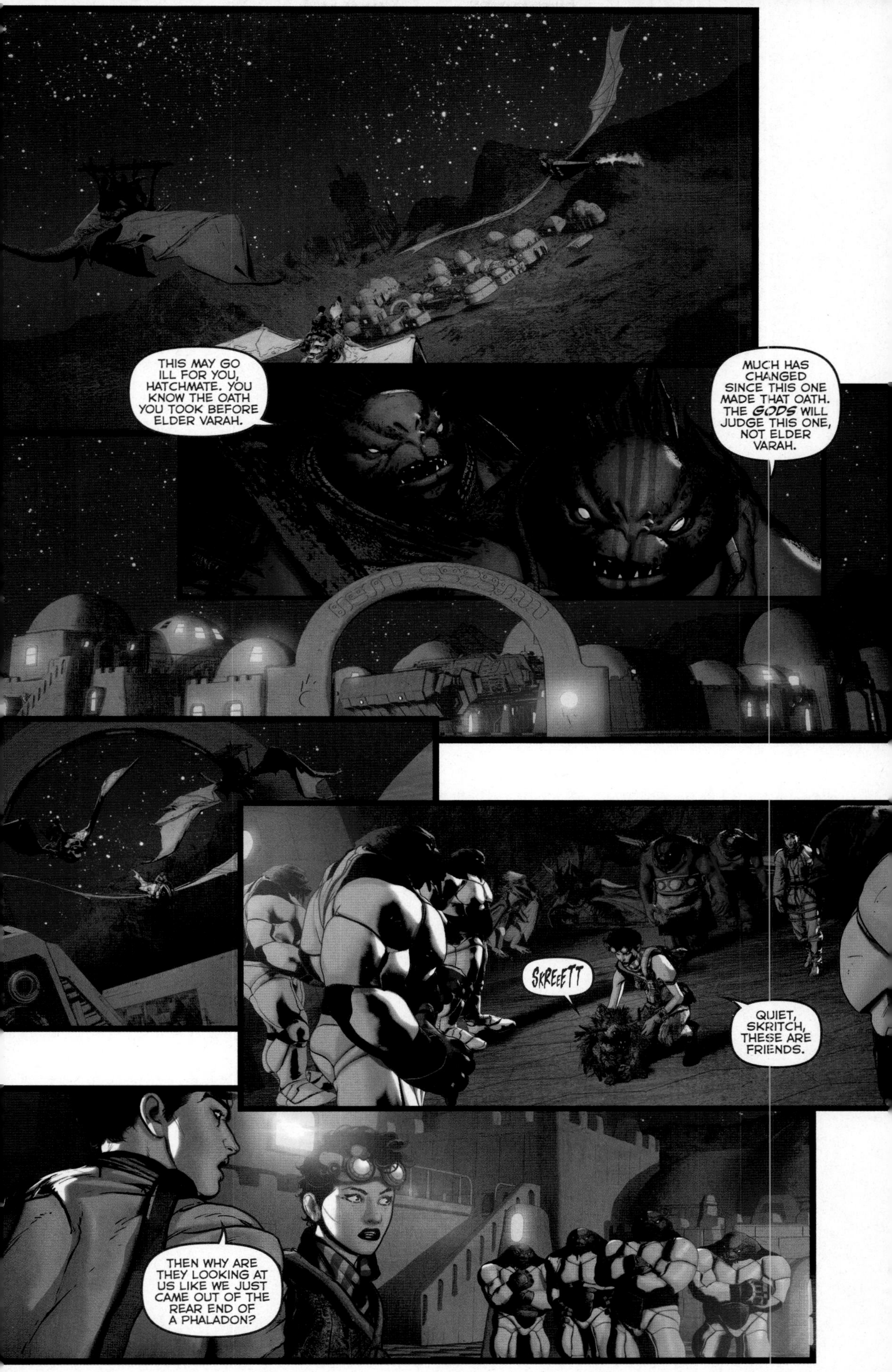
THIS MAY GO ILL FOR YOU, HATCHMATE. YOU KNOW THE OATH YOU TOOK BEFORE ELDER VARAH.
MUCH HAS CHANGED SINCE THIS ONE MADE THAT OATH. THE GODS WILL JUDGE THIS ONE, NOT ELDER VARAH.
SKREEETT
QUIET, SKRITCH, THESE ARE FRIENDS.
THEN WHY ARE THEY LOOKING AT US LIKE WE JUST CAME OUT OF THE REAR END OF A PHALADON?

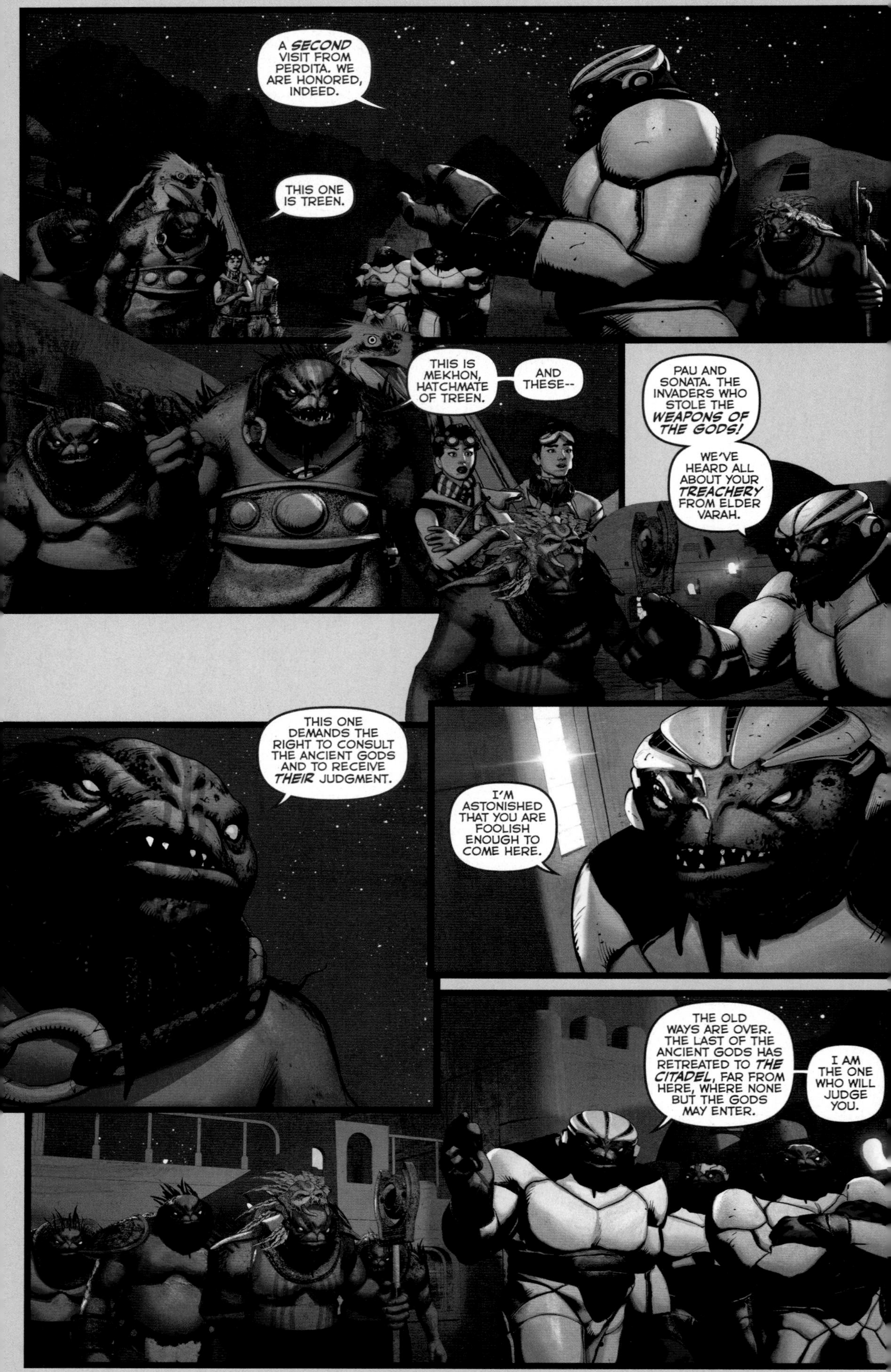
A SECOND VISIT FROM PERDITA. WE ARE HONORED, INDEED.
THIS ONE IS TREEN.
THIS IS MEKHON, HATCHMATE OF TREEN.
AND THESE--
PAU AND SONATA. THE INVADERS WHO STOLE THE WEAPONS OF THE GODS!
WE'VE HEARD ALL ABOUT YOUR TREACHERY FROM ELDER VARAH.
THIS ONE DEMANDS THE RIGHT TO CONSULT THE ANCIENT GODS AND TO RECEIVE THEIR JUDGMENT.
I'M ASTONISHED THAT YOU ARE FOOLISH ENOUGH TO COME HERE.
THE OLD WAYS ARE OVER. THE LAST OF THE ANCIENT GODS HAS RETREATED TO THE CITADEL, FAR FROM HERE, WHERE NONE BUT THE GODS MAY ENTER.
I AM THE ONE WHO WILL JUDGE YOU.

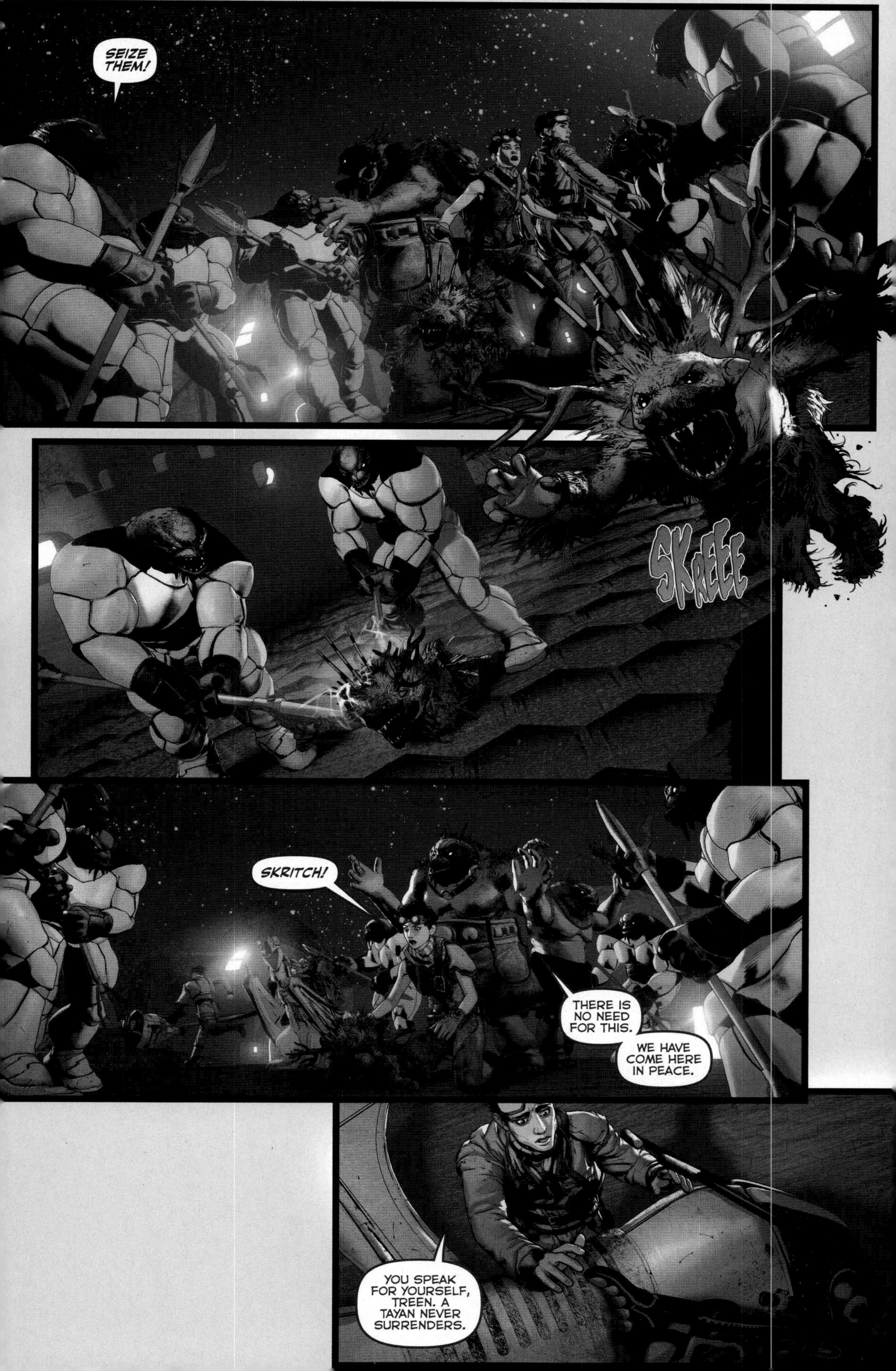
SEIZE THEM!
SKREEE
SKRITCH!
THERE IS NO NEED FOR THIS.
WE HAVE COME HERE IN PEACE.
YOU SPEAK FOR YOURSELF, TREEN. A TAYAN NEVER SURRENDERS.

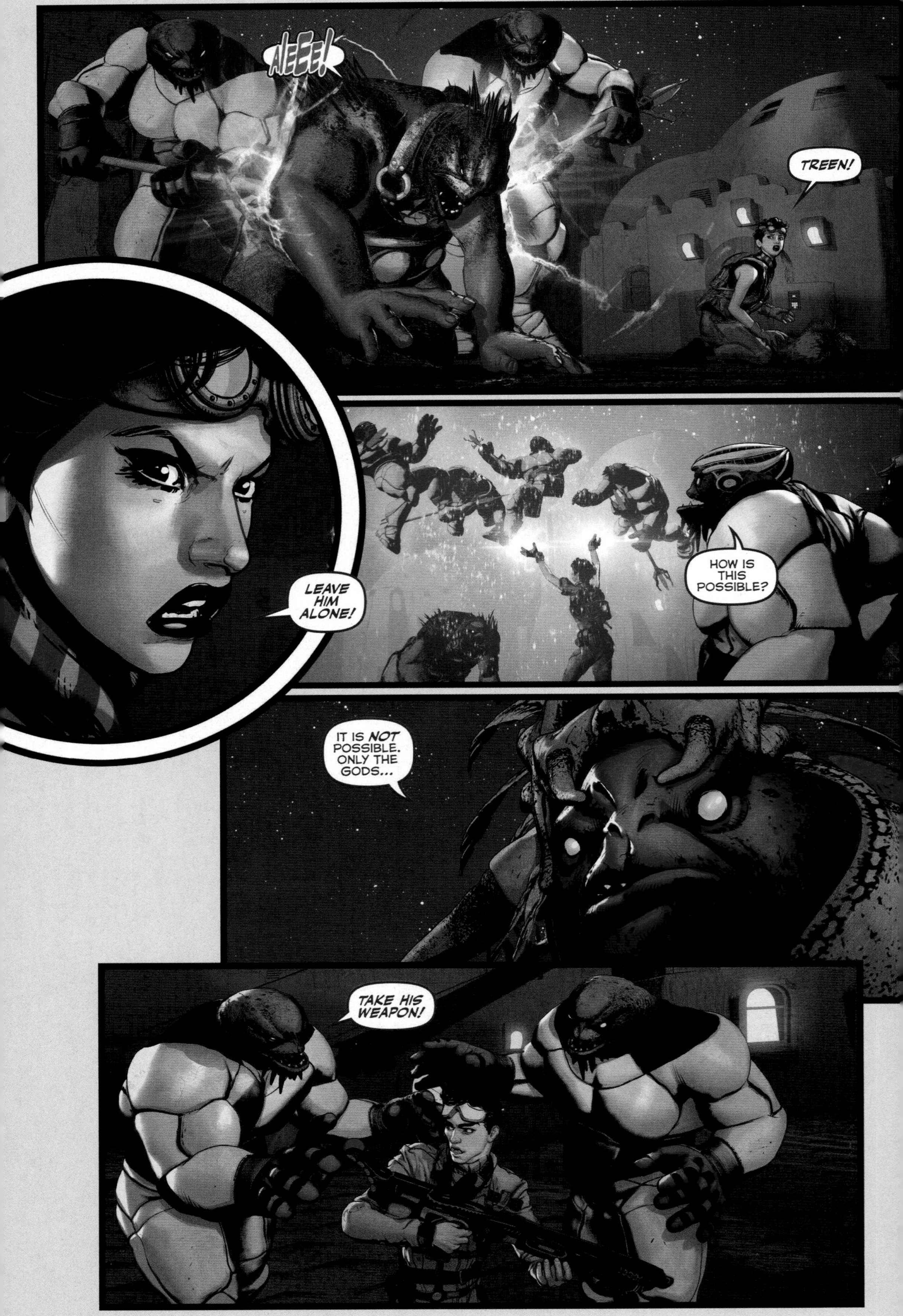
AIEEE!
TREEN!
LEAVE HIM ALONE!
HOW IS THIS POSSIBLE?
IT IS NOT POSSIBLE. ONLY THE GODS...
TAKE HIS WEAPON!

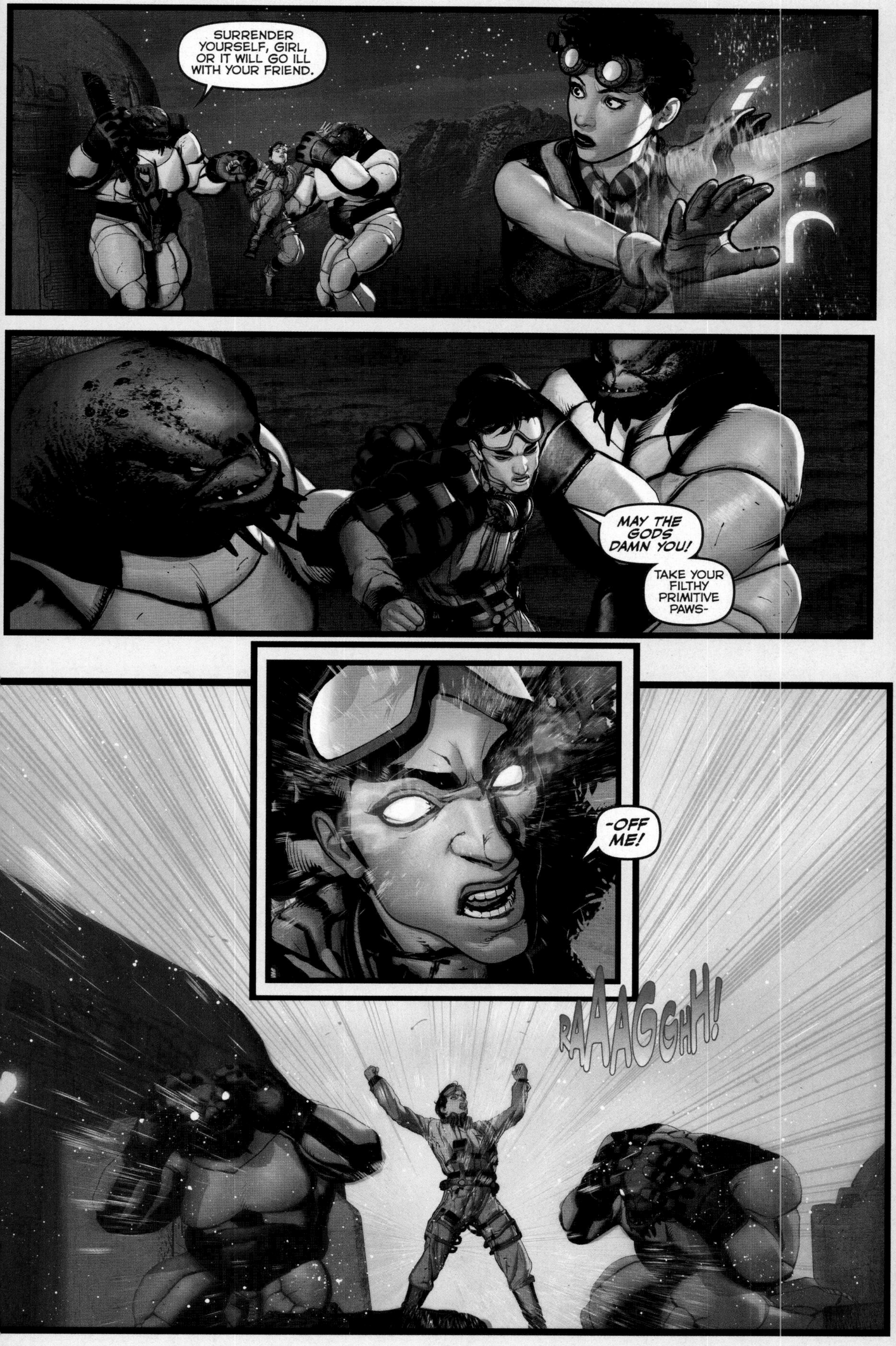
SURRENDER YOURSELF, GIRL, OR IT WILL GO ILL WITH YOUR FRIEND.
MAY THE GODS DAMN YOU!
TAKE YOUR FILTHY PRIMITIVE PAWS-
-OFF ME!
RAAAGGHH!

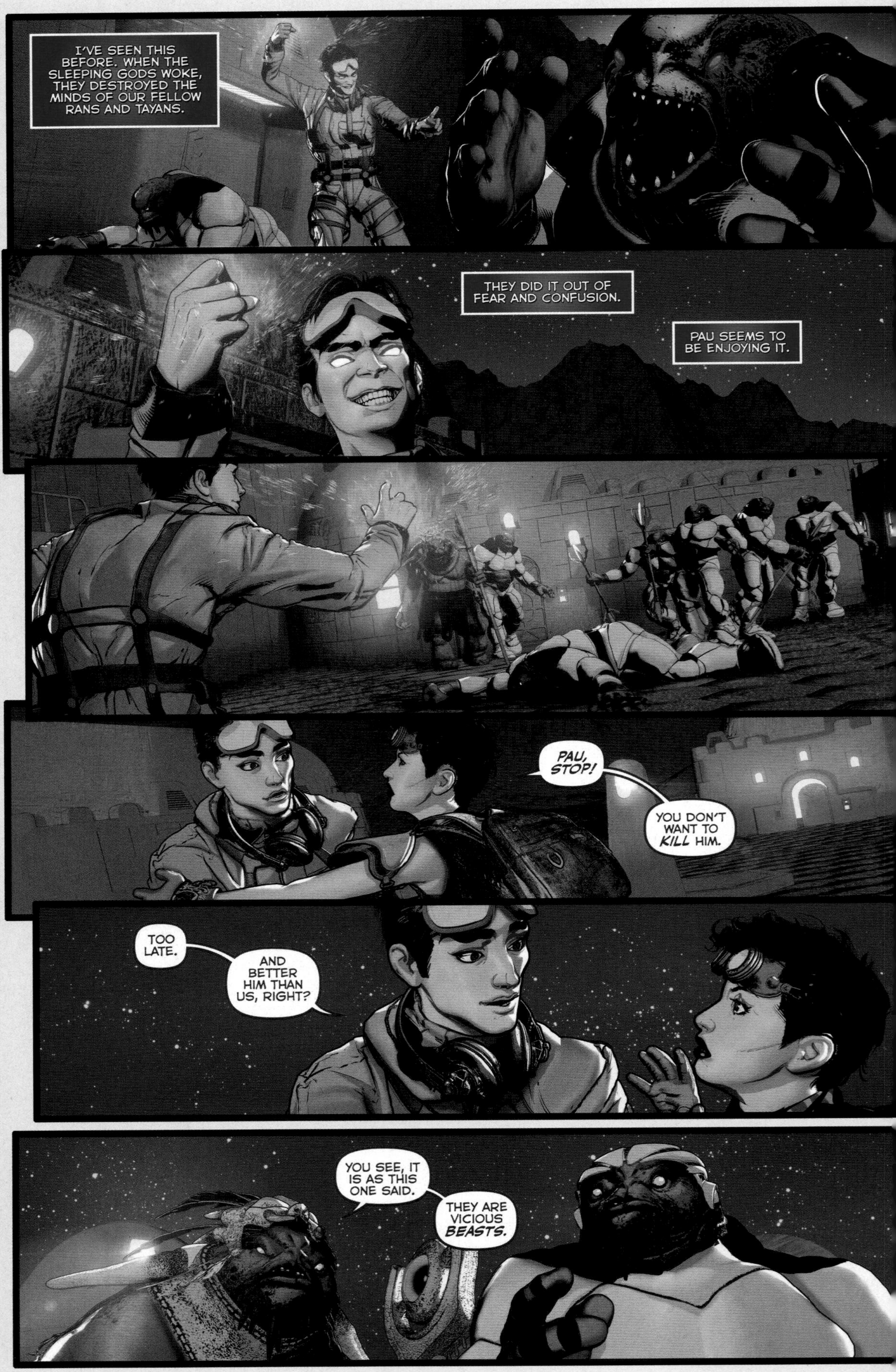
I'VE SEEN THIS BEFORE. WHEN THE SLEEPING GODS WOKE, THEY DESTROYED THE MINDS OF OUR FELLOW RANS AND TAYANS.
THEY DID IT OUT OF FEAR AND CONFUSION.
PAU SEEMS TO BE ENJOYING IT.
PAU, STOP!
YOU DON'T WANT TO KILL HIM.
TOO LATE.
AND BETTER HIM THAN US, RIGHT?
YOU SEE, IT IS AS THIS ONE SAID.
THEY ARE VICIOUS BEASTS.

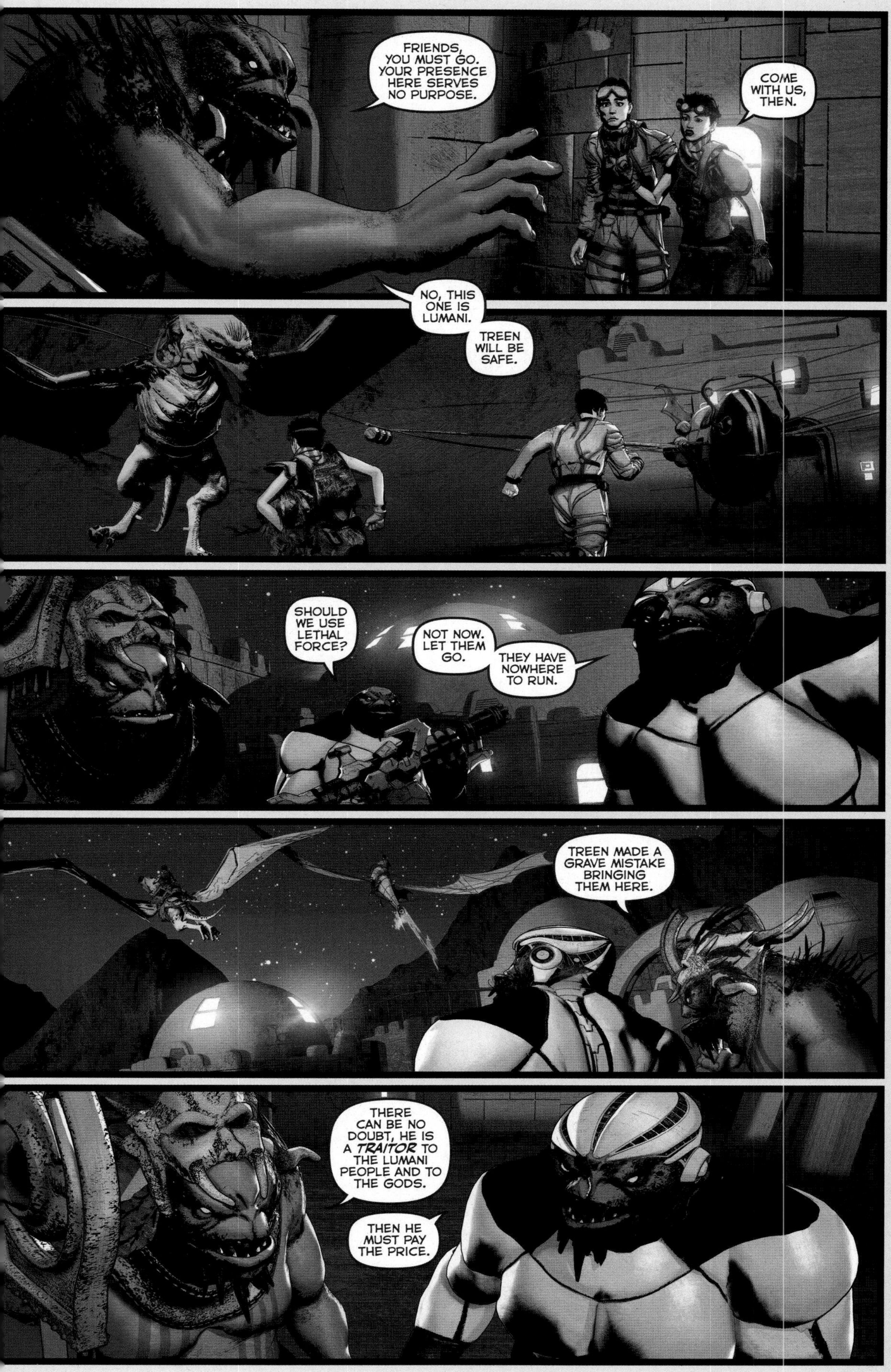
FRIENDS, YOU MUST GO. YOUR PRESENCE HERE SERVES NO PURPOSE.
COME WITH US, THEN.
NO, THIS ONE IS LUMANI.
TREEN WILL BE SAFE.
SHOULD WE USE LETHAL FORCE?
NOT NOW. LET THEM GO.
THEY HAVE NOWHERE TO RUN.
TREEN MADE A GRAVE MISTAKE BRINGING THEM HERE.
THERE CAN BE NO DOUBT, HE IS A TRAITOR TO THE LUMANI PEOPLE AND TO THE GODS.
THEN HE MUST PAY THE PRICE.

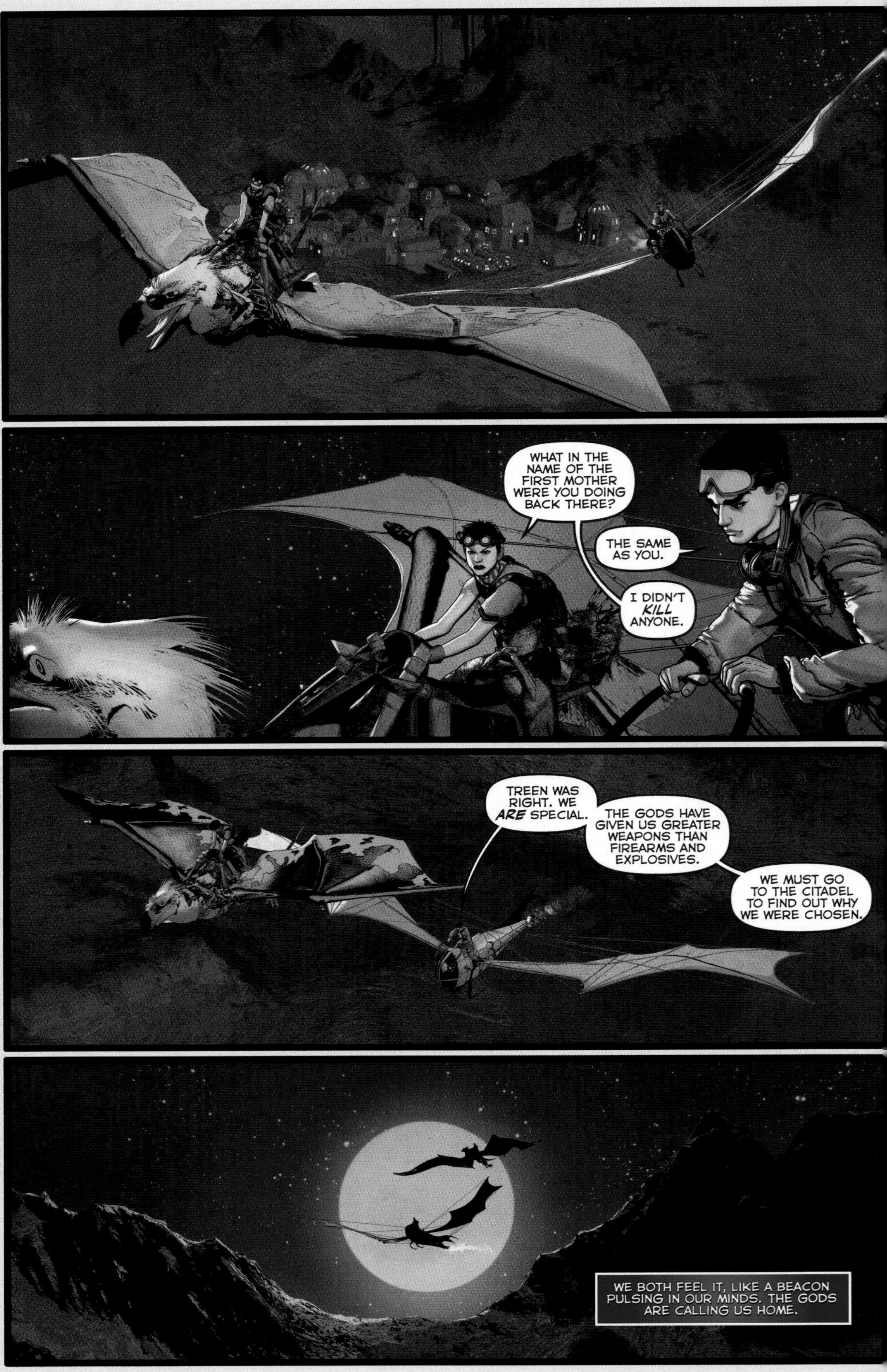
WHAT IN THE NAME OF THE FIRST MOTHER WERE YOU DOING BACK THERE?
THE SAME AS YOU.
I DIDN'T *KILL* ANYONE.
TREEN WAS RIGHT. WE *ARE* SPECIAL.
THE GODS HAVE GIVEN US GREATER WEAPONS THAN FIREARMS AND EXPLOSIVES.
WE MUST GO TO THE CITADEL TO FIND OUT WHY WE WERE CHOSEN.
WE BOTH FEEL IT, LIKE A BEACON PULSING IN OUR MINDS. THE GODS ARE CALLING US HOME.

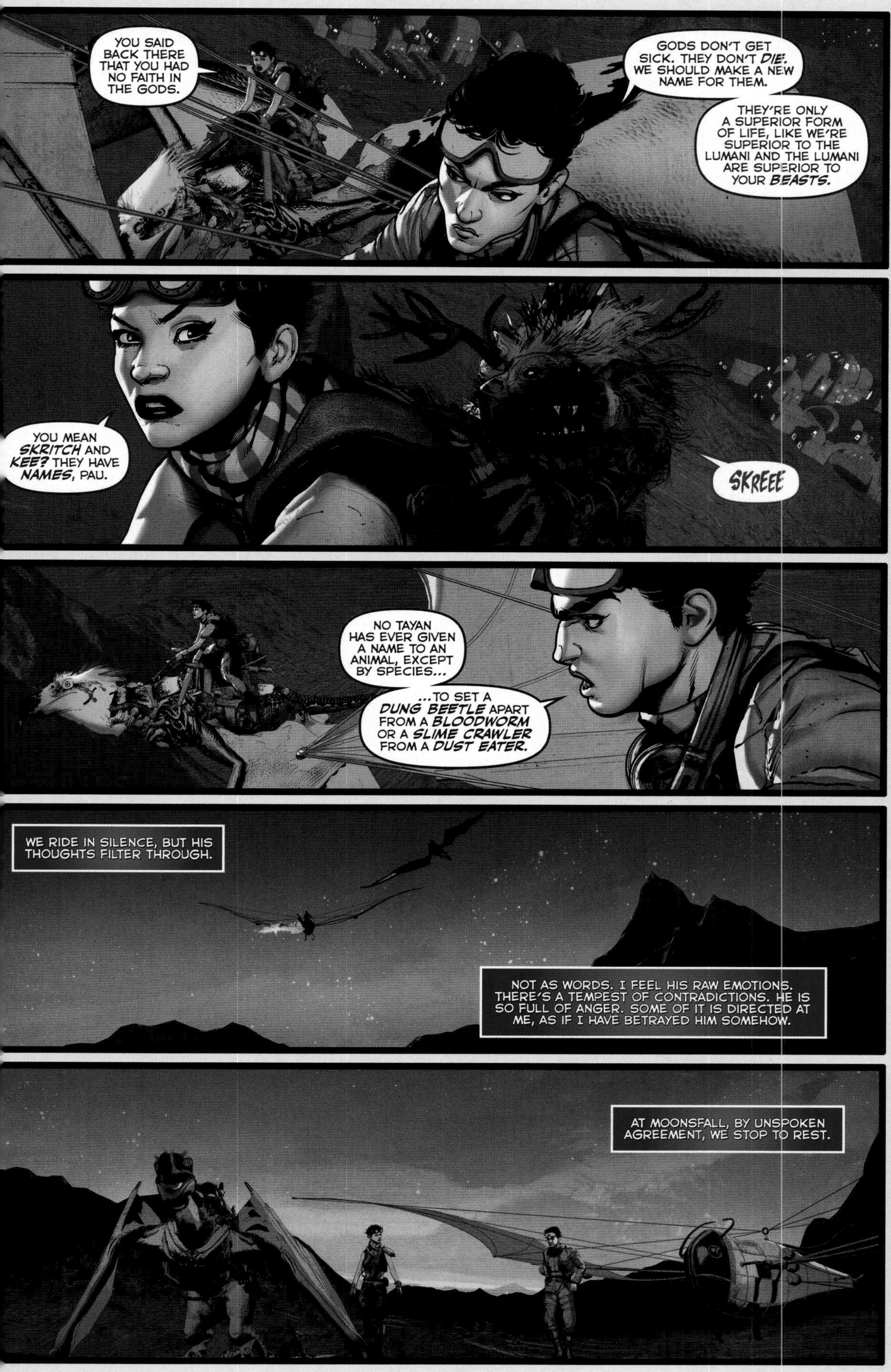

YOU SAID BACK THERE THAT YOU HAD NO FAITH IN THE GODS.
GODS DON'T GET SICK. THEY DON'T DIE. WE SHOULD MAKE A NEW NAME FOR THEM.
THEY'RE ONLY A SUPERIOR FORM OF LIFE, LIKE WE'RE SUPERIOR TO THE LUMANI AND THE LUMANI ARE SUPERIOR TO YOUR BEASTS.
YOU MEAN SKRITCH AND KEE? THEY HAVE NAMES, PAU.
SKREEE
NO TAYAN HAS EVER GIVEN A NAME TO AN ANIMAL, EXCEPT BY SPECIES...
...TO SET A DUNG BEETLE APART FROM A BLOODWORM OR A SLIME CRAWLER FROM A DUST EATER.
WE RIDE IN SILENCE, BUT HIS THOUGHTS FILTER THROUGH.
NOT AS WORDS. I FEEL HIS RAW EMOTIONS. THERE'S A TEMPEST OF CONTRADICTIONS. HE IS SO FULL OF ANGER. SOME OF IT IS DIRECTED AT ME, AS IF I HAVE BETRAYED HIM SOMEHOW.
AT MOONSFALL, BY UNSPOKEN AGREEMENT, WE STOP TO REST.

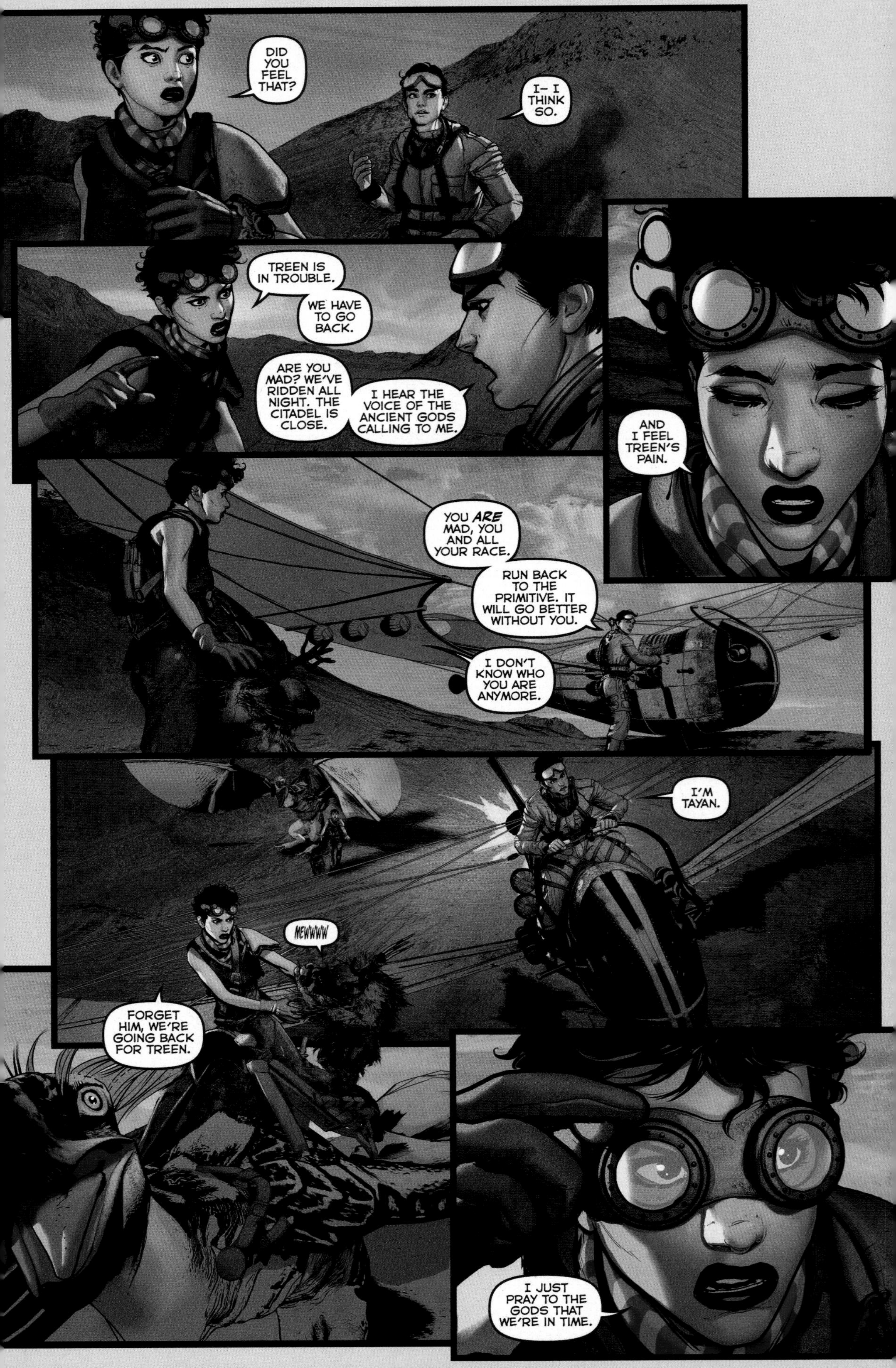
DID YOU FEEL THAT?
I– I THINK SO.
TREEN IS IN TROUBLE.
WE HAVE TO GO BACK.
ARE YOU MAD? WE'VE RIDDEN ALL NIGHT. THE CITADEL IS CLOSE.
I HEAR THE VOICE OF THE ANCIENT GODS CALLING TO ME.
AND I FEEL TREEN'S PAIN.
YOU ARE MAD, YOU AND ALL YOUR RACE.
RUN BACK TO THE PRIMITIVE. IT WILL GO BETTER WITHOUT YOU.
I DON'T KNOW WHO YOU ARE ANYMORE.
I'M TAYAN.
MEWWWW
FORGET HIM, WE'RE GOING BACK FOR TREEN.
I JUST PRAY TO THE GODS THAT WE'RE IN TIME.

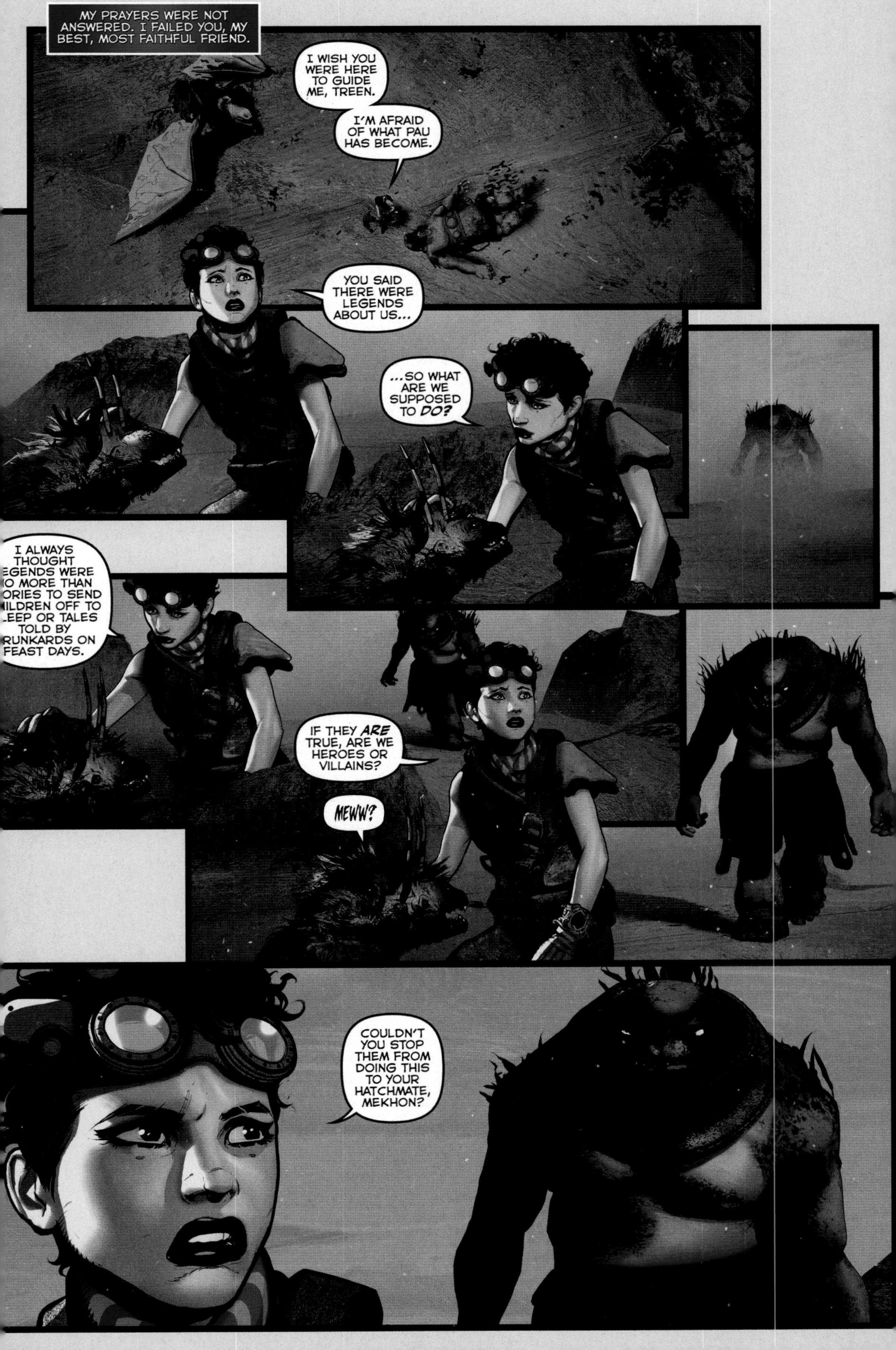

MY PRAYERS WERE NOT ANSWERED. I FAILED YOU, MY BEST, MOST FAITHFUL FRIEND.
I WISH YOU WERE HERE TO GUIDE ME, TREEN.
I'M AFRAID OF WHAT PAU HAS BECOME.
YOU SAID THERE WERE LEGENDS ABOUT US...
...SO WHAT ARE WE SUPPOSED TO *DO?*
I ALWAYS THOUGHT EGENDS WERE O MORE THAN ORIES TO SEND HILDREN OFF TO LEEP OR TALES TOLD BY RUNKARDS ON FEAST DAYS.
IF THEY *ARE* TRUE, ARE WE HEROES OR VILLAINS?
MEWW?
COULDN'T YOU STOP THEM FROM DOING THIS TO YOUR HATCHMATE, MEKHON?

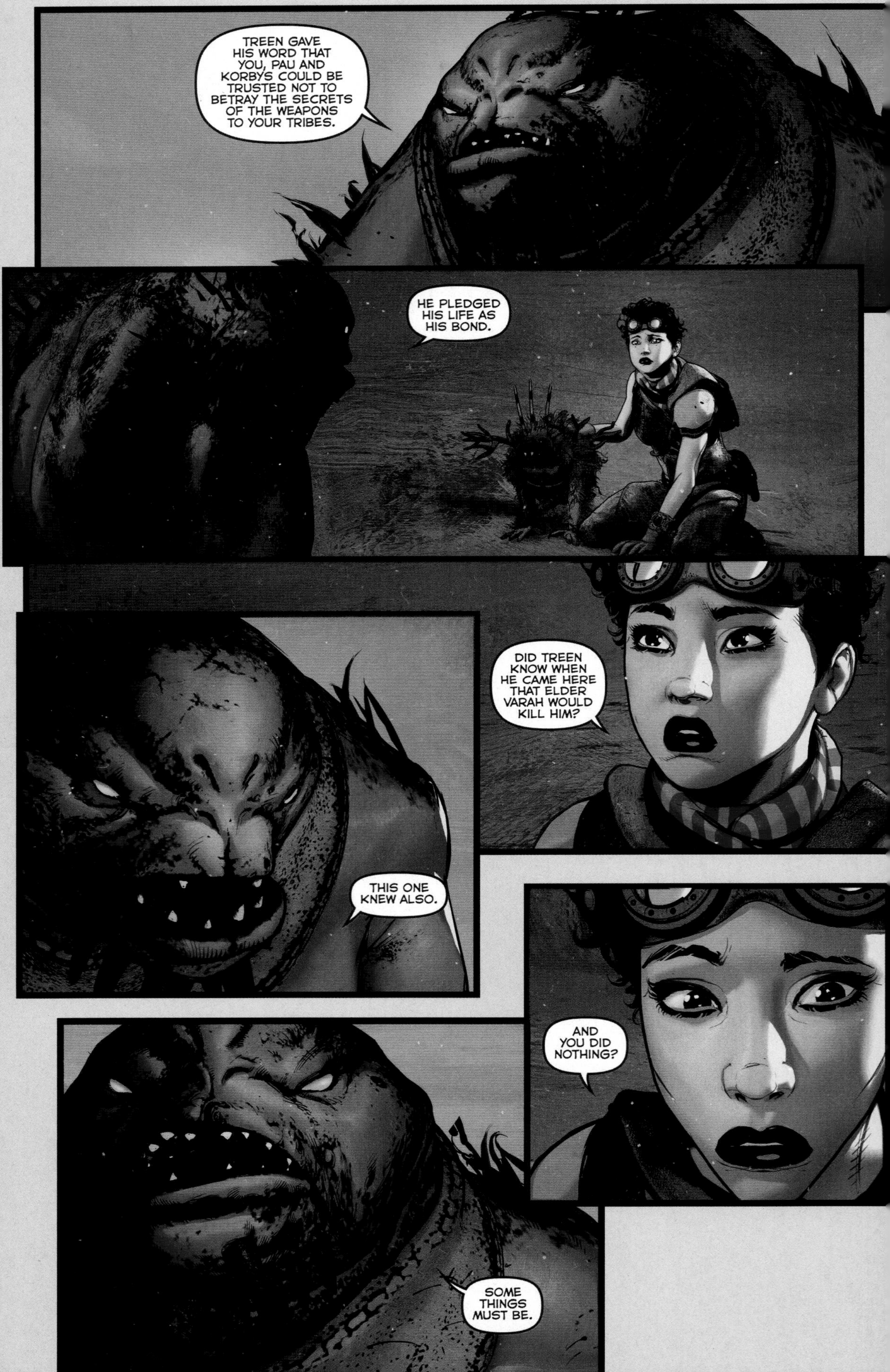
TREEN GAVE HIS WORD THAT YOU, PAU AND KORBYS COULD BE TRUSTED NOT TO BETRAY THE SECRETS OF THE WEAPONS TO YOUR TRIBES.
HE PLEDGED HIS LIFE AS HIS BOND.
DID TREEN KNOW WHEN HE CAME HERE THAT ELDER VARAH WOULD KILL HIM?
THIS ONE KNEW ALSO.
AND YOU DID NOTHING?
SOME THINGS MUST BE.

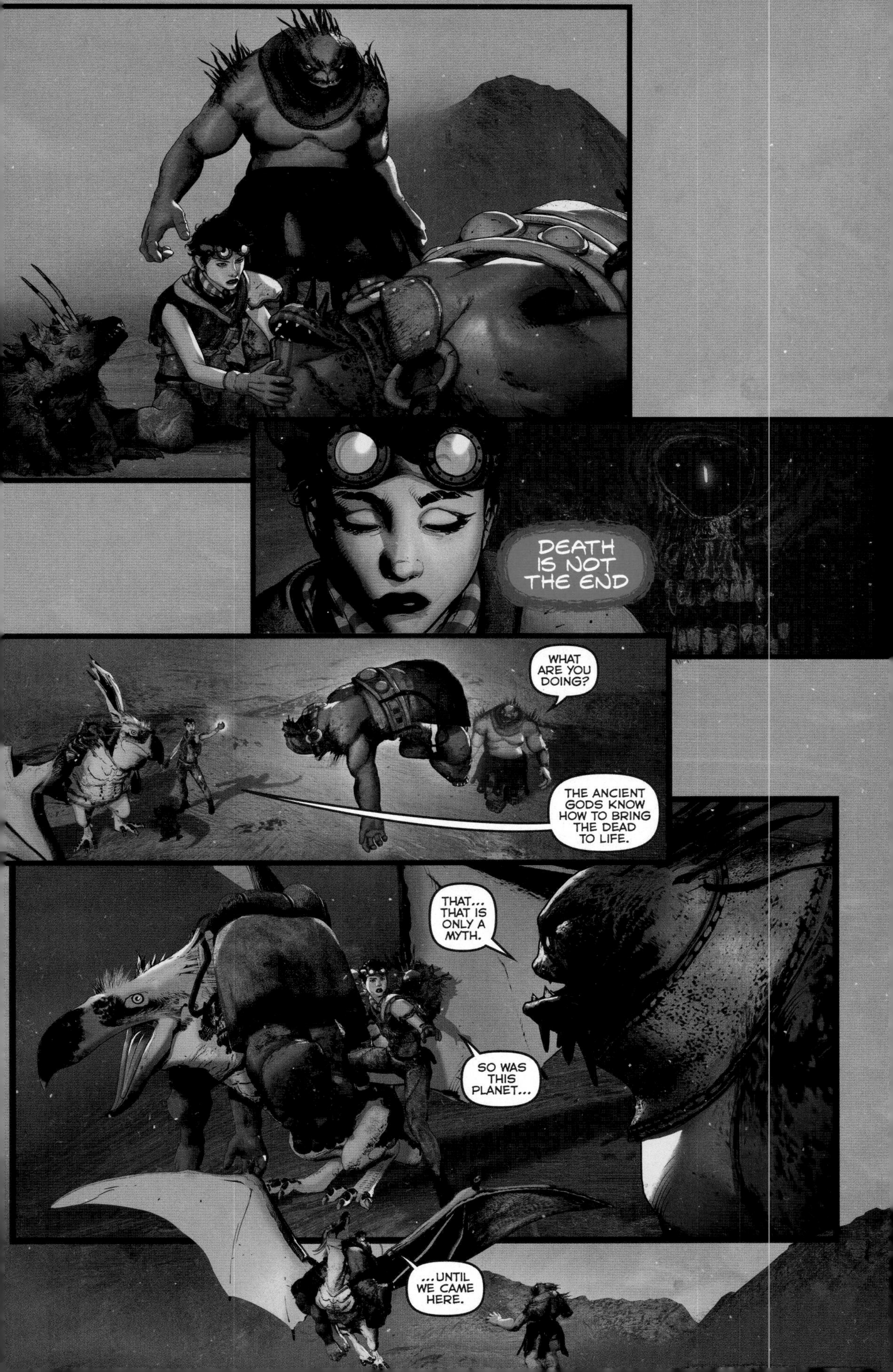
DEATH IS NOT THE END
WHAT ARE YOU DOING?
THE ANCIENT GODS KNOW HOW TO BRING THE DEAD TO LIFE.
THAT... THAT IS ONLY A MYTH.
SO WAS THIS PLANET...
...UNTIL WE CAME HERE.

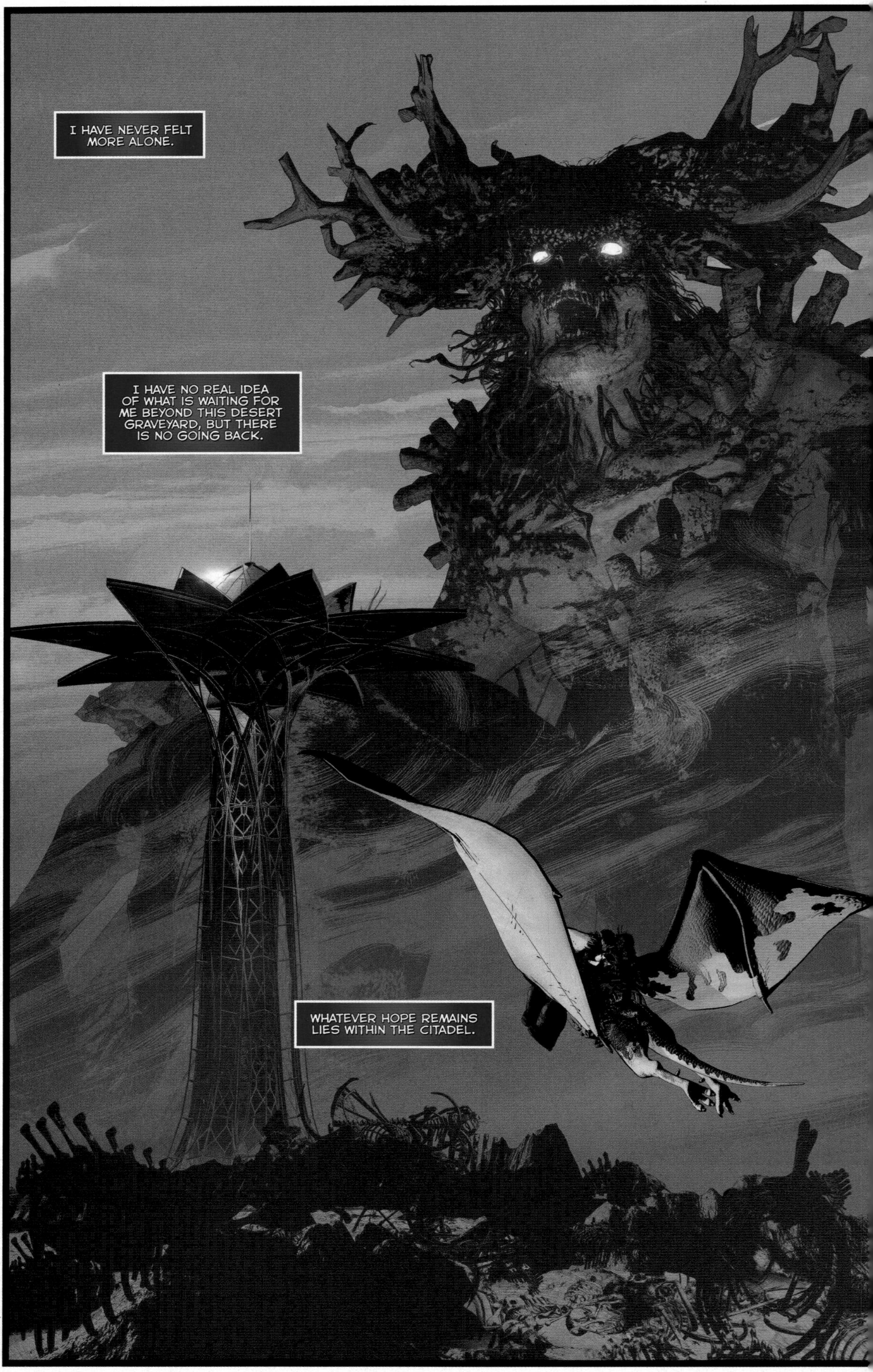
I HAVE NEVER FELT MORE ALONE.
I HAVE NO REAL IDEA OF WHAT IS WAITING FOR ME BEYOND THIS DESERT GRAVEYARD, BUT THERE IS NO GOING BACK.
WHATEVER HOPE REMAINS LIES WITHIN THE CITADEL.

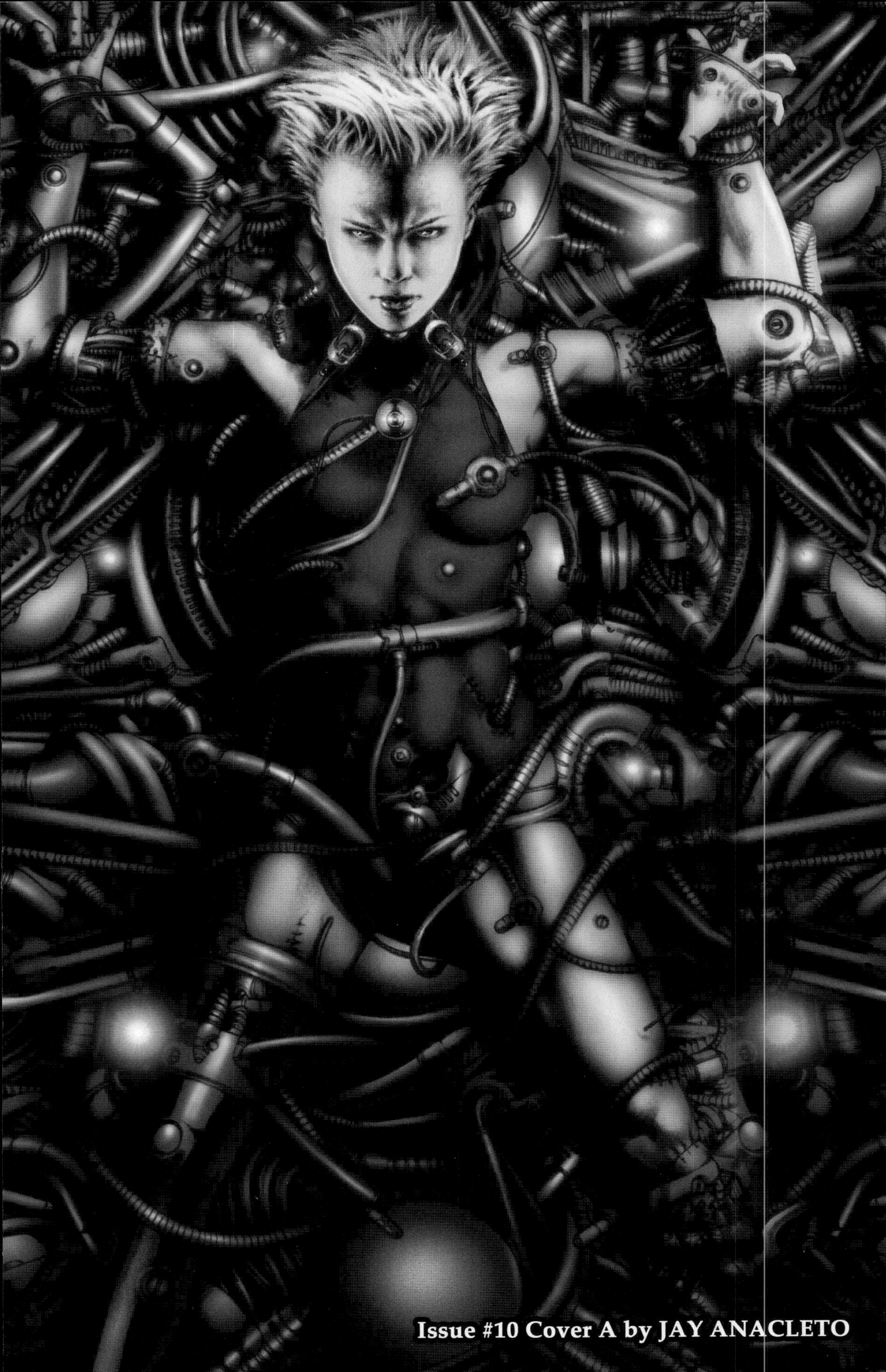

Issue #10 Cover A by JAY ANACLETO

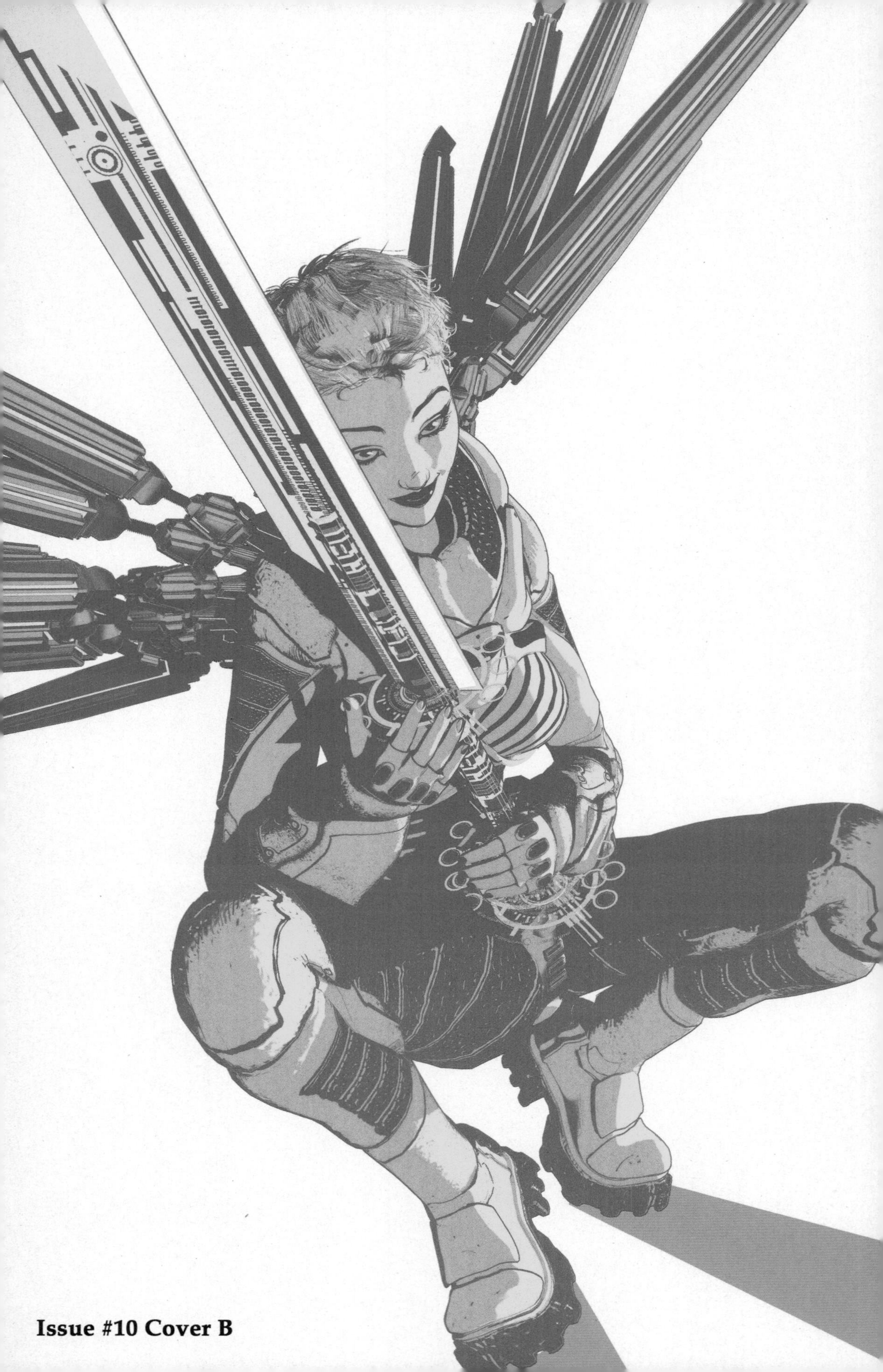

Issue #10 Cover B

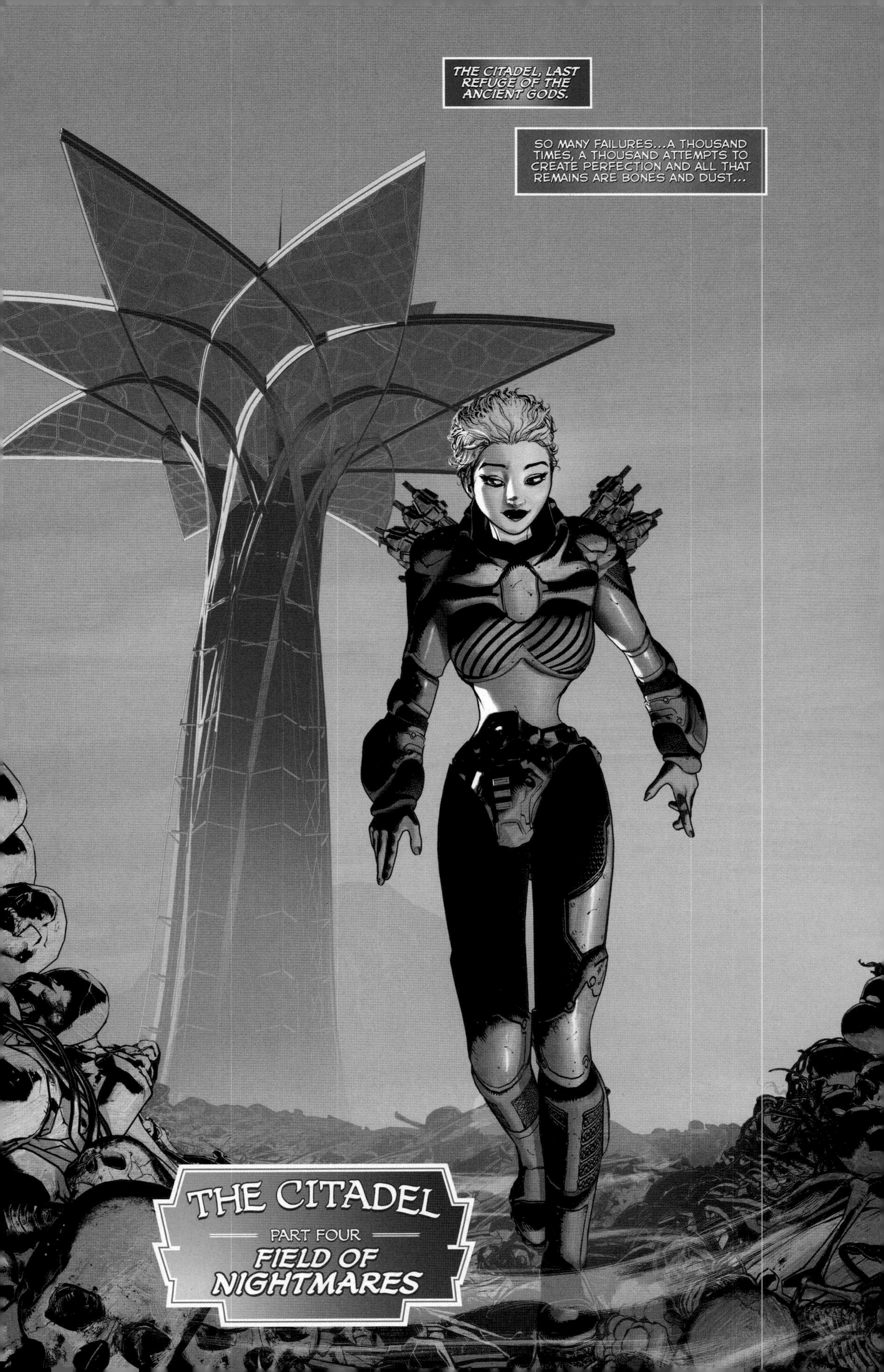
THE CITADEL, LAST REFUGE OF THE ANCIENT GODS.
SO MANY FAILURES...A THOUSAND TIMES, A THOUSAND ATTEMPTS TO CREATE PERFECTION AND ALL THAT REMAINS ARE BONES AND DUST...
THE CITADEL
PART FOUR
FIELD OF NIGHTMARES

THE PUTREFYING CORPSES HAVE MADE THIS SOIL FERTILE. A PITY THAT THE PLANTS ARE AS FLAWED AS THE BODIES THAT NOURISH THEM.

DID YOU LIVE LONG ENOUGH TO DREAM OF IMMORTALITY?

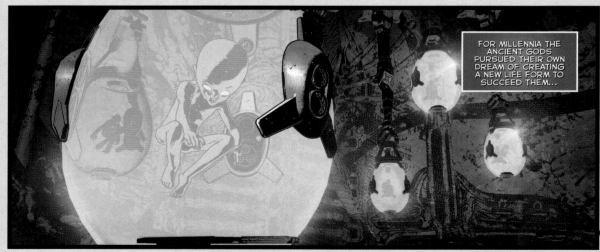

FOR MILLENNIA THE ANCIENT GODS PURSUED THEIR OWN DREAM OF CREATING A NEW LIFE FORM TO SUCCEED THEM...

...AND FOR MILLENNIA THEY FAILED...

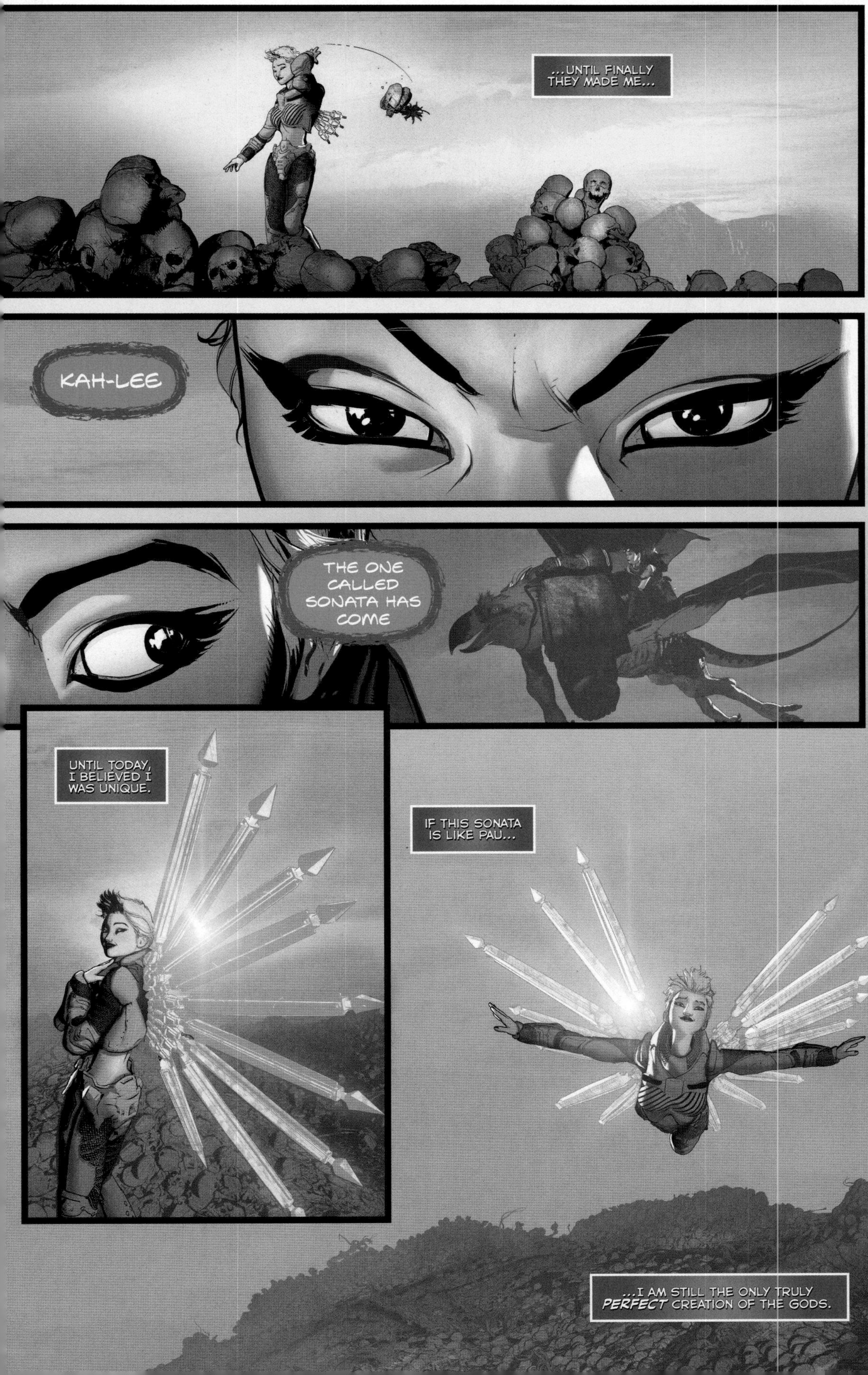
...UNTIL FINALLY THEY MADE ME...
KAH-LEE
THE ONE CALLED SONATA HAS COME
UNTIL TODAY, I BELIEVED I WAS UNIQUE.
IF THIS SONATA IS LIKE PAU...
...I AM STILL THE ONLY TRULY *PERFECT* CREATION OF THE GODS.

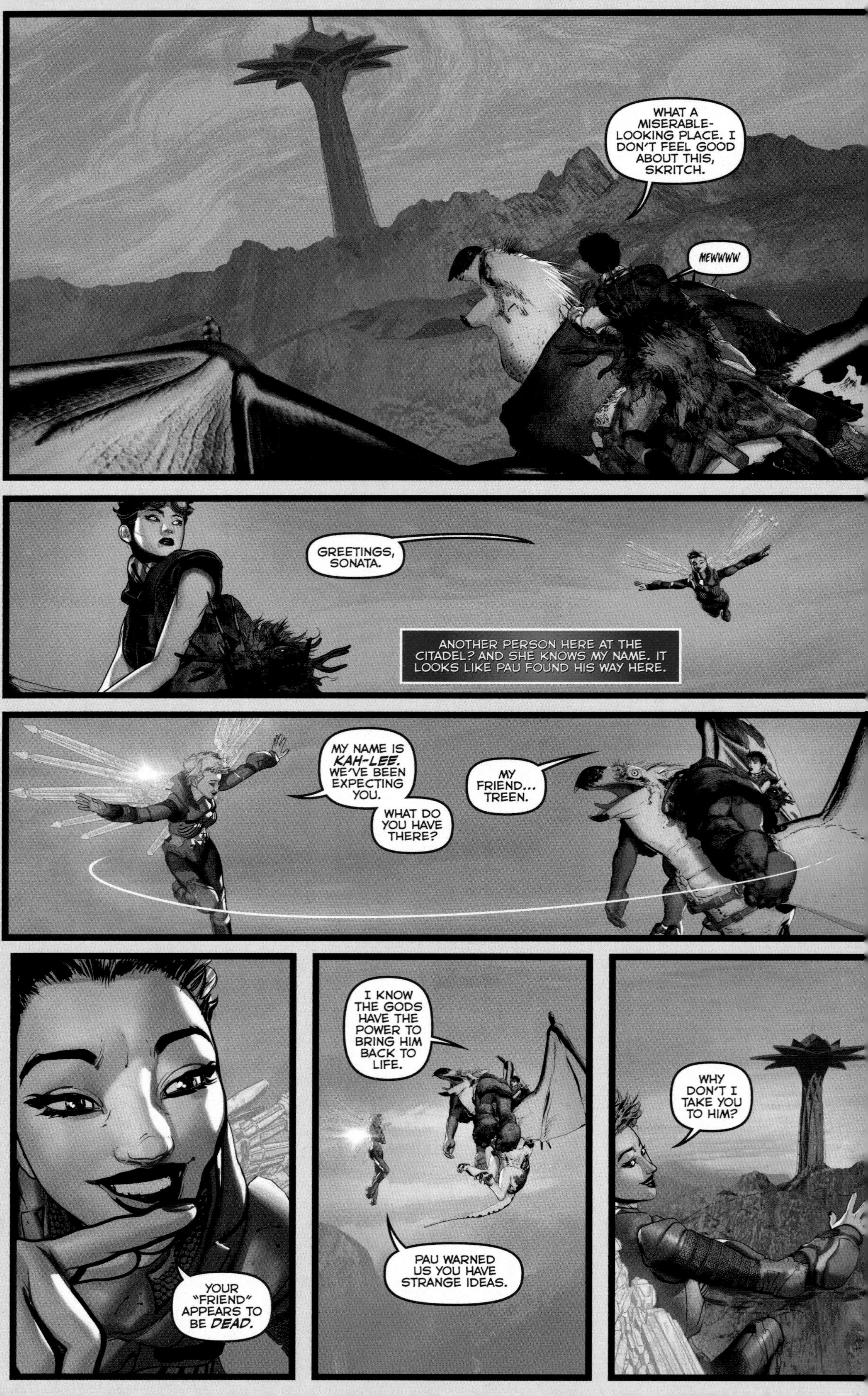
WHAT A MISERABLE-LOOKING PLACE. I DON'T FEEL GOOD ABOUT THIS, SKRITCH.
MEWWWW
GREETINGS, SONATA.
ANOTHER PERSON HERE AT THE CITADEL? AND SHE KNOWS MY NAME. IT LOOKS LIKE PAU FOUND HIS WAY HERE.
MY NAME IS KAH-LEE. WE'VE BEEN EXPECTING YOU.
WHAT DO YOU HAVE THERE?
MY FRIEND... TREEN.
YOUR "FRIEND" APPEARS TO BE DEAD.
I KNOW THE GODS HAVE THE POWER TO BRING HIM BACK TO LIFE.
PAU WARNED US YOU HAVE STRANGE IDEAS.
WHY DON'T I TAKE YOU TO HIM?

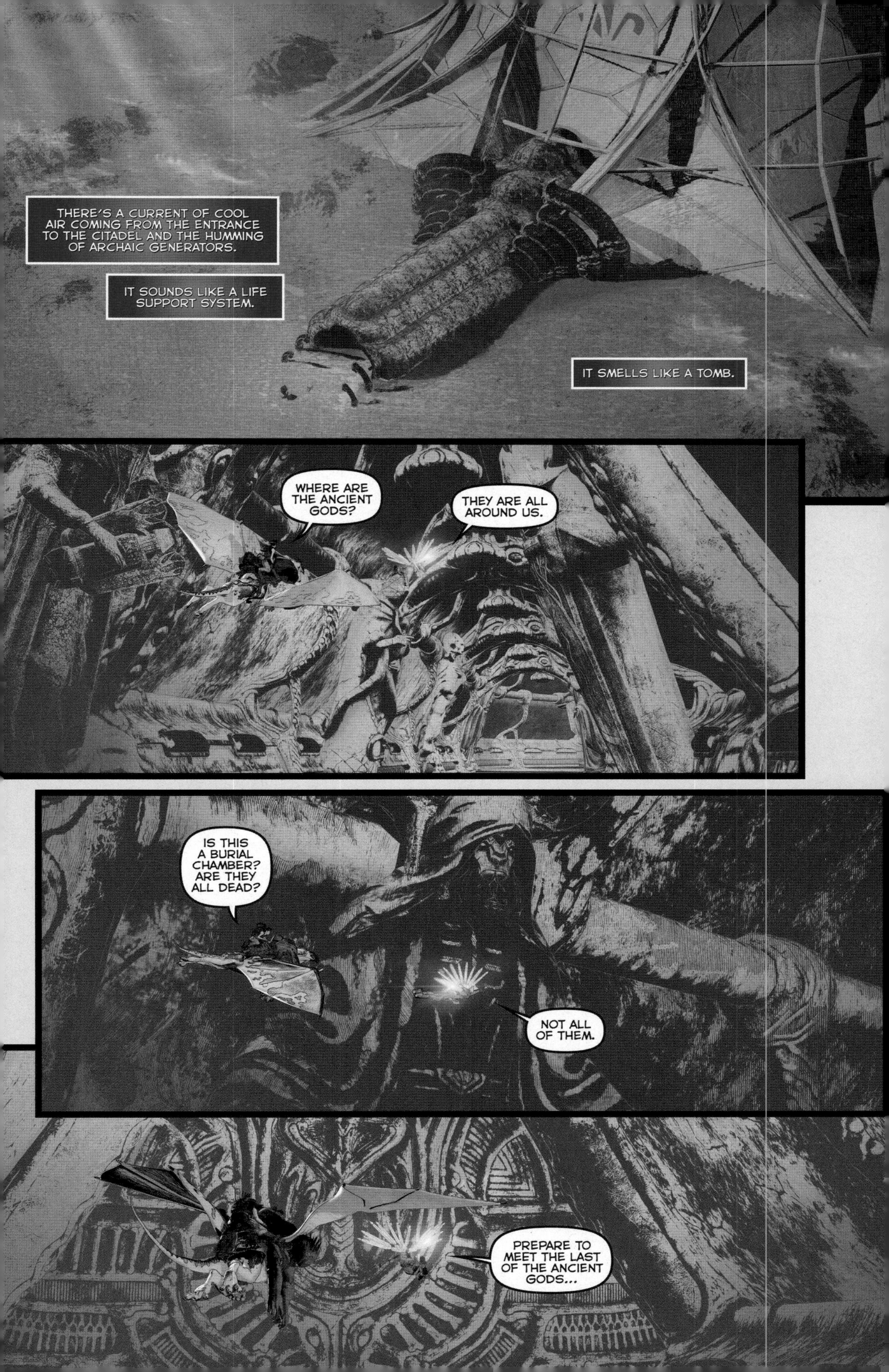
THERE'S A CURRENT OF COOL AIR COMING FROM THE ENTRANCE TO THE CITADEL AND THE HUMMING OF ARCHAIC GENERATORS.
IT SOUNDS LIKE A LIFE SUPPORT SYSTEM.
IT SMELLS LIKE A TOMB.
WHERE ARE THE ANCIENT GODS?
THEY ARE ALL AROUND US.
IS THIS A BURIAL CHAMBER? ARE THEY ALL DEAD?
NOT ALL OF THEM.
PREPARE TO MEET THE LAST OF THE ANCIENT GODS...

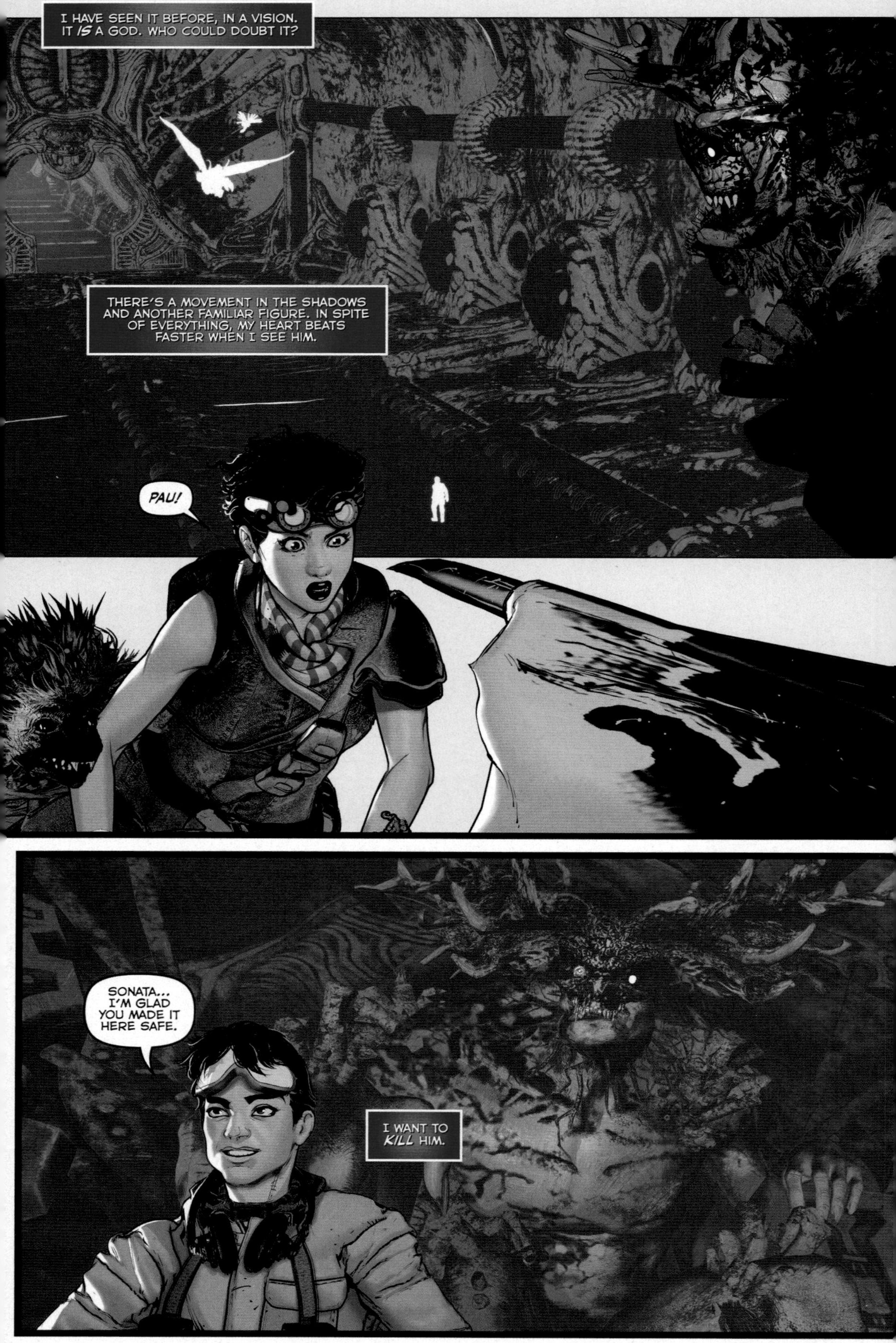
I HAVE SEEN IT BEFORE, IN A VISION. IT IS A GOD. WHO COULD DOUBT IT?
THERE'S A MOVEMENT IN THE SHADOWS AND ANOTHER FAMILIAR FIGURE. IN SPITE OF EVERYTHING, MY HEART BEATS FASTER WHEN I SEE HIM.
PAU!
SONATA... I'M GLAD YOU MADE IT HERE SAFE.
I WANT TO KILL HIM.

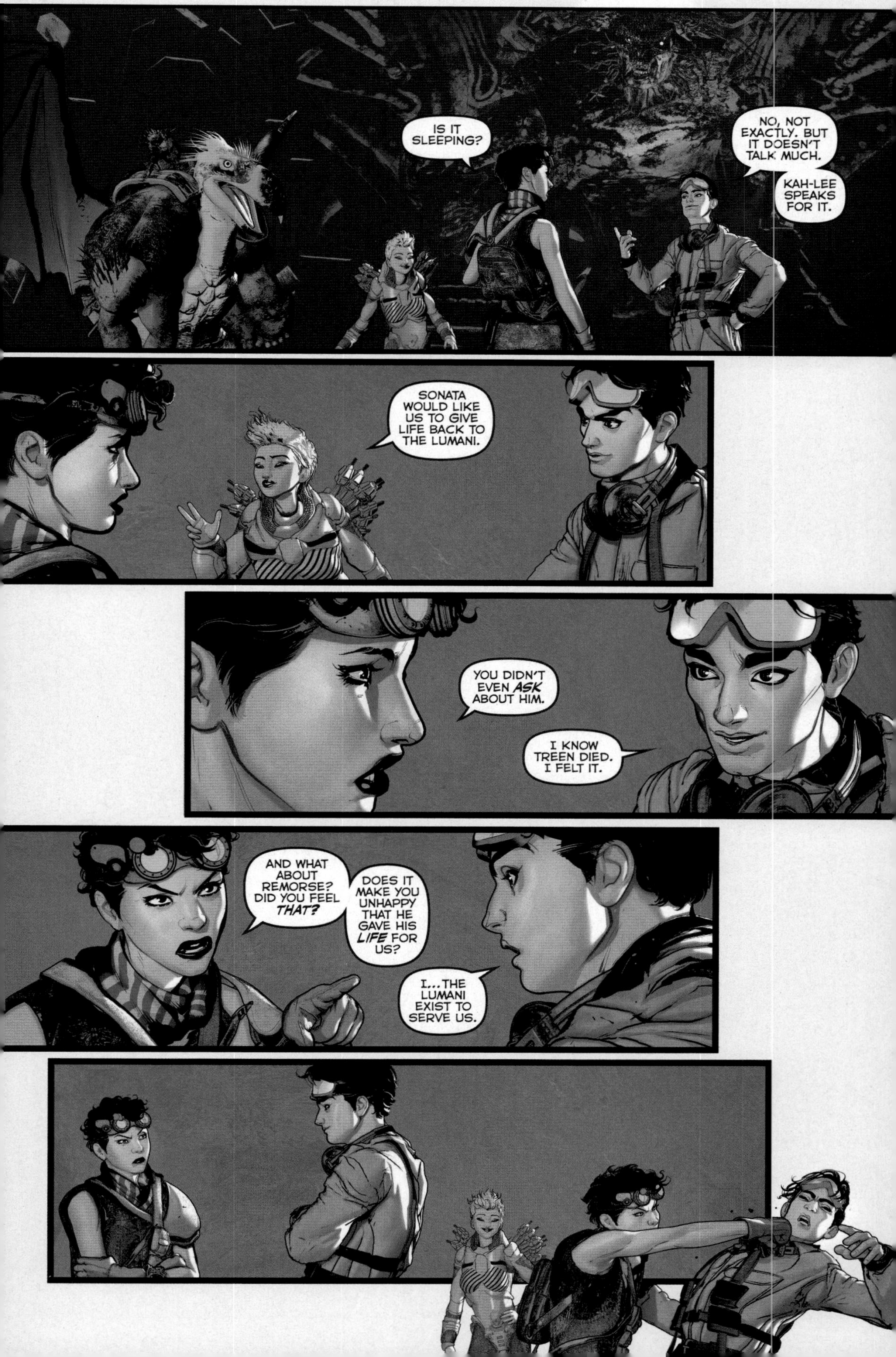
IS IT SLEEPING?
NO, NOT EXACTLY. BUT IT DOESN'T TALK MUCH.
KAH-LEE SPEAKS FOR IT.
SONATA WOULD LIKE US TO GIVE LIFE BACK TO THE LUMANI.
YOU DIDN'T EVEN *ASK* ABOUT HIM.
I KNOW TREEN DIED. I FELT IT.
AND WHAT ABOUT REMORSE? DID YOU FEEL *THAT?*
DOES IT MAKE YOU UNHAPPY THAT HE GAVE HIS *LIFE* FOR US?
I...THE LUMANI EXIST TO SERVE US.

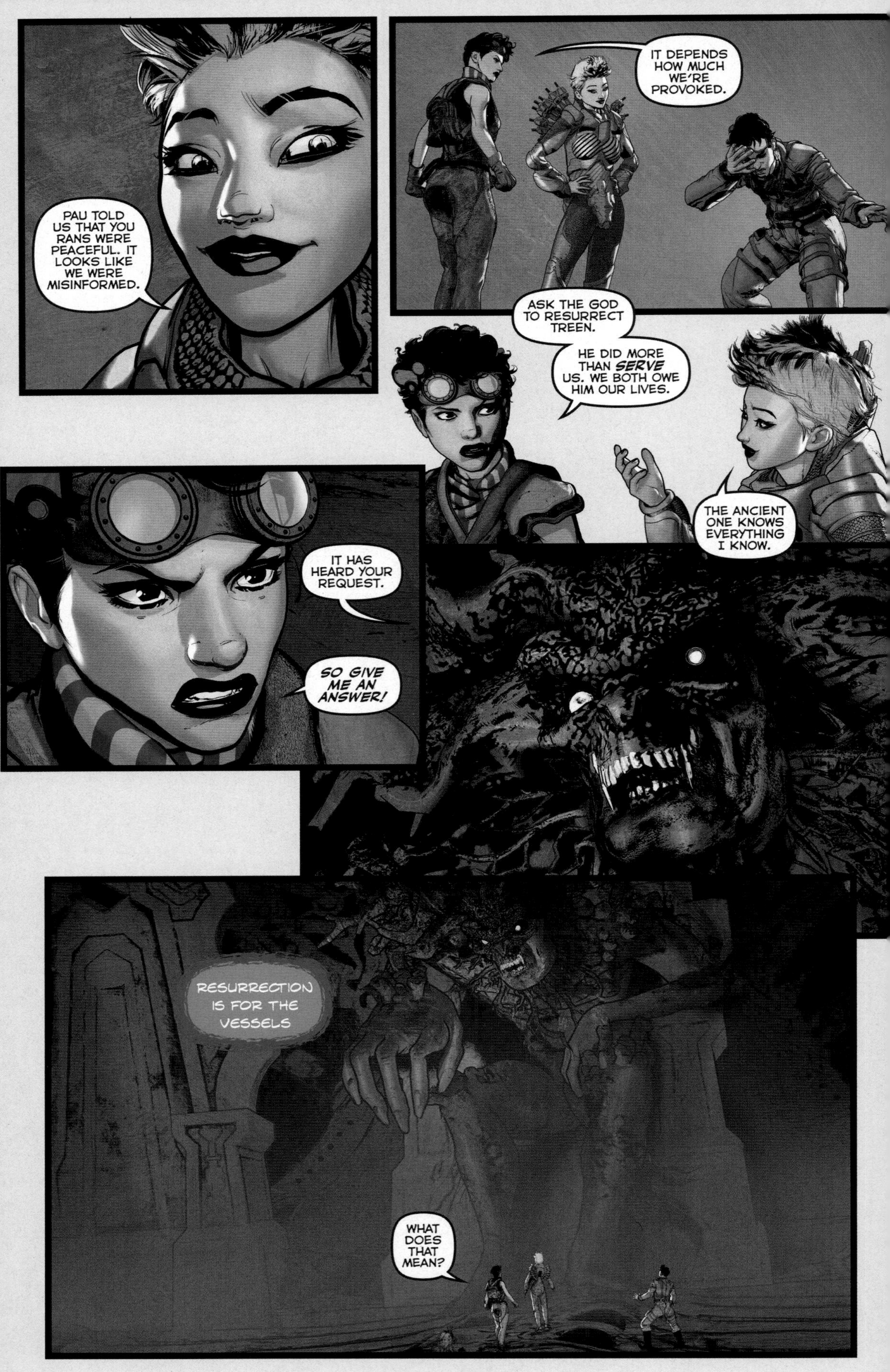
PAU TOLD US THAT YOU RANS WERE PEACEFUL. IT LOOKS LIKE WE WERE MISINFORMED.
IT DEPENDS HOW MUCH WE'RE PROVOKED.
ASK THE GOD TO RESURRECT TREEN.
HE DID MORE THAN SERVE US. WE BOTH OWE HIM OUR LIVES.
THE ANCIENT ONE KNOWS EVERYTHING I KNOW.
IT HAS HEARD YOUR REQUEST.
SO GIVE ME AN ANSWER!
RESURRECTION IS FOR THE VESSELS
WHAT DOES THAT MEAN?

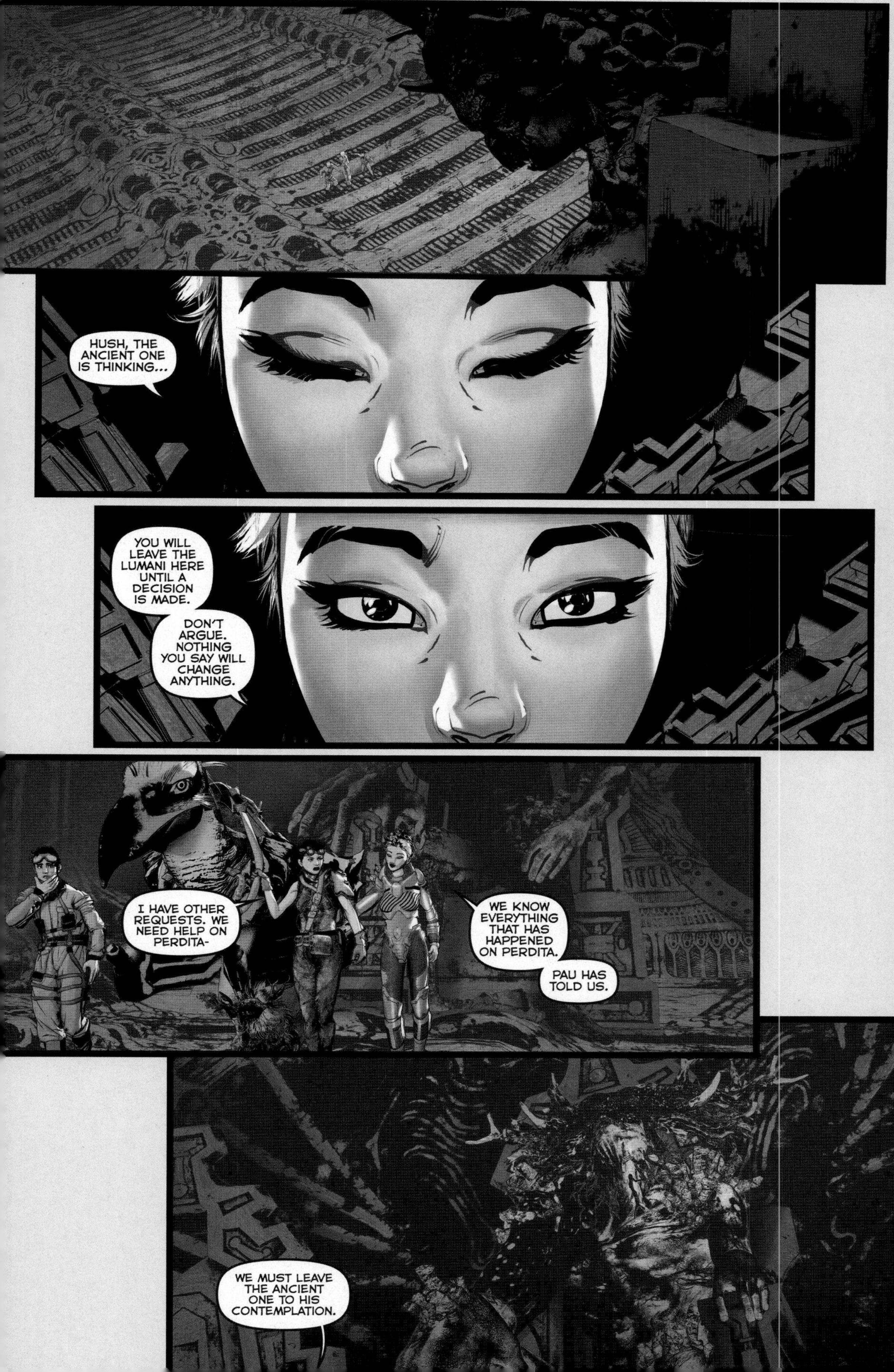
HUSH, THE ANCIENT ONE IS THINKING...
YOU WILL LEAVE THE LUMANI HERE UNTIL A DECISION IS MADE.
DON'T ARGUE. NOTHING YOU SAY WILL CHANGE ANYTHING.
I HAVE OTHER REQUESTS. WE NEED HELP ON PERDITA-
WE KNOW EVERYTHING THAT HAS HAPPENED ON PERDITA.
PAU HAS TOLD US.
WE MUST LEAVE THE ANCIENT ONE TO HIS CONTEMPLATION.

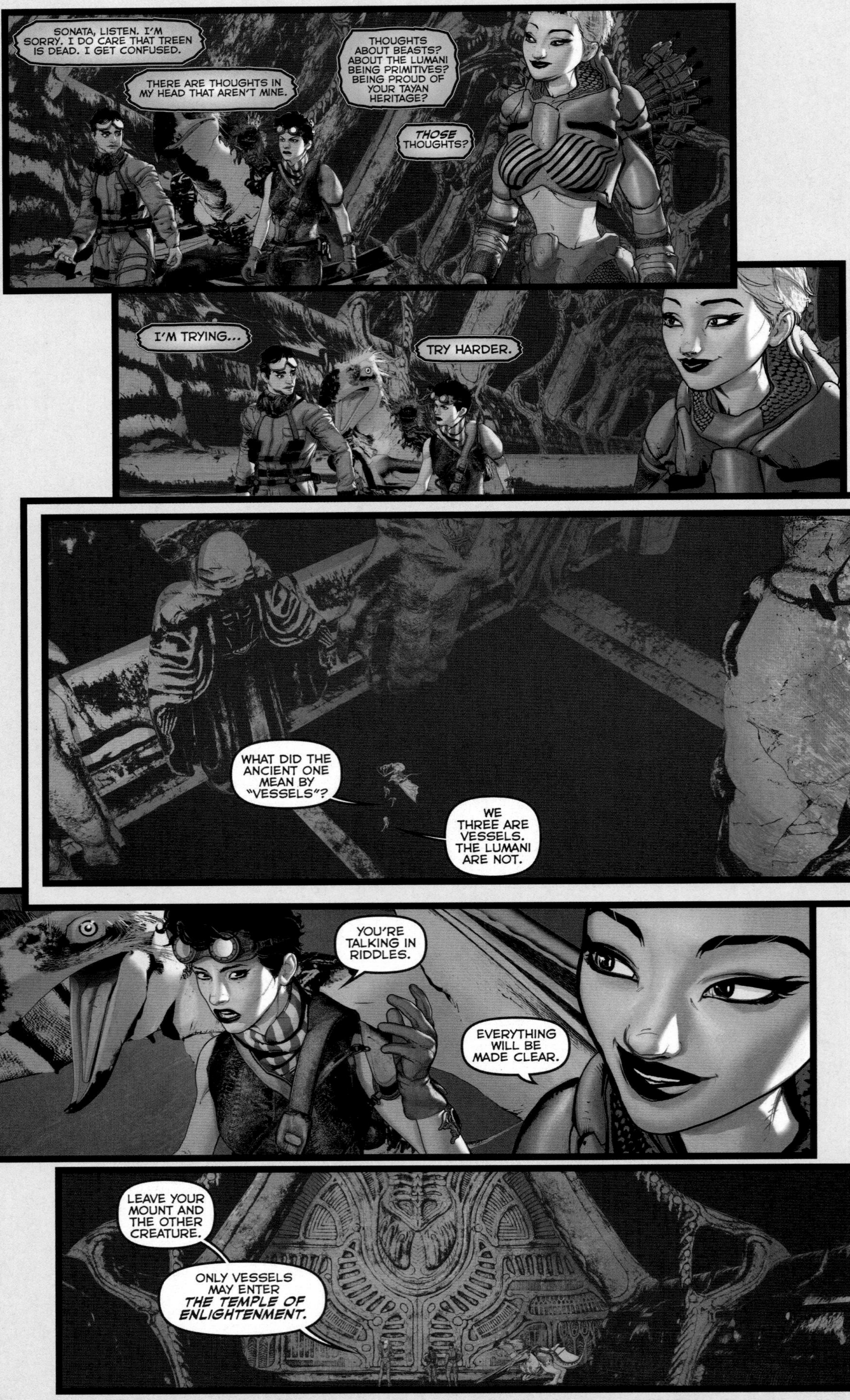
SONATA, LISTEN. I'M SORRY. I DO CARE THAT TREEN IS DEAD. I GET CONFUSED.
THERE ARE THOUGHTS IN MY HEAD THAT AREN'T MINE.
THOUGHTS ABOUT BEASTS? ABOUT THE LUMANI BEING PRIMITIVES? BEING PROUD OF YOUR TAYAN HERITAGE?
THOSE THOUGHTS?
I'M TRYING...
TRY HARDER.
WHAT DID THE ANCIENT ONE MEAN BY "VESSELS"?
WE THREE ARE VESSELS. THE LUMANI ARE NOT.
YOU'RE TALKING IN RIDDLES.
EVERYTHING WILL BE MADE CLEAR.
LEAVE YOUR MOUNT AND THE OTHER CREATURE.
ONLY VESSELS MAY ENTER ***THE TEMPLE OF ENLIGHTENMENT.***

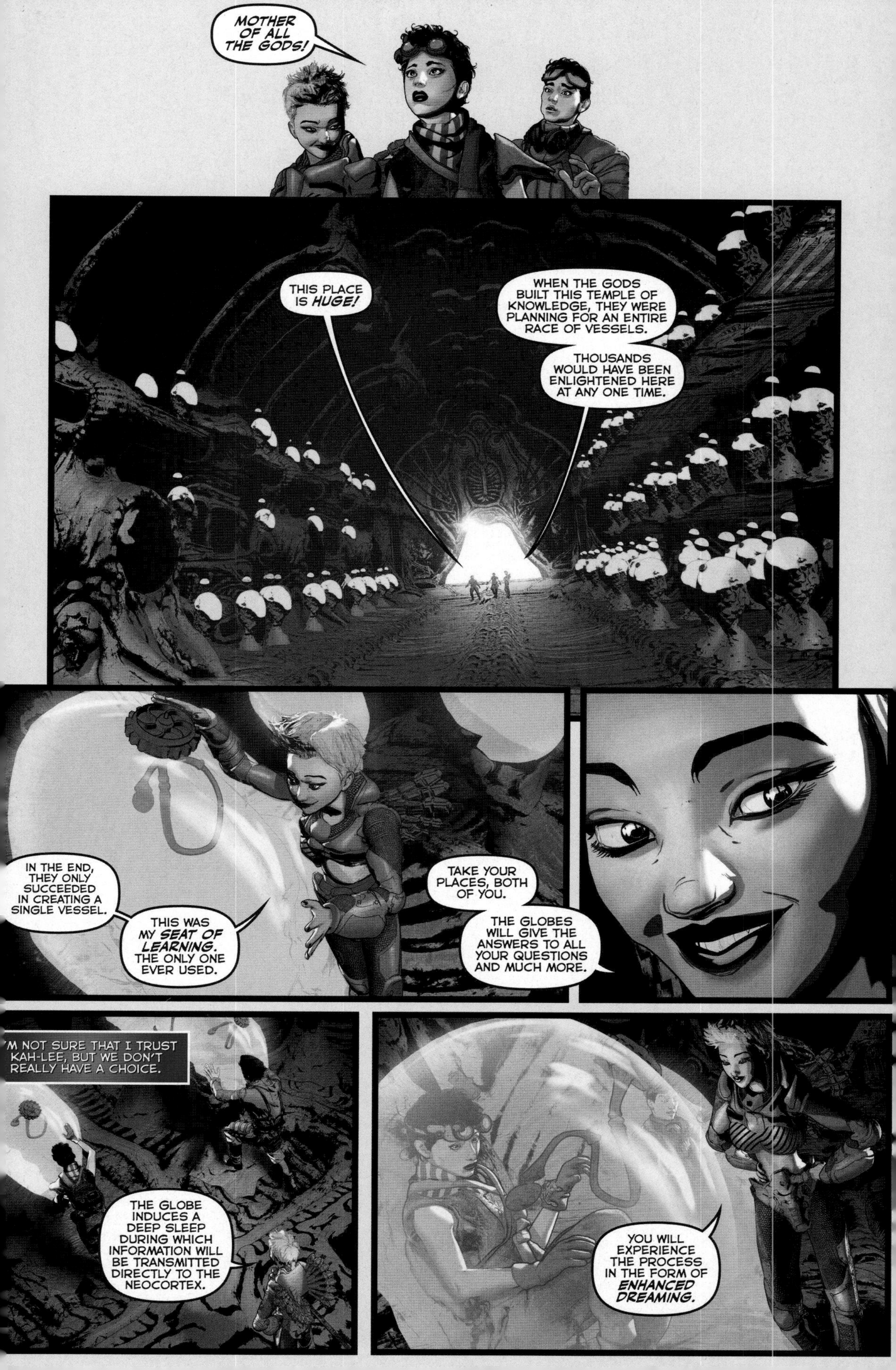
MOTHER OF ALL THE GODS!
THIS PLACE IS HUGE!
WHEN THE GODS BUILT THIS TEMPLE OF KNOWLEDGE, THEY WERE PLANNING FOR AN ENTIRE RACE OF VESSELS.
THOUSANDS WOULD HAVE BEEN ENLIGHTENED HERE AT ANY ONE TIME.
IN THE END, THEY ONLY SUCCEEDED IN CREATING A SINGLE VESSEL.
THIS WAS MY SEAT OF LEARNING. THE ONLY ONE EVER USED.
TAKE YOUR PLACES, BOTH OF YOU.
THE GLOBES WILL GIVE THE ANSWERS TO ALL YOUR QUESTIONS AND MUCH MORE.
'M NOT SURE THAT I TRUST KAH-LEE, BUT WE DON'T REALLY HAVE A CHOICE.
THE GLOBE INDUCES A DEEP SLEEP DURING WHICH INFORMATION WILL BE TRANSMITTED DIRECTLY TO THE NEOCORTEX.
YOU WILL EXPERIENCE THE PROCESS IN THE FORM OF ENHANCED DREAMING.

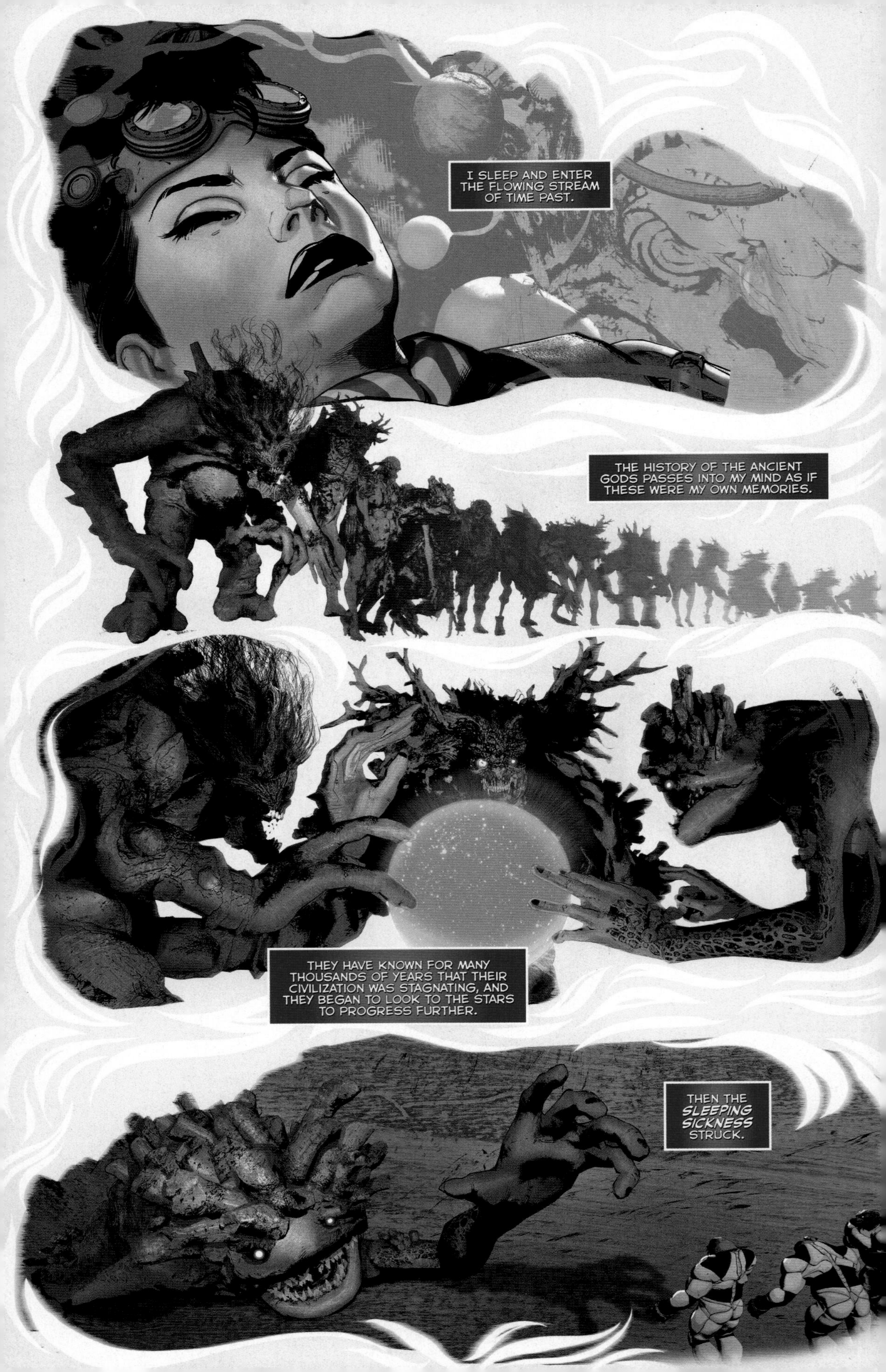
I SLEEP AND ENTER THE FLOWING STREAM OF TIME PAST.
THE HISTORY OF THE ANCIENT GODS PASSES INTO MY MIND AS IF THESE WERE MY OWN MEMORIES.
THEY HAVE KNOWN FOR MANY THOUSANDS OF YEARS THAT THEIR CIVILIZATION WAS STAGNATING, AND THEY BEGAN TO LOOK TO THE STARS TO PROGRESS FURTHER.
THEN THE *SLEEPING SICKNESS* STRUCK.

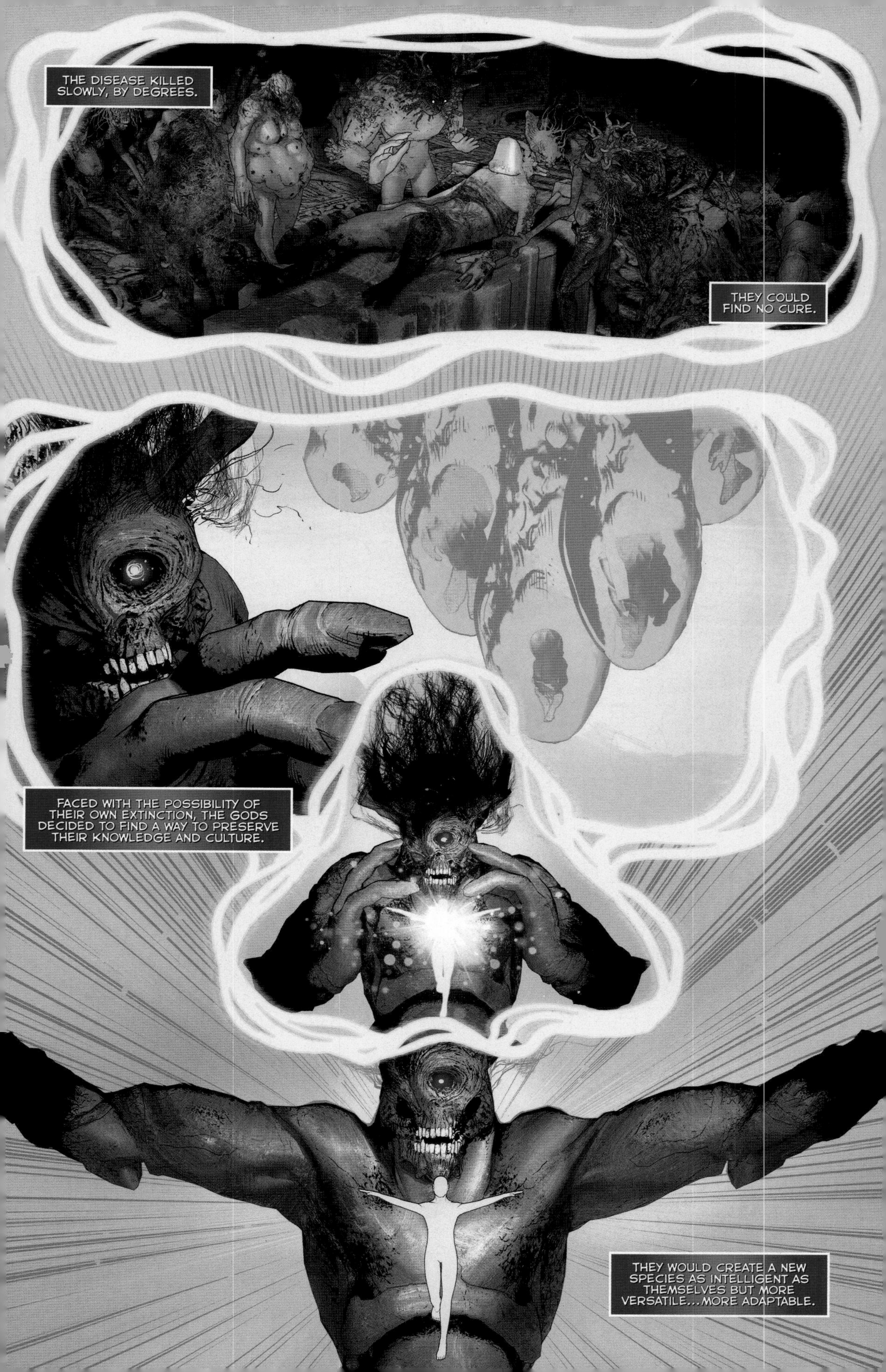
THE DISEASE KILLED SLOWLY, BY DEGREES.
THEY COULD FIND NO CURE.
FACED WITH THE POSSIBILITY OF THEIR OWN EXTINCTION, THE GODS DECIDED TO FIND A WAY TO PRESERVE THEIR KNOWLEDGE AND CULTURE.
THEY WOULD CREATE A NEW SPECIES AS INTELLIGENT AS THEMSELVES BUT MORE VERSATILE...MORE ADAPTABLE.

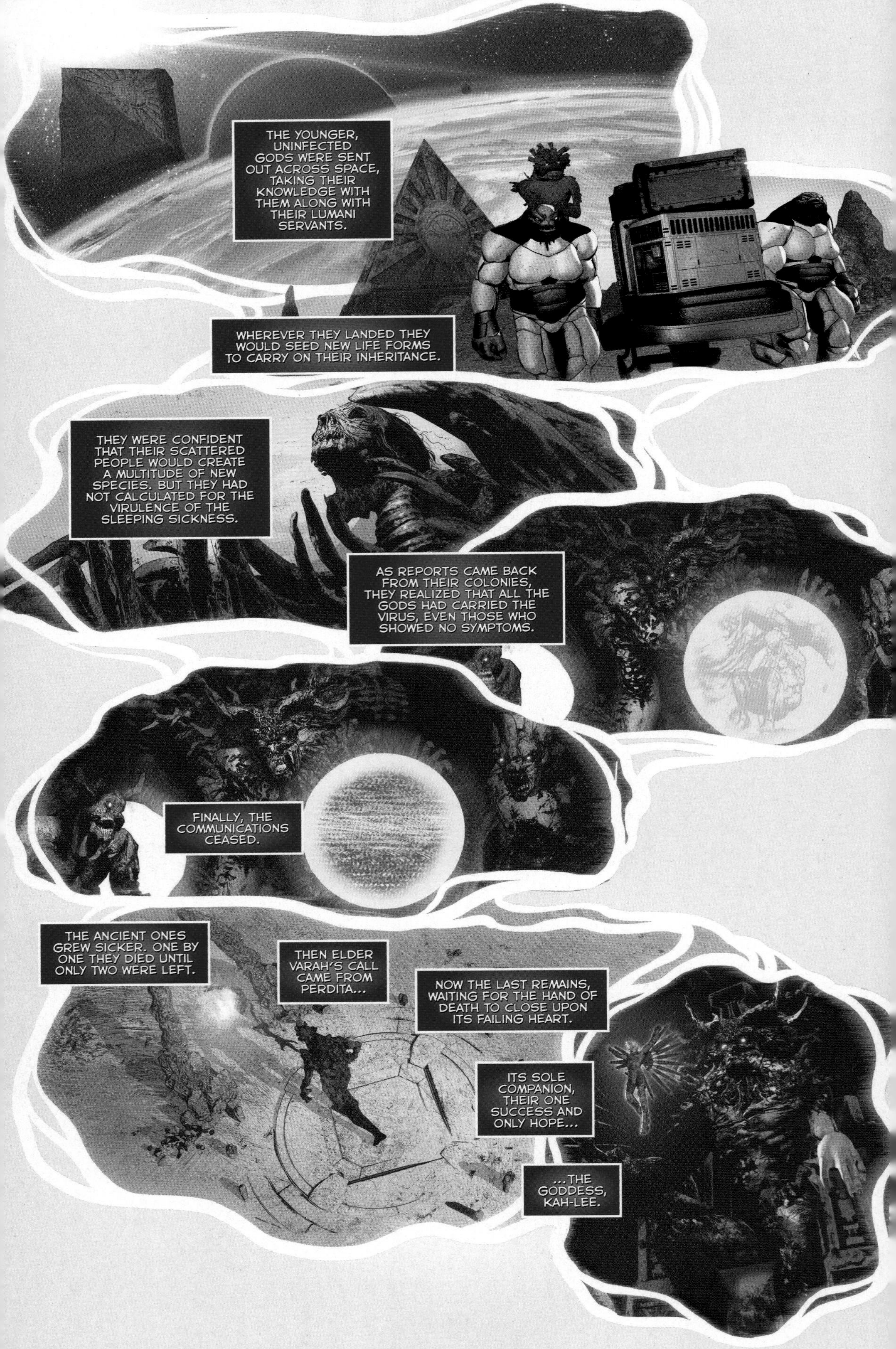
THE YOUNGER, UNINFECTED GODS WERE SENT OUT ACROSS SPACE, TAKING THEIR KNOWLEDGE WITH THEM ALONG WITH THEIR LUMANI SERVANTS.
WHEREVER THEY LANDED THEY WOULD SEED NEW LIFE FORMS TO CARRY ON THEIR INHERITANCE.
THEY WERE CONFIDENT THAT THEIR SCATTERED PEOPLE WOULD CREATE A MULTITUDE OF NEW SPECIES. BUT THEY HAD NOT CALCULATED FOR THE VIRULENCE OF THE SLEEPING SICKNESS.
AS REPORTS CAME BACK FROM THEIR COLONIES, THEY REALIZED THAT ALL THE GODS HAD CARRIED THE VIRUS, EVEN THOSE WHO SHOWED NO SYMPTOMS.
FINALLY, THE COMMUNICATIONS CEASED.
THE ANCIENT ONES GREW SICKER. ONE BY ONE THEY DIED UNTIL ONLY TWO WERE LEFT.
THEN ELDER VARAH'S CALL CAME FROM PERDITA...
NOW THE LAST REMAINS, WAITING FOR THE HAND OF DEATH TO CLOSE UPON ITS FAILING HEART.
ITS SOLE COMPANION, THEIR ONE SUCCESS AND ONLY HOPE...
...THE GODDESS, KAH-LEE.

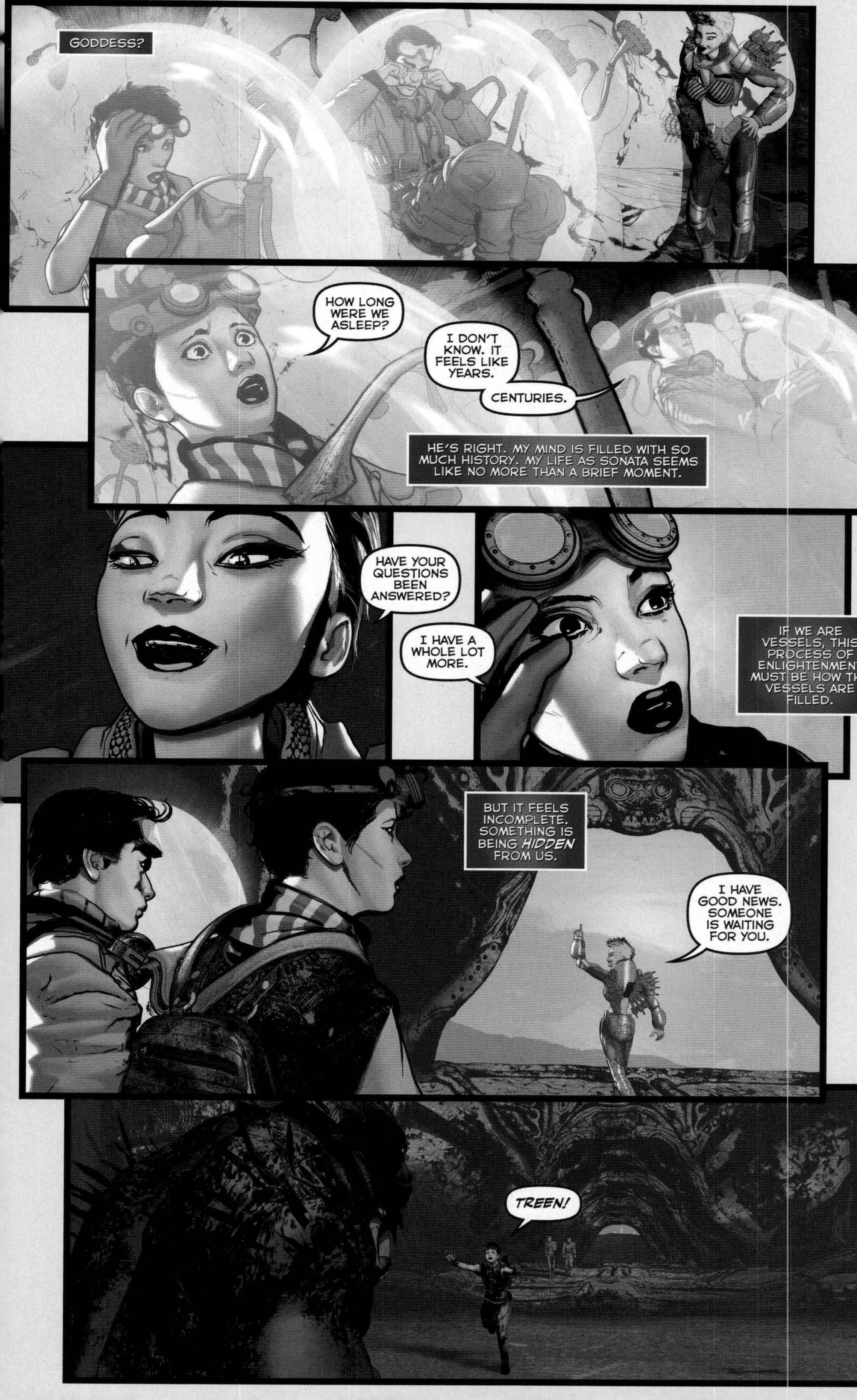
GODDESS?
HOW LONG WERE WE ASLEEP?
I DON'T KNOW. IT FEELS LIKE YEARS.
CENTURIES.
HE'S RIGHT. MY MIND IS FILLED WITH SO MUCH HISTORY. MY LIFE AS SONATA SEEMS LIKE NO MORE THAN A BRIEF MOMENT.
HAVE YOUR QUESTIONS BEEN ANSWERED?
I HAVE A WHOLE LOT MORE.
IF WE ARE VESSELS, THIS PROCESS OF ENLIGHTENMENT MUST BE HOW THE VESSELS ARE FILLED.
BUT IT FEELS INCOMPLETE. SOMETHING IS BEING *HIDDEN* FROM US.
I HAVE GOOD NEWS. SOMEONE IS WAITING FOR YOU.
TREEN!

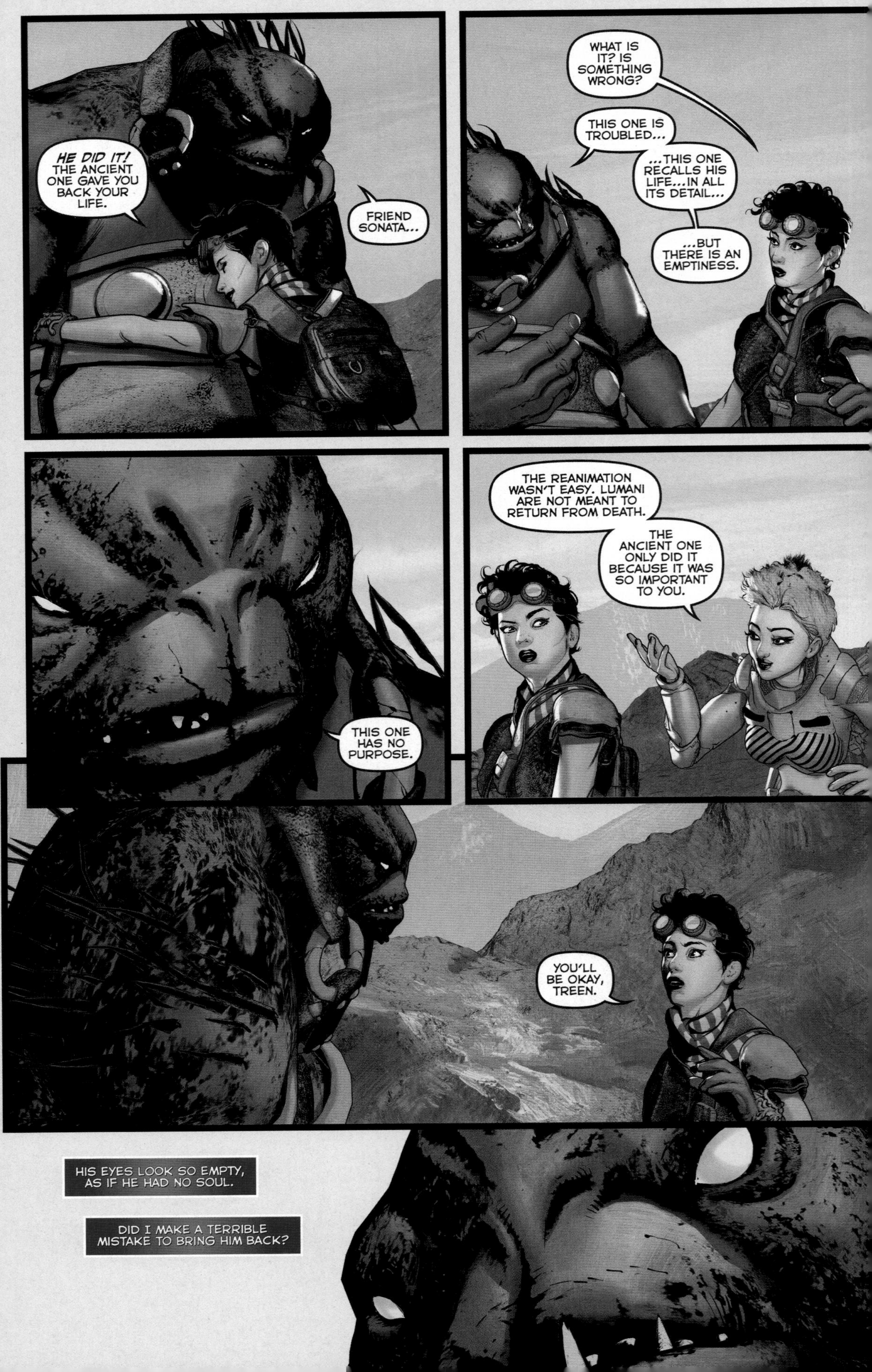
HE DID IT! THE ANCIENT ONE GAVE YOU BACK YOUR LIFE.
FRIEND SONATA...
WHAT IS IT? IS SOMETHING WRONG?
THIS ONE IS TROUBLED...
...THIS ONE RECALLS HIS LIFE...IN ALL ITS DETAIL...
...BUT THERE IS AN EMPTINESS.
THIS ONE HAS NO PURPOSE.
THE REANIMATION WASN'T EASY. LUMANI ARE NOT MEANT TO RETURN FROM DEATH.
THE ANCIENT ONE ONLY DID IT BECAUSE IT WAS SO IMPORTANT TO YOU.
YOU'LL BE OKAY, TREEN.
HIS EYES LOOK SO EMPTY, AS IF HE HAD NO SOUL.
DID I MAKE A TERRIBLE MISTAKE TO BRING HIM BACK?

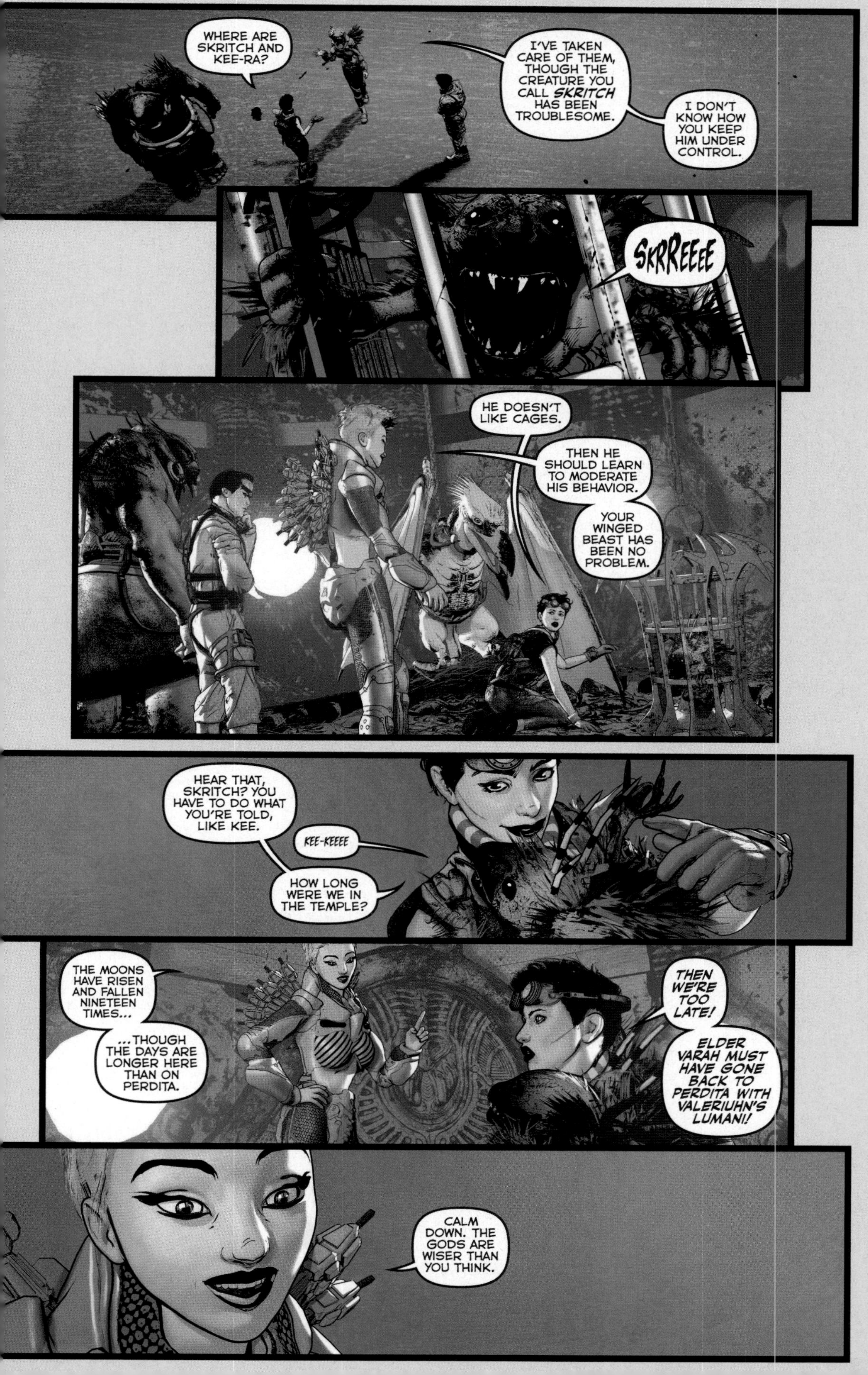
WHERE ARE SKRITCH AND KEE-RA?
I'VE TAKEN CARE OF THEM, THOUGH THE CREATURE YOU CALL SKRITCH HAS BEEN TROUBLESOME.
I DON'T KNOW HOW YOU KEEP HIM UNDER CONTROL.
SKRREEEE
HE DOESN'T LIKE CAGES.
THEN HE SHOULD LEARN TO MODERATE HIS BEHAVIOR.
YOUR WINGED BEAST HAS BEEN NO PROBLEM.
HEAR THAT, SKRITCH? YOU HAVE TO DO WHAT YOU'RE TOLD, LIKE KEE.
KEE-KEEEE
HOW LONG WERE WE IN THE TEMPLE?
THE MOONS HAVE RISEN AND FALLEN NINETEEN TIMES...
...THOUGH THE DAYS ARE LONGER HERE THAN ON PERDITA.
THEN WE'RE TOO LATE!
ELDER VARAH MUST HAVE GONE BACK TO PERDITA WITH VALERIUHN'S LUMANI!
CALM DOWN. THE GODS ARE WISER THAN YOU THINK.

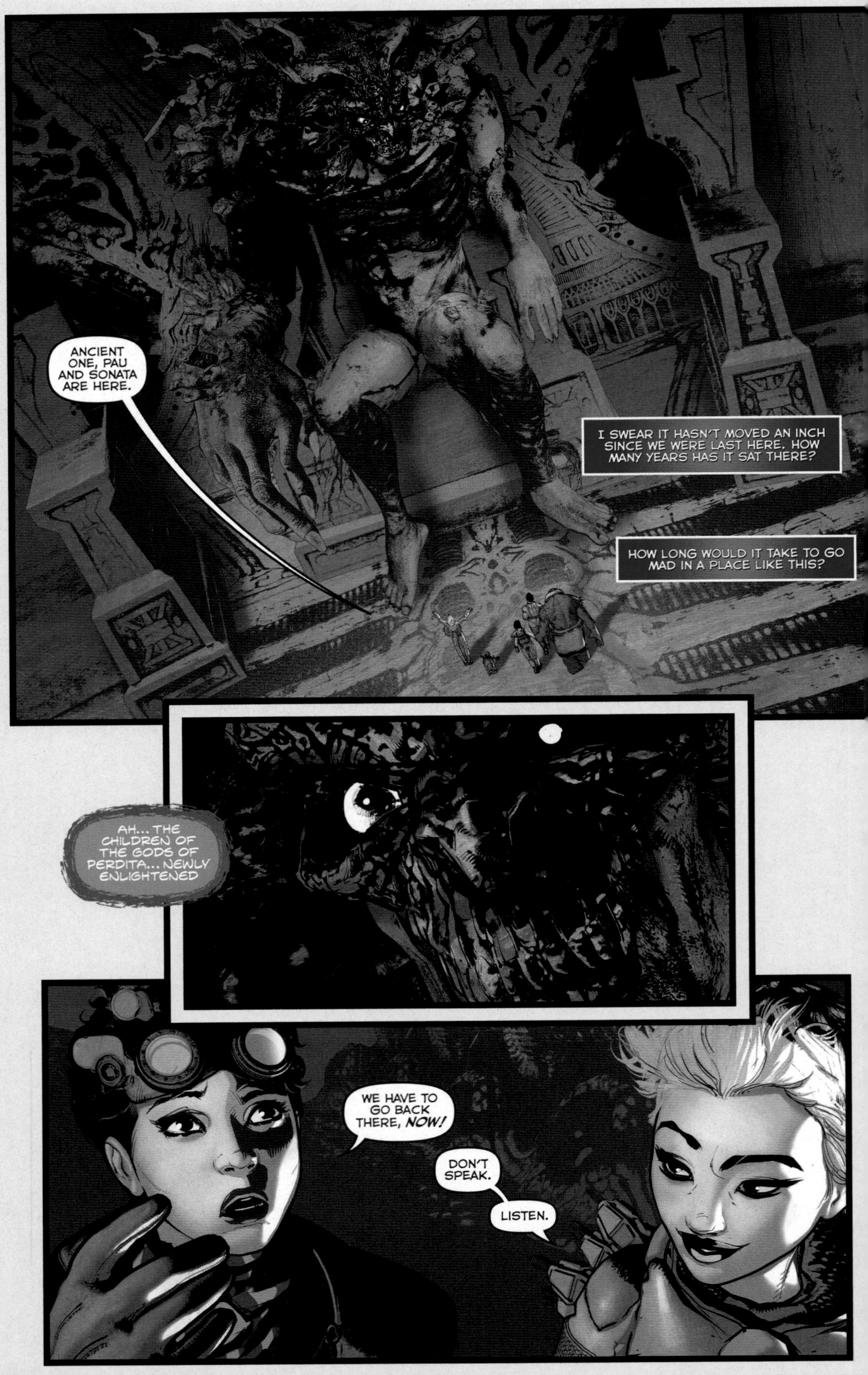
ANCIENT ONE, PAU AND SONATA ARE HERE.
I SWEAR IT HASN'T MOVED AN INCH SINCE WE WERE LAST HERE. HOW MANY YEARS HAS IT SAT THERE?
HOW LONG WOULD IT TAKE TO GO MAD IN A PLACE LIKE THIS?
AH... THE CHILDREN OF THE GODS OF PERDITA... NEWLY ENLIGHTENED
WE HAVE TO GO BACK THERE, NOW!
DON'T SPEAK.
LISTEN.

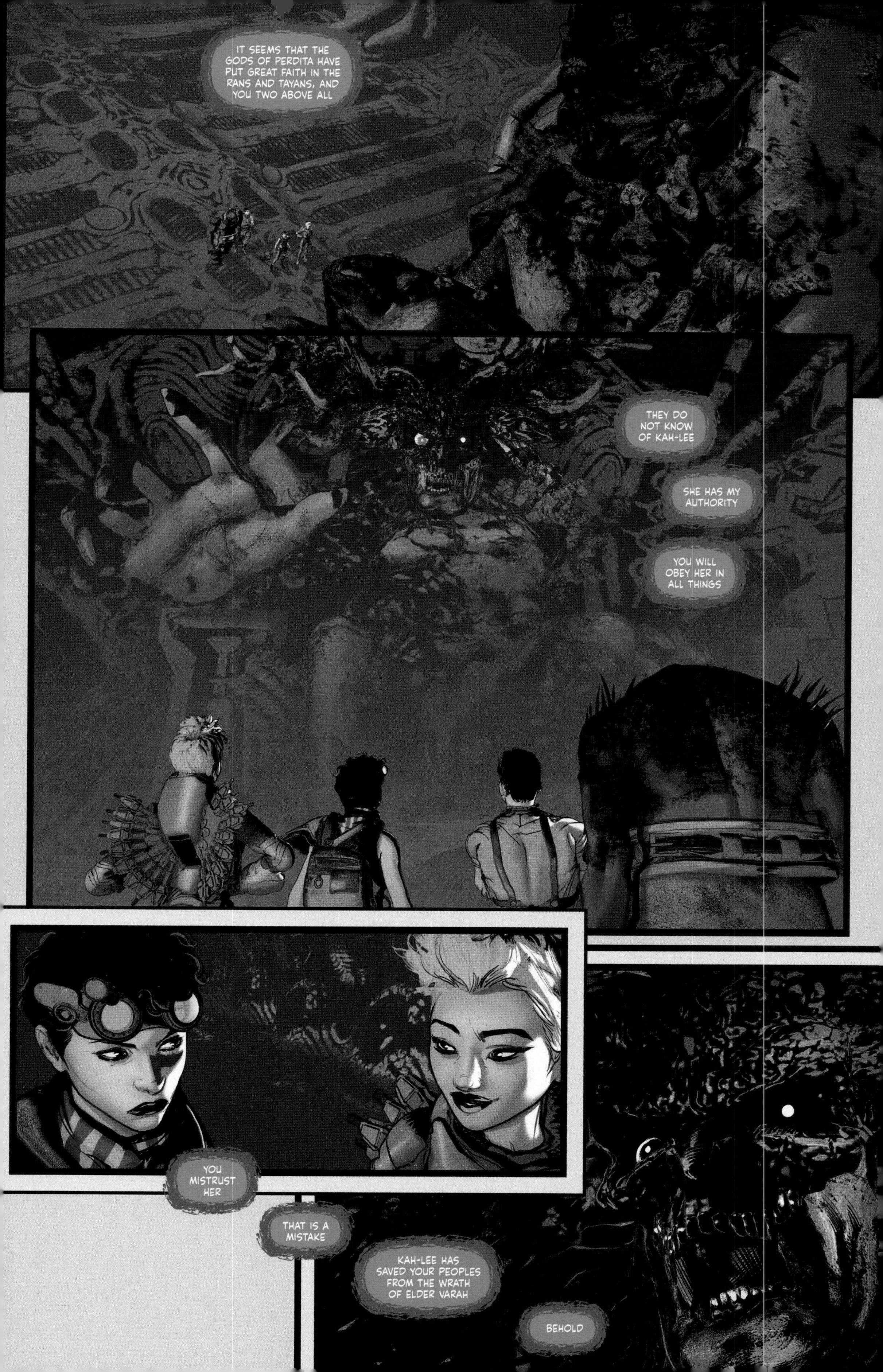
IT SEEMS THAT THE GODS OF PERDITA HAVE PUT GREAT FAITH IN THE RANS AND TAYANS, AND YOU TWO ABOVE ALL
THEY DO NOT KNOW OF KAH-LEE
SHE HAS MY AUTHORITY
YOU WILL OBEY HER IN ALL THINGS
YOU MISTRUST HER
THAT IS A MISTAKE
KAH-LEE HAS SAVED YOUR PEOPLES FROM THE WRATH OF ELDER VARAH
BEHOLD

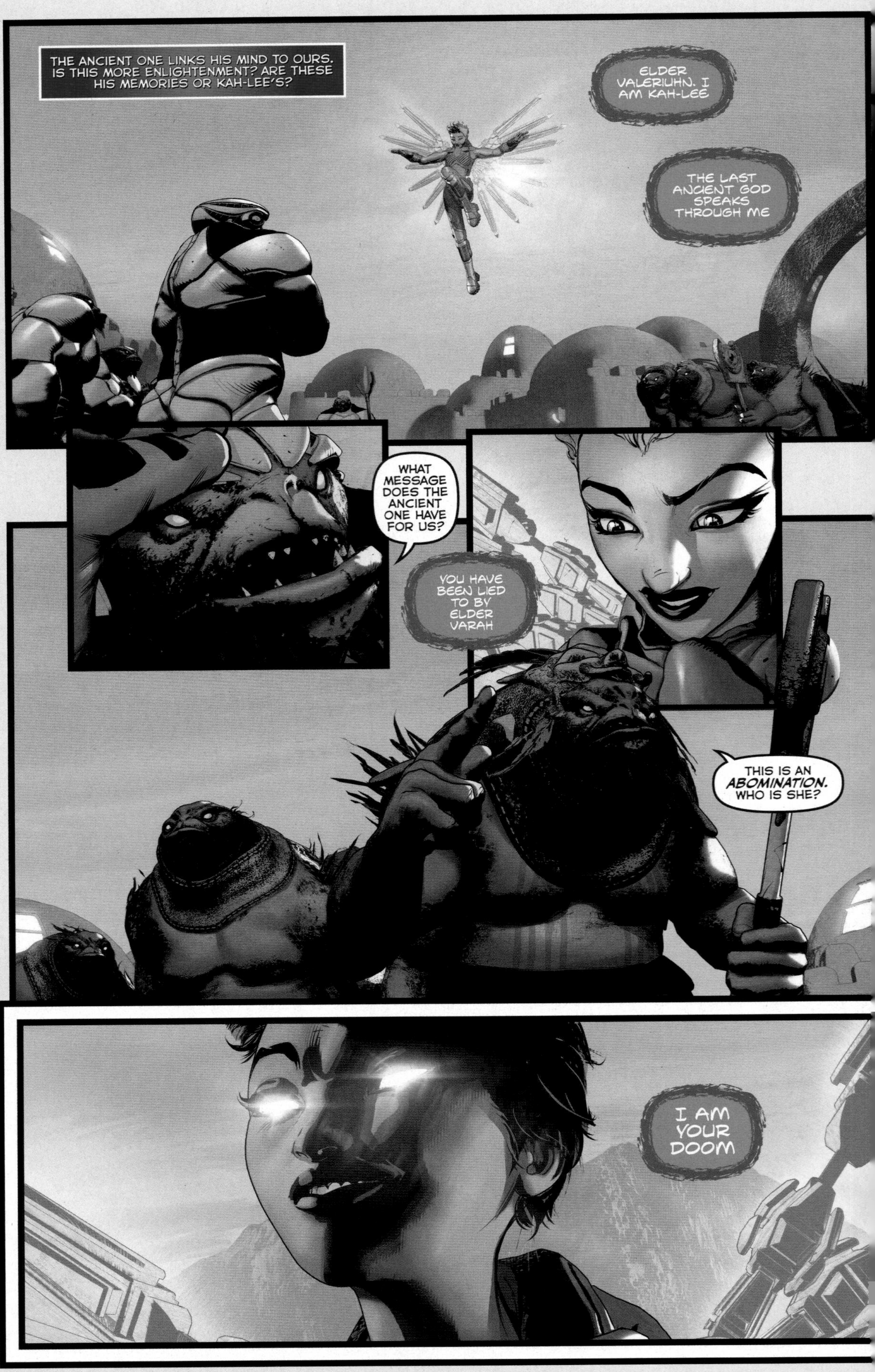
THE ANCIENT ONE LINKS HIS MIND TO OURS. IS THIS MORE ENLIGHTENMENT? ARE THESE HIS MEMORIES OR KAH-LEE'S?
ELDER VALERIUHN. I AM KAH-LEE
THE LAST ANCIENT GOD SPEAKS THROUGH ME
WHAT MESSAGE DOES THE ANCIENT ONE HAVE FOR US?
YOU HAVE BEEN LIED TO BY ELDER VARAH
THIS IS AN *ABOMINATION.* WHO IS SHE?
I AM YOUR DOOM

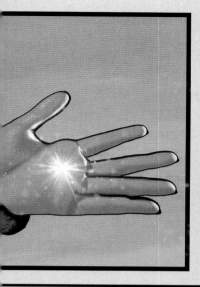

SHE IS EVEN MORE BRUTAL THAN THE TAYANS, YET THERE IS A FLUIDITY IN HER MOVEMENTS...A POETRY OF VIOLENCE...

IN HER OWN WAY SHE *IS* PERFECT.

VALERIUHN... PREPARE YOUR LUMANI FOR THE JOURNEY TO PERDITA...

WE ARE YOURS TO COMMAND.

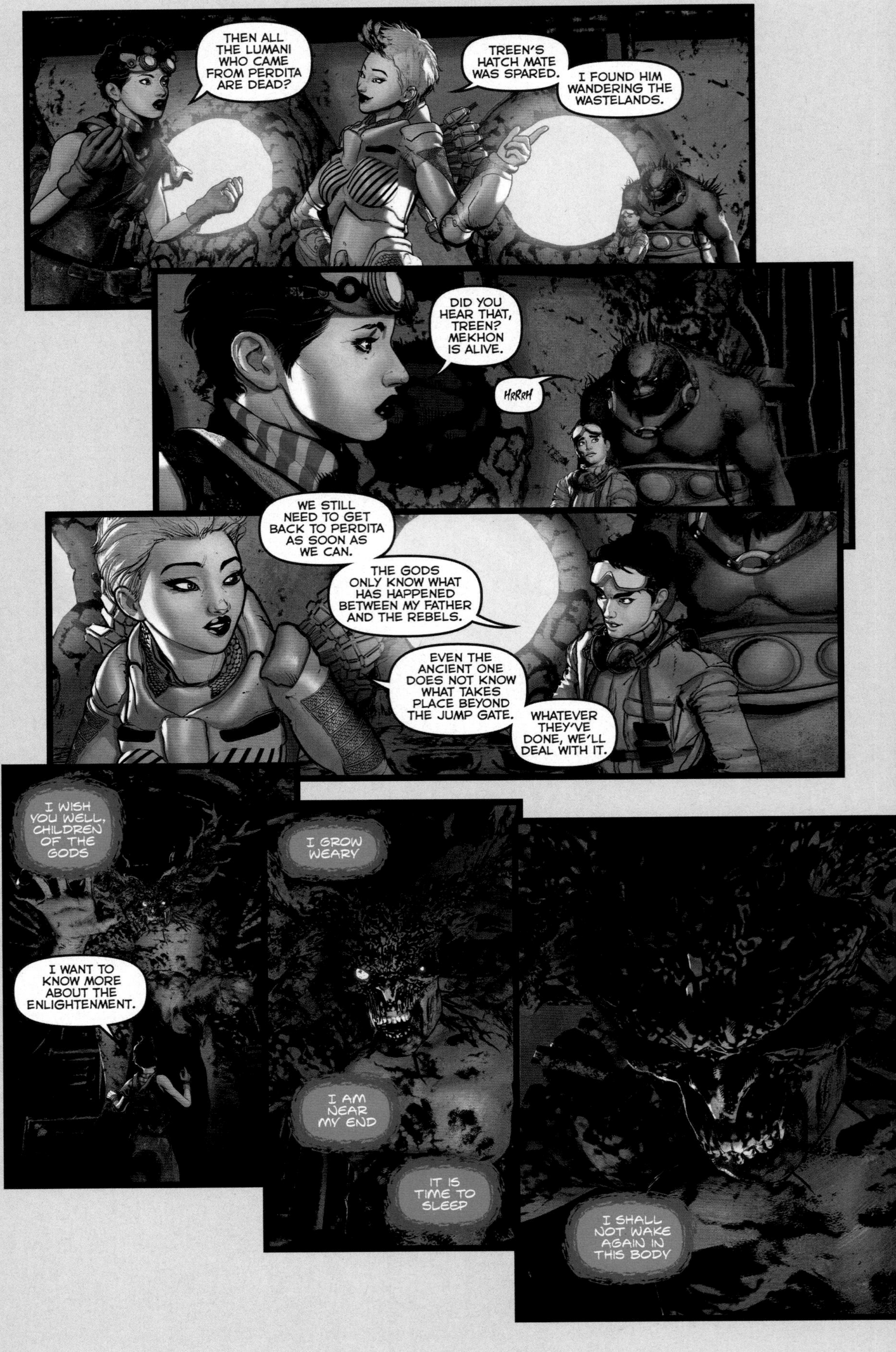
THEN ALL THE LUMANI WHO CAME FROM PERDITA ARE DEAD?
TREEN'S HATCH MATE WAS SPARED.
I FOUND HIM WANDERING THE WASTELANDS.
DID YOU HEAR THAT, TREEN? MEKHON IS ALIVE.
HRRRH
WE STILL NEED TO GET BACK TO PERDITA AS SOON AS WE CAN.
THE GODS ONLY KNOW WHAT HAS HAPPENED BETWEEN MY FATHER AND THE REBELS.
EVEN THE ANCIENT ONE DOES NOT KNOW WHAT TAKES PLACE BEYOND THE JUMP GATE.
WHATEVER THEY'VE DONE, WE'LL DEAL WITH IT.
I WISH YOU WELL, CHILDREN OF THE GODS
I WANT TO KNOW MORE ABOUT THE ENLIGHTENMENT.
I GROW WEARY
I AM NEAR MY END
IT IS TIME TO SLEEP
I SHALL NOT WAKE AGAIN IN THIS BODY

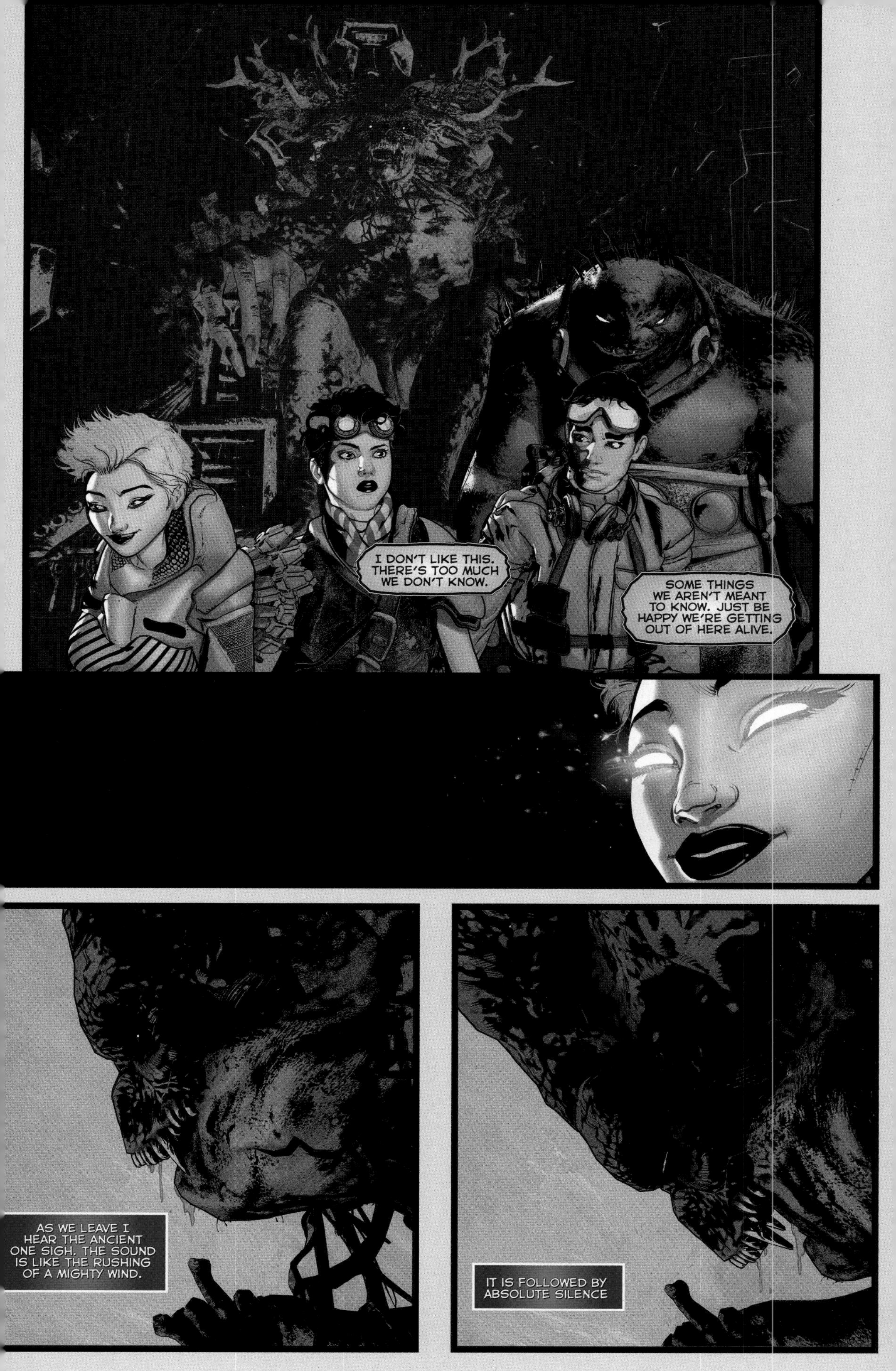
I DON'T LIKE THIS. THERE'S TOO MUCH WE DON'T KNOW.
SOME THINGS WE AREN'T MEANT TO KNOW. JUST BE HAPPY WE'RE GETTING OUT OF HERE ALIVE.
AS WE LEAVE I HEAR THE ANCIENT ONE SIGH. THE SOUND IS LIKE THE RUSHING OF A MIGHTY WIND.
IT IS FOLLOWED BY ABSOLUTE SILENCE

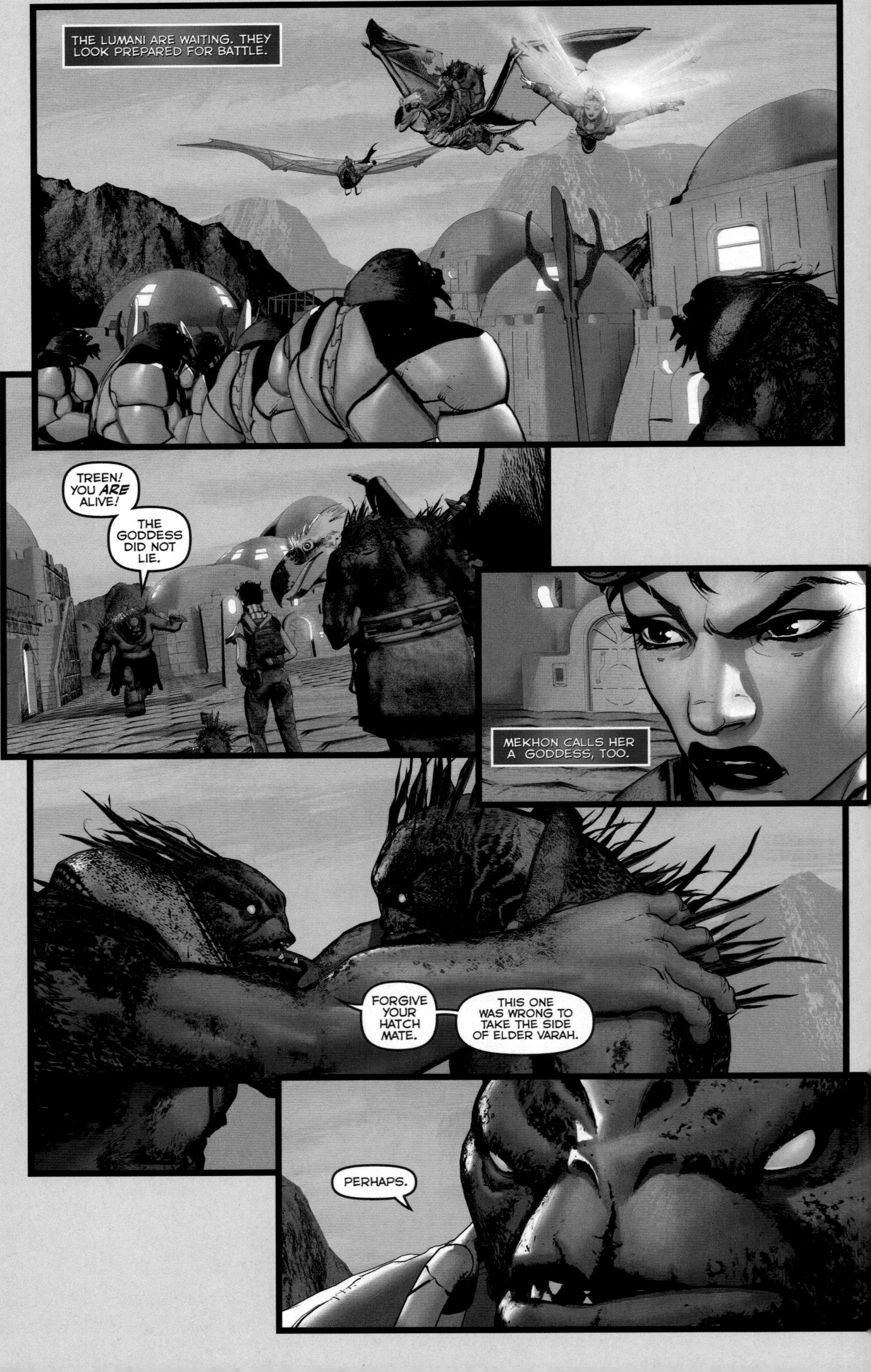
THE LUMANI ARE WAITING. THEY LOOK PREPARED FOR BATTLE.
TREEN! YOU ARE ALIVE!
THE GODDESS DID NOT LIE.
MEKHON CALLS HER A GODDESS, TOO.
FORGIVE YOUR HATCH MATE.
THIS ONE WAS WRONG TO TAKE THE SIDE OF ELDER VARAH.
PERHAPS.

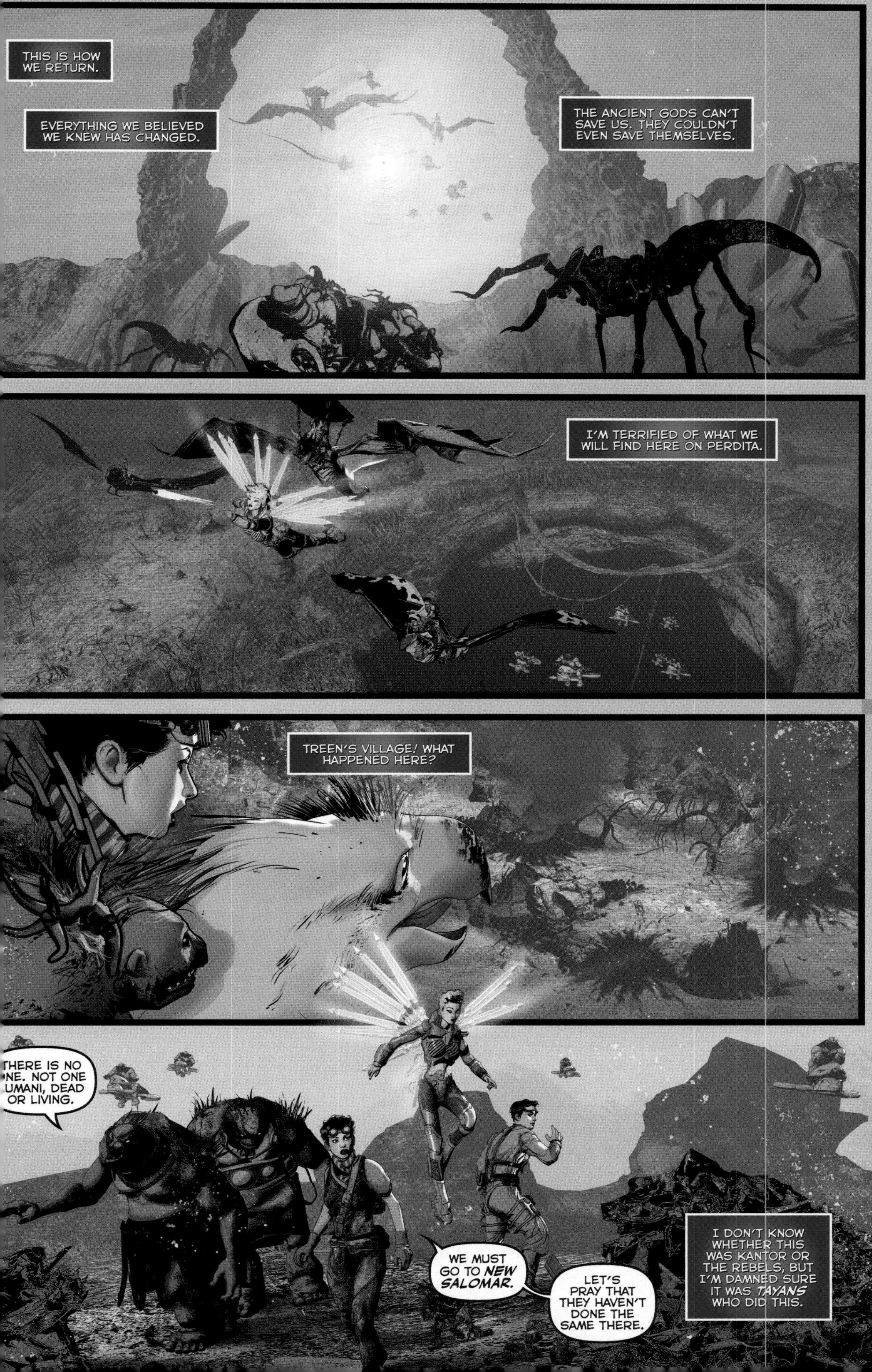
THIS IS HOW WE RETURN.
EVERYTHING WE BELIEVED WE KNEW HAS CHANGED.
THE ANCIENT GODS CAN'T SAVE US. THEY COULDN'T EVEN SAVE THEMSELVES.
I'M TERRIFIED OF WHAT WE WILL FIND HERE ON PERDITA.
TREEN'S VILLAGE! WHAT HAPPENED HERE?
THERE IS NO NE. NOT ONE UMANI, DEAD OR LIVING.
I DON'T KNOW WHETHER THIS WAS KANTOR OR THE REBELS, BUT I'M DAMNED SURE IT WAS TAYANS WHO DID THIS.
WE MUST GO TO NEW SALOMAR.
LET'S PRAY THAT THEY HAVEN'T DONE THE SAME THERE.

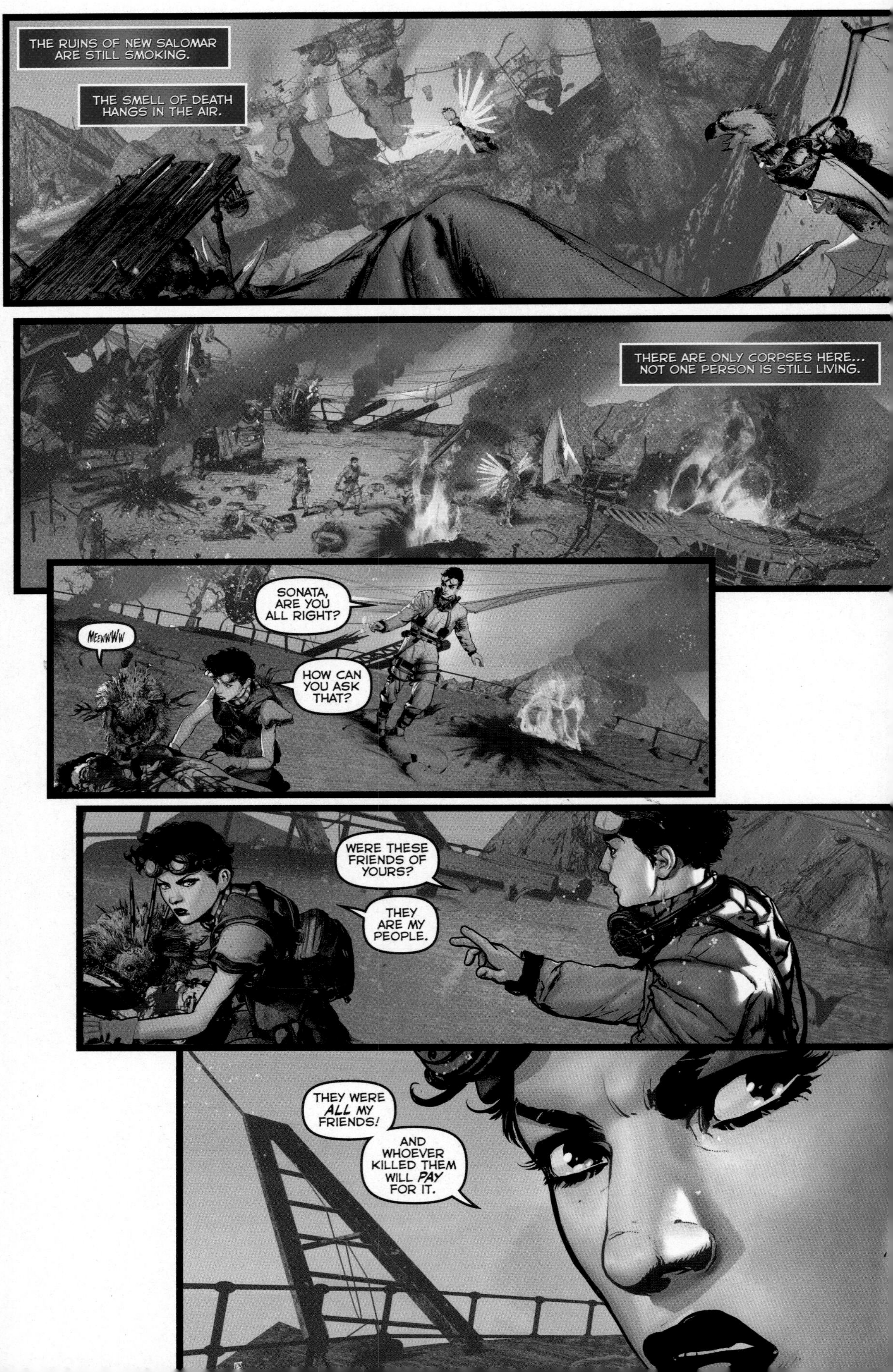

THE RUINS OF NEW SALOMAR ARE STILL SMOKING.
THE SMELL OF DEATH HANGS IN THE AIR.
THERE ARE ONLY CORPSES HERE... NOT ONE PERSON IS STILL LIVING.
SONATA, ARE YOU ALL RIGHT?
MEEWWWW
HOW CAN YOU ASK THAT?
WERE THESE FRIENDS OF YOURS?
THEY ARE MY PEOPLE.
THEY WERE *ALL* MY FRIENDS!
AND WHOEVER KILLED THEM WILL *PAY* FOR IT.

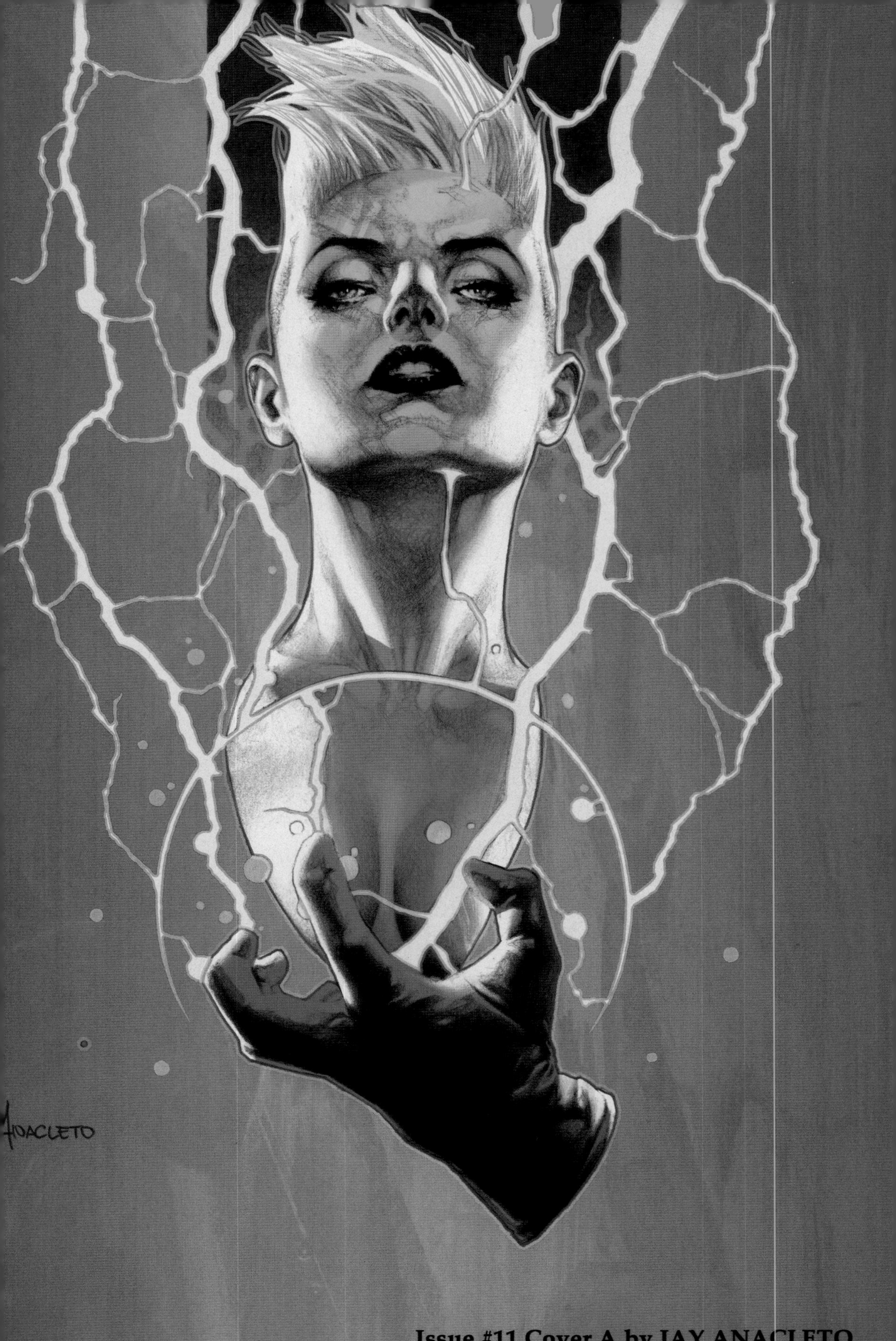
ANACLETO

Issue #11 Cover A by JAY ANACLETO

Issue #11 Cover B

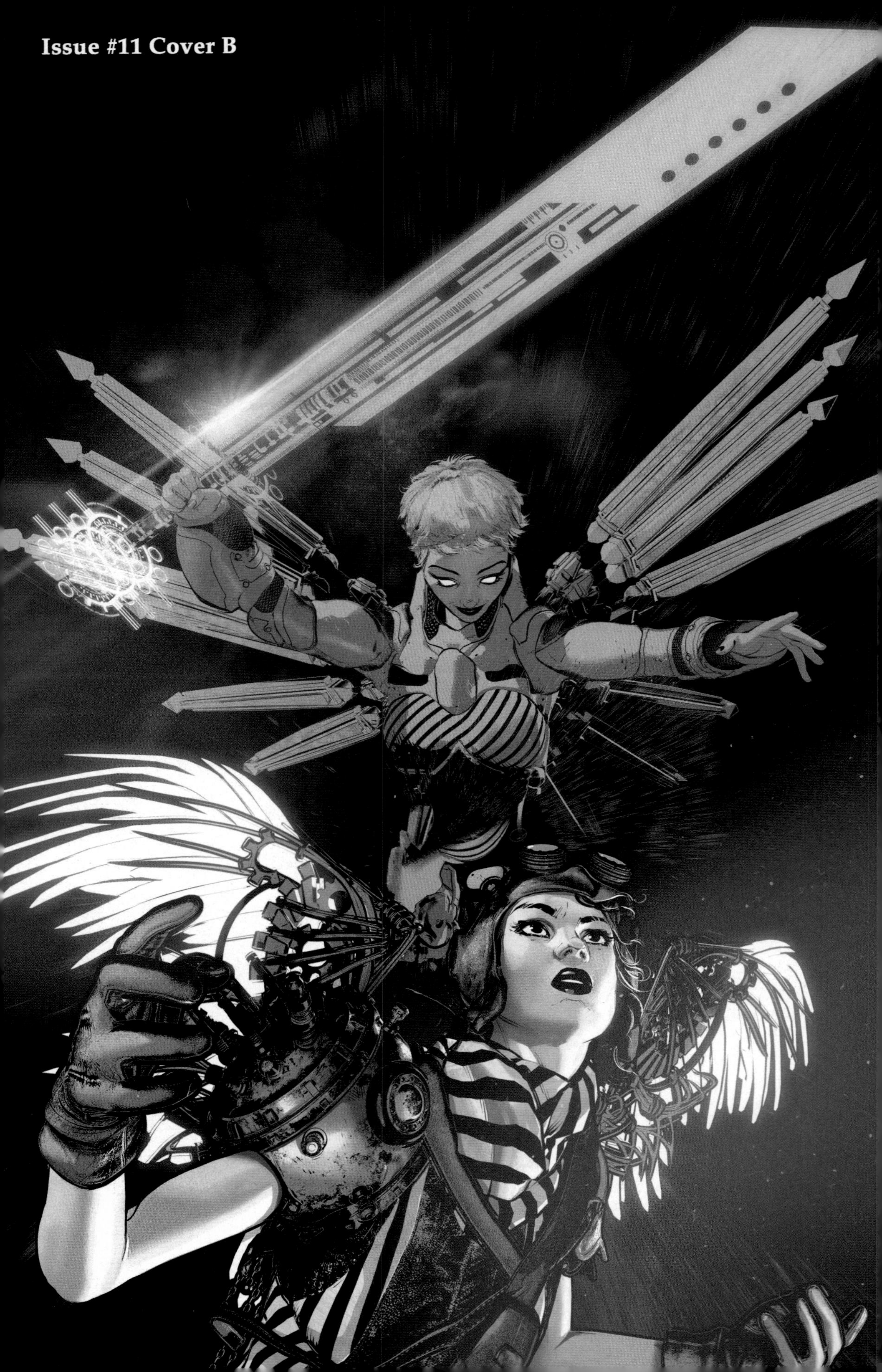

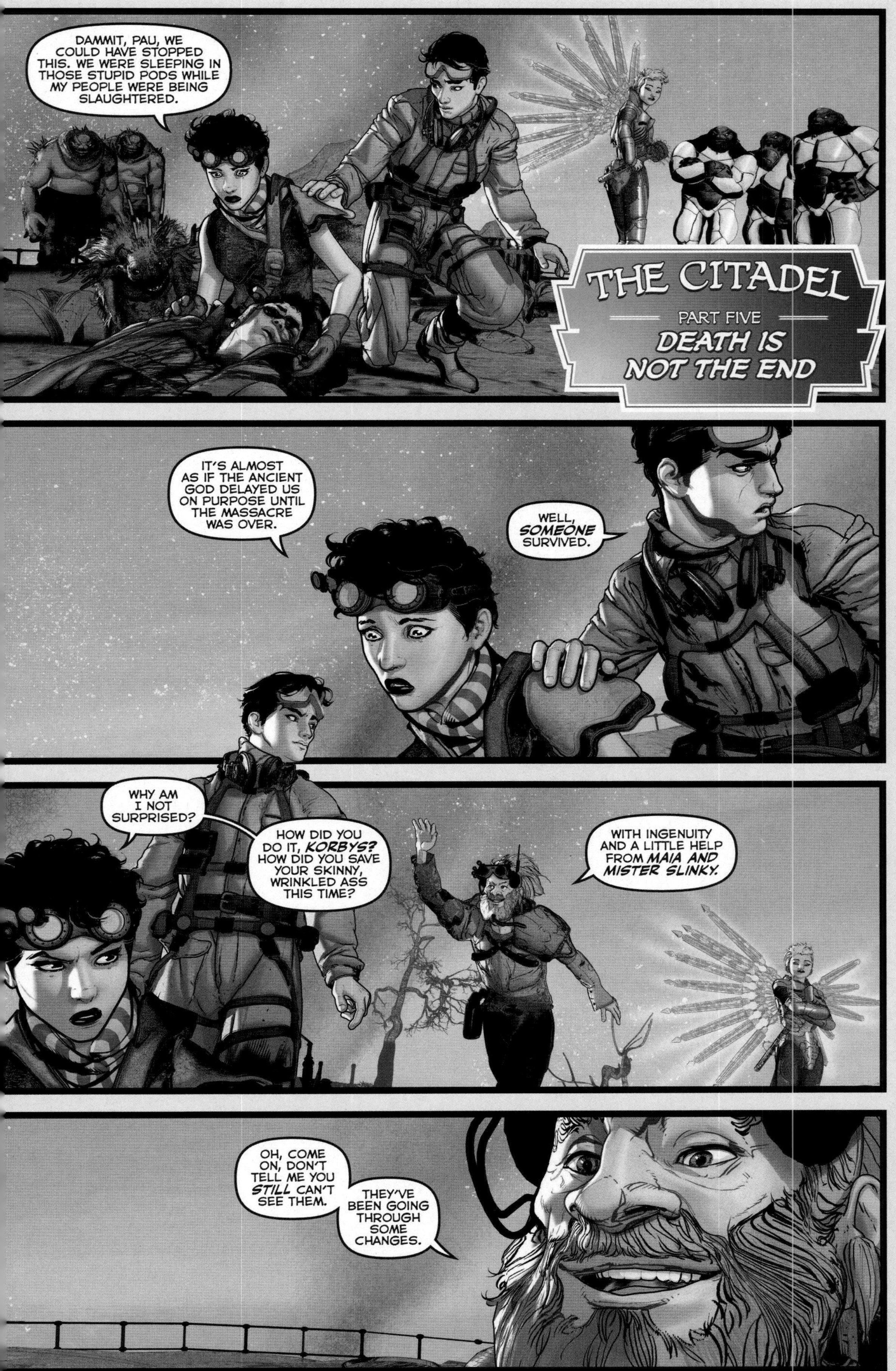
DAMMIT, PAU, WE COULD HAVE STOPPED THIS. WE WERE SLEEPING IN THOSE STUPID PODS WHILE MY PEOPLE WERE BEING SLAUGHTERED.
THE CITADEL
PART FIVE
DEATH IS NOT THE END
IT'S ALMOST AS IF THE ANCIENT GOD DELAYED US ON PURPOSE UNTIL THE MASSACRE WAS OVER.
WELL, SOMEONE SURVIVED.
WHY AM I NOT SURPRISED?
HOW DID YOU DO IT, KORBYS? HOW DID YOU SAVE YOUR SKINNY, WRINKLED ASS THIS TIME?
WITH INGENUITY AND A LITTLE HELP FROM MAIA AND MISTER SLINKY.
OH, COME ON, DON'T TELL ME YOU STILL CAN'T SEE THEM.
THEY'VE BEEN GOING THROUGH SOME CHANGES.

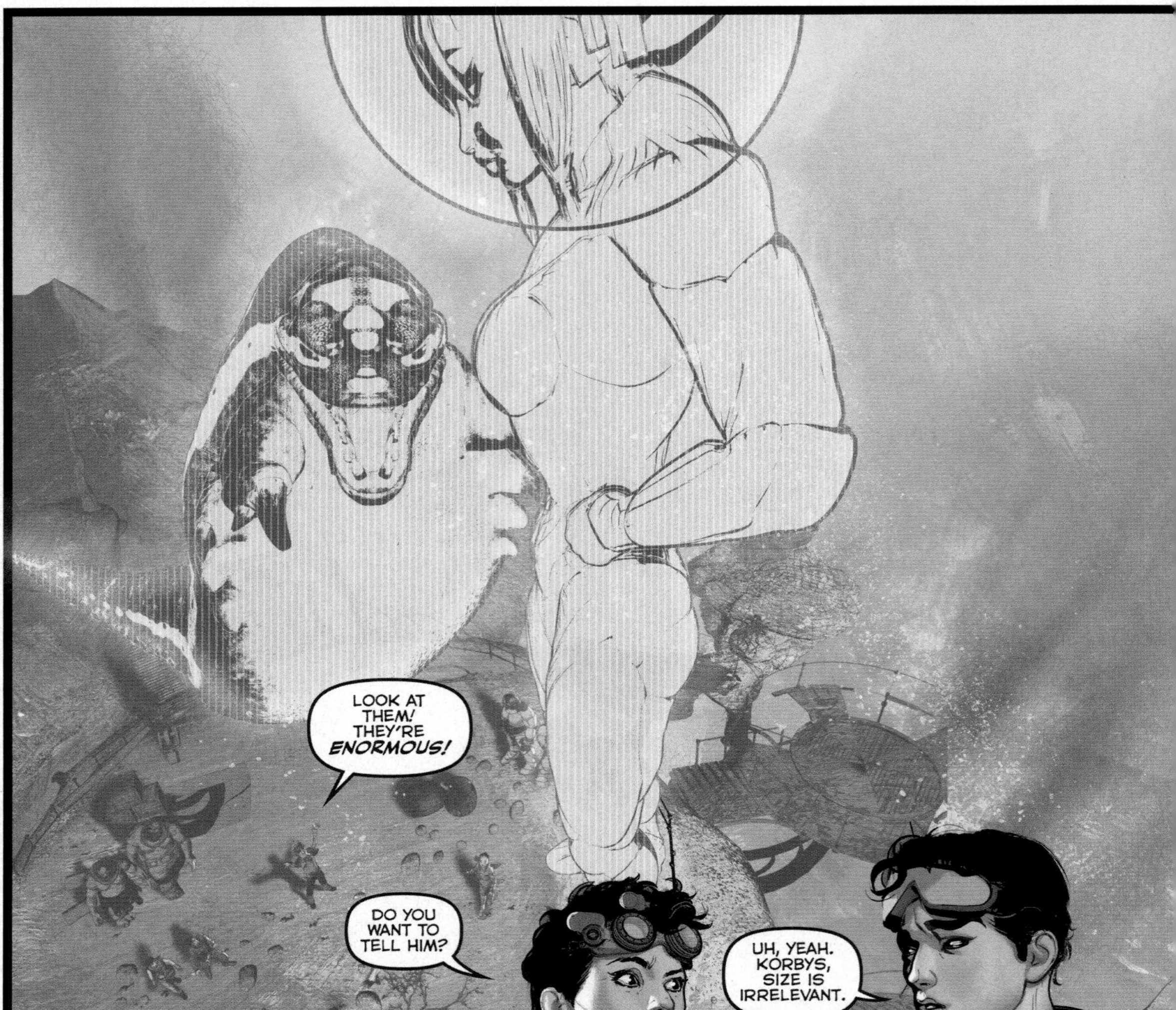
LOOK AT THEM! THEY'RE ENORMOUS!
DO YOU WANT TO TELL HIM?
UH, YEAH. KORBYS, SIZE IS IRRELEVANT.
THEY'RE STILL IMAGINARY FRIENDS.

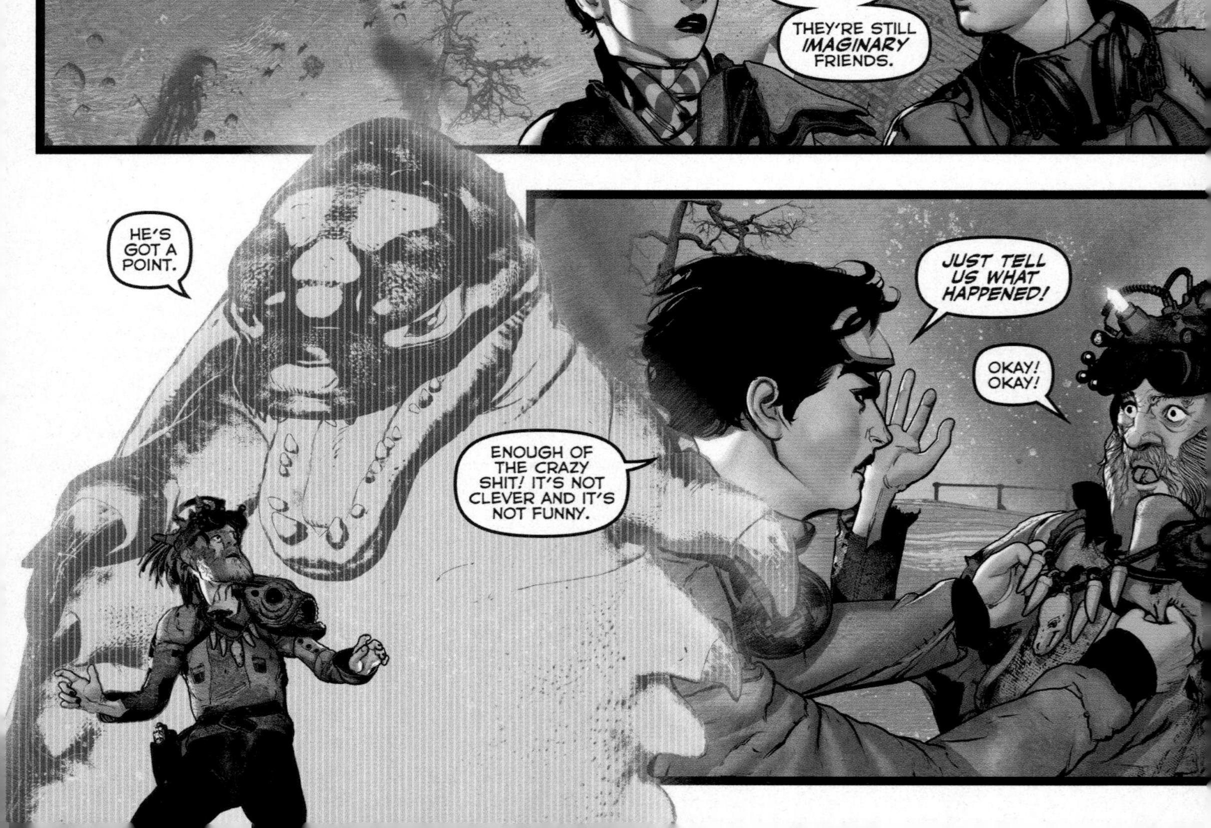
HE'S GOT A POINT.
JUST TELL US WHAT HAPPENED!
OKAY! OKAY!
ENOUGH OF THE CRAZY SHIT! IT'S NOT CLEVER AND IT'S NOT FUNNY.

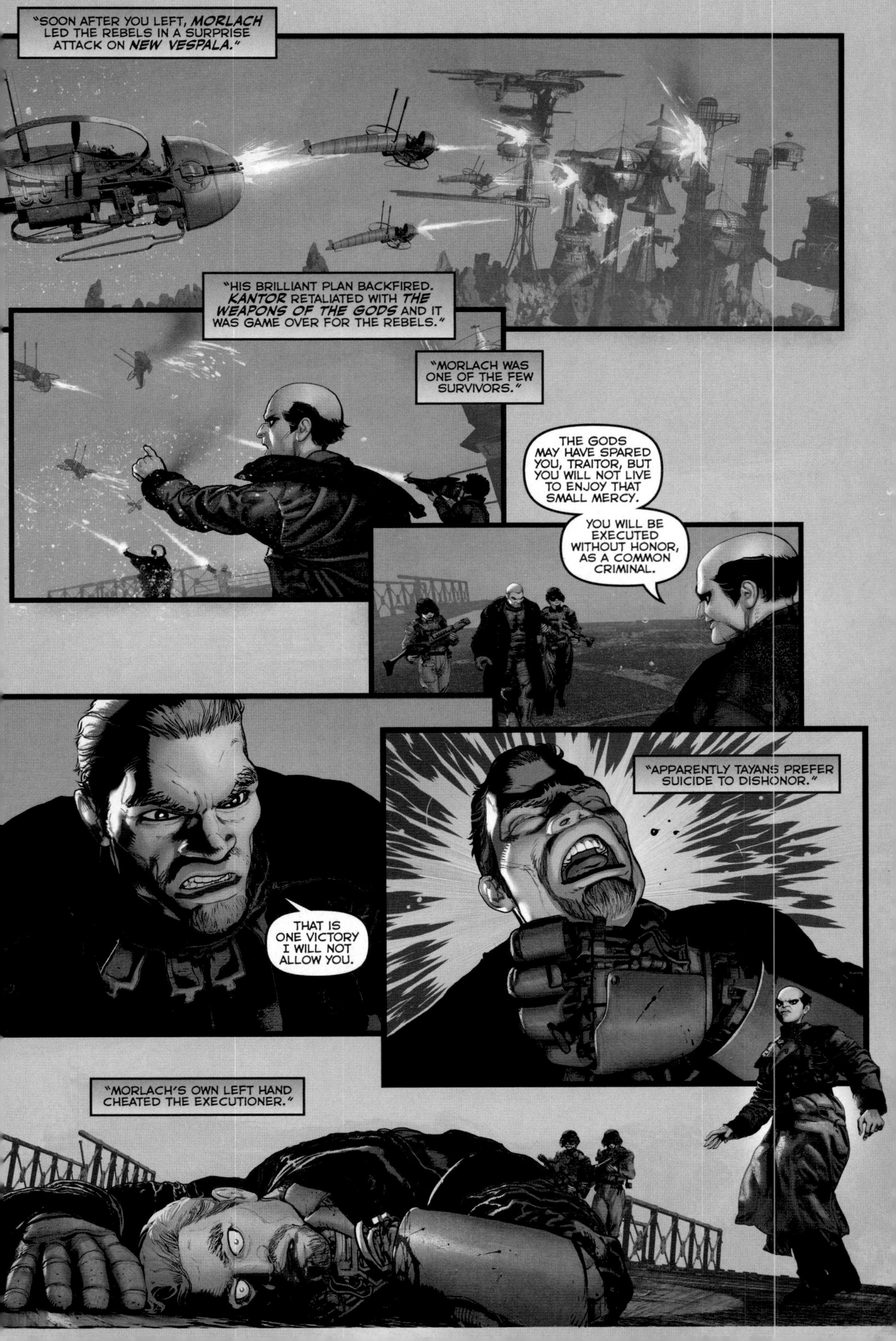
"SOON AFTER YOU LEFT, MORLACH LED THE REBELS IN A SURPRISE ATTACK ON NEW VESPALA."
"HIS BRILLIANT PLAN BACKFIRED. KANTOR RETALIATED WITH THE WEAPONS OF THE GODS AND IT WAS GAME OVER FOR THE REBELS."
"MORLACH WAS ONE OF THE FEW SURVIVORS."
THE GODS MAY HAVE SPARED YOU, TRAITOR, BUT YOU WILL NOT LIVE TO ENJOY THAT SMALL MERCY.
YOU WILL BE EXECUTED WITHOUT HONOR, AS A COMMON CRIMINAL.
THAT IS ONE VICTORY I WILL NOT ALLOW YOU.
"APPARENTLY TAYANS PREFER SUICIDE TO DISHONOR."
"MORLACH'S OWN LEFT HAND CHEATED THE EXECUTIONER."

"KANTOR ATTACKED *NEW SALOMAR* THE NEXT DAY."

"OUR PEOPLE BARELY FOUGHT BACK. *BRAMAN* KNEW THEY COULDN'T WIN. HE MUST HAVE HOPED THAT BY SURRENDERING QUICKLY THEY MIGHT HAVE A BETTER CHANCE OF MERCY."

"KANTOR ONLY HAD MORE CONTEMPT FOR THEM. HE MADE IT CLEAR THAT HE WOULD EXTERMINATE EVERY LAST RAN ON THE PLANET."

"ONLY *FEDALA* ARGUED AGAINST IT, THOUGH I HAD THE FEELING SHE WAS JUST LOOKING FOR A REASON TO CONFRONT HIM."

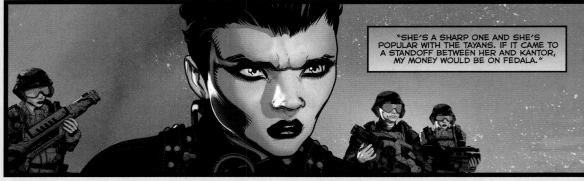

"SHE'S A SHARP ONE AND SHE'S POPULAR WITH THE TAYANS. IF IT CAME TO A STANDOFF BETWEEN HER AND KANTOR, MY MONEY WOULD BE ON FEDALA."

"KANTOR GAVE IN, BUT IF I'M ANY JUDGE OF PSYCHOPATHS, HE WAS ONLY PLANNING TO LET THEM LIVE FOR ABOUT A MINUTE AFTER HE KILLED FEDALA."

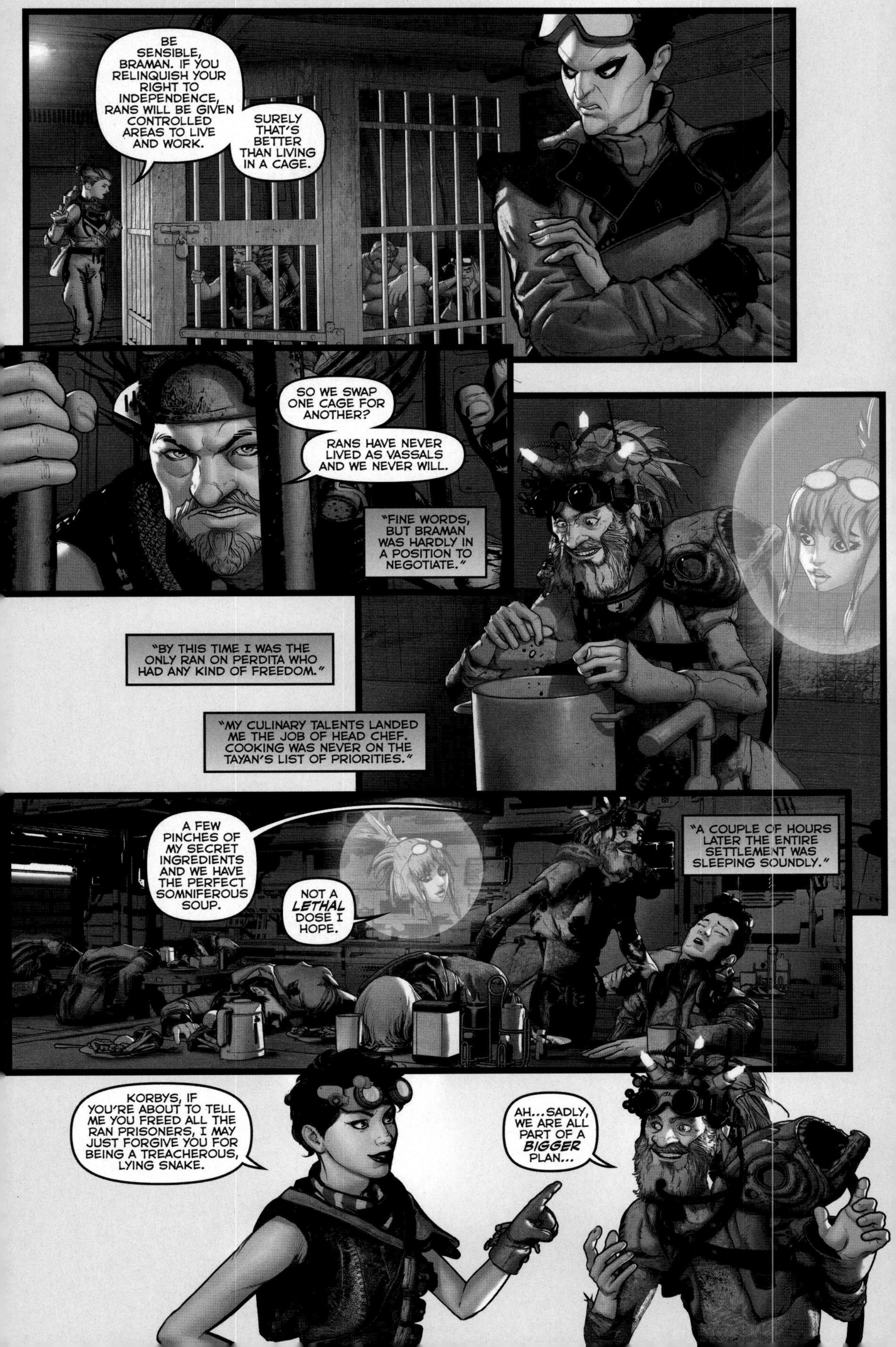
BE SENSIBLE, BRAMAN. IF YOU RELINQUISH YOUR RIGHT TO INDEPENDENCE, RANS WILL BE GIVEN CONTROLLED AREAS TO LIVE AND WORK.
SURELY THAT'S BETTER THAN LIVING IN A CAGE.
SO WE SWAP ONE CAGE FOR ANOTHER?
RANS HAVE NEVER LIVED AS VASSALS AND WE NEVER WILL.
"FINE WORDS, BUT BRAMAN WAS HARDLY IN A POSITION TO NEGOTIATE."
"BY THIS TIME I WAS THE ONLY RAN ON PERDITA WHO HAD ANY KIND OF FREEDOM."
"MY CULINARY TALENTS LANDED ME THE JOB OF HEAD CHEF. COOKING WAS NEVER ON THE TAYAN'S LIST OF PRIORITIES."
A FEW PINCHES OF MY SECRET INGREDIENTS AND WE HAVE THE PERFECT SOMNIFEROUS SOUP.
NOT A *LETHAL* DOSE I HOPE.
"A COUPLE OF HOURS LATER THE ENTIRE SETTLEMENT WAS SLEEPING SOUNDLY."
KORBYS, IF YOU'RE ABOUT TO TELL ME YOU FREED ALL THE RAN PRISONERS, I MAY JUST FORGIVE YOU FOR BEING A TREACHEROUS, LYING SNAKE.
AH...SADLY, WE ARE ALL PART OF A *BIGGER* PLAN...

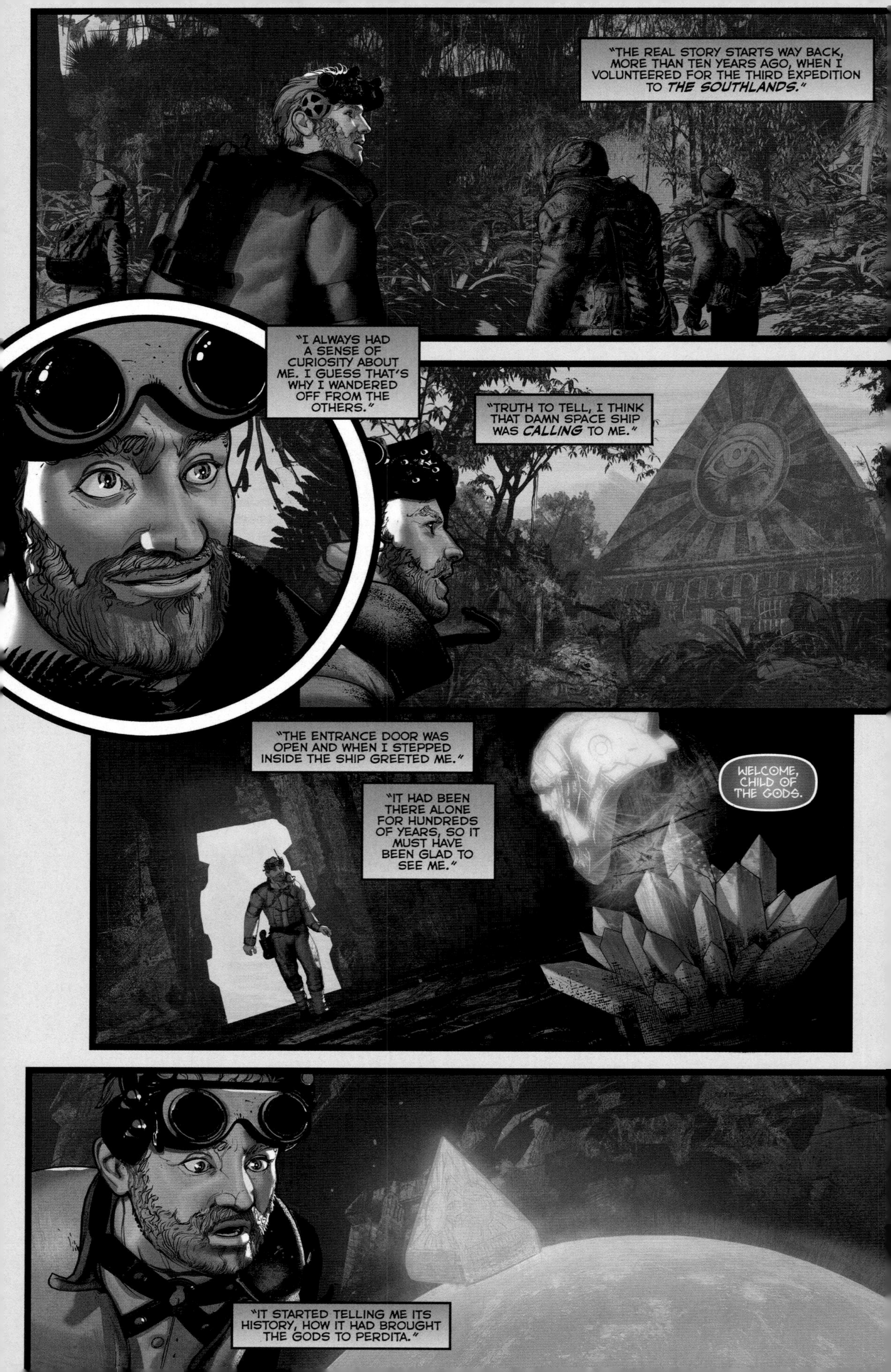
"THE REAL STORY STARTS WAY BACK, MORE THAN TEN YEARS AGO, WHEN I VOLUNTEERED FOR THE THIRD EXPEDITION TO THE SOUTHLANDS."
"I ALWAYS HAD A SENSE OF CURIOSITY ABOUT ME. I GUESS THAT'S WHY I WANDERED OFF FROM THE OTHERS."
"TRUTH TO TELL, I THINK THAT DAMN SPACE SHIP WAS CALLING TO ME."
"THE ENTRANCE DOOR WAS OPEN AND WHEN I STEPPED INSIDE THE SHIP GREETED ME."
"IT HAD BEEN THERE ALONE FOR HUNDREDS OF YEARS, SO IT MUST HAVE BEEN GLAD TO SEE ME."
WELCOME, CHILD OF THE GODS.
"IT STARTED TELLING ME ITS HISTORY, HOW IT HAD BROUGHT THE GODS TO PERDITA."

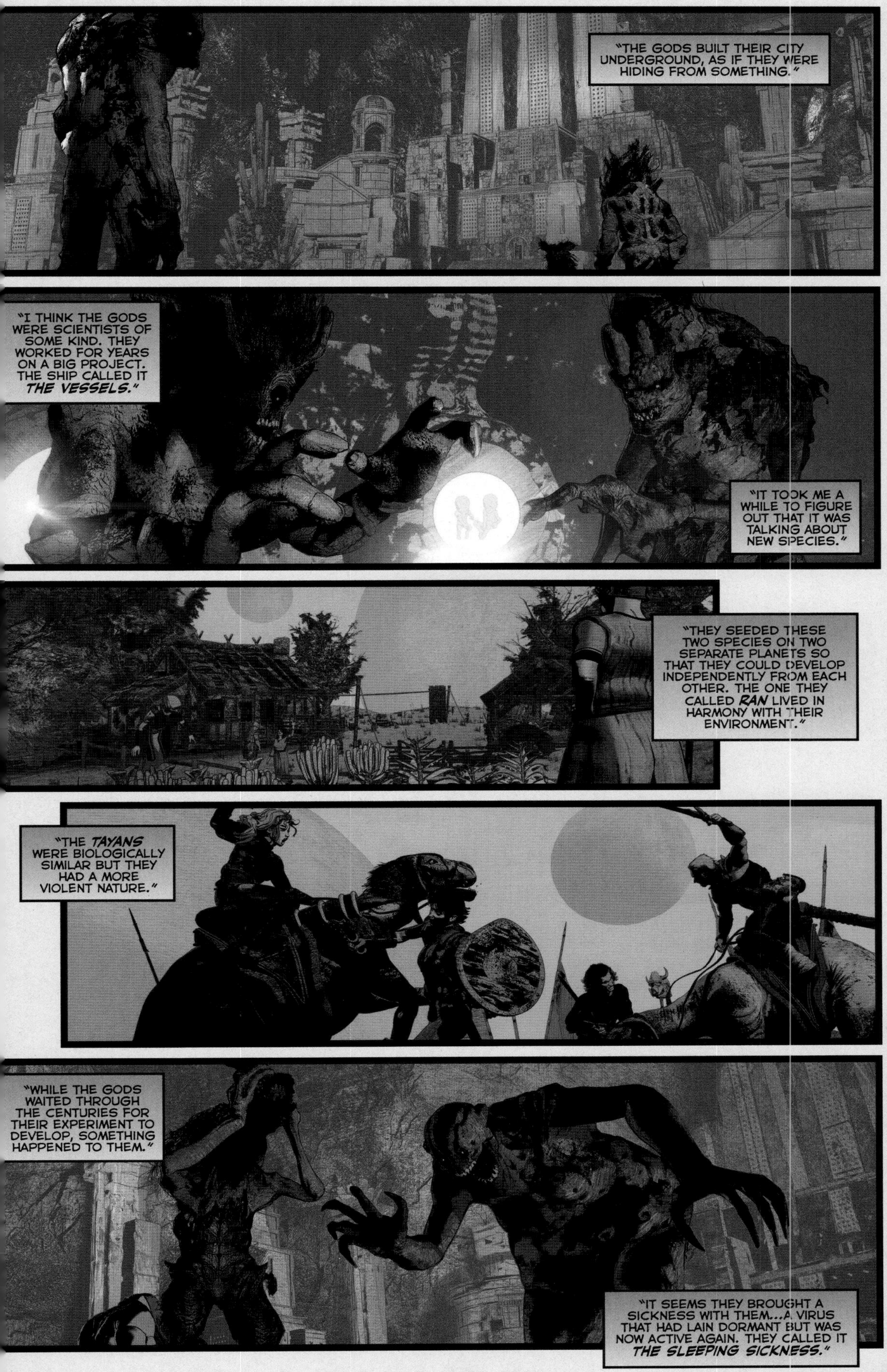
"THE GODS BUILT THEIR CITY UNDERGROUND, AS IF THEY WERE HIDING FROM SOMETHING."
"I THINK THE GODS WERE SCIENTISTS OF SOME KIND. THEY WORKED FOR YEARS ON A BIG PROJECT. THE SHIP CALLED IT *THE VESSELS*."
"IT TOOK ME A WHILE TO FIGURE OUT THAT IT WAS TALKING ABOUT NEW SPECIES."
"THEY SEEDED THESE TWO SPECIES ON TWO SEPARATE PLANETS SO THAT THEY COULD DEVELOP INDEPENDENTLY FROM EACH OTHER. THE ONE THEY CALLED *RAN* LIVED IN HARMONY WITH THEIR ENVIRONMENT."
"THE *TAYANS* WERE BIOLOGICALLY SIMILAR BUT THEY HAD A MORE VIOLENT NATURE."
"WHILE THE GODS WAITED THROUGH THE CENTURIES FOR THEIR EXPERIMENT TO DEVELOP, SOMETHING HAPPENED TO THEM."
"IT SEEMS THEY BROUGHT A SICKNESS WITH THEM...A VIRUS THAT HAD LAIN DORMANT BUT WAS NOW ACTIVE AGAIN. THEY CALLED IT *THE SLEEPING SICKNESS*."

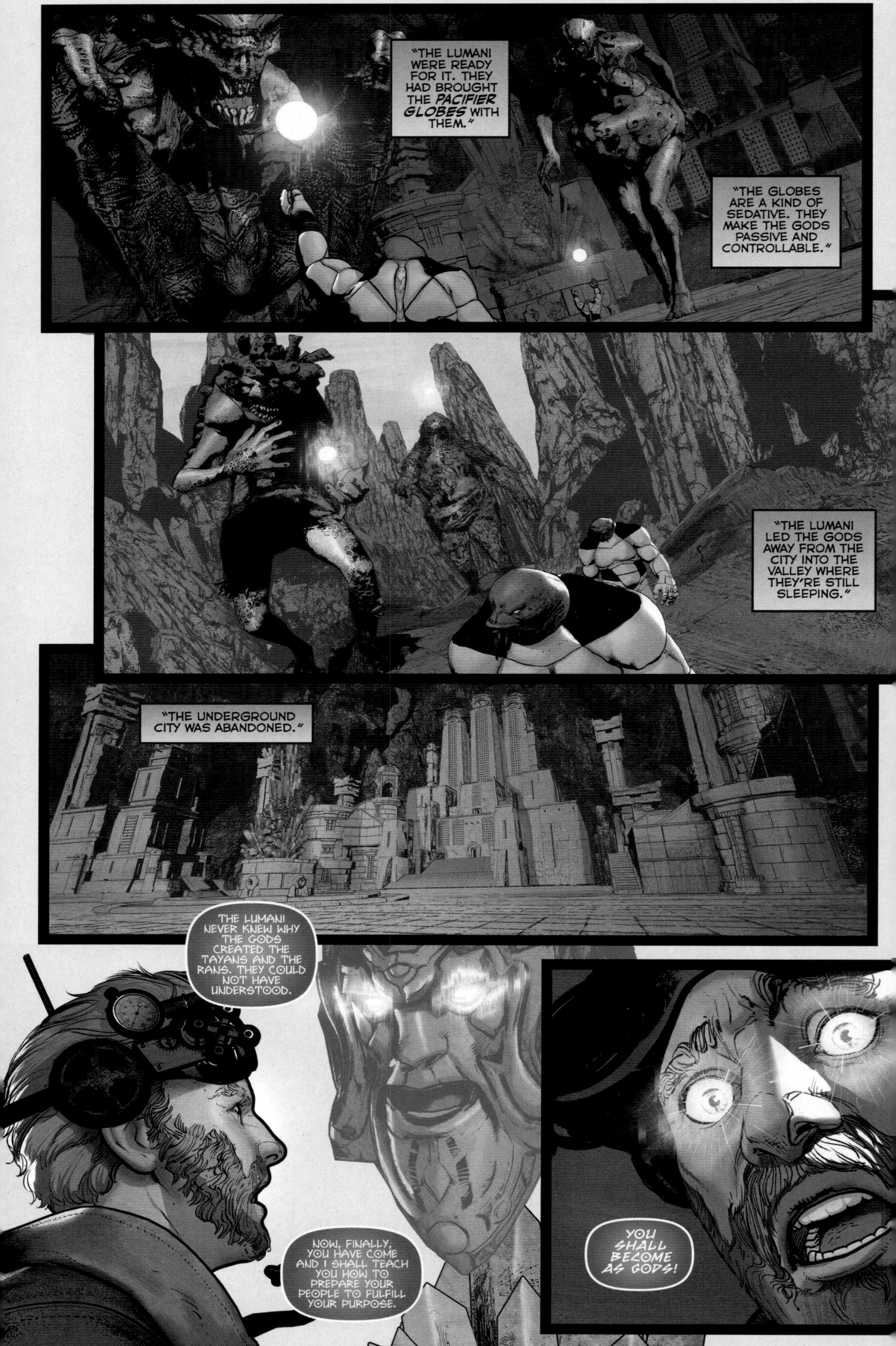
"THE LUMANI WERE READY FOR IT. THEY HAD BROUGHT THE PACIFIER GLOBES WITH THEM."
"THE GLOBES ARE A KIND OF SEDATIVE. THEY MAKE THE GODS PASSIVE AND CONTROLLABLE."
"THE LUMANI LED THE GODS AWAY FROM THE CITY INTO THE VALLEY WHERE THEY'RE STILL SLEEPING."
"THE UNDERGROUND CITY WAS ABANDONED."
THE LUMANI NEVER KNEW WHY THE GODS CREATED THE TAYANS AND THE RANS. THEY COULD NOT HAVE UNDERSTOOD.
NOW, FINALLY, YOU HAVE COME AND I SHALL TEACH YOU HOW TO PREPARE YOUR PEOPLE TO FULFILL YOUR PURPOSE.
YOU SHALL BECOME AS GODS!

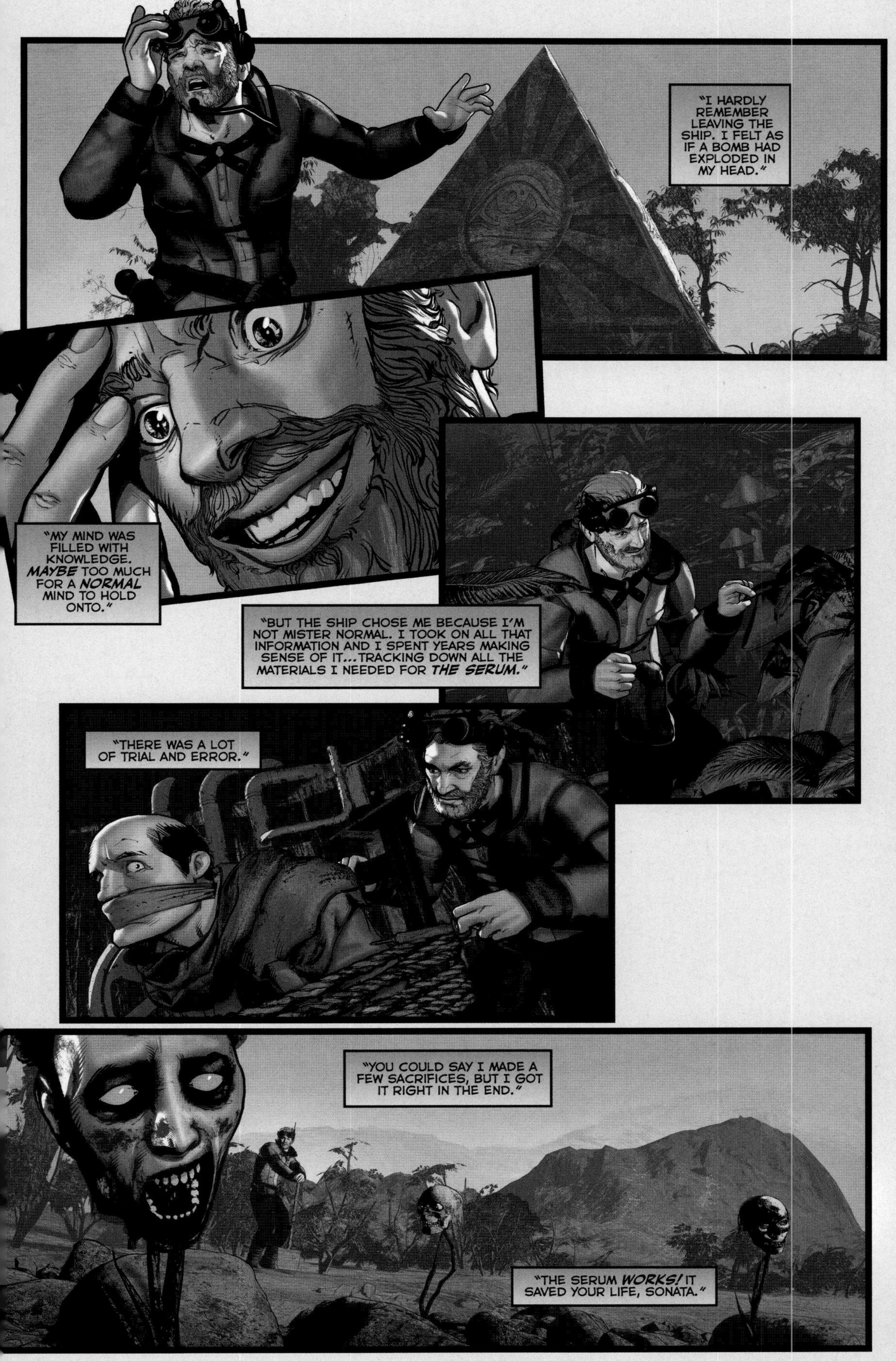
"I HARDLY REMEMBER LEAVING THE SHIP. I FELT AS IF A BOMB HAD EXPLODED IN MY HEAD."
"MY MIND WAS FILLED WITH KNOWLEDGE. *MAYBE* TOO MUCH FOR A *NORMAL* MIND TO HOLD ONTO."
"BUT THE SHIP CHOSE ME BECAUSE I'M NOT MISTER NORMAL. I TOOK ON ALL THAT INFORMATION AND I SPENT YEARS MAKING SENSE OF IT...TRACKING DOWN ALL THE MATERIALS I NEEDED FOR *THE SERUM.*"
"THERE WAS A LOT OF TRIAL AND ERROR."
"YOU COULD SAY I MADE A FEW SACRIFICES, BUT I GOT IT RIGHT IN THE END."
"THE SERUM *WORKS!* IT SAVED YOUR LIFE, SONATA."

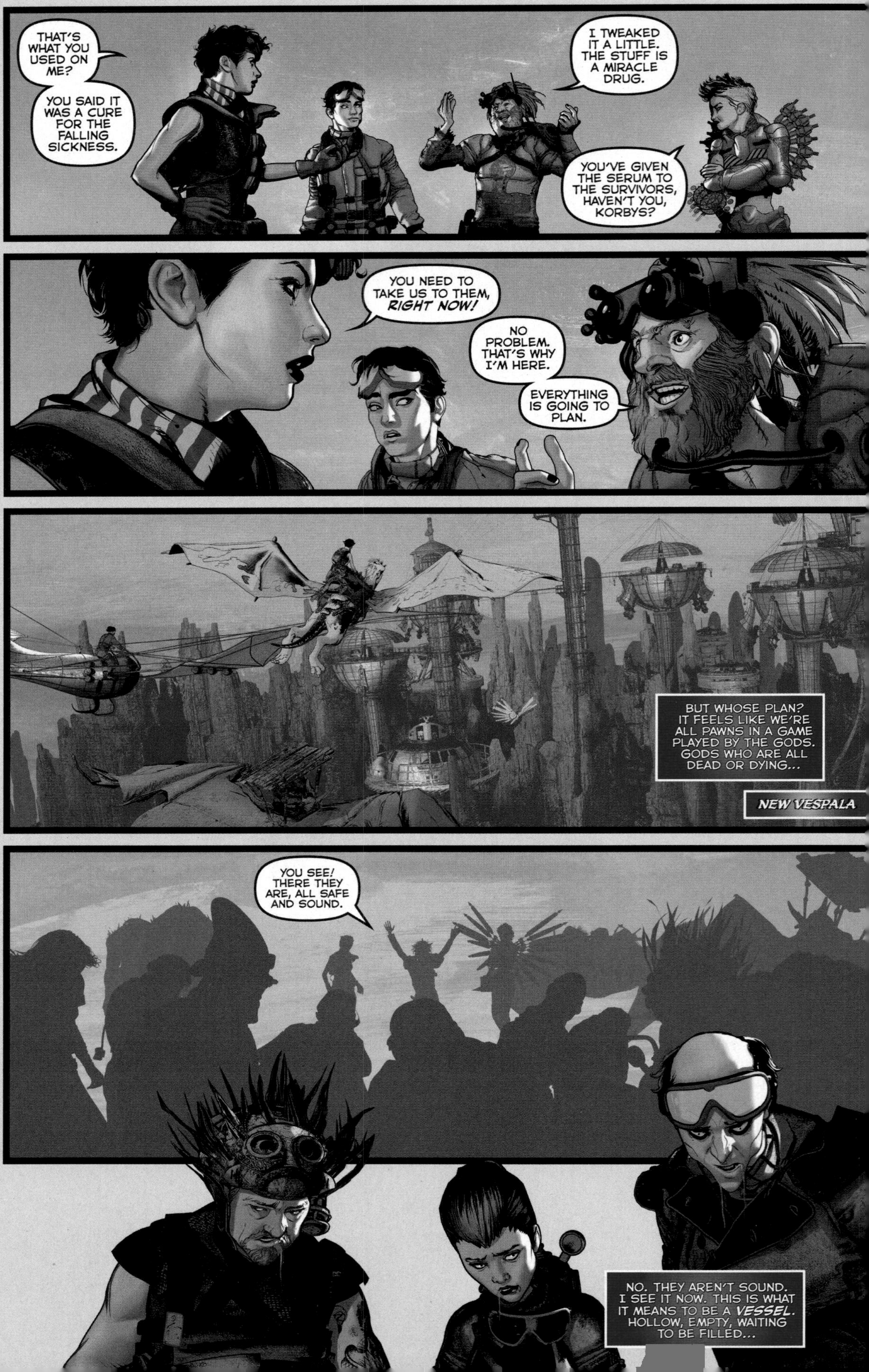
THAT'S WHAT YOU USED ON ME?
YOU SAID IT WAS A CURE FOR THE FALLING SICKNESS.
I TWEAKED IT A LITTLE. THE STUFF IS A MIRACLE DRUG.
YOU'VE GIVEN THE SERUM TO THE SURVIVORS, HAVEN'T YOU, KORBYS?
YOU NEED TO TAKE US TO THEM, RIGHT NOW!
NO PROBLEM. THAT'S WHY I'M HERE.
EVERYTHING IS GOING TO PLAN.
BUT WHOSE PLAN? IT FEELS LIKE WE'RE ALL PAWNS IN A GAME PLAYED BY THE GODS. GODS WHO ARE ALL DEAD OR DYING...
NEW VESPALA
YOU SEE! THERE THEY ARE, ALL SAFE AND SOUND.
NO. THEY AREN'T SOUND. I SEE IT NOW. THIS IS WHAT IT MEANS TO BE A VESSEL. HOLLOW, EMPTY, WAITING TO BE FILLED...

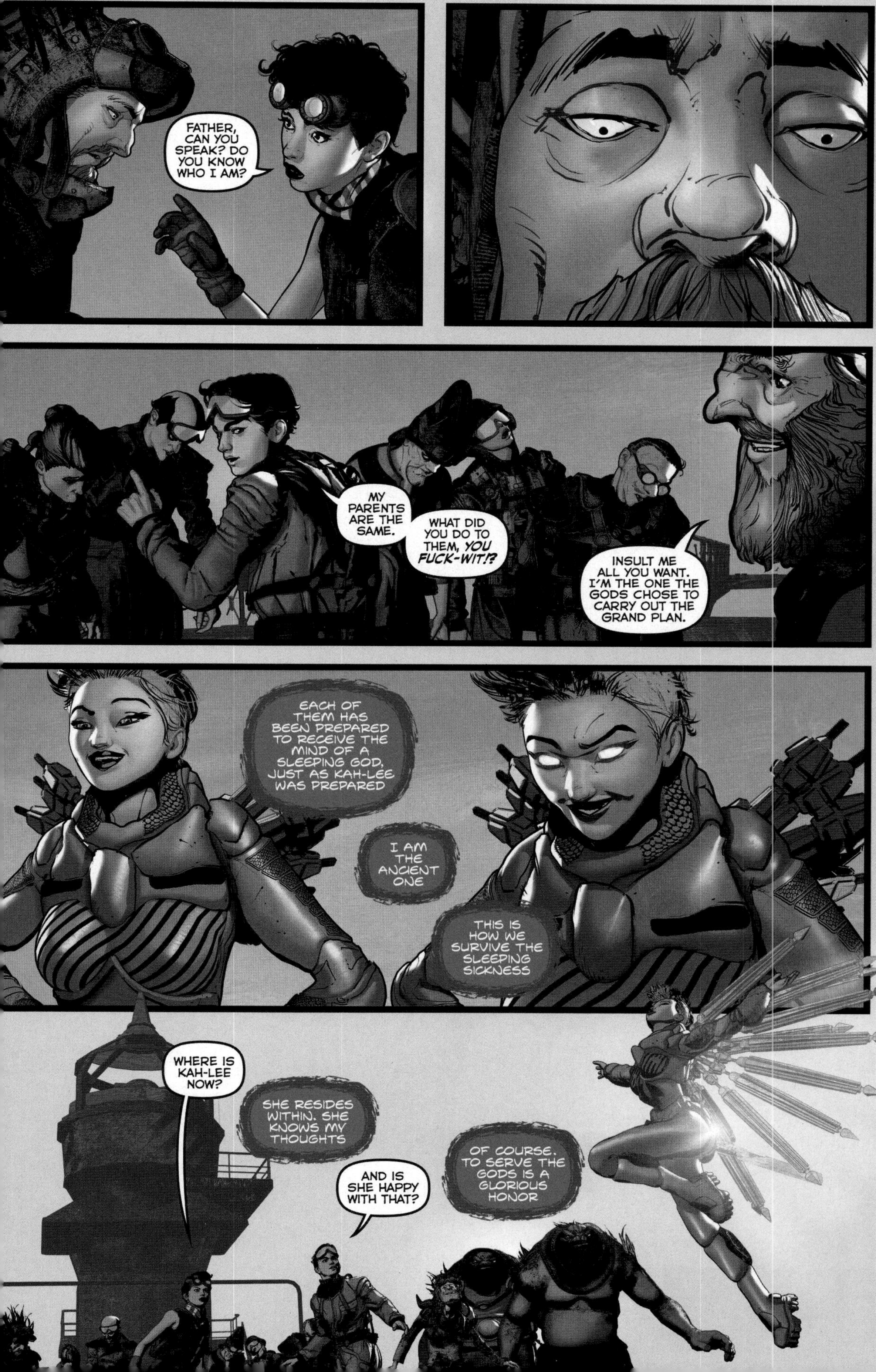
FATHER, CAN YOU SPEAK? DO YOU KNOW WHO I AM?
MY PARENTS ARE THE SAME.
WHAT DID YOU DO TO THEM, YOU FUCK-WIT!?
INSULT ME ALL YOU WANT. I'M THE ONE THE GODS CHOSE TO CARRY OUT THE GRAND PLAN.
EACH OF THEM HAS BEEN PREPARED TO RECEIVE THE MIND OF A SLEEPING GOD, JUST AS KAH-LEE WAS PREPARED
I AM THE ANCIENT ONE
THIS IS HOW WE SURVIVE THE SLEEPING SICKNESS
WHERE IS KAH-LEE NOW?
SHE RESIDES WITHIN. SHE KNOWS MY THOUGHTS
AND IS SHE HAPPY WITH THAT?
OF COURSE. TO SERVE THE GODS IS A GLORIOUS HONOR

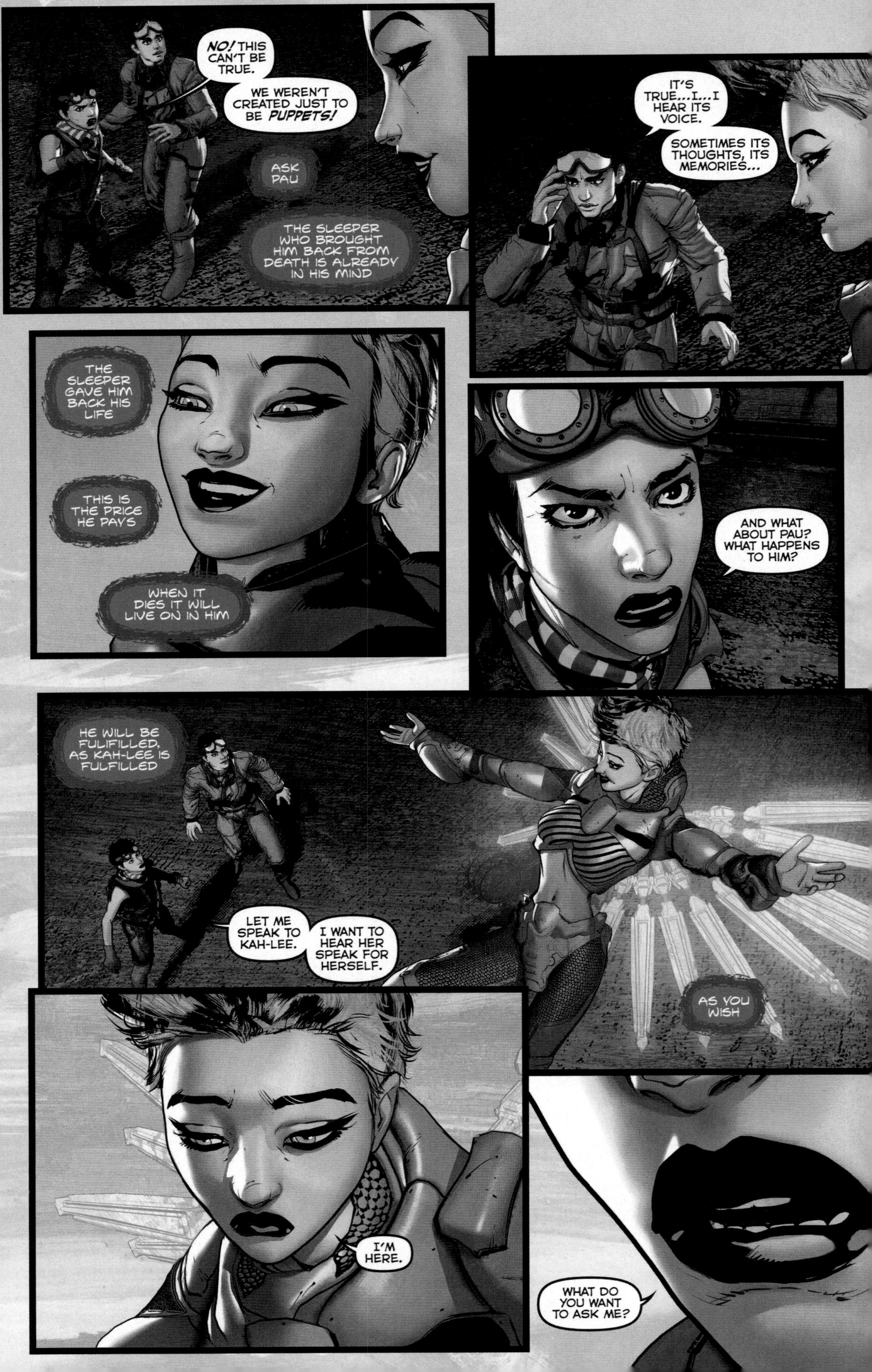
NO! THIS CAN'T BE TRUE.
WE WEREN'T CREATED JUST TO BE PUPPETS!
ASK PAU
THE SLEEPER WHO BROUGHT HIM BACK FROM DEATH IS ALREADY IN HIS MIND
IT'S TRUE...I...I HEAR ITS VOICE.
SOMETIMES ITS THOUGHTS, ITS MEMORIES...
THE SLEEPER GAVE HIM BACK HIS LIFE
THIS IS THE PRICE HE PAYS
WHEN IT DIES IT WILL LIVE ON IN HIM
AND WHAT ABOUT PAU? WHAT HAPPENS TO HIM?
HE WILL BE FULIFILLED, AS KAH-LEE IS FULFILLED
LET ME SPEAK TO KAH-LEE.
I WANT TO HEAR HER SPEAK FOR HERSELF.
AS YOU WISH
I'M HERE.
WHAT DO YOU WANT TO ASK ME?

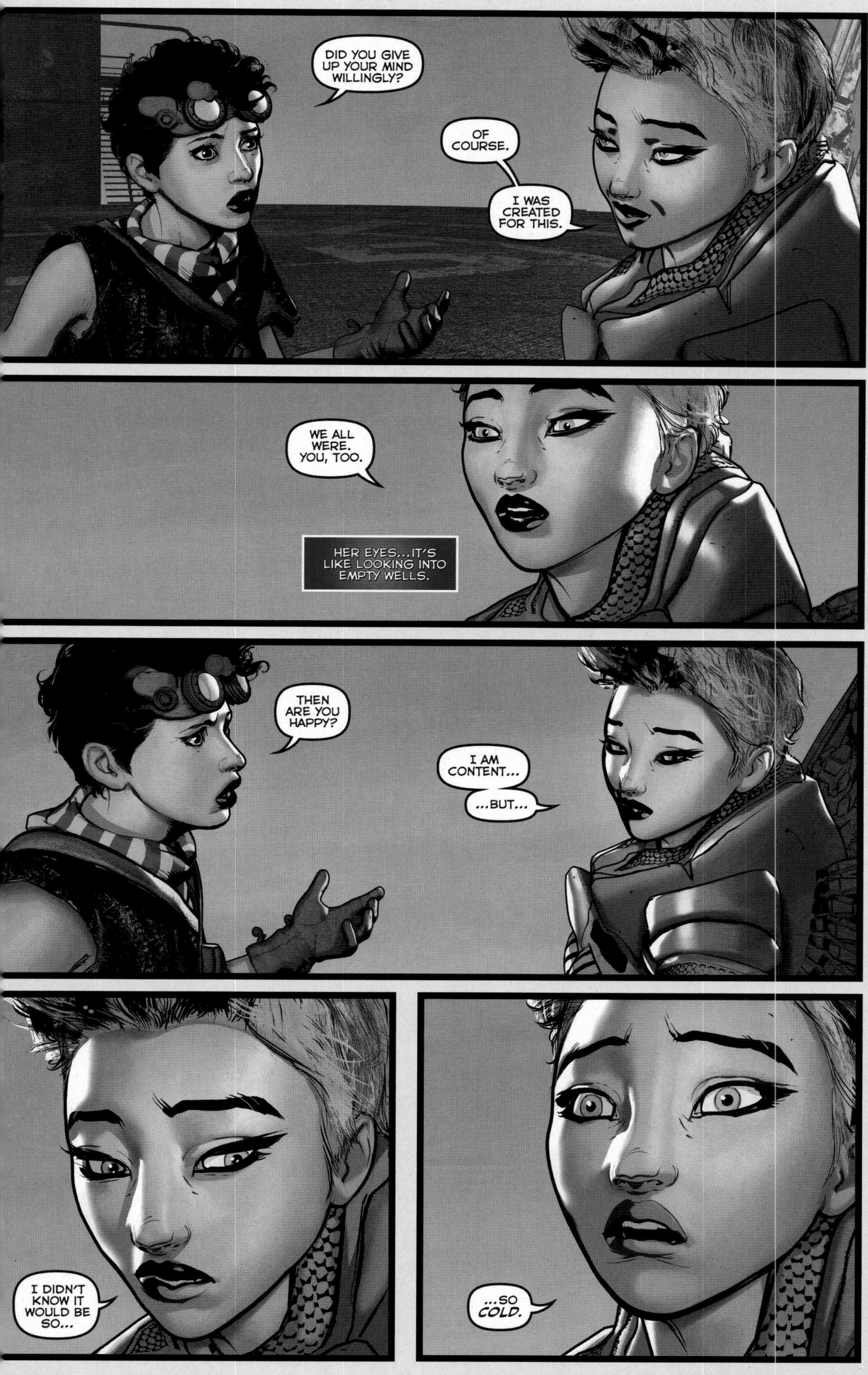
DID YOU GIVE UP YOUR MIND WILLINGLY?
OF COURSE.
I WAS CREATED FOR THIS.
WE ALL WERE. YOU, TOO.
HER EYES...IT'S LIKE LOOKING INTO EMPTY WELLS.
THEN ARE YOU HAPPY?
I AM CONTENT...
...BUT...
I DIDN'T KNOW IT WOULD BE SO...
...SO *COLD.*

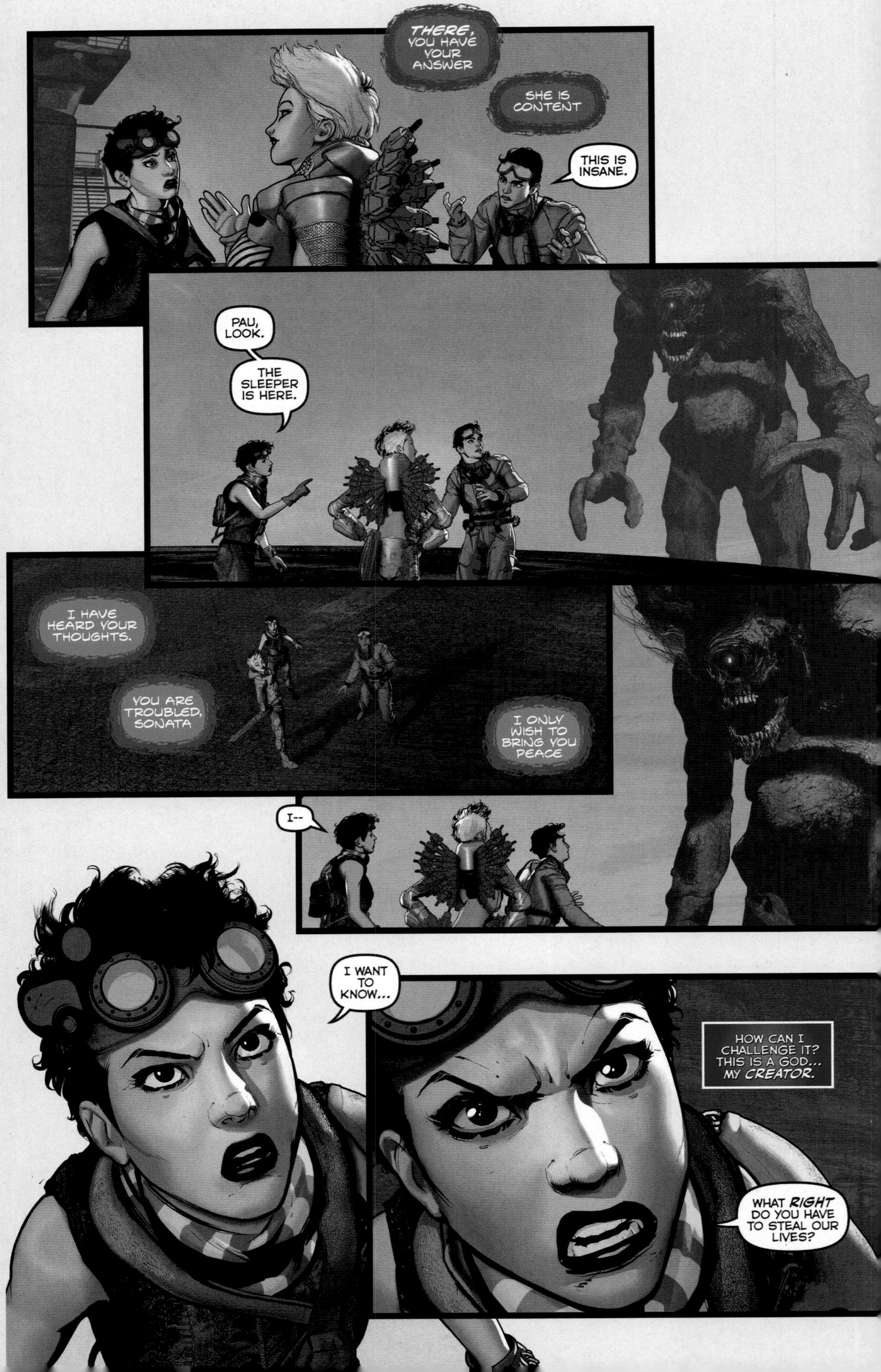
THERE, YOU HAVE YOUR ANSWER
SHE IS CONTENT
THIS IS INSANE.
PAU, LOOK.
THE SLEEPER IS HERE.
I HAVE HEARD YOUR THOUGHTS.
YOU ARE TROUBLED, SONATA
I ONLY WISH TO BRING YOU PEACE
I--
I WANT TO KNOW...
HOW CAN I CHALLENGE IT? THIS IS A GOD... MY CREATOR.
WHAT RIGHT DO YOU HAVE TO STEAL OUR LIVES?

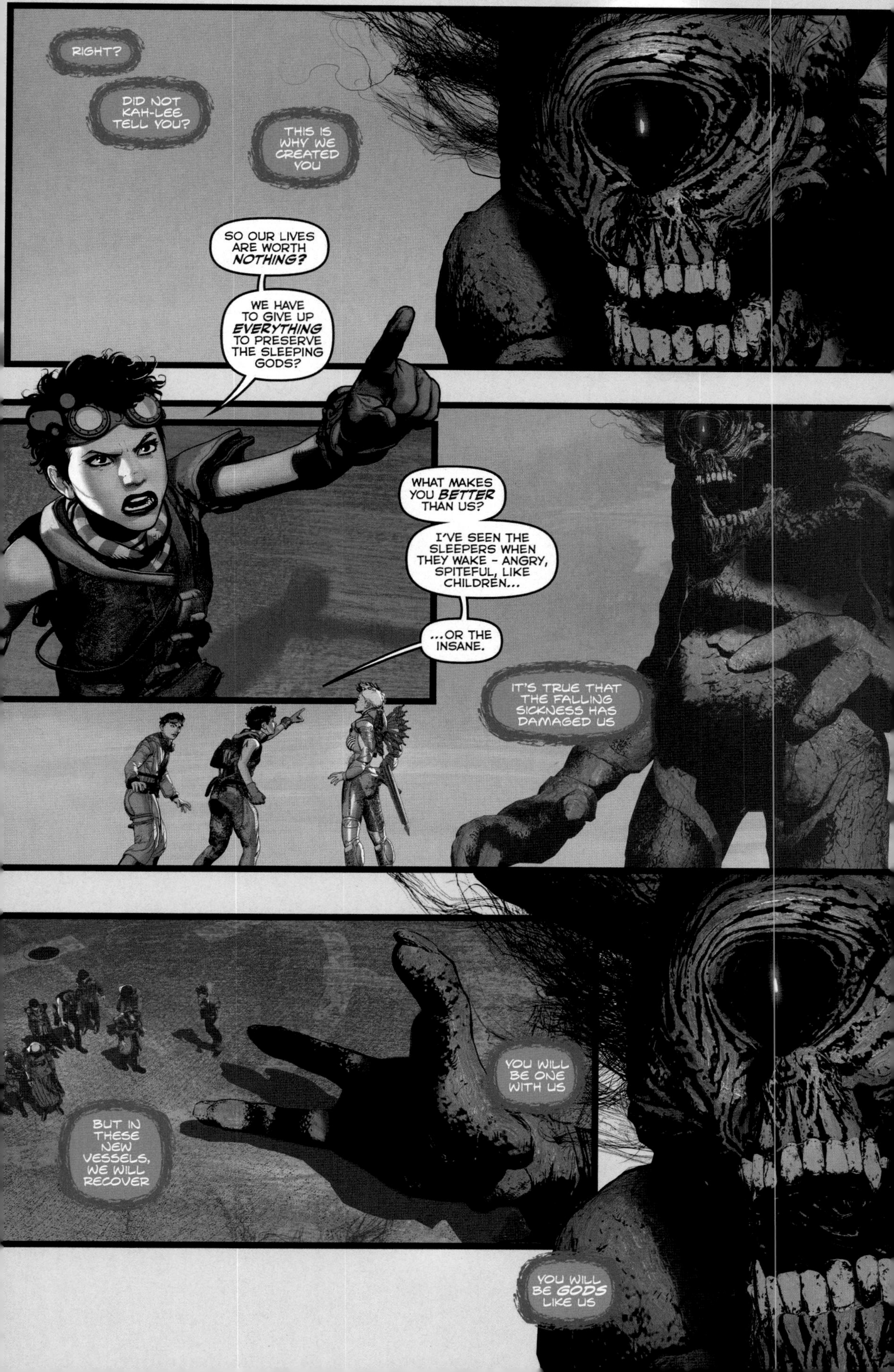
RIGHT?
DID NOT KAH-LEE TELL YOU?
THIS IS WHY WE CREATED YOU
SO OUR LIVES ARE WORTH NOTHING?
WE HAVE TO GIVE UP EVERYTHING TO PRESERVE THE SLEEPING GODS?
WHAT MAKES YOU BETTER THAN US?
I'VE SEEN THE SLEEPERS WHEN THEY WAKE - ANGRY, SPITEFUL, LIKE CHILDREN...
...OR THE INSANE.
IT'S TRUE THAT THE FALLING SICKNESS HAS DAMAGED US
BUT IN THESE NEW VESSELS, WE WILL RECOVER
YOU WILL BE ONE WITH US
YOU WILL BE GODS LIKE US

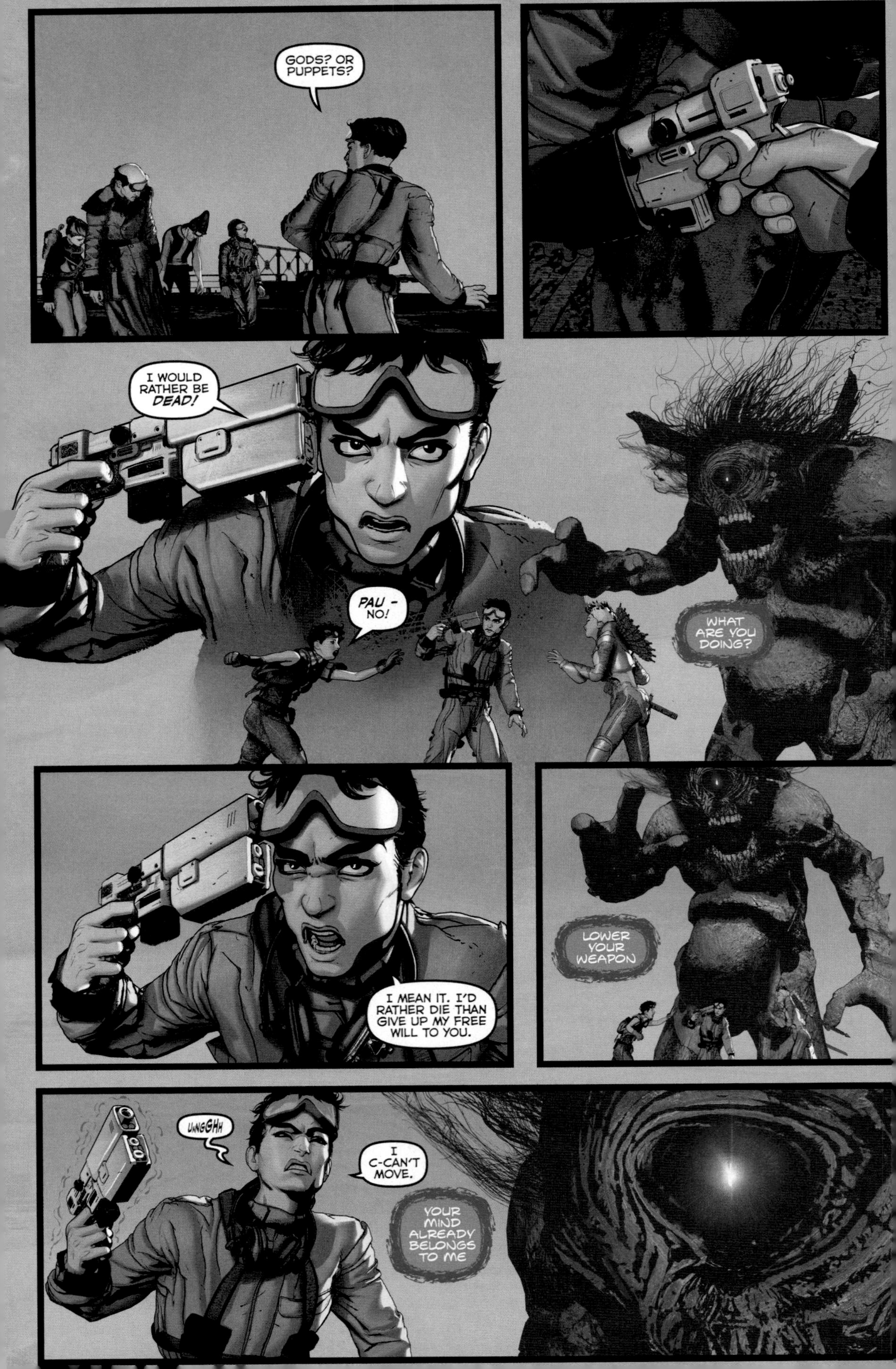
GODS? OR PUPPETS?
I WOULD RATHER BE DEAD!
PAU - NO!
WHAT ARE YOU DOING?
I MEAN IT. I'D RATHER DIE THAN GIVE UP MY FREE WILL TO YOU.
LOWER YOUR WEAPON
UNNGGHH
I C-CAN'T MOVE.
YOUR MIND ALREADY BELONGS TO ME

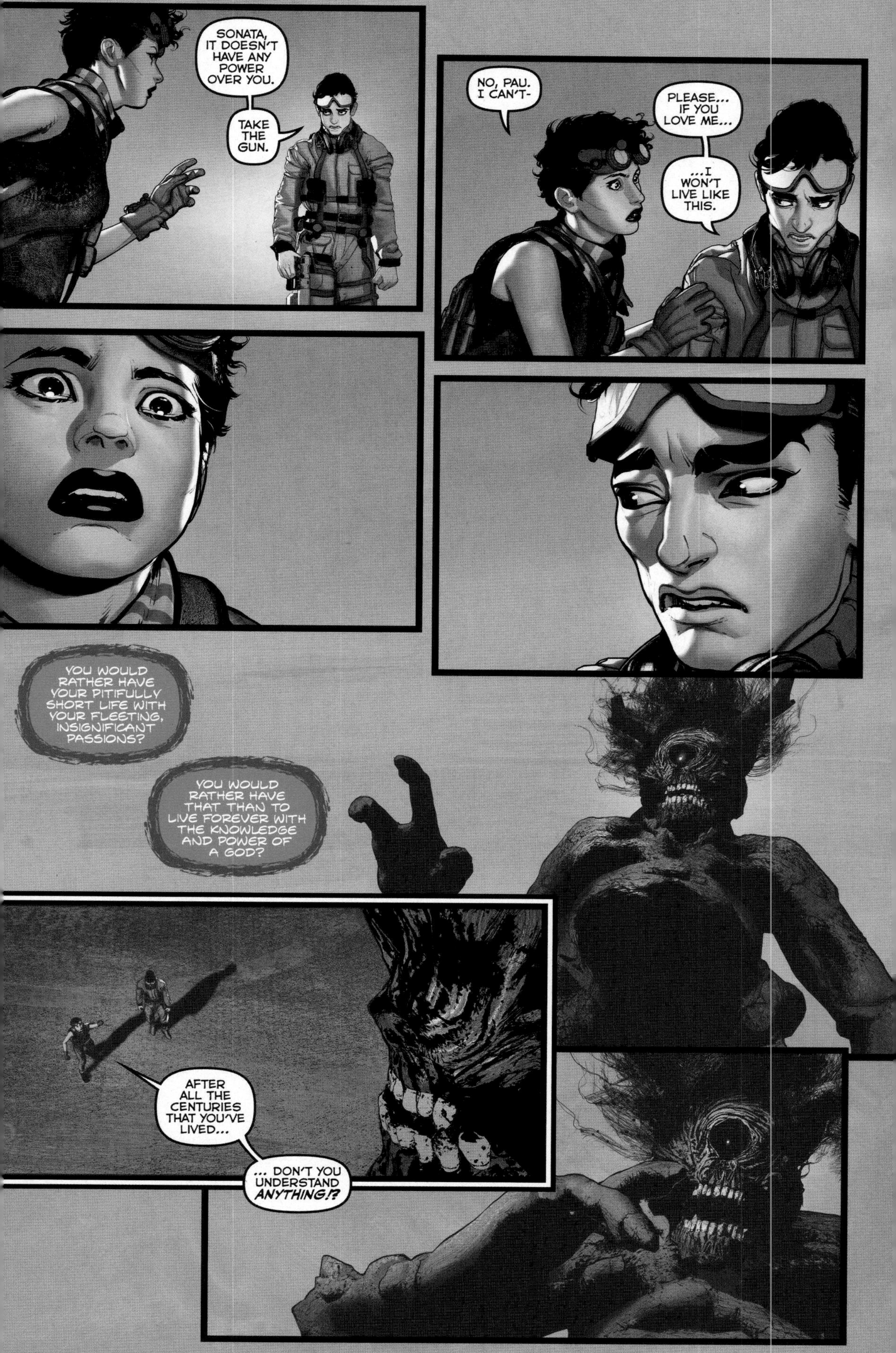
SONATA, IT DOESN'T HAVE ANY POWER OVER YOU.
TAKE THE GUN.
NO, PAU. I CAN'T-
PLEASE... IF YOU LOVE ME...
...I WON'T LIVE LIKE THIS.
YOU WOULD RATHER HAVE YOUR PITIFULLY SHORT LIFE WITH YOUR FLEETING, INSIGNIFICANT PASSIONS?
YOU WOULD RATHER HAVE THAT THAN TO LIVE FOREVER WITH THE KNOWLEDGE AND POWER OF A GOD?
AFTER ALL THE CENTURIES THAT YOU'VE LIVED...
... DON'T YOU UNDERSTAND ANYTHING!?

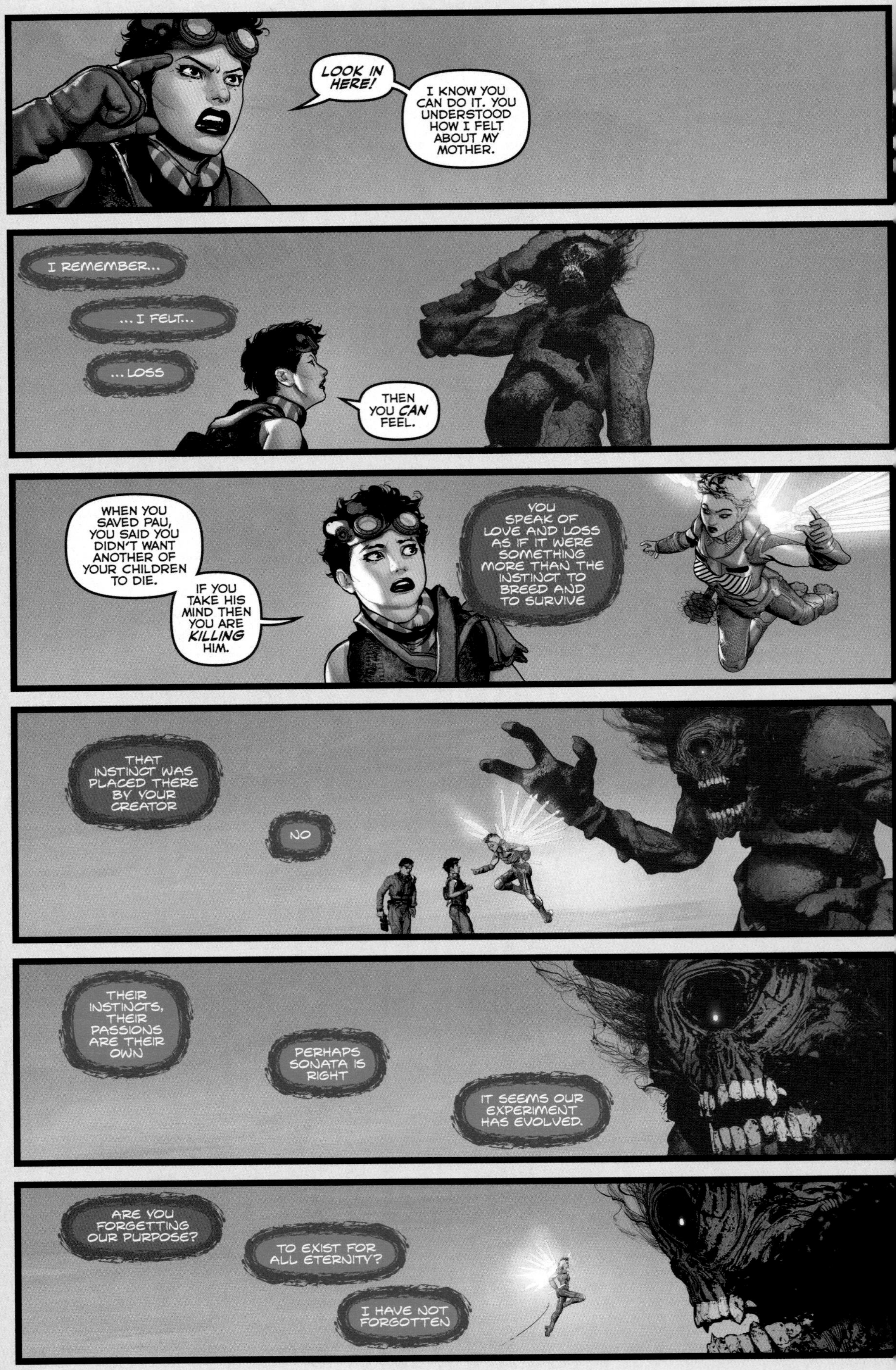
LOOK IN HERE!
I KNOW YOU CAN DO IT. YOU UNDERSTOOD HOW I FELT ABOUT MY MOTHER.
I REMEMBER...
... I FELT...
... LOSS
THEN YOU CAN FEEL.
WHEN YOU SAVED PAU, YOU SAID YOU DIDN'T WANT ANOTHER OF YOUR CHILDREN TO DIE.
IF YOU TAKE HIS MIND THEN YOU ARE KILLING HIM.
YOU SPEAK OF LOVE AND LOSS AS IF IT WERE SOMETHING MORE THAN THE INSTINCT TO BREED AND TO SURVIVE
THAT INSTINCT WAS PLACED THERE BY YOUR CREATOR
NO
THEIR INSTINCTS, THEIR PASSIONS ARE THEIR OWN
PERHAPS SONATA IS RIGHT
IT SEEMS OUR EXPERIMENT HAS EVOLVED.
ARE YOU FORGETTING OUR PURPOSE?
TO EXIST FOR ALL ETERNITY?
I HAVE NOT FORGOTTEN

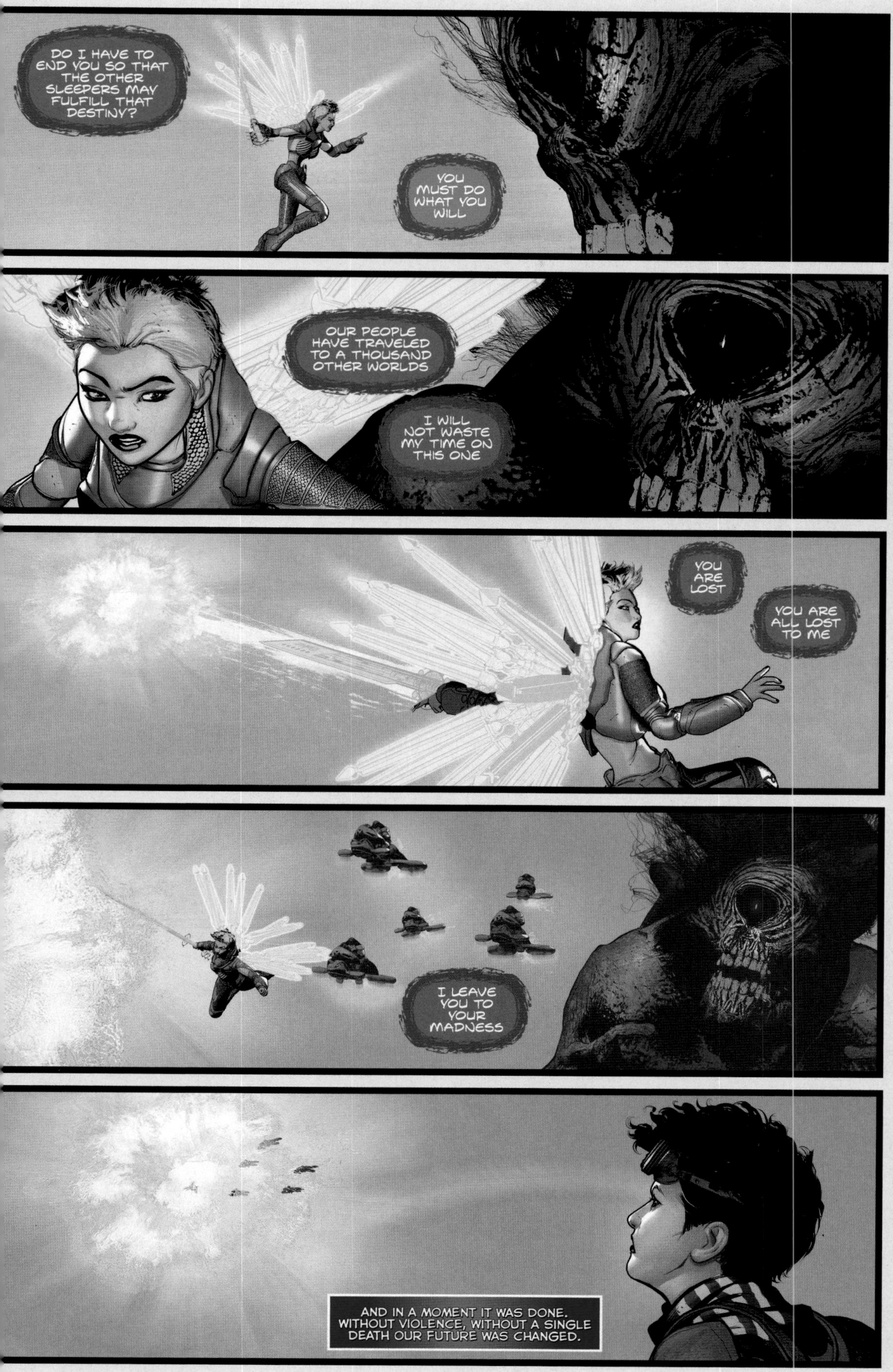
DO I HAVE TO END YOU SO THAT THE OTHER SLEEPERS MAY FULFILL THAT DESTINY?
YOU MUST DO WHAT YOU WILL
OUR PEOPLE HAVE TRAVELED TO A THOUSAND OTHER WORLDS
I WILL NOT WASTE MY TIME ON THIS ONE
YOU ARE LOST
YOU ARE ALL LOST TO ME
I LEAVE YOU TO YOUR MADNESS
AND IN A MOMENT IT WAS DONE. WITHOUT VIOLENCE, WITHOUT A SINGLE DEATH OUR FUTURE WAS CHANGED.

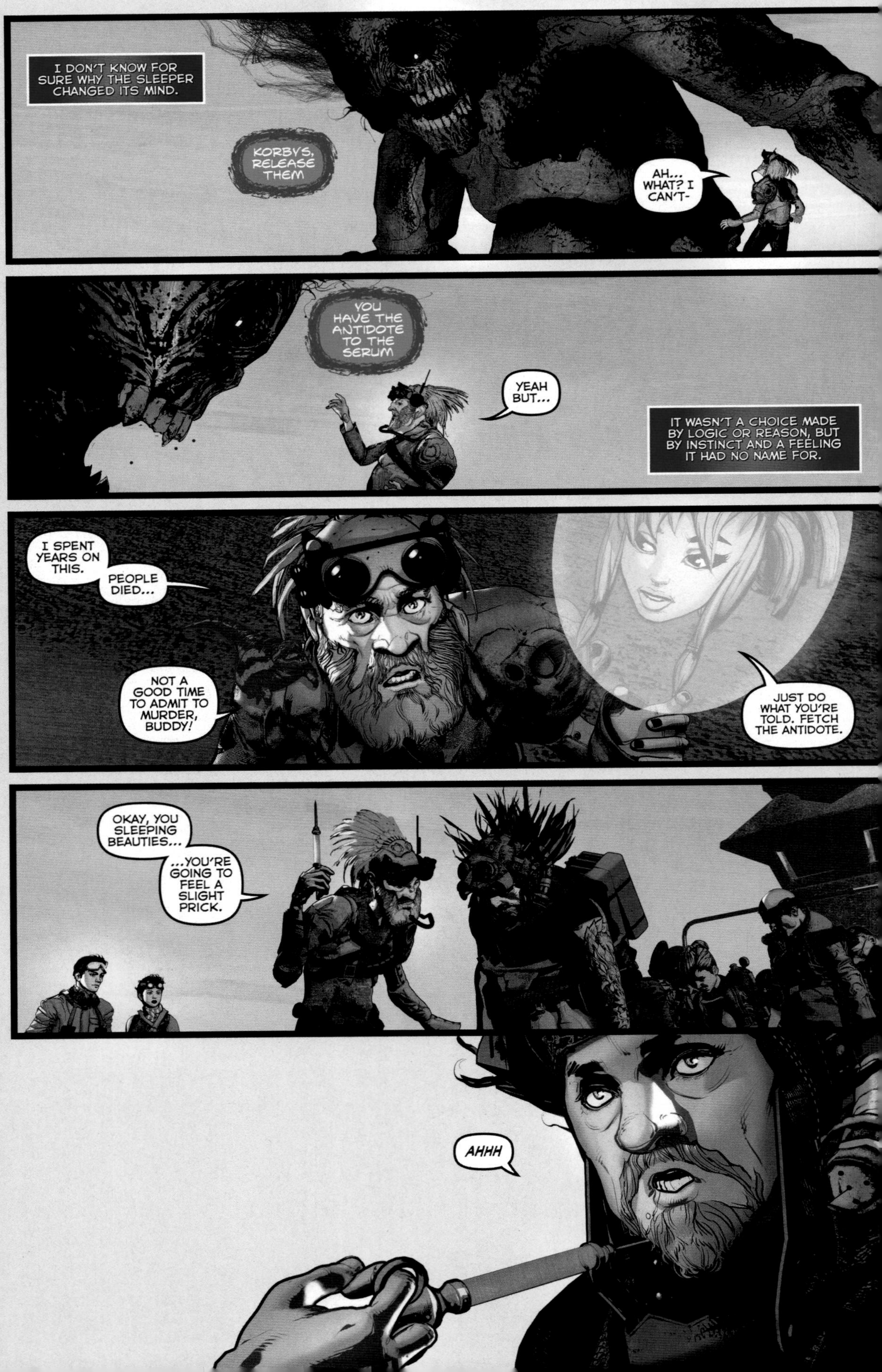
I DON'T KNOW FOR SURE WHY THE SLEEPER CHANGED ITS MIND.
KORBYS, RELEASE THEM
AH... WHAT? I CAN'T-
YOU HAVE THE ANTIDOTE TO THE SERUM
YEAH BUT...
IT WASN'T A CHOICE MADE BY LOGIC OR REASON, BUT BY INSTINCT AND A FEELING IT HAD NO NAME FOR.
I SPENT YEARS ON THIS.
PEOPLE DIED...
NOT A GOOD TIME TO ADMIT TO MURDER, BUDDY!
JUST DO WHAT YOU'RE TOLD. FETCH THE ANTIDOTE.
OKAY, YOU SLEEPING BEAUTIES...
...YOU'RE GOING TO FEEL A SLIGHT PRICK.
AHHH

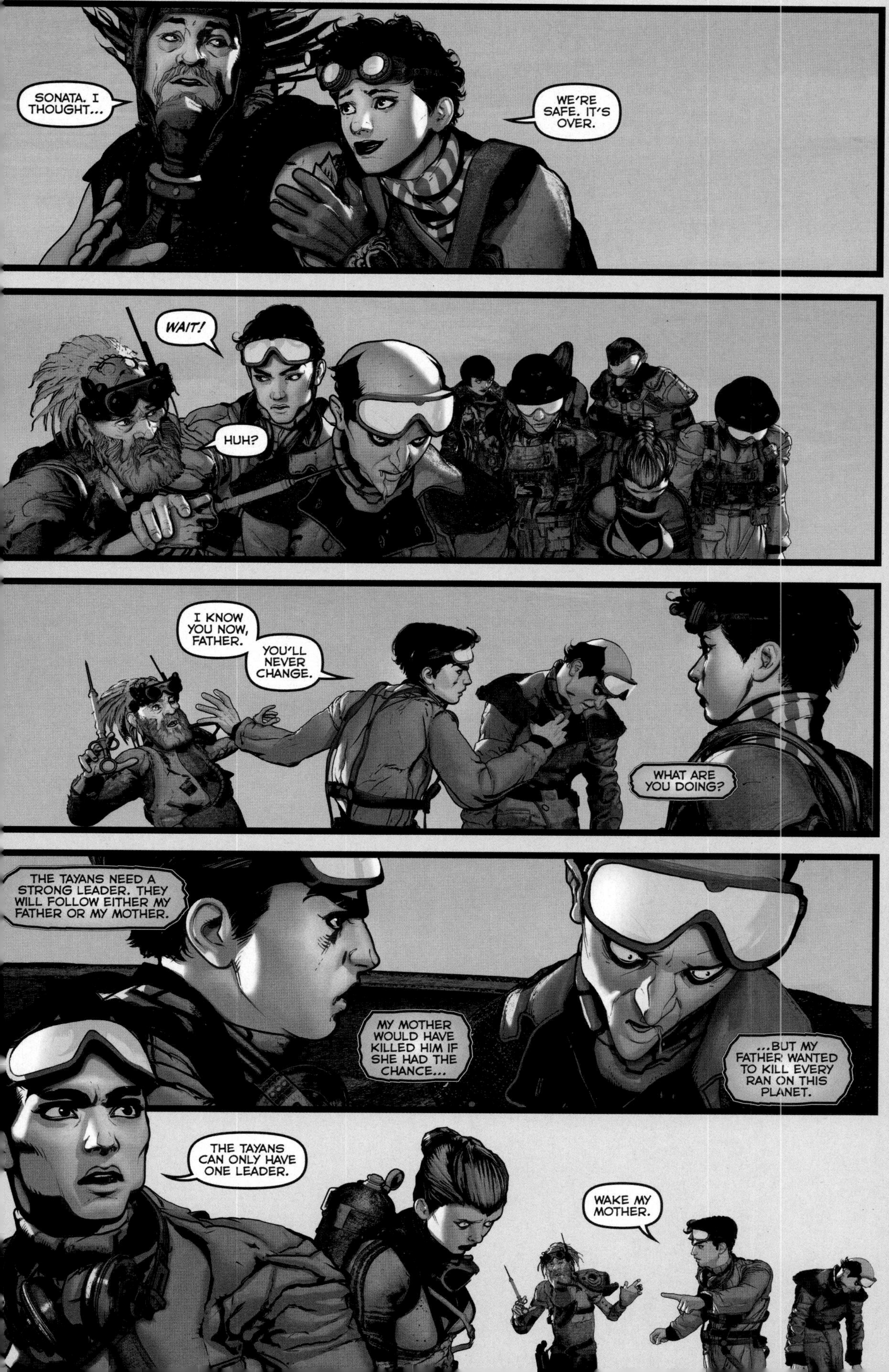
SONATA. I THOUGHT...
WE'RE SAFE. IT'S OVER.
WAIT!
HUH?
I KNOW YOU NOW, FATHER.
YOU'LL NEVER CHANGE.
WHAT ARE YOU DOING?
THE TAYANS NEED A STRONG LEADER. THEY WILL FOLLOW EITHER MY FATHER OR MY MOTHER.
MY MOTHER WOULD HAVE KILLED HIM IF SHE HAD THE CHANCE...
...BUT MY FATHER WANTED TO KILL EVERY RAN ON THIS PLANET.
THE TAYANS CAN ONLY HAVE ONE LEADER.
WAKE MY MOTHER.

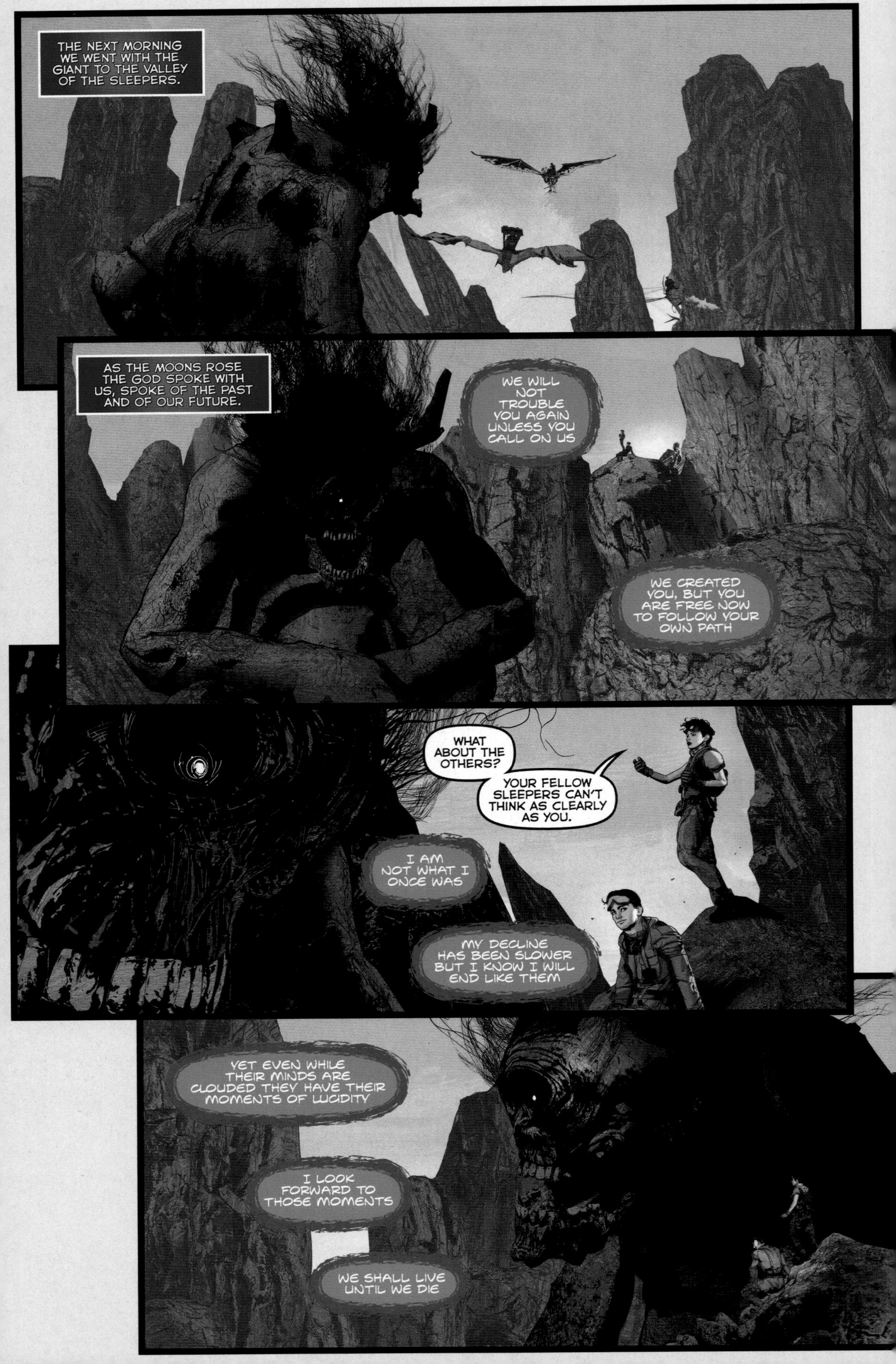
THE NEXT MORNING WE WENT WITH THE GIANT TO THE VALLEY OF THE SLEEPERS.
AS THE MOONS ROSE THE GOD SPOKE WITH US, SPOKE OF THE PAST AND OF OUR FUTURE.
WE WILL NOT TROUBLE YOU AGAIN UNLESS YOU CALL ON US
WE CREATED YOU, BUT YOU ARE FREE NOW TO FOLLOW YOUR OWN PATH
WHAT ABOUT THE OTHERS?
YOUR FELLOW SLEEPERS CAN'T THINK AS CLEARLY AS YOU.
I AM NOT WHAT I ONCE WAS
MY DECLINE HAS BEEN SLOWER BUT I KNOW I WILL END LIKE THEM
YET EVEN WHILE THEIR MINDS ARE CLOUDED THEY HAVE THEIR MOMENTS OF LUCIDITY
I LOOK FORWARD TO THOSE MOMENTS
WE SHALL LIVE UNTIL WE DIE

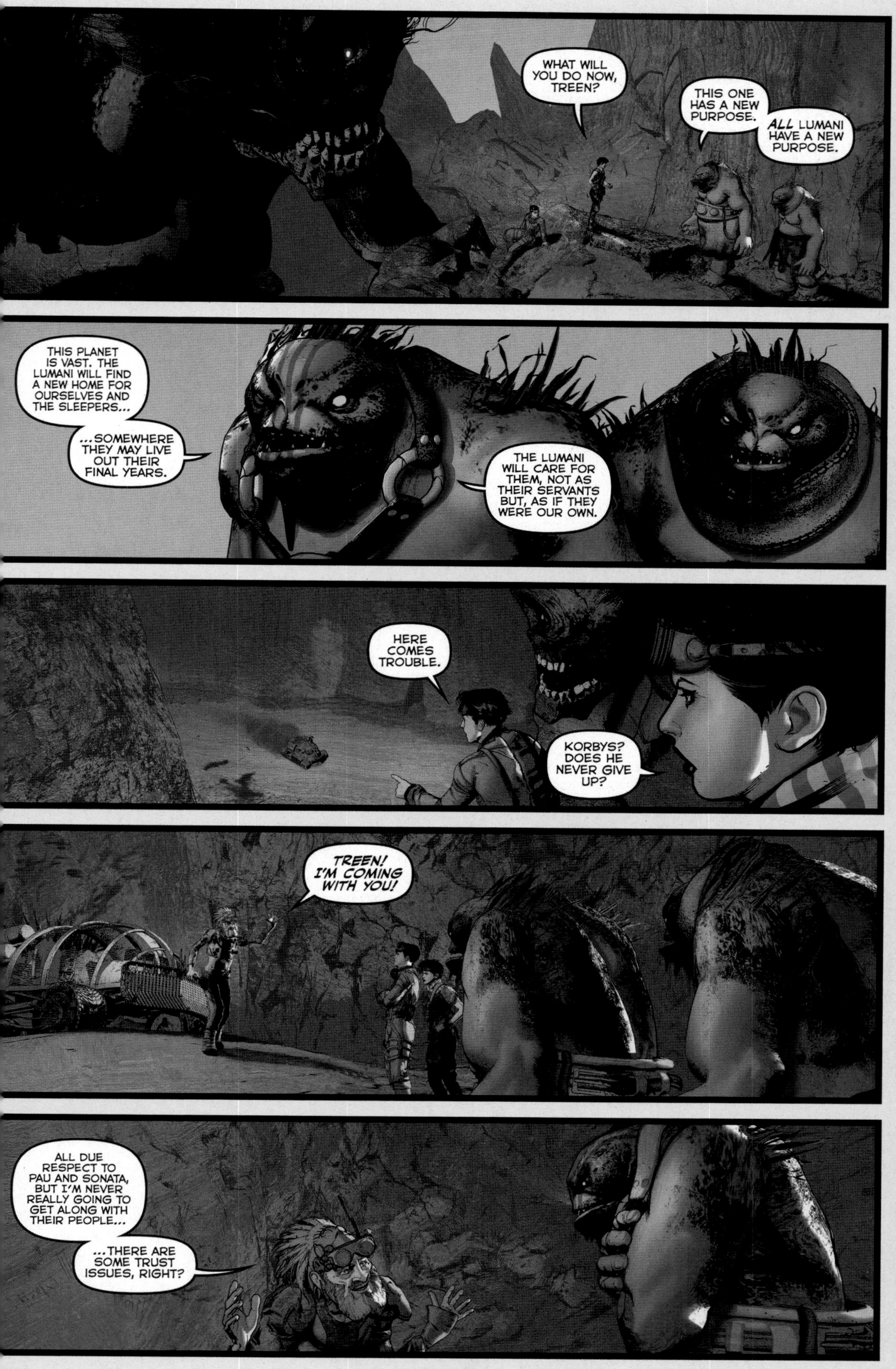
WHAT WILL YOU DO NOW, TREEN?
THIS ONE HAS A NEW PURPOSE.
ALL LUMANI HAVE A NEW PURPOSE.
THIS PLANET IS VAST. THE LUMANI WILL FIND A NEW HOME FOR OURSELVES AND THE SLEEPERS...
...SOMEWHERE THEY MAY LIVE OUT THEIR FINAL YEARS.
THE LUMANI WILL CARE FOR THEM, NOT AS THEIR SERVANTS BUT, AS IF THEY WERE OUR OWN.
HERE COMES TROUBLE.
KORBYS? DOES HE NEVER GIVE UP?
TREEN! I'M COMING WITH YOU!
ALL DUE RESPECT TO PAU AND SONATA, BUT I'M NEVER REALLY GOING TO GET ALONG WITH THEIR PEOPLE...
...THERE ARE SOME TRUST ISSUES, RIGHT?

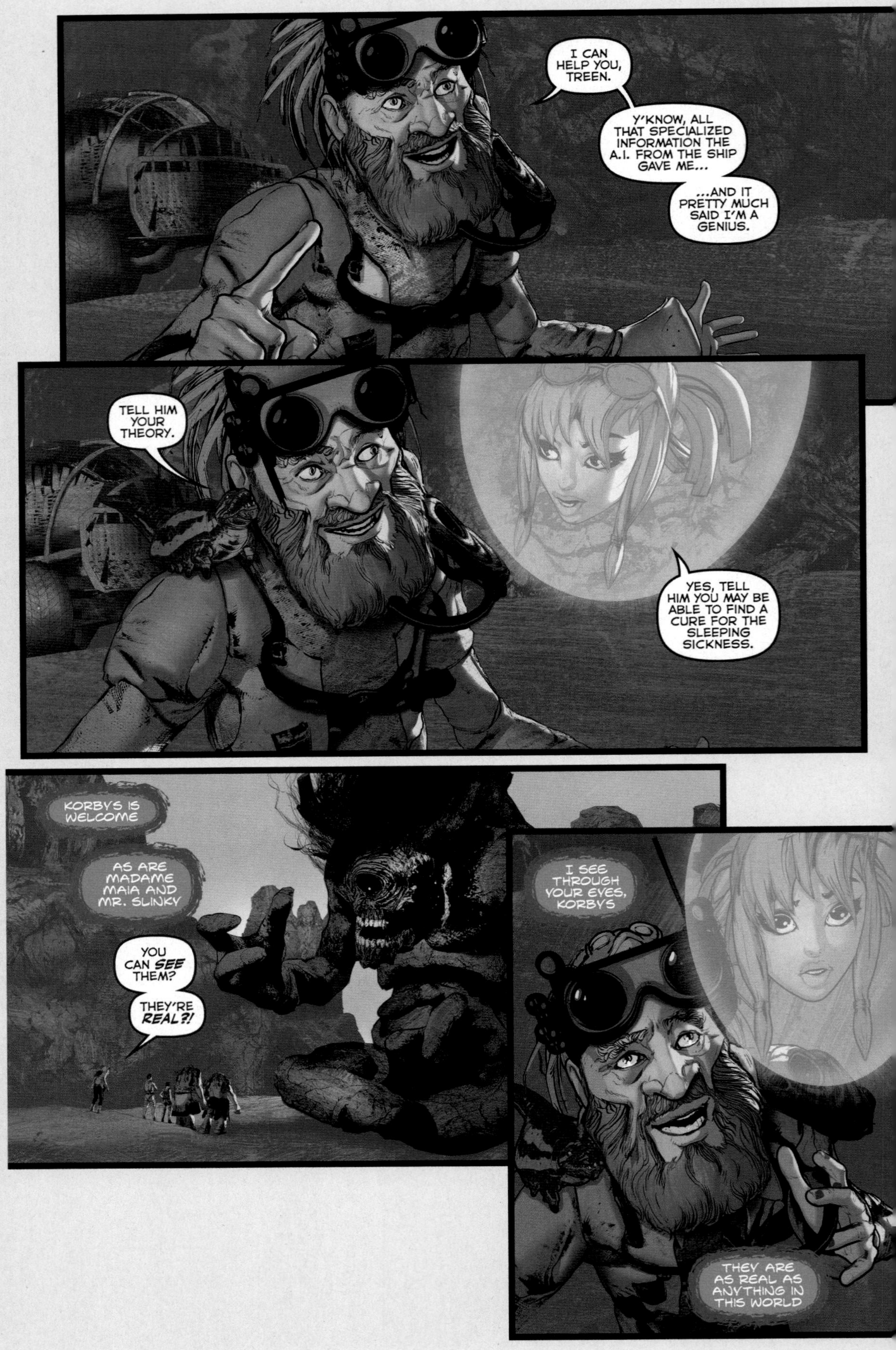
I CAN HELP YOU, TREEN.
Y'KNOW, ALL THAT SPECIALIZED INFORMATION THE A.I. FROM THE SHIP GAVE ME...
...AND IT PRETTY MUCH SAID I'M A GENIUS.
TELL HIM YOUR THEORY.
YES, TELL HIM YOU MAY BE ABLE TO FIND A CURE FOR THE SLEEPING SICKNESS.
KORBYS IS WELCOME
AS ARE MADAME MAIA AND MR. SLINKY
YOU CAN SEE THEM?
THEY'RE REAL?!
I SEE THROUGH YOUR EYES, KORBYS
THEY ARE AS REAL AS ANYTHING IN THIS WORLD

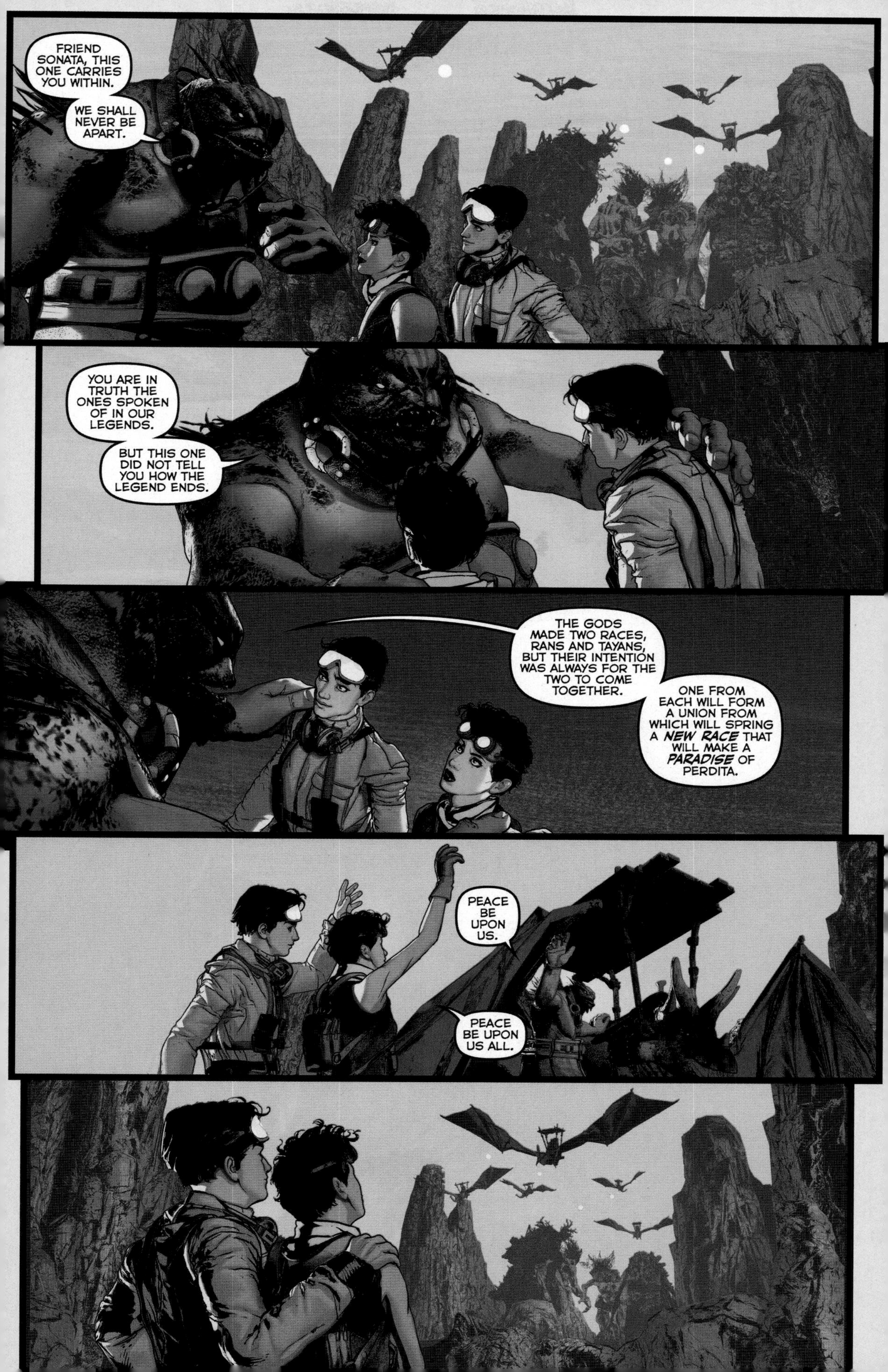
FRIEND SONATA, THIS ONE CARRIES YOU WITHIN.
WE SHALL NEVER BE APART.
YOU ARE IN TRUTH THE ONES SPOKEN OF IN OUR LEGENDS.
BUT THIS ONE DID NOT TELL YOU HOW THE LEGEND ENDS.
THE GODS MADE TWO RACES, RANS AND TAYANS, BUT THEIR INTENTION WAS ALWAYS FOR THE TWO TO COME TOGETHER.
ONE FROM EACH WILL FORM A UNION FROM WHICH WILL SPRING A *NEW RACE* THAT WILL MAKE A *PARADISE* OF PERDITA.
PEACE BE UPON US.
PEACE BE UPON US ALL.

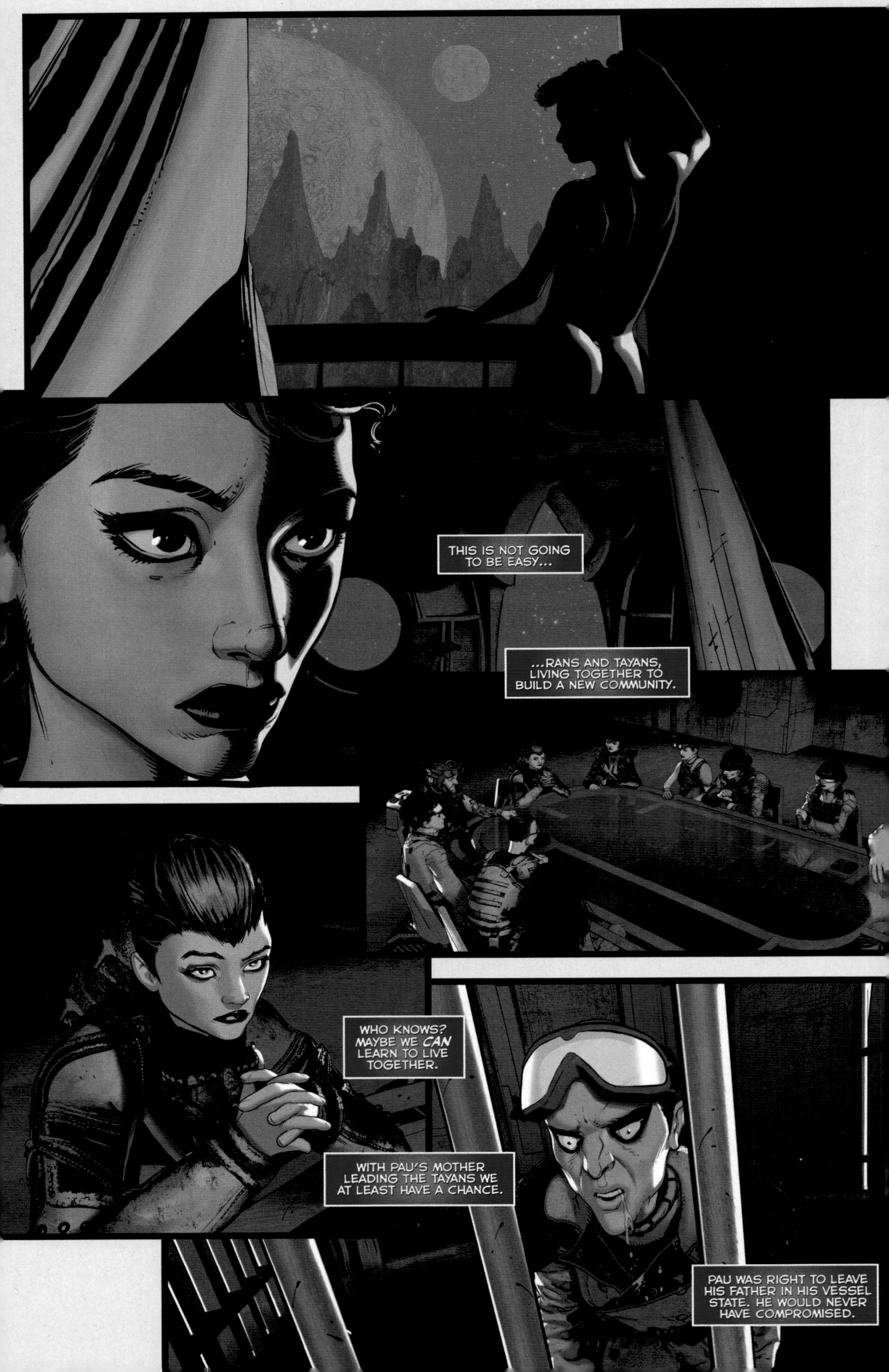
THIS IS NOT GOING TO BE EASY...
...RANS AND TAYANS, LIVING TOGETHER TO BUILD A NEW COMMUNITY.
WHO KNOWS? MAYBE WE CAN LEARN TO LIVE TOGETHER.
WITH PAU'S MOTHER LEADING THE TAYANS WE AT LEAST HAVE A CHANCE.
PAU WAS RIGHT TO LEAVE HIS FATHER IN HIS VESSEL STATE. HE WOULD NEVER HAVE COMPROMISED.

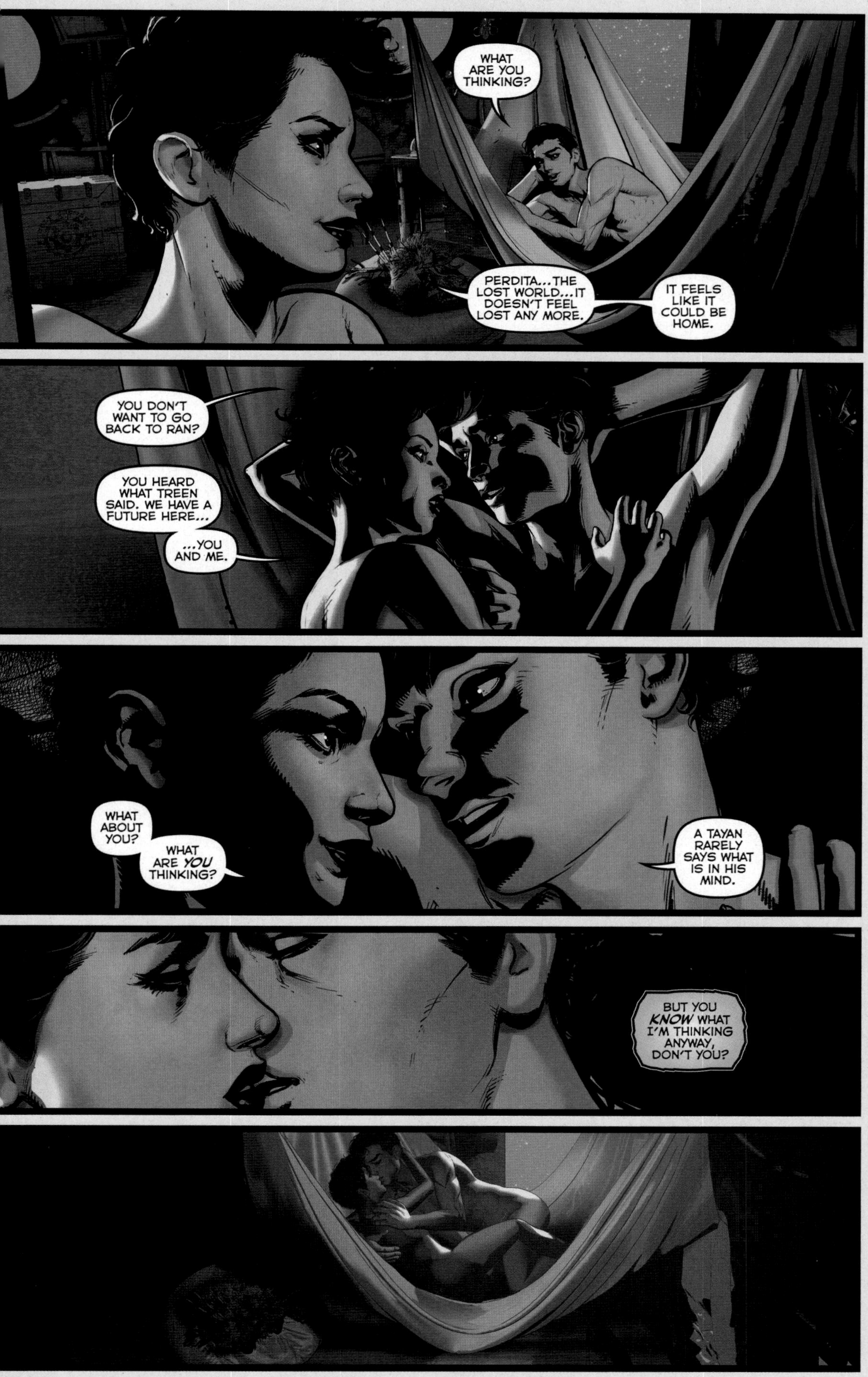
WHAT ARE YOU THINKING?
PERDITA...THE LOST WORLD...IT DOESN'T FEEL LOST ANY MORE.
IT FEELS LIKE IT COULD BE HOME.
YOU DON'T WANT TO GO BACK TO RAN?
YOU HEARD WHAT TREEN SAID. WE HAVE A FUTURE HERE...
...YOU AND ME.
WHAT ABOUT YOU?
WHAT ARE *YOU* THINKING?
A TAYAN RARELY SAYS WHAT IS IN HIS MIND.
BUT YOU ***KNOW*** WHAT I'M THINKING ANYWAY, DON'T YOU?

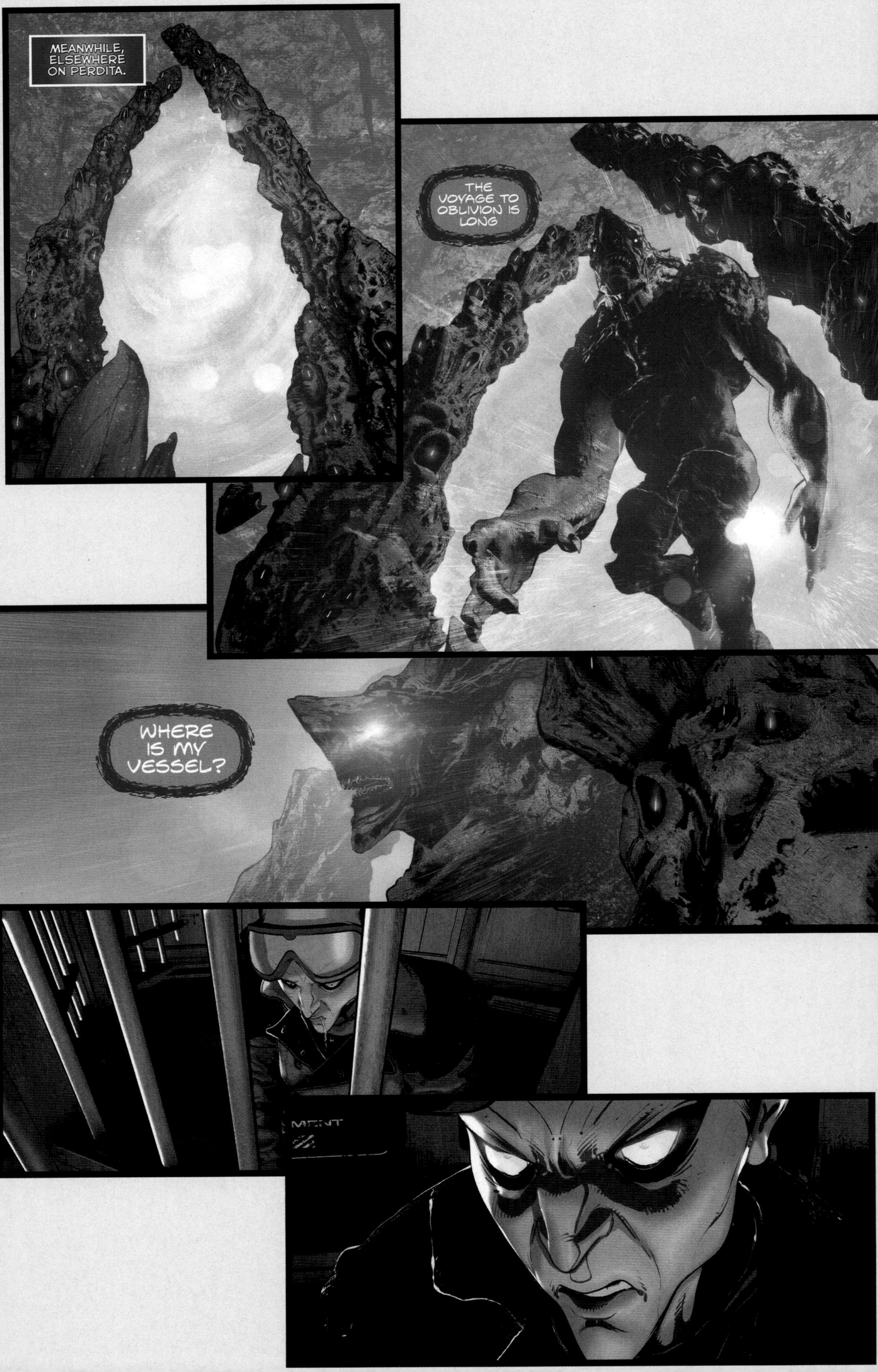
MEANWHILE, ELSEWHERE ON PERDITA.
THE VOYAGE TO OBLIVION IS LONG
WHERE IS MY VESSEL?

Issue #12 Cover

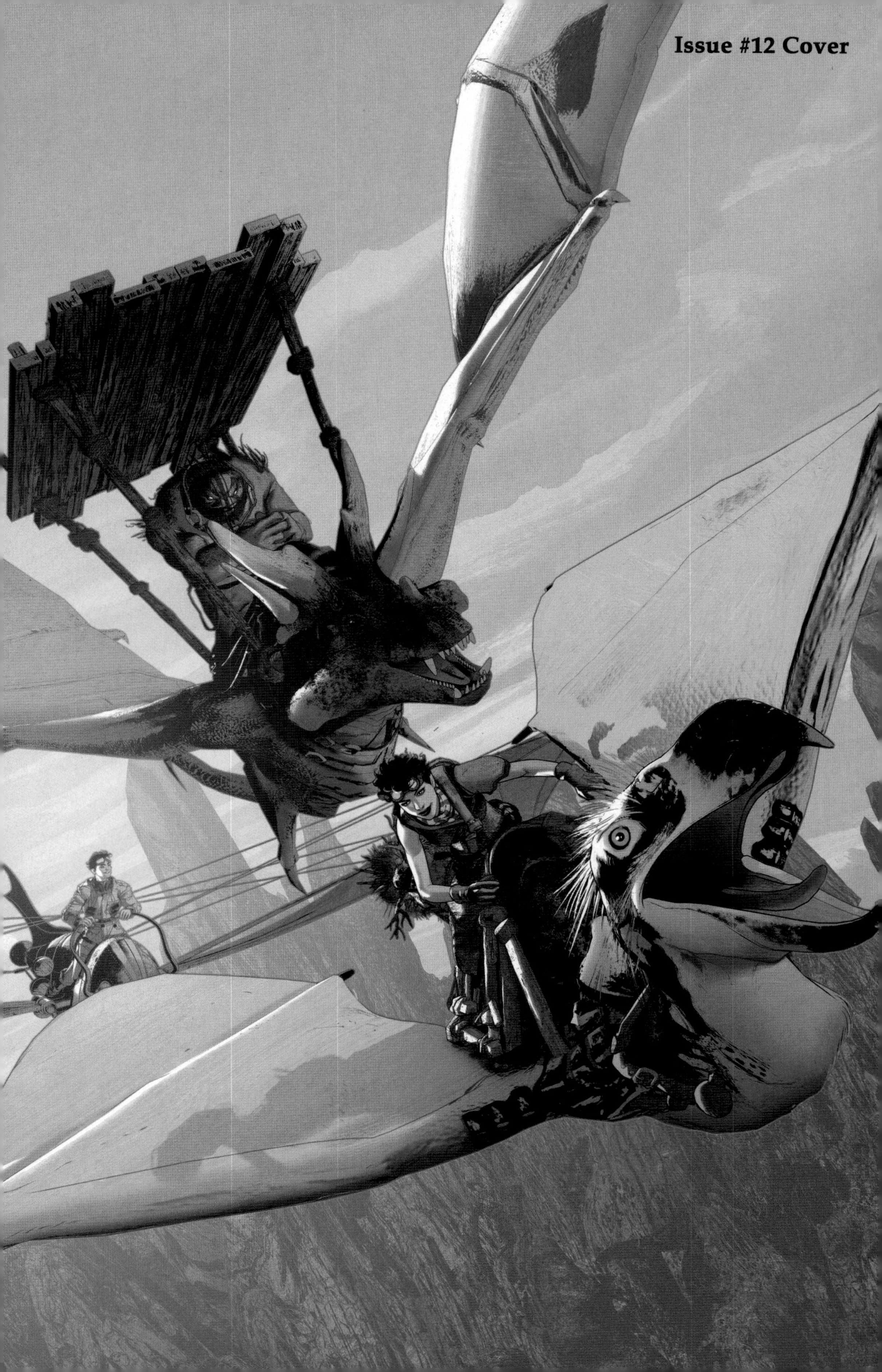

Unpublished art for SONATA TV pitch

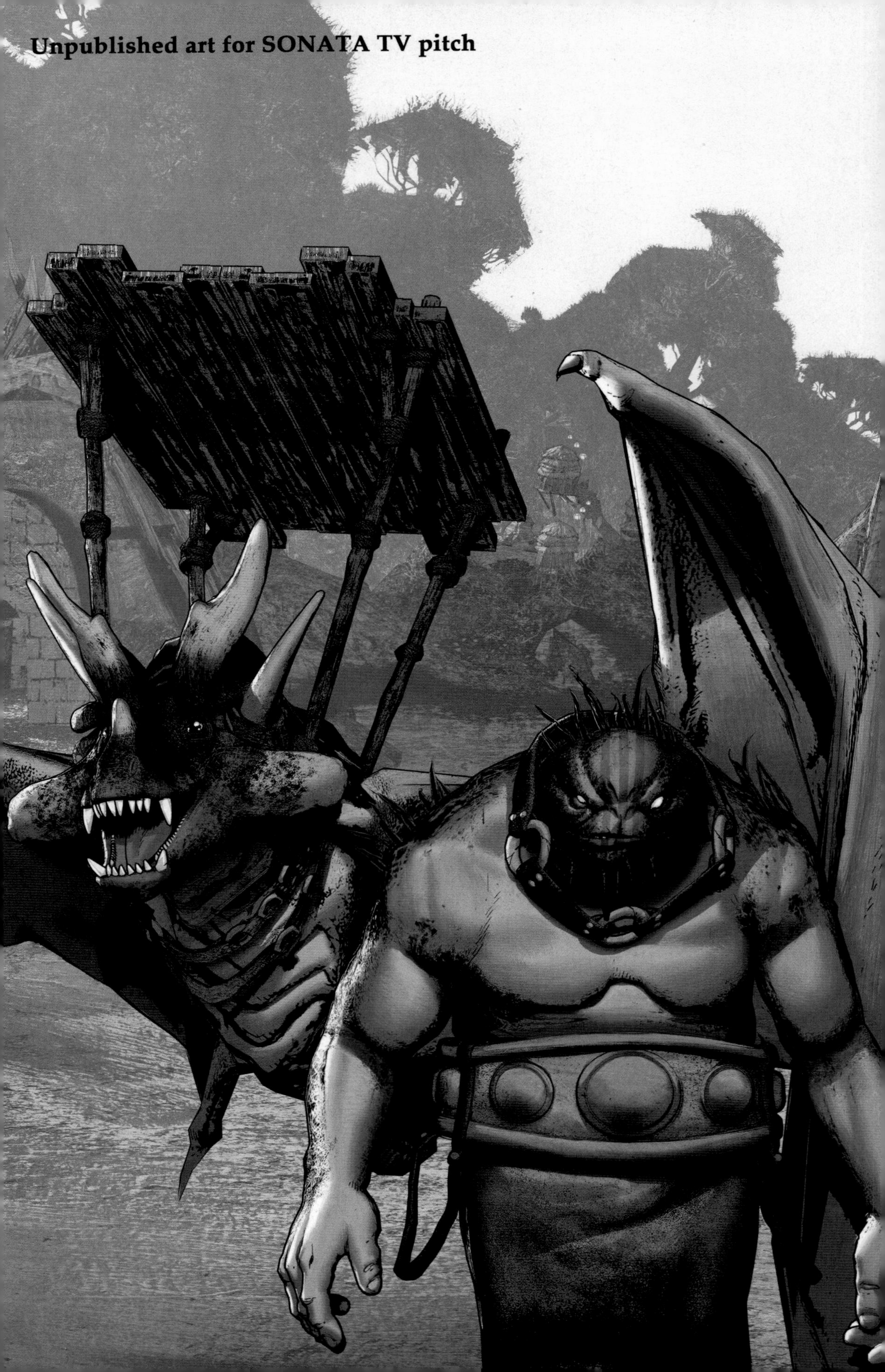

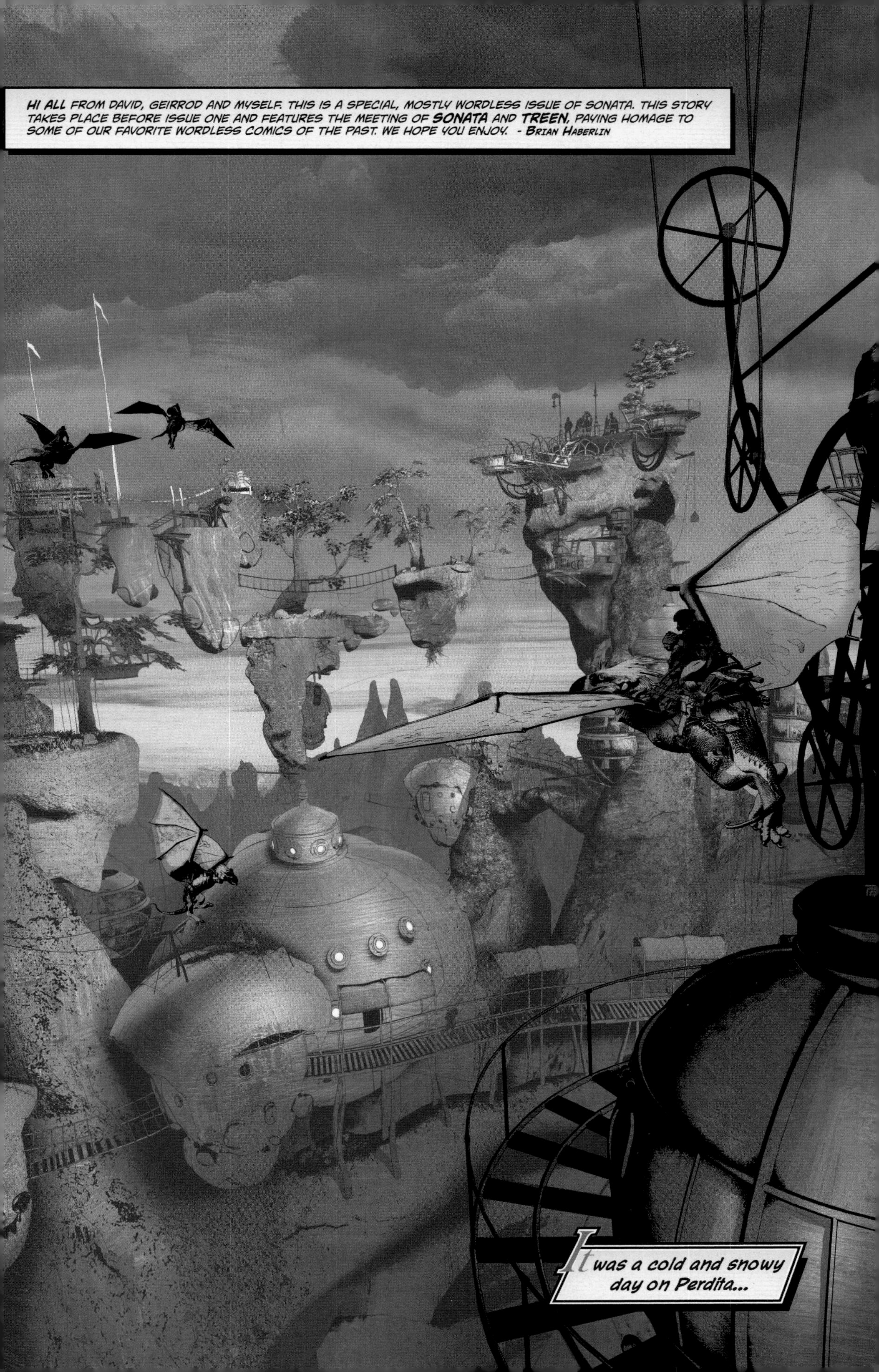
HI ALL FROM DAVID, GEIRROD AND MYSELF. THIS IS A SPECIAL, MOSTLY WORDLESS ISSUE OF SONATA. THIS STORY TAKES PLACE BEFORE ISSUE ONE AND FEATURES THE MEETING OF SONATA AND TREEN, PAYING HOMAGE TO SOME OF OUR FAVORITE WORDLESS COMICS OF THE PAST. WE HOPE YOU ENJOY. - BRIAN HABERLIN
It was a cold and snowy day on Perdita...

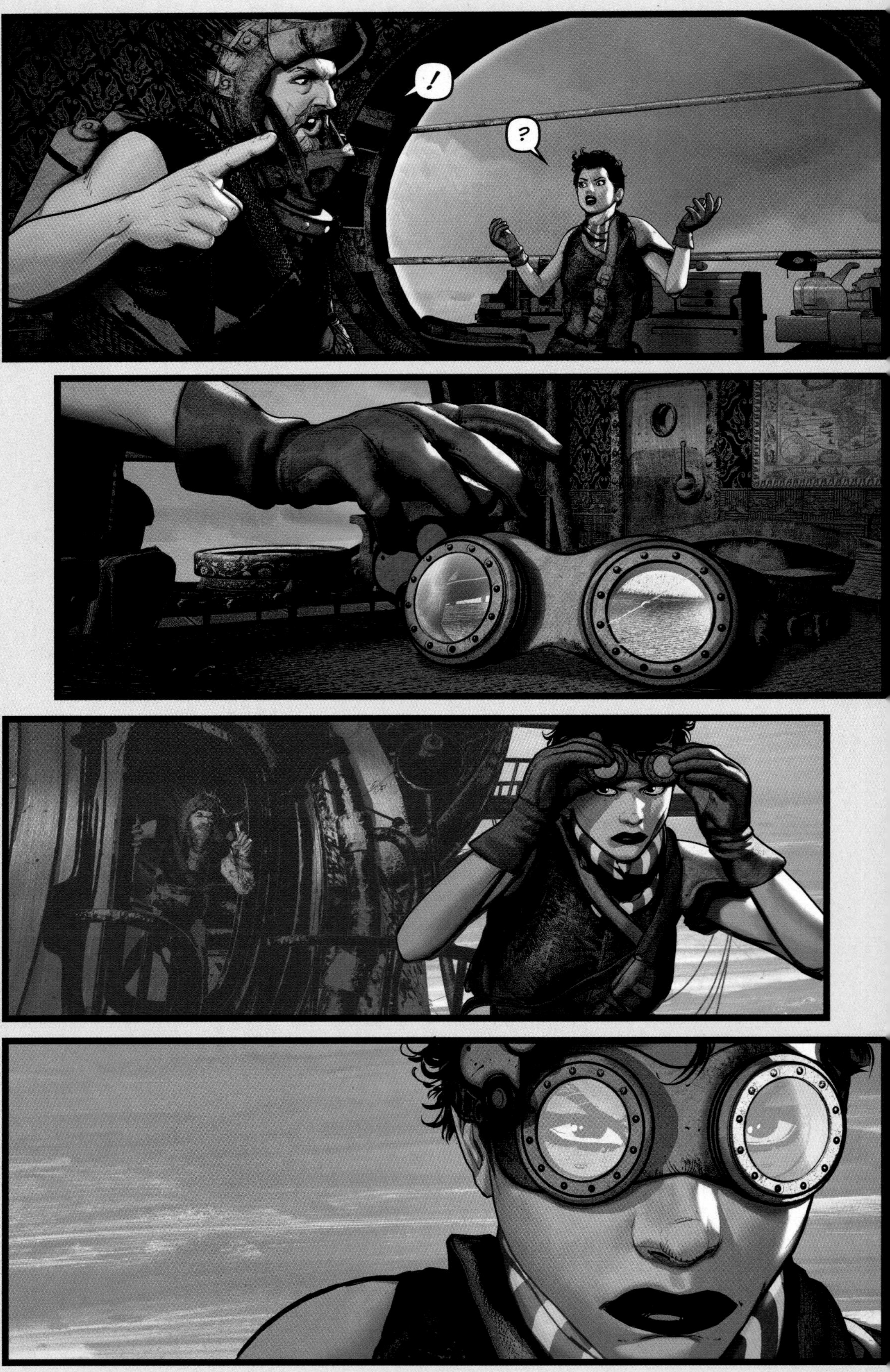
!
?

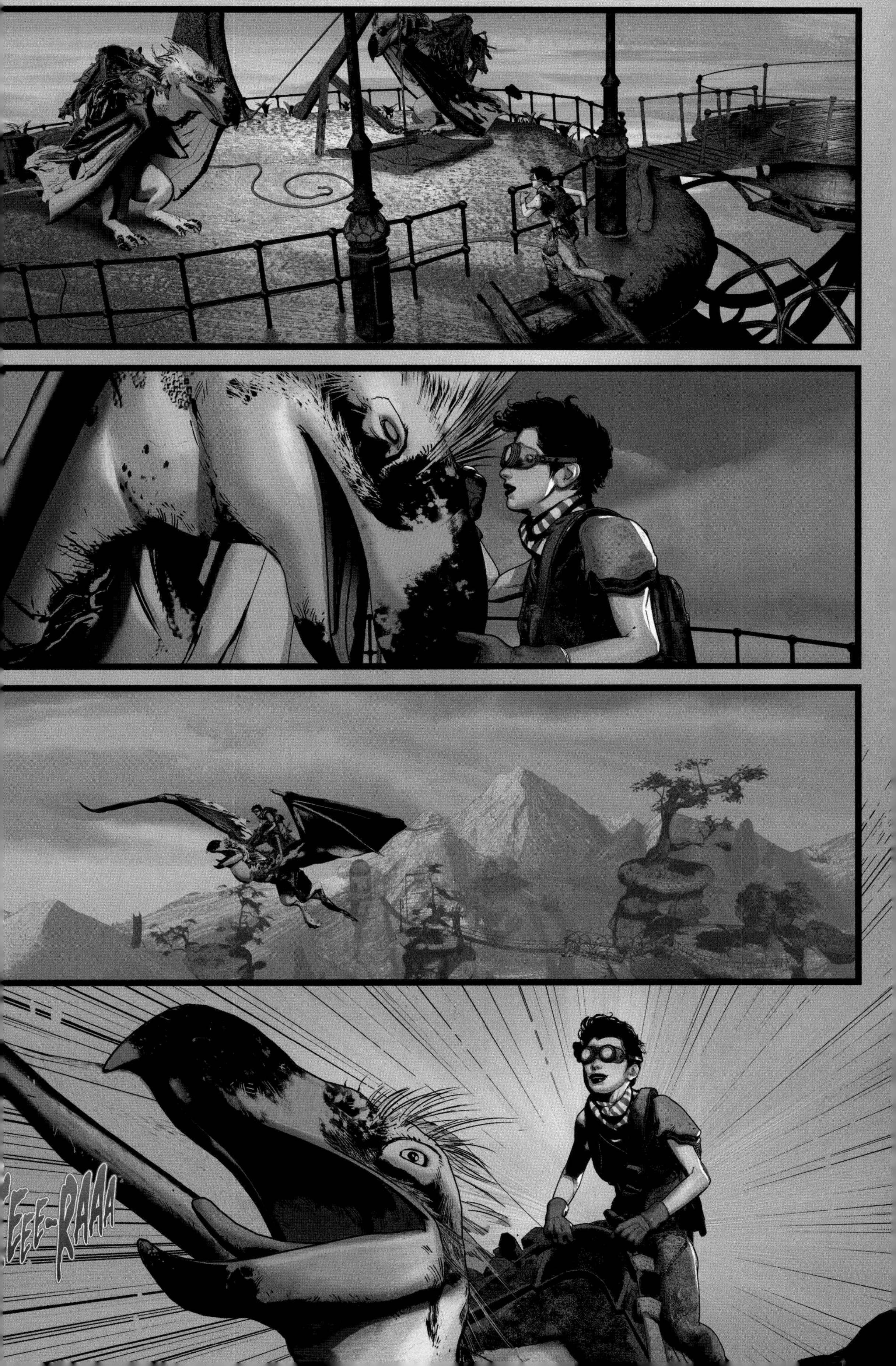
EEE-RAAA

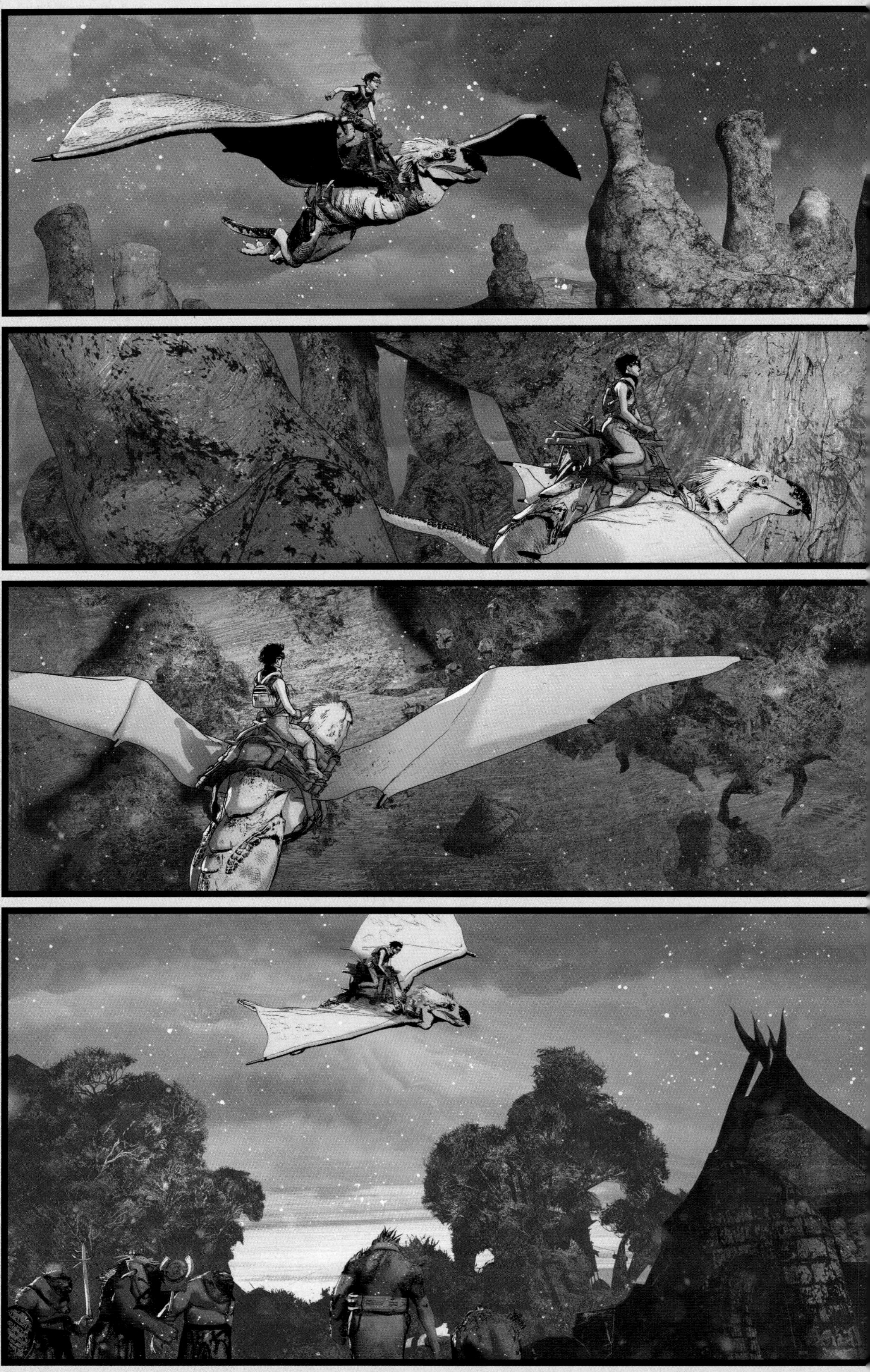

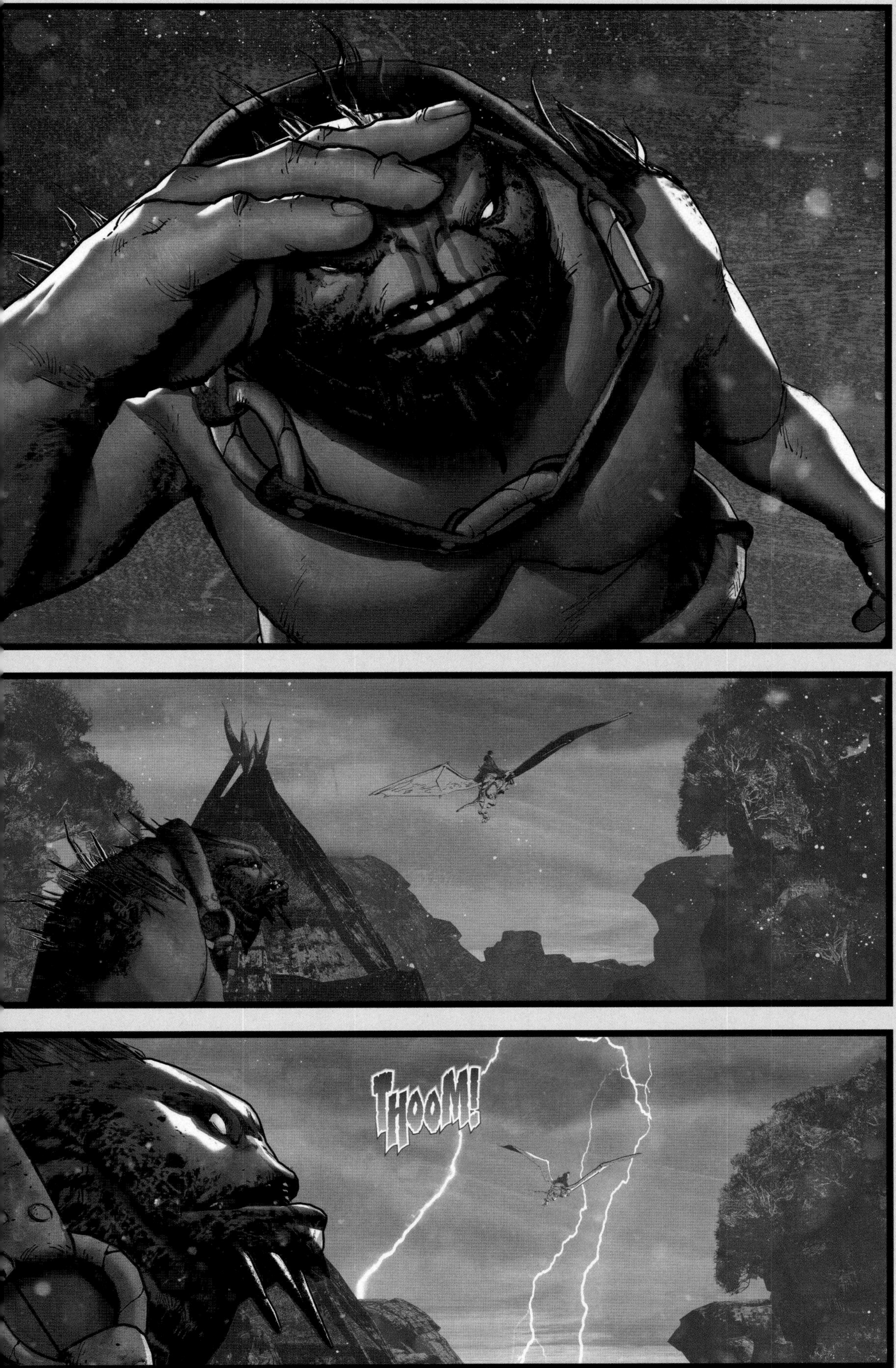
THOOM!

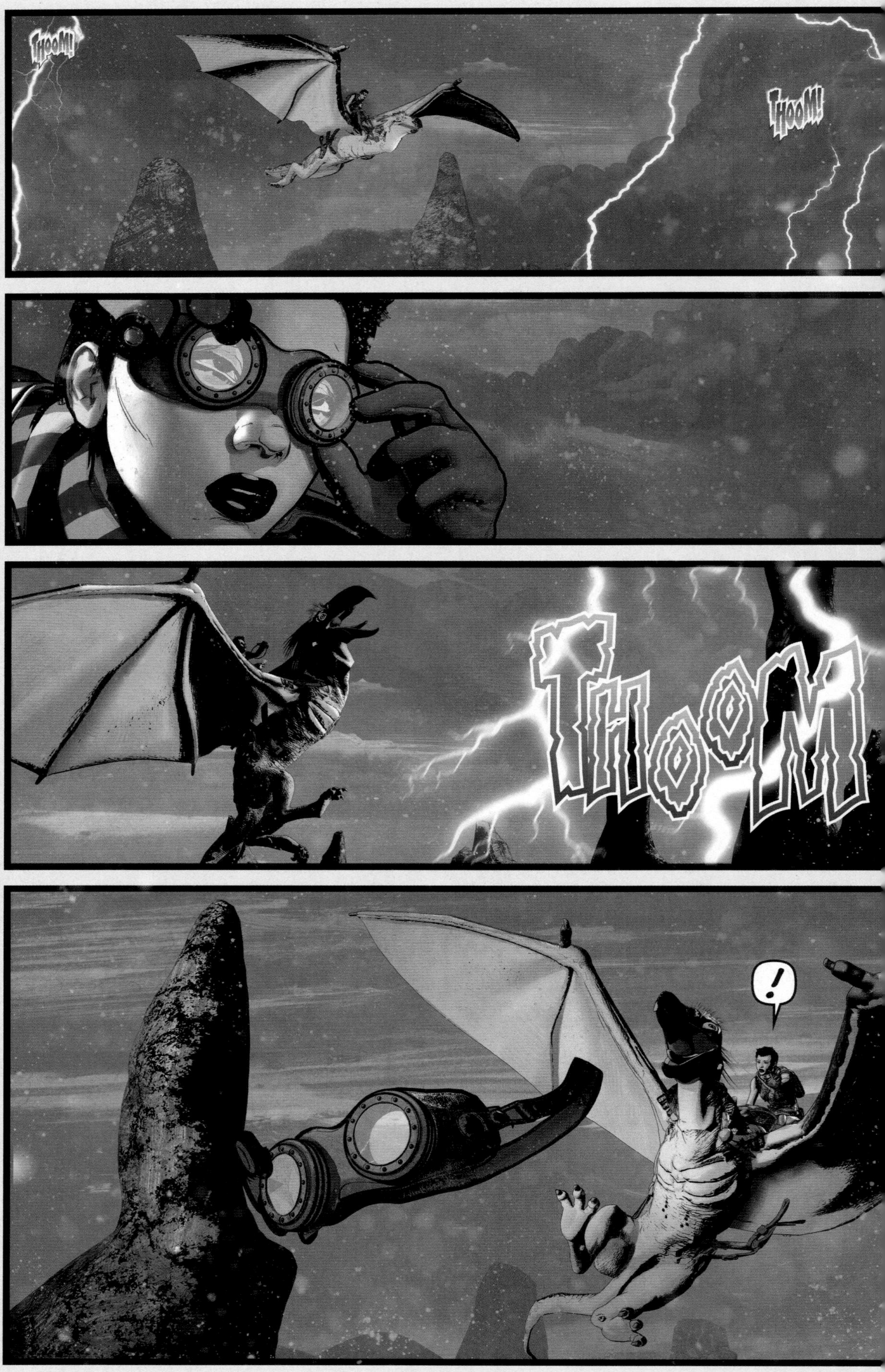
THOOM!
THOOM!
THOOM
!

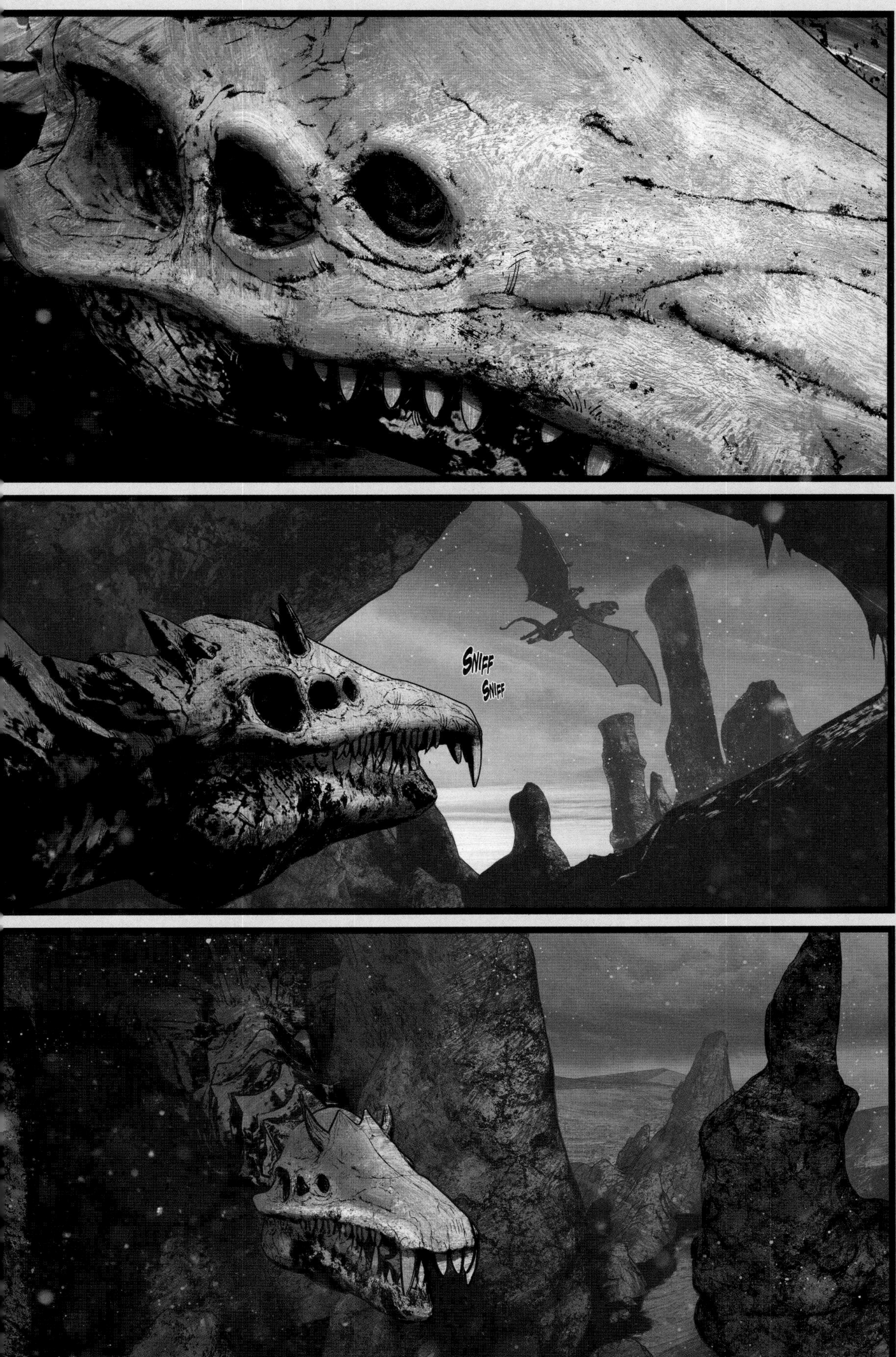
SNIFF
SNIFF

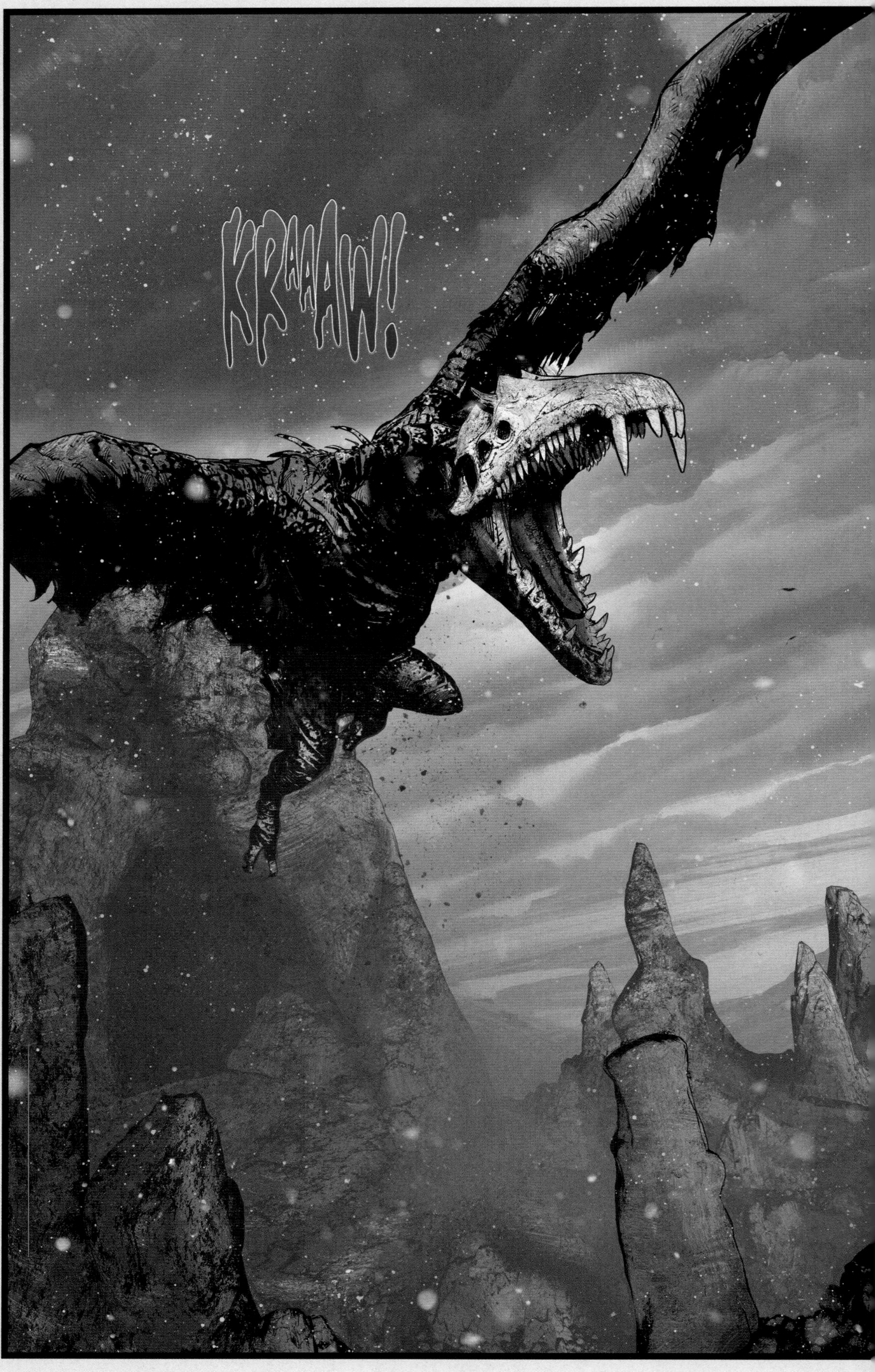
KRAAAW!

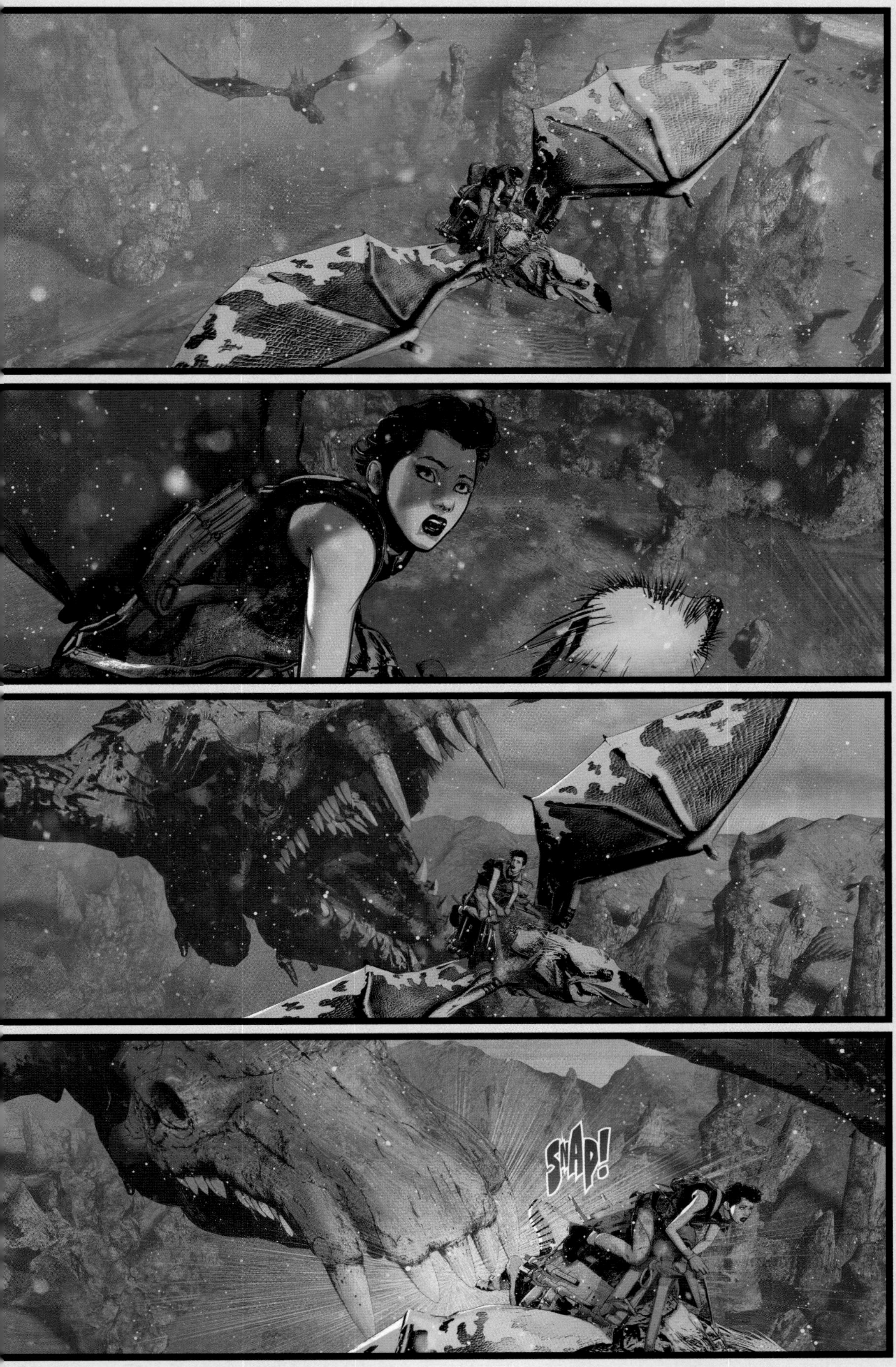
SNAP!

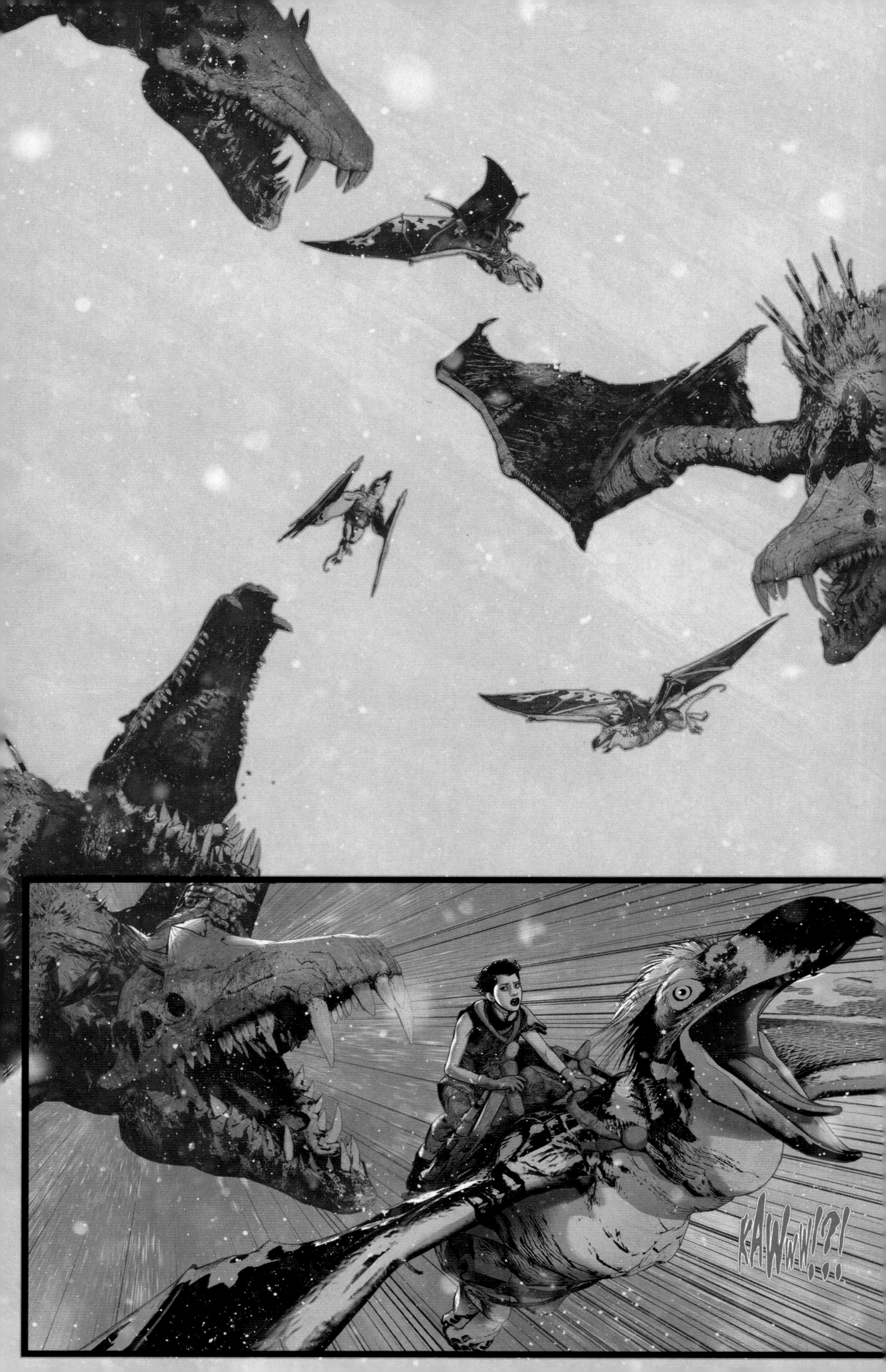
KAWwww!?!

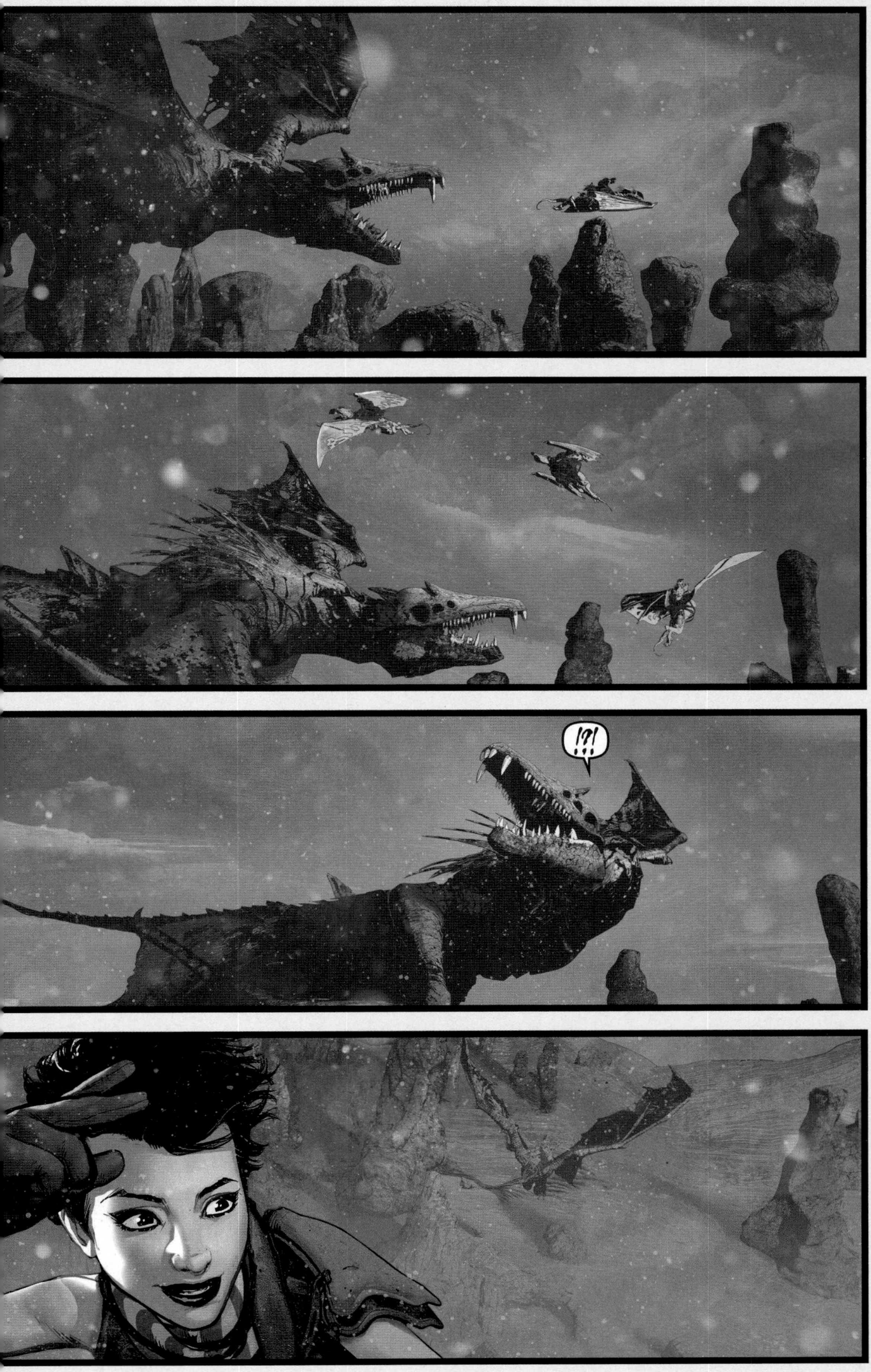
!?!

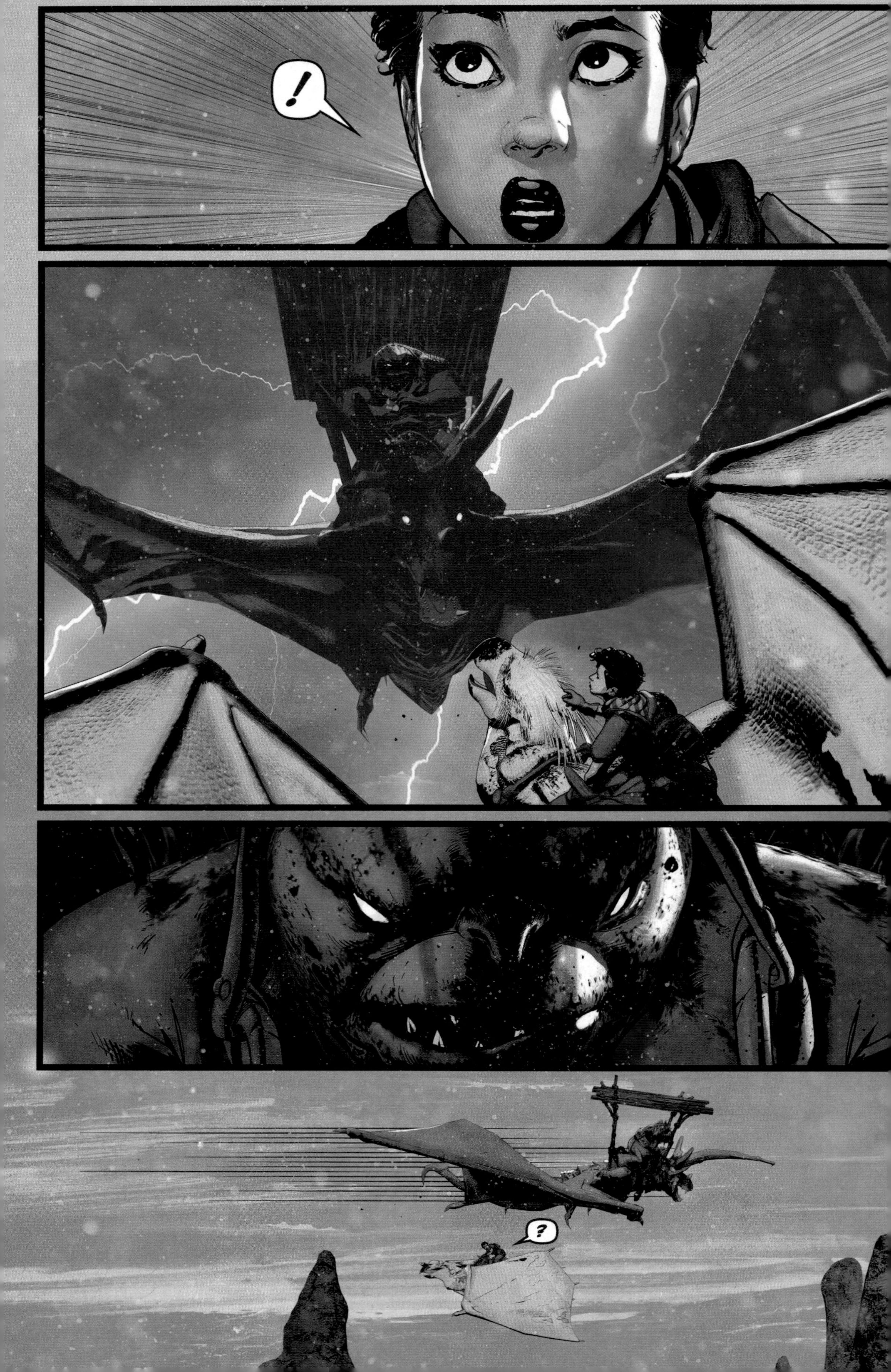
!
?

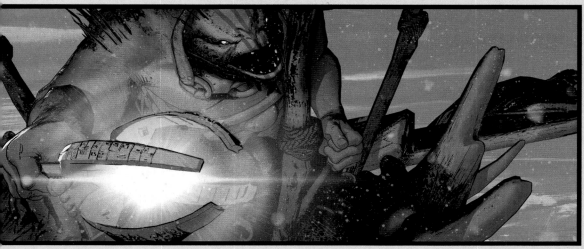

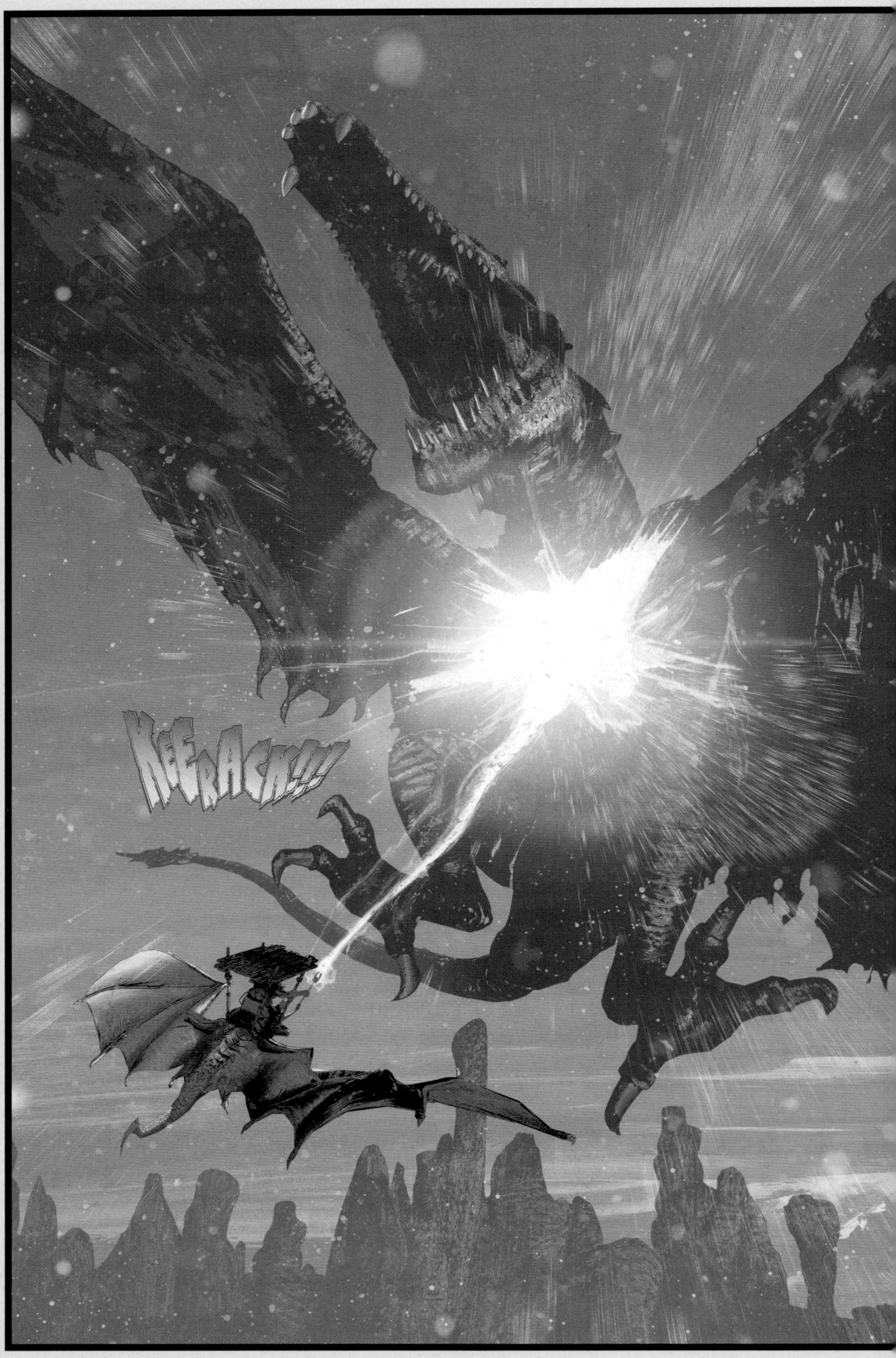
KEERACK!!!

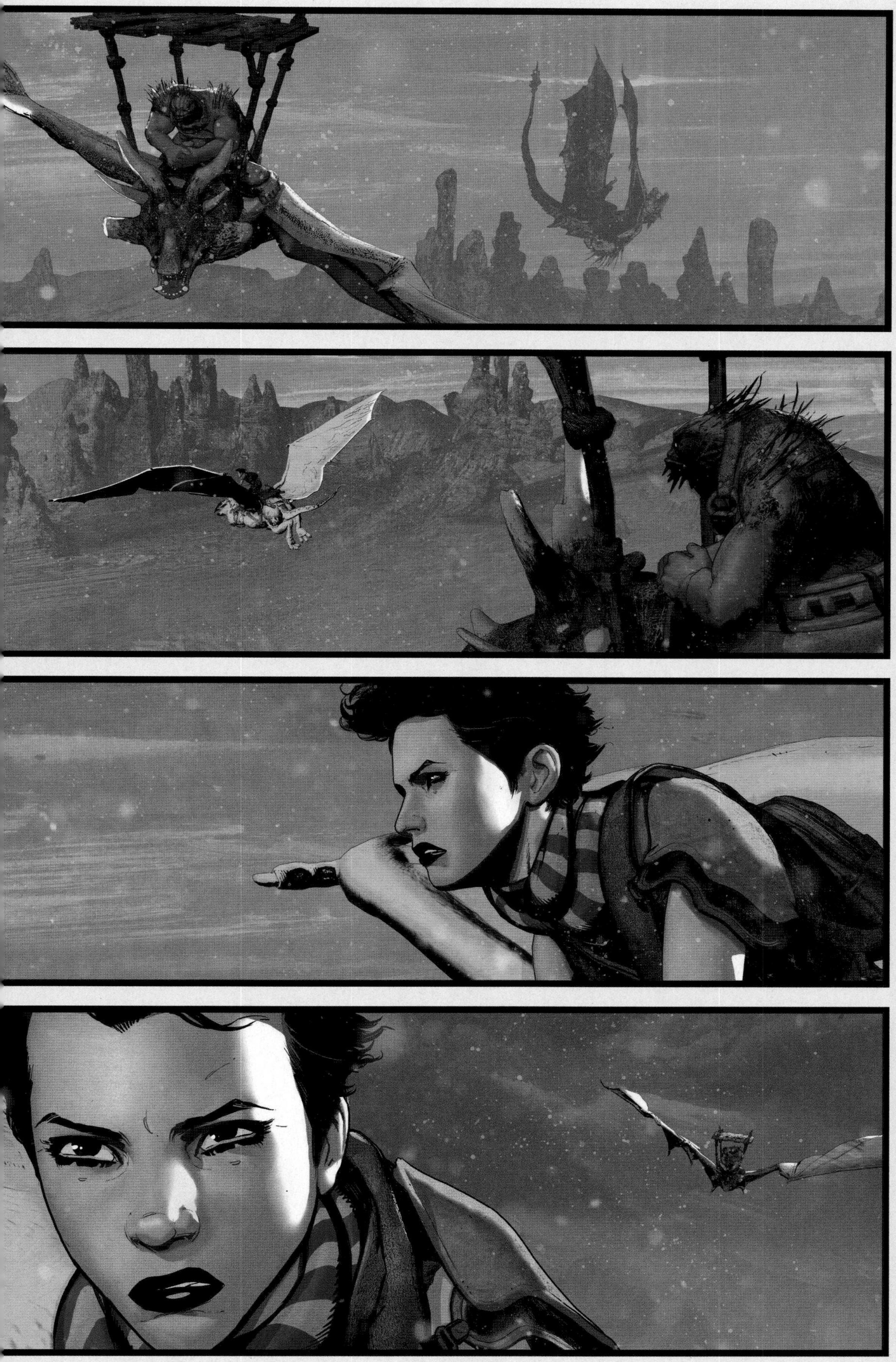

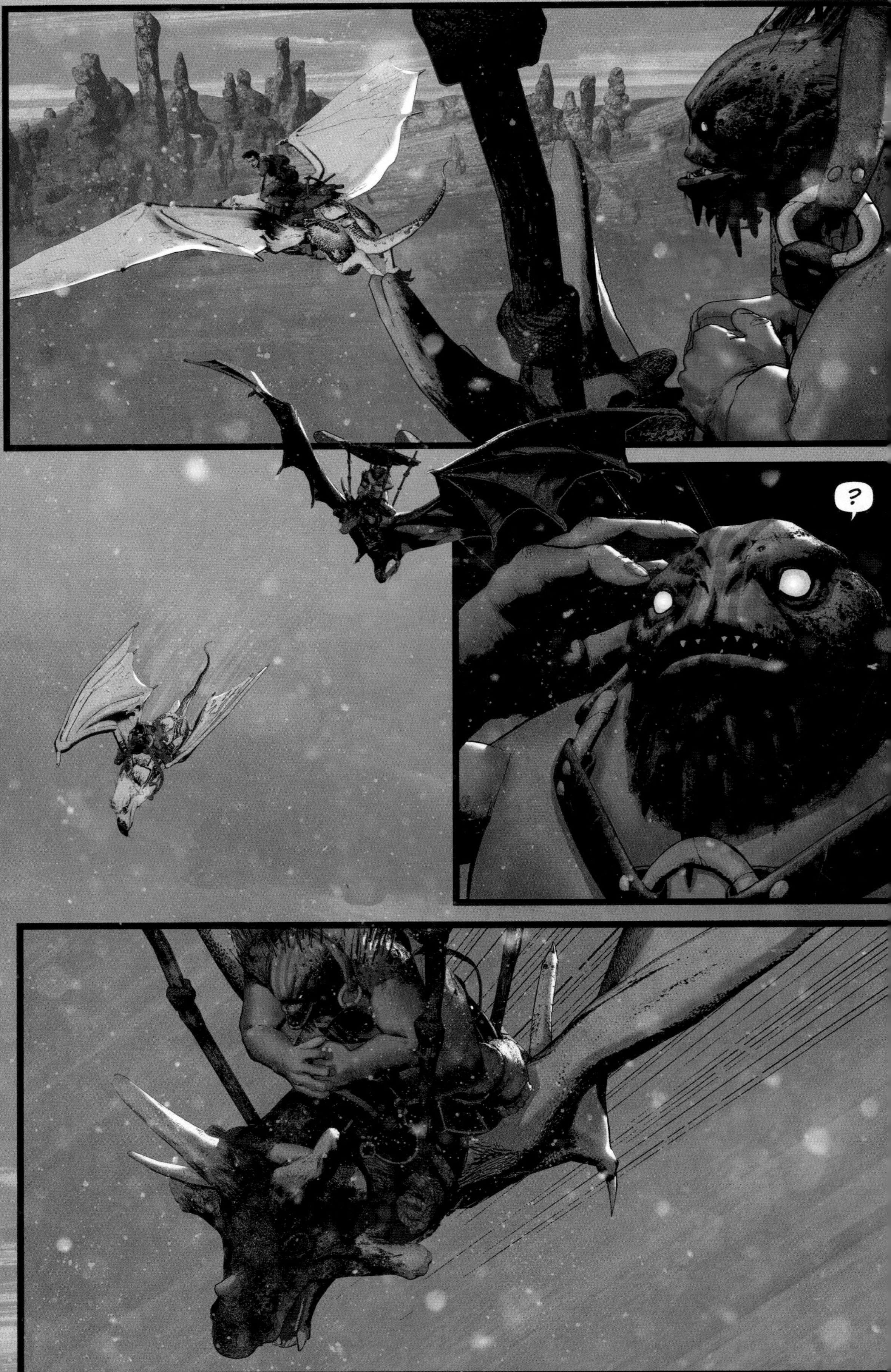
?

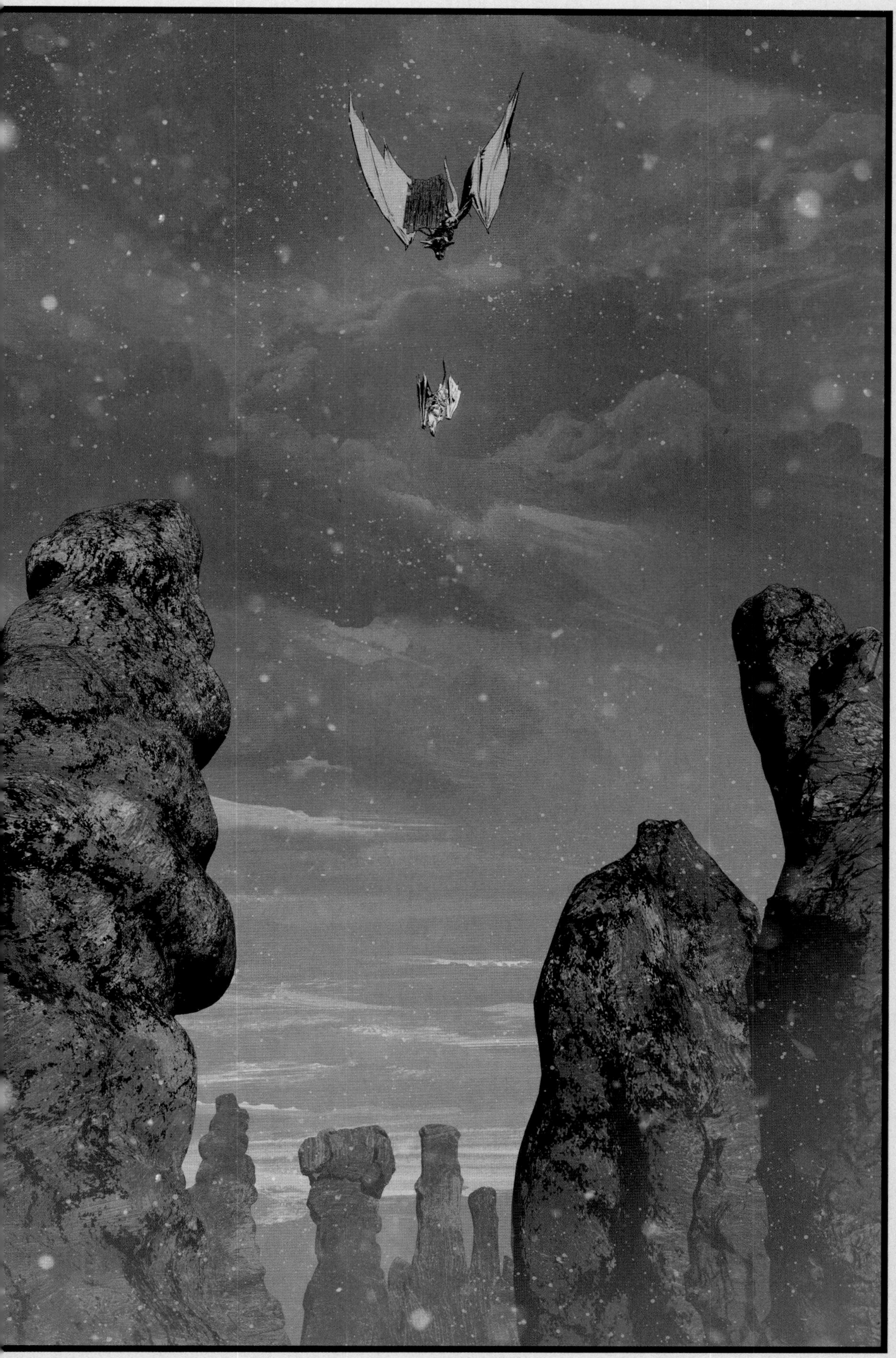

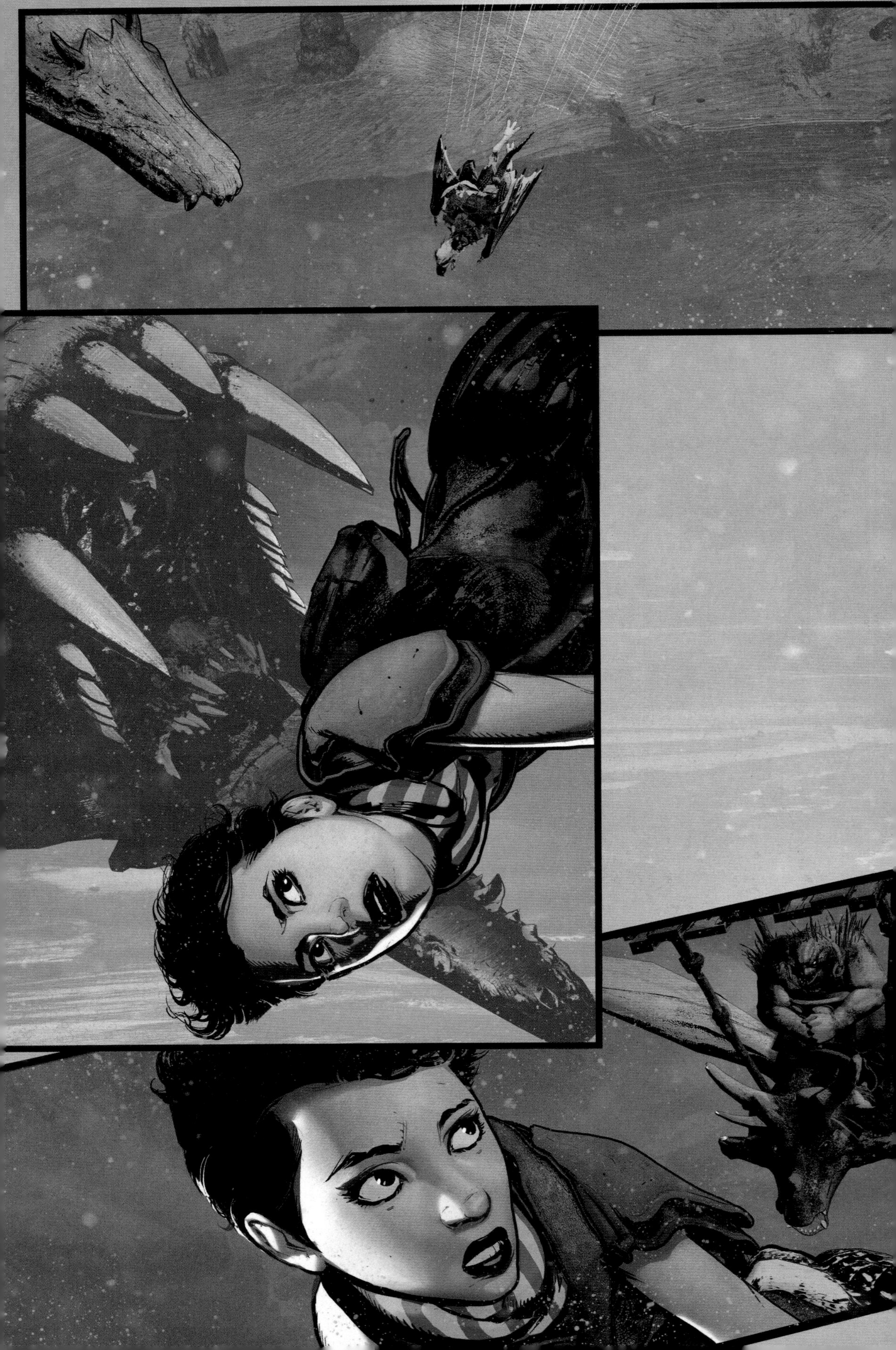

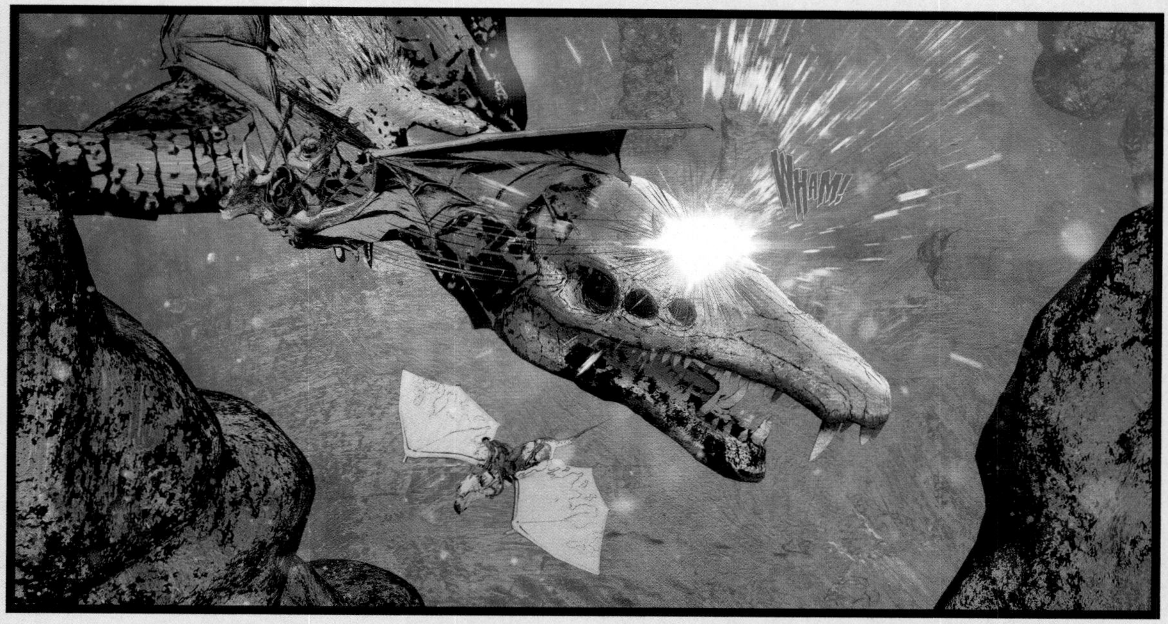
WHAM!
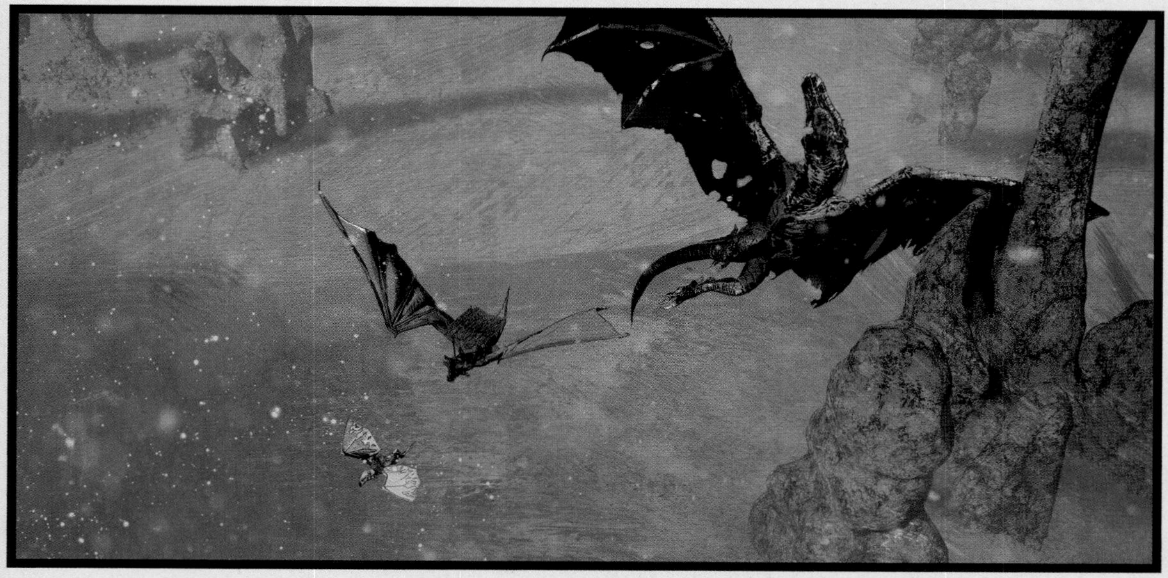
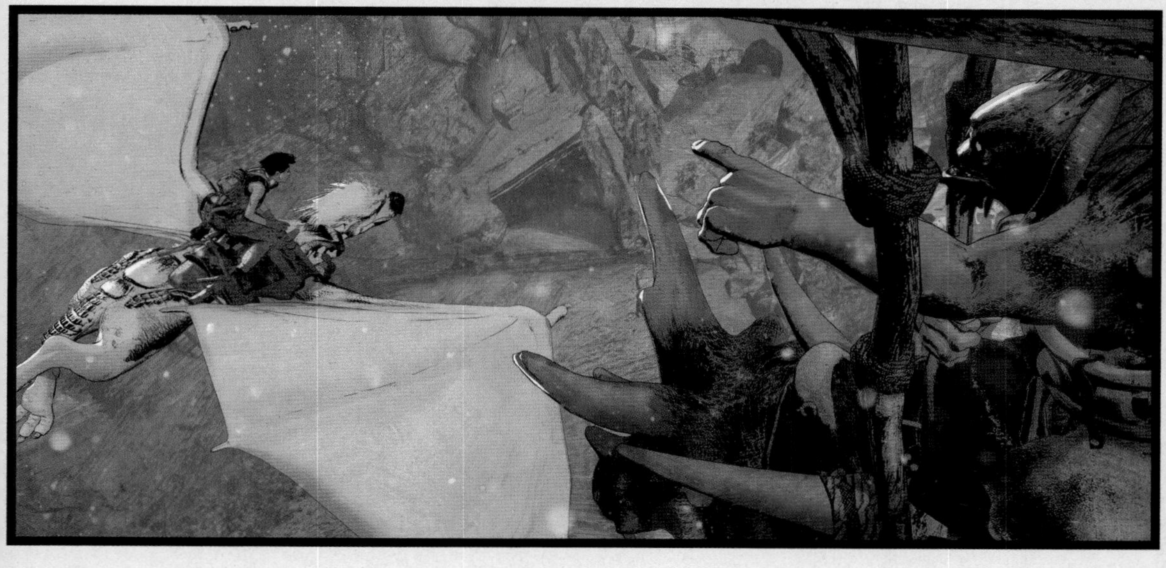

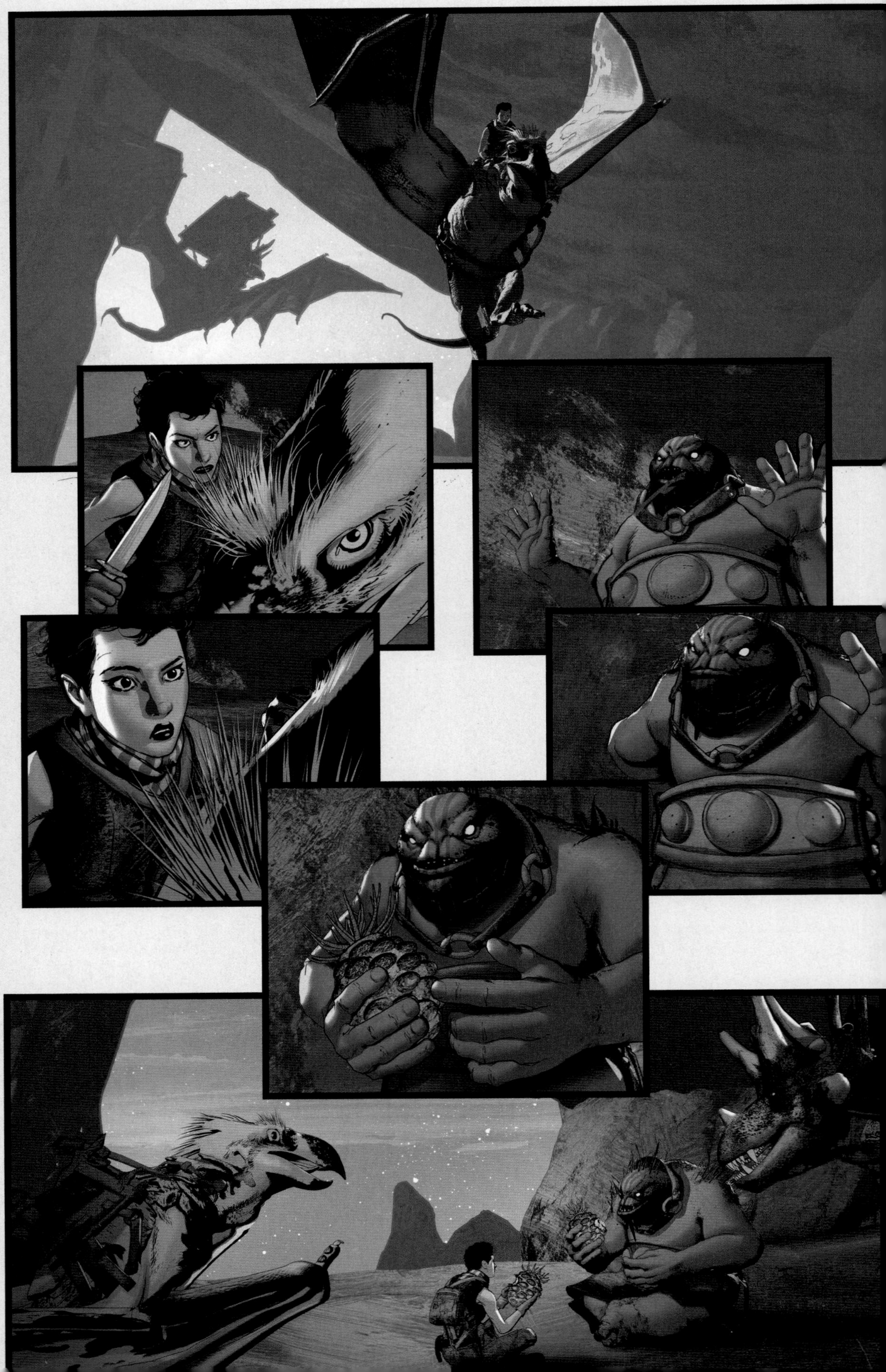

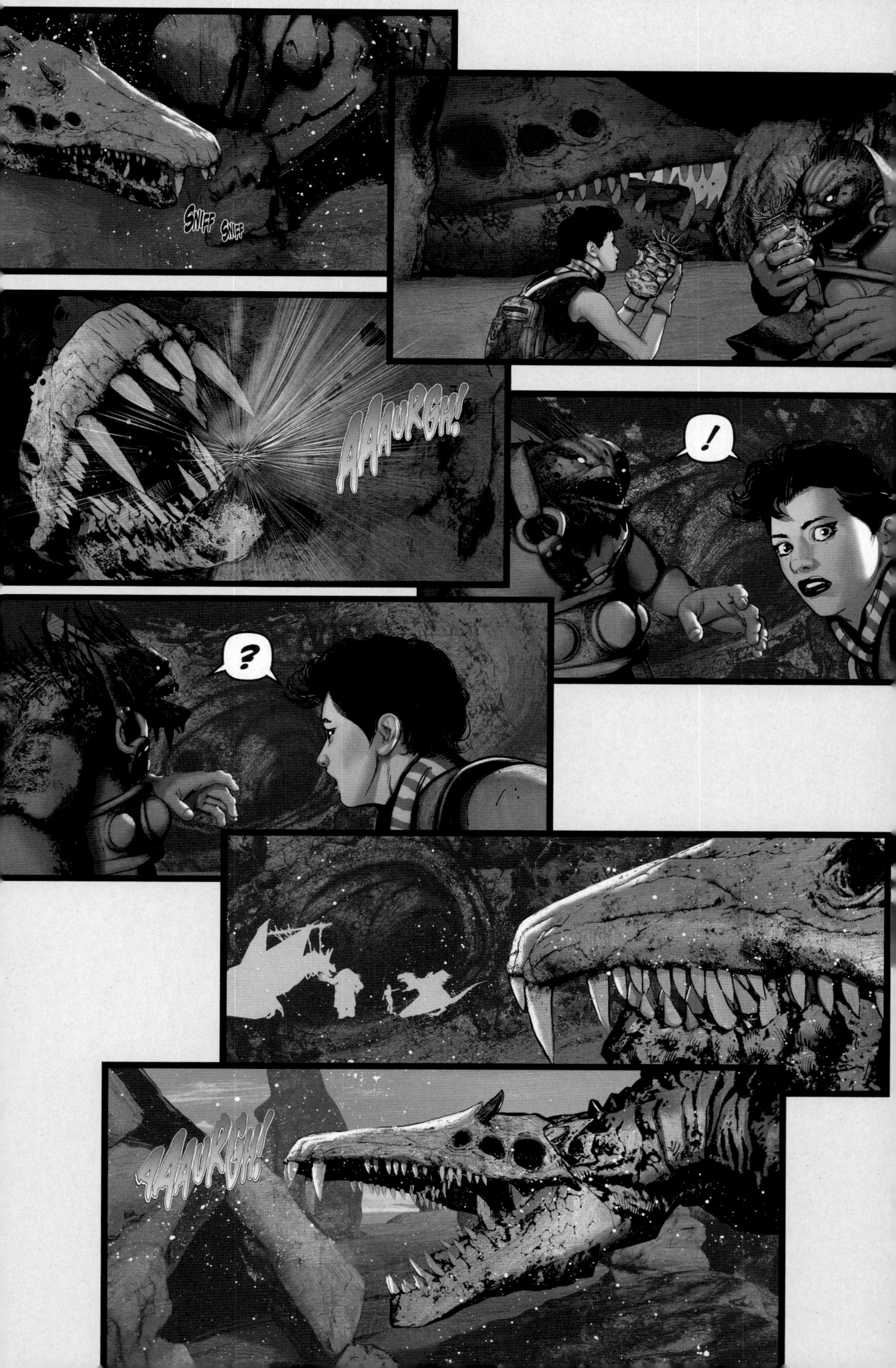
SNIFF SNIFF
AAAURGH!
!
?
AAAURGH!

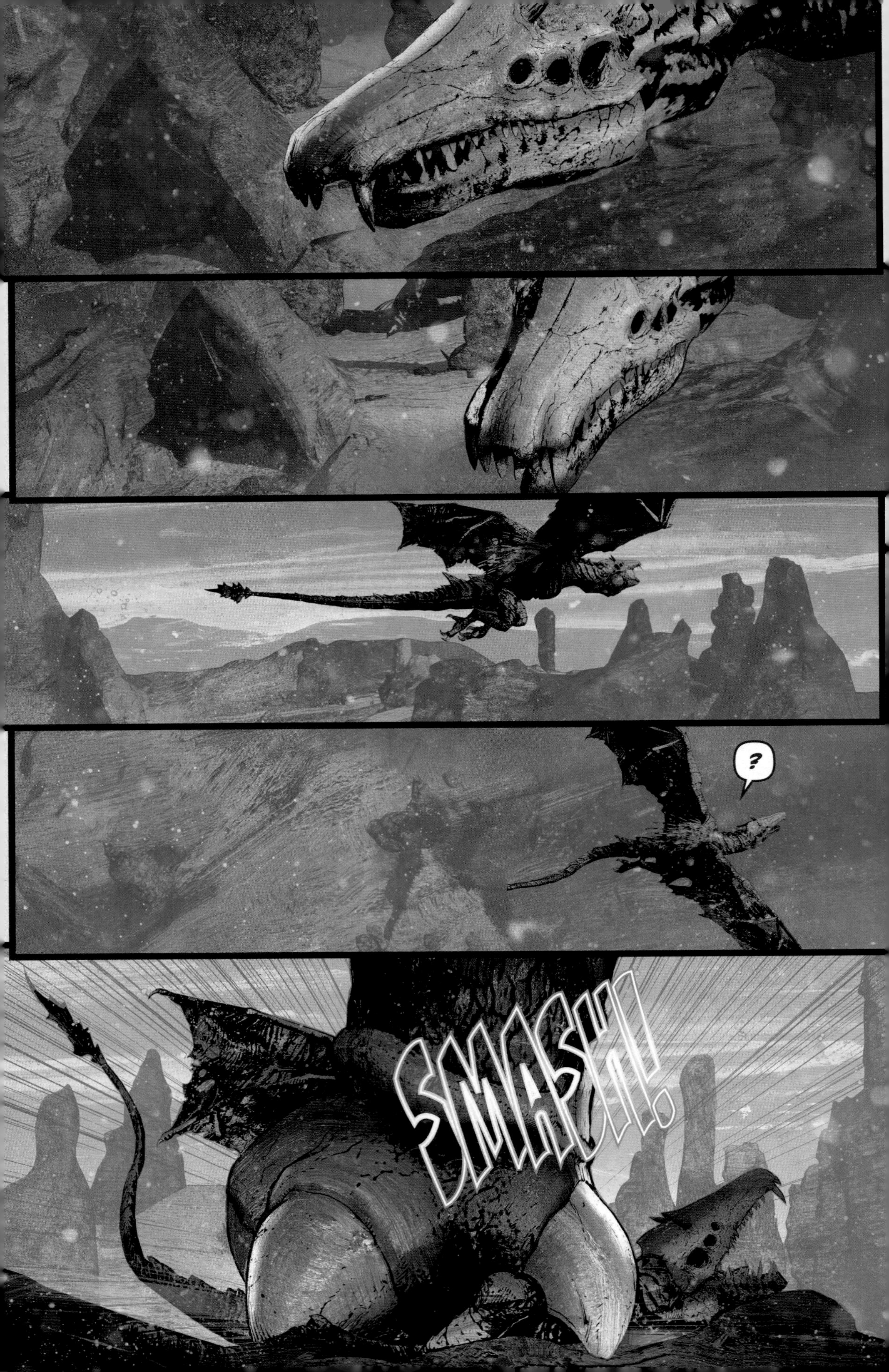
?
SMASH!!

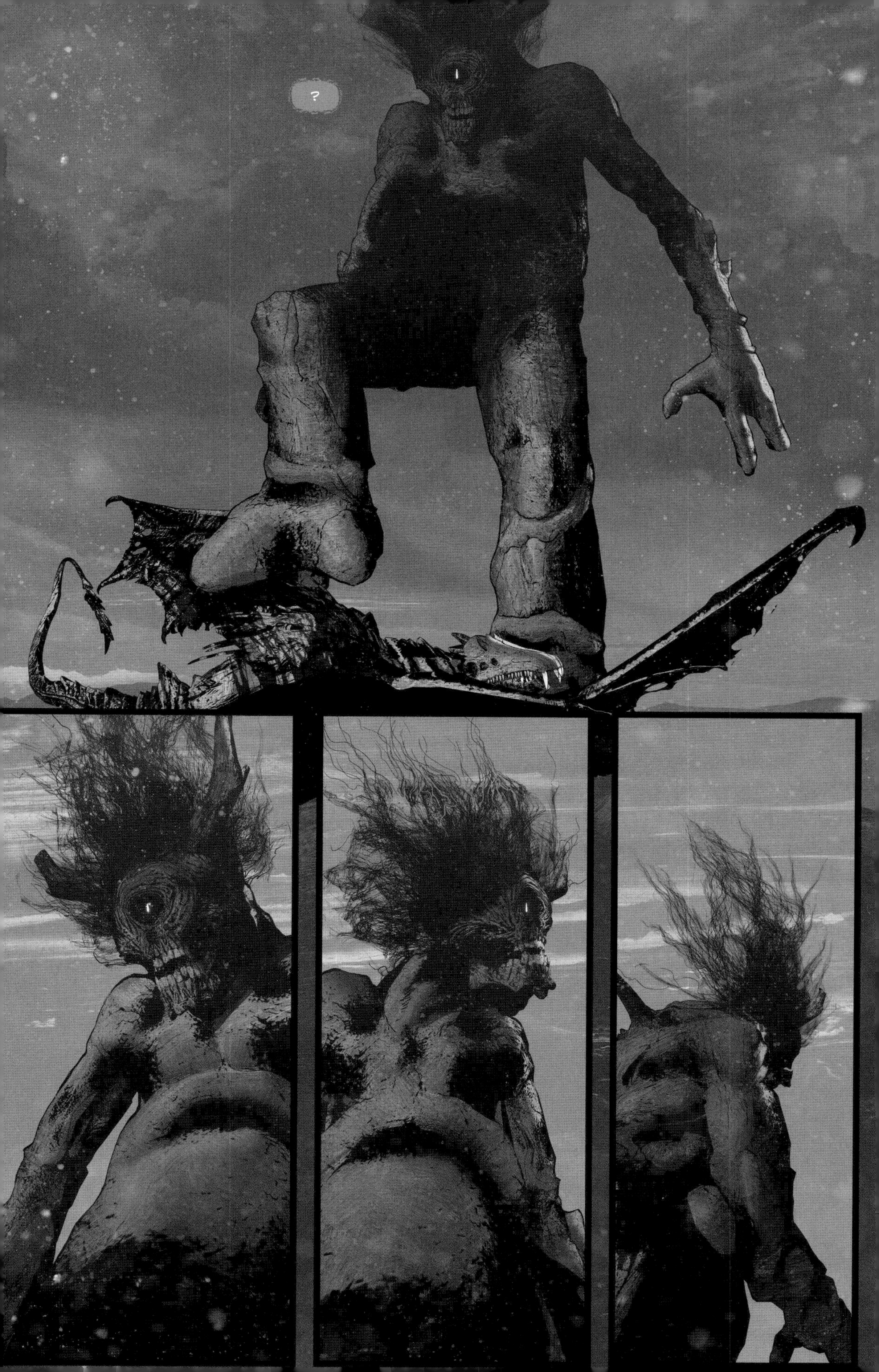
?

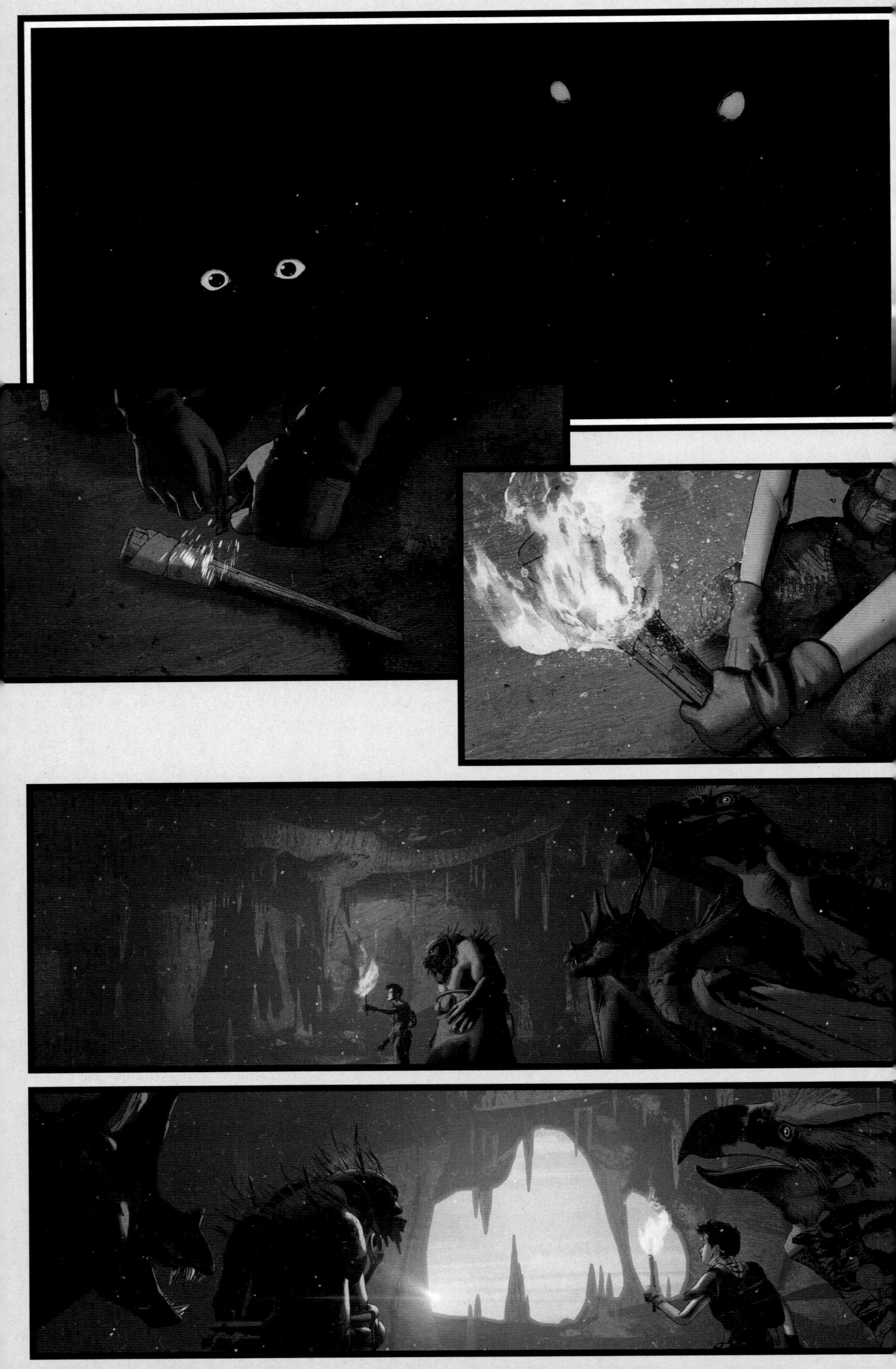

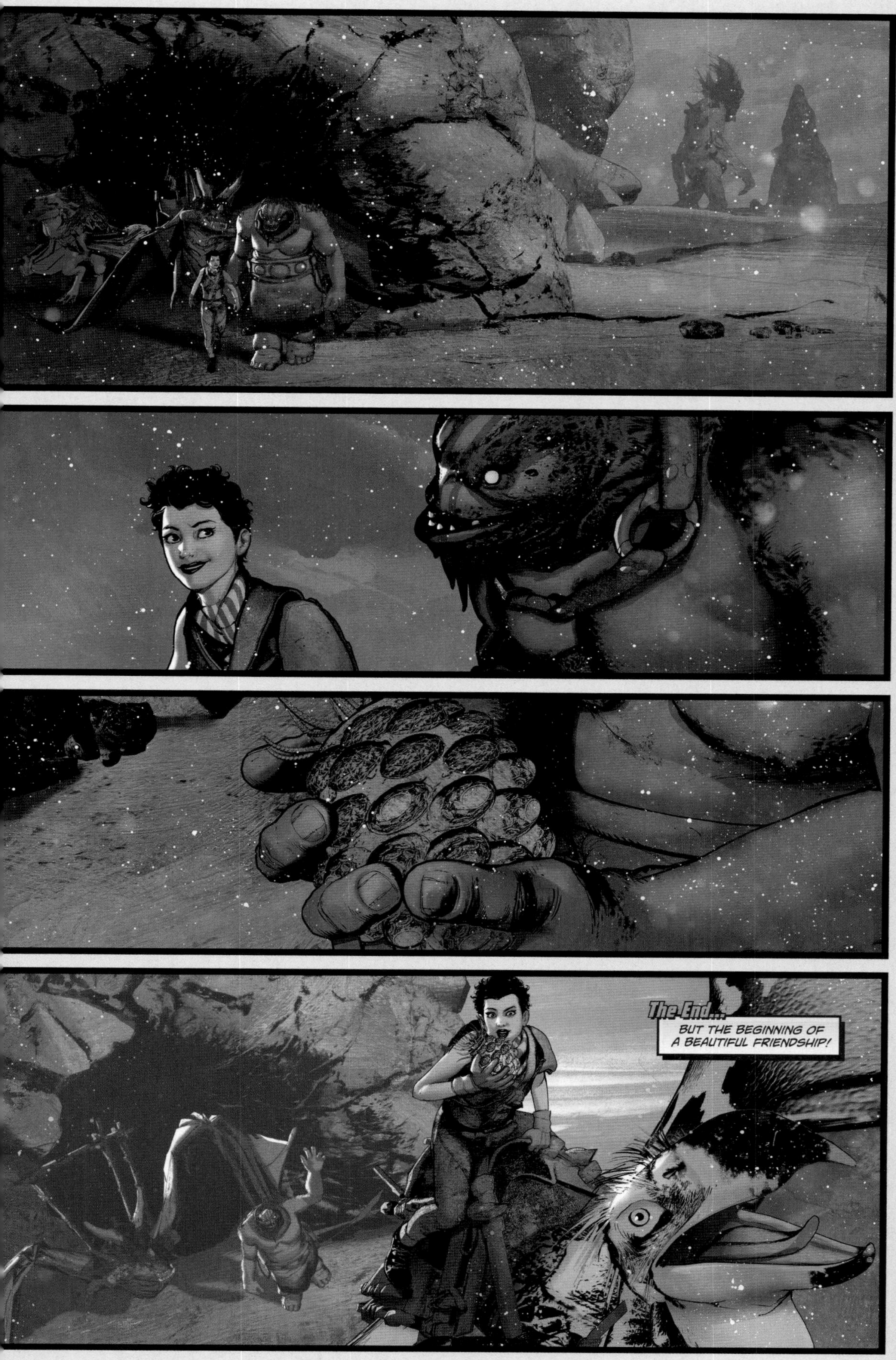
The End...
BUT THE BEGINNING OF A BEAUTIFUL FRIENDSHIP!

Unpublished art for SONATA TV pitch

The following story originally appeared
in the anthology
WHERE WE LIVE
published by IMAGE COMICS

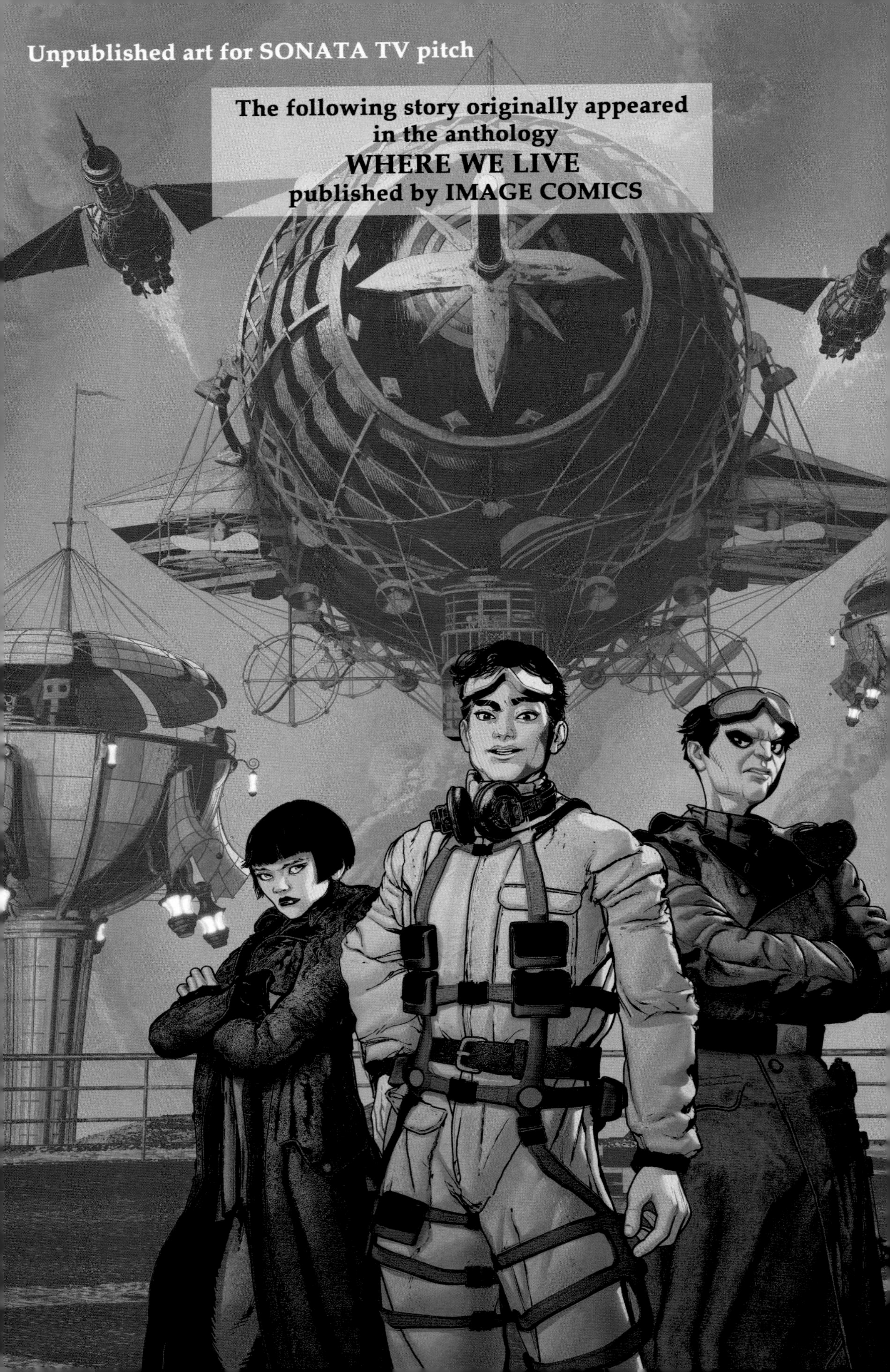

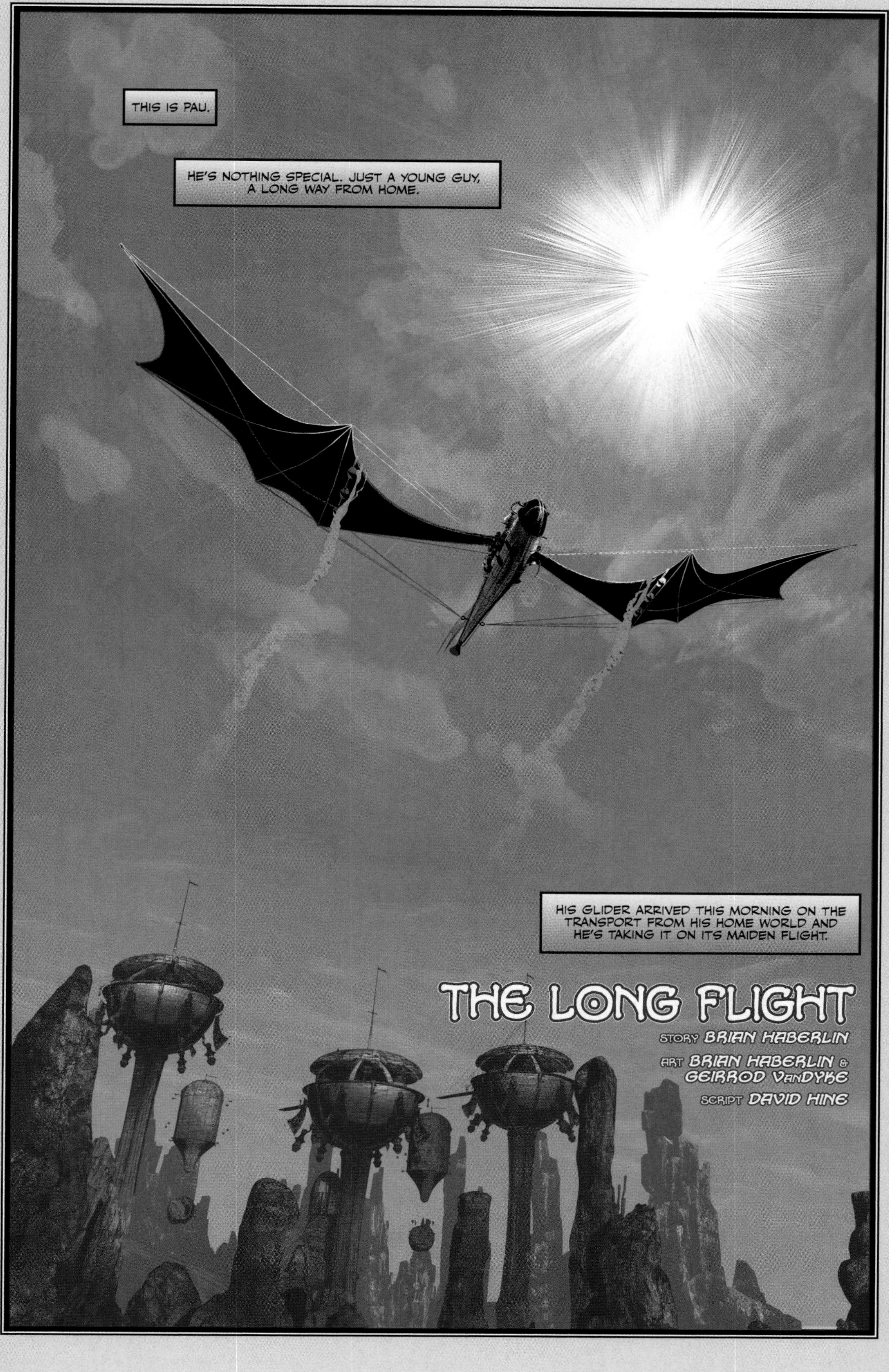
THIS IS PAU.
HE'S NOTHING SPECIAL. JUST A YOUNG GUY, A LONG WAY FROM HOME.
HIS GLIDER ARRIVED THIS MORNING ON THE TRANSPORT FROM HIS HOME WORLD AND HE'S TAKING IT ON ITS MAIDEN FLIGHT.
THE LONG FLIGHT
STORY BRIAN HABERLIN
ART BRIAN HABERLIN & GEIRROD VANDYKE
SCRIPT DAVID HINE

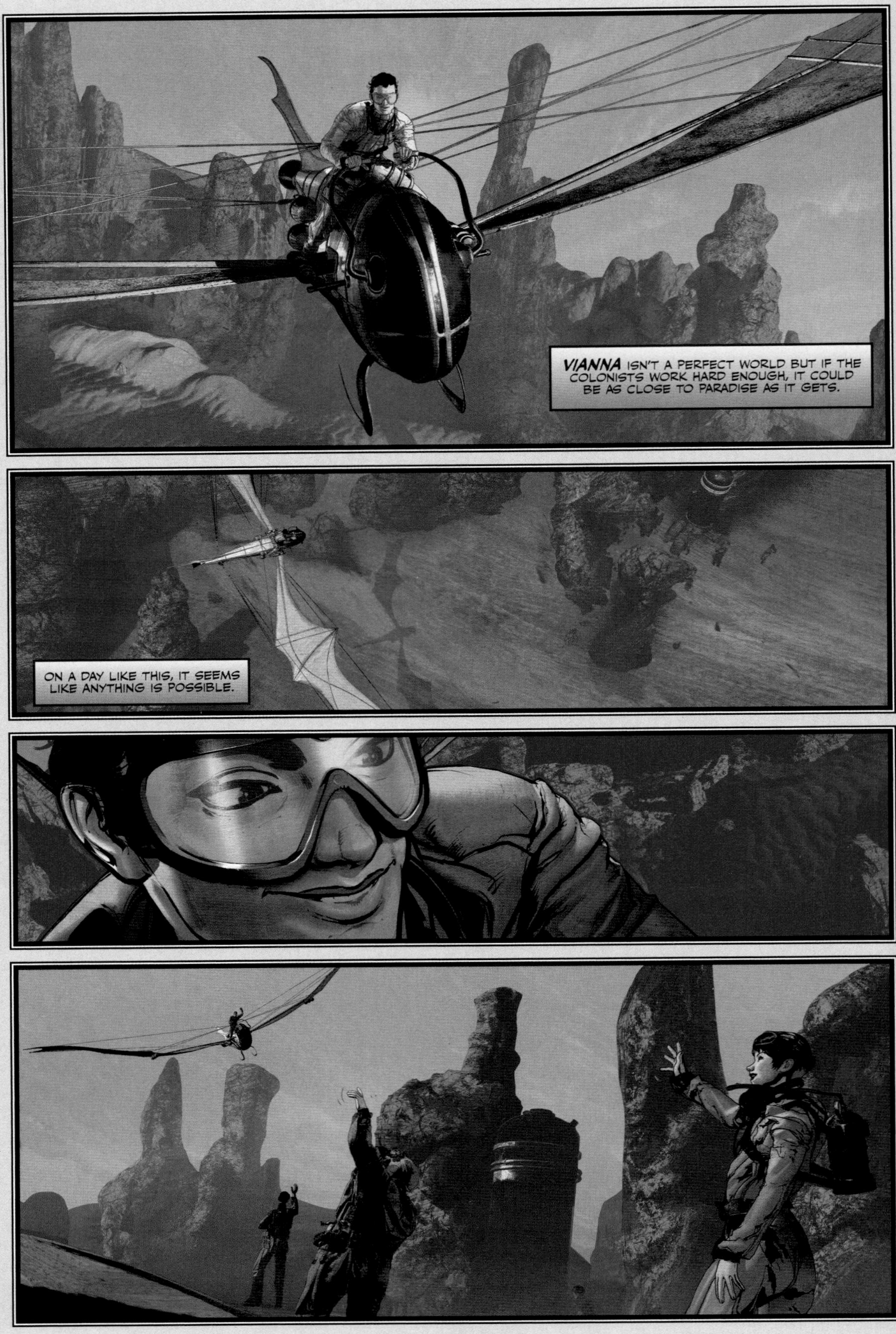
VIANNA ISN'T A PERFECT WORLD BUT IF THE COLONISTS WORK HARD ENOUGH, IT COULD BE AS CLOSE TO PARADISE AS IT GETS.
ON A DAY LIKE THIS, IT SEEMS LIKE ANYTHING IS POSSIBLE.

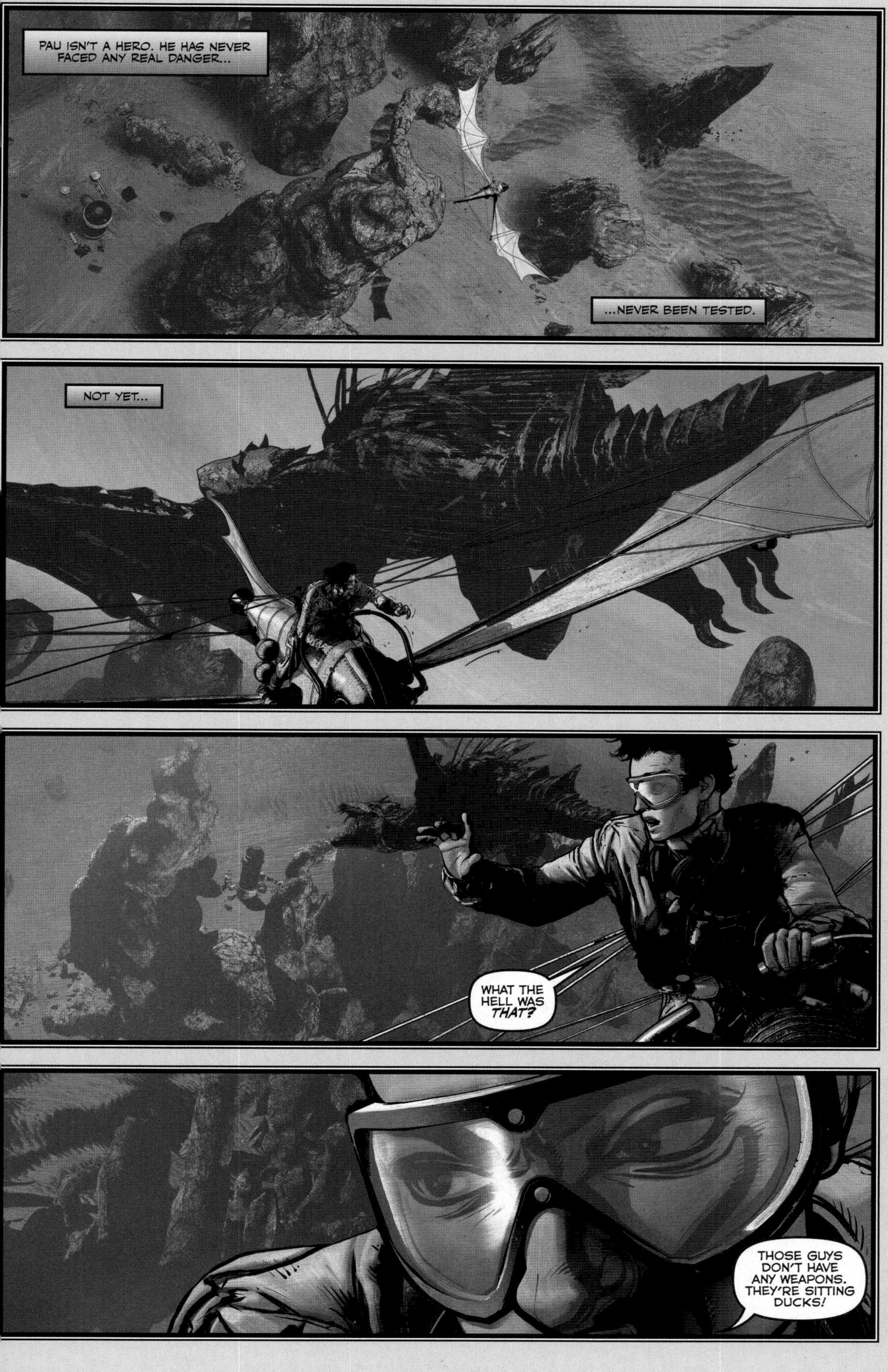
PAU ISN'T A HERO. HE HAS NEVER FACED ANY REAL DANGER...
...NEVER BEEN TESTED.
NOT YET...
WHAT THE HELL WAS *THAT?*
THOSE GUYS DON'T HAVE ANY WEAPONS. THEY'RE SITTING DUCKS!

IN TIMES OF DANGER, WHEN THE ADRENALINE KICKS IN, THERE ARE TWO NATURAL HUMAN REACTIONS...

...CONFRONT THE DANGER, OR RUN AWAY FROM IT...

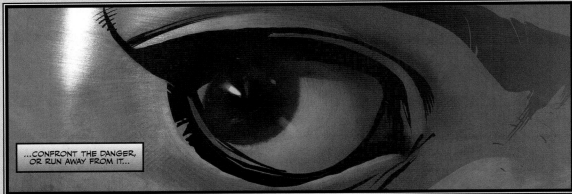

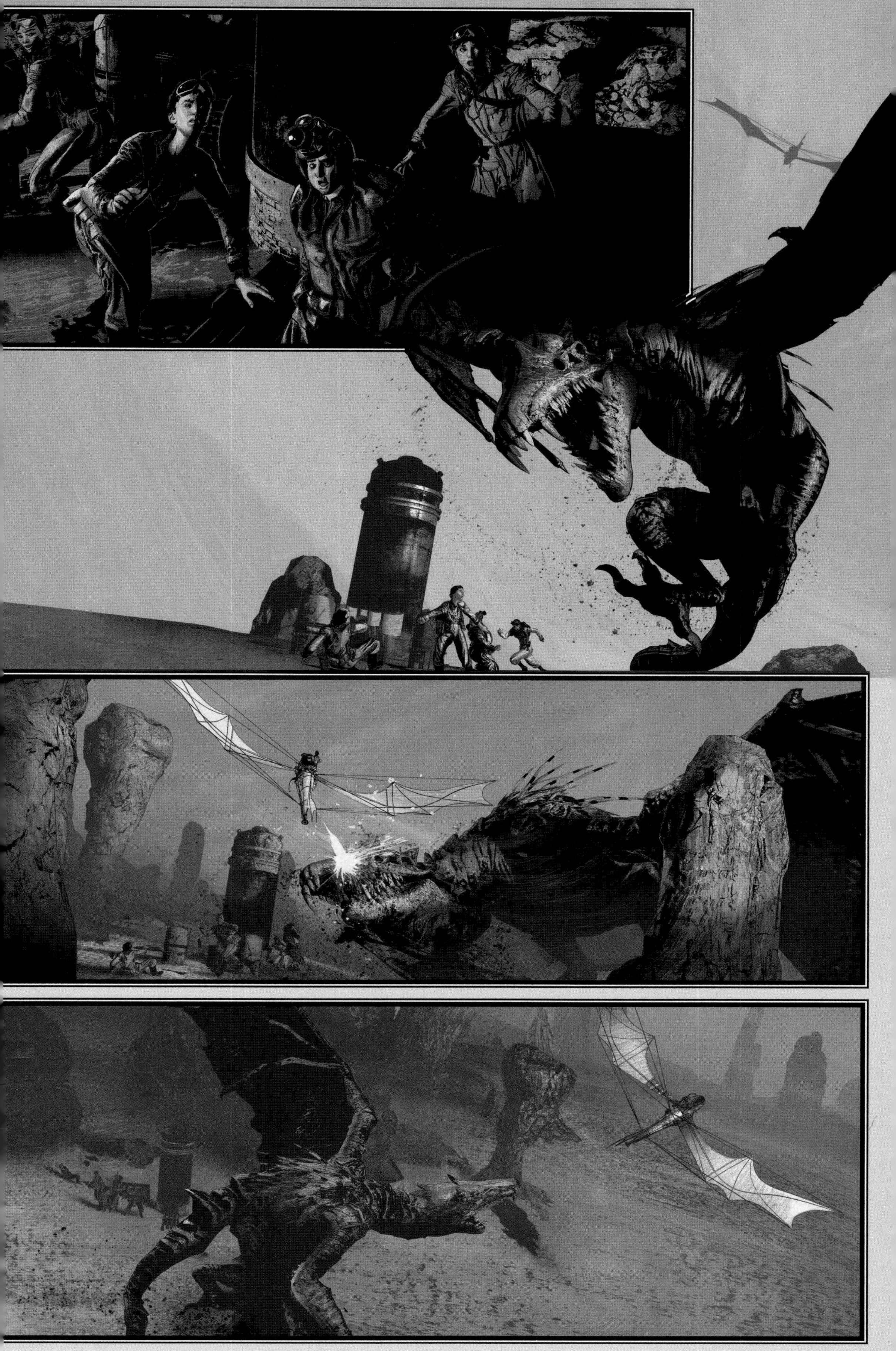

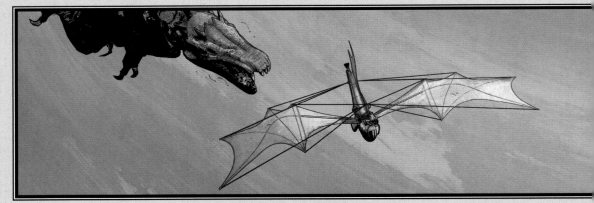

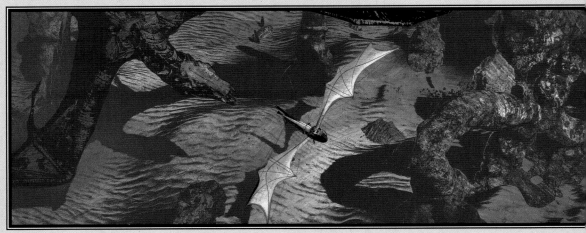

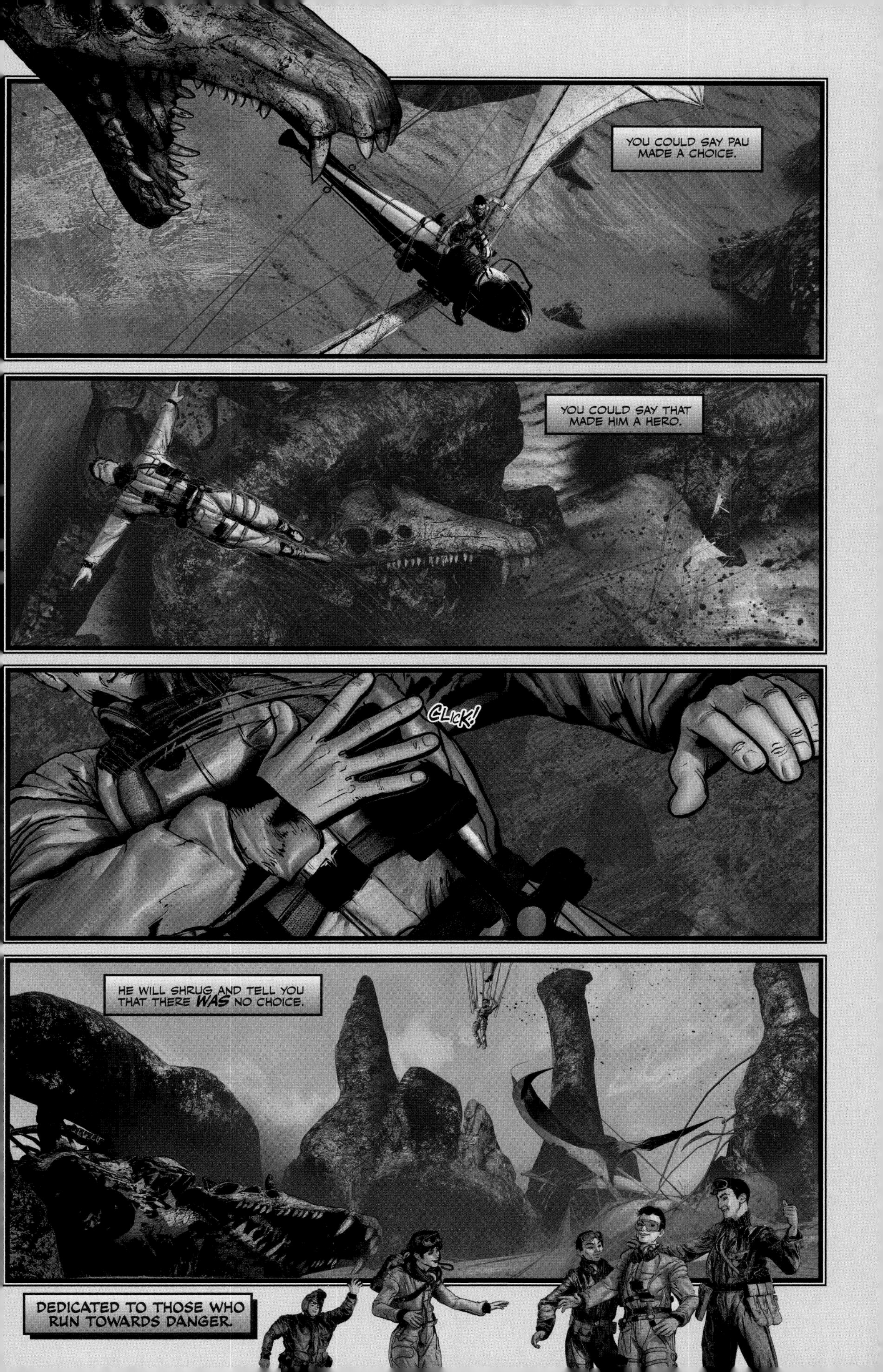
YOU COULD SAY PAU MADE A CHOICE.
YOU COULD SAY THAT MADE HIM A HERO.
CLICK!
HE WILL SHRUG AND TELL YOU THAT THERE *WAS* NO CHOICE.
DEDICATED TO THOSE WHO RUN TOWARDS DANGER.

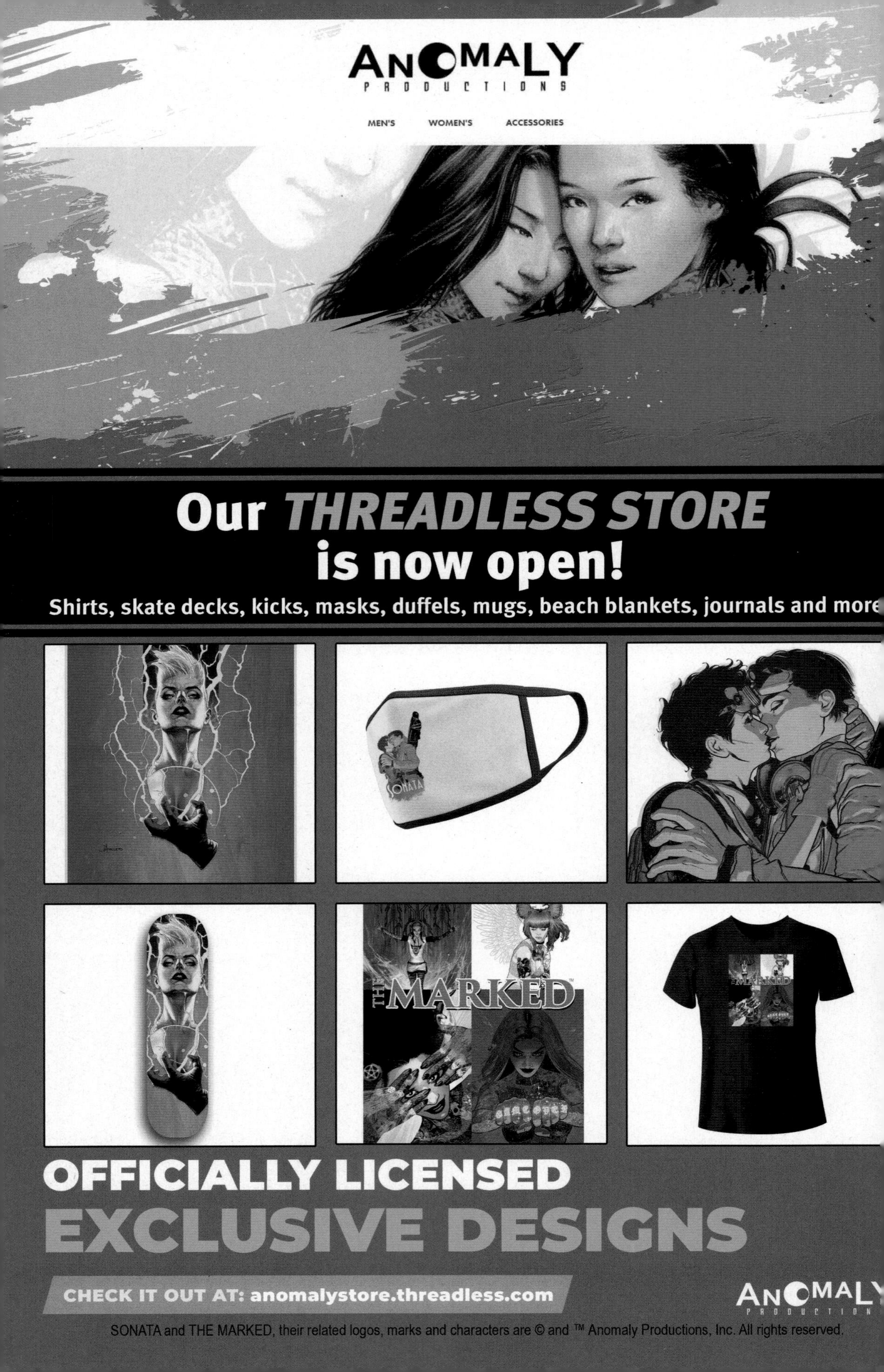
ANOMALY PRODUCTIONS
MEN'S
WOMEN'S
ACCESSORIES
Our THREADLESS STORE is now open!
Shirts, skate decks, kicks, masks, duffels, mugs, beach blankets, journals and more
SONATA
THE MARKED
OFFICIALLY LICENSED
EXCLUSIVE DESIGNS
CHECK IT OUT AT: anomalystore.threadless.com
ANOMALY PRODUCTIONS
SONATA and THE MARKED, their related logos, marks and characters are © and ™ Anomaly Productions, Inc. All rights reserved.

More books by Brian Haberlin you're bound to enjoy...

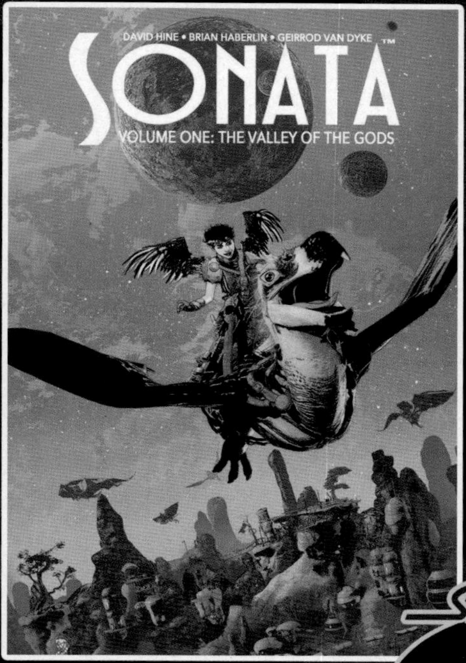
DAVID HINE • BRIAN HABERLIN • GEIRROD VAN DYKE
SONATA
VOLUME ONE: THE VALLEY OF THE GODS

Vol. 1: VALLEY OF THE GODS

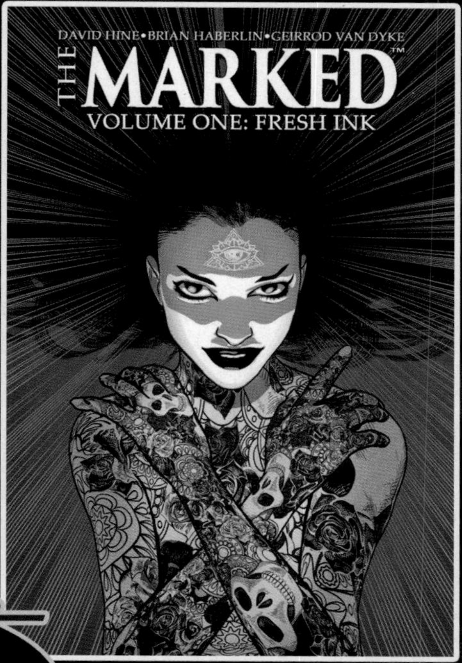
DAVID HINE•BRIAN HABERLIN•GEIRROD VAN DYKE
THE MARKED
VOLUME ONE: FRESH INK

Vol. 1: FRESH INK

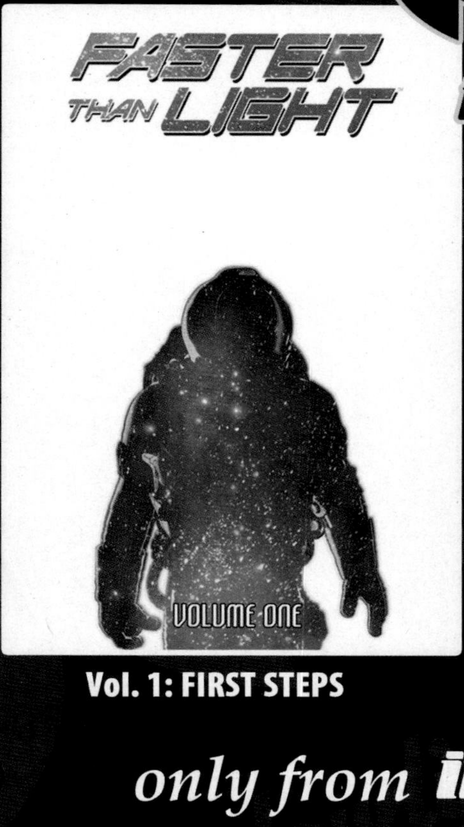
FASTER THAN LIGHT
VOLUME ONE

Vol. 1: FIRST STEPS

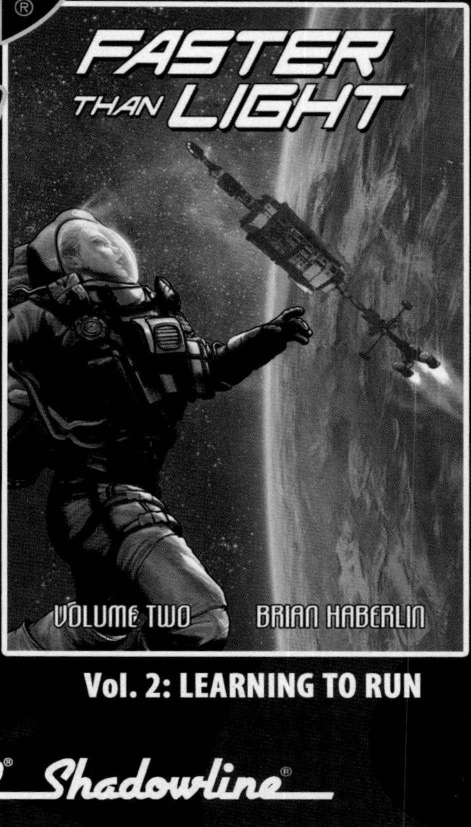
FASTER THAN LIGHT
VOLUME TWO
BRIAN HABERLIN

Vol. 2: LEARNING TO RUN

only from **image**® *Shadowline*®

AVAILABLE AT FINER COMICS SHOPS EVERYWHERE!

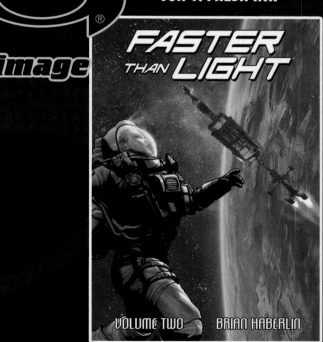

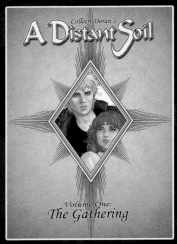

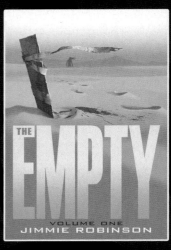

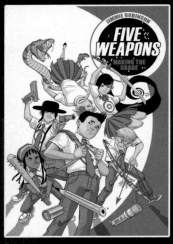